Freya North

a North is the author of 11 bestselling novels which have, in a career spanning 15 years, been translated into ny languages. Though often hailed as one of the founders Chick Lit, she can't stand the term, preferring to classify er novels 'feisty romps'. From teenage girls to elderly ntlemen, Freya's novels have won the hearts of legions of readers worldwide. In 2008, she won the Romantic Novel of the Year Award for *Pillow Talk*.

:hool, Freya was constantly reprimanded for day-dreaming he still can't quite believe that essentially, this is what she is ow paid to do. She was born in London but lives in rural ertfordshire with her family and other animals, where she writes from a stable in her back garden.

To find out more about Freya and her books, log onto www.freyanorth.com or join her at

Acclaim for...

secrets:

'As addictive as it is tantalising... this novel has all the charm
we have come to expect from North'
Sunday Express

'A perfect curl-up and chill-out read... another sure-fire hit for Freya' *Heat*

'A fab read' *Closer*

'Freya North always manages to create such believable heroines (and very sexy
love scenes!) that you get sucked into her beautifully observed world' *Bella*

'Funny and feel-good, but has bite too' *Cosmopolitan*

'An addictive mix of sex, mystery and romance' *Woman & Home*

pillow talk:

'Fast paced, page-turning and full of endearing, interesting characters.
I defy anyone who doesn't fall in love with it' *Glamour*

'Warm, sexy, satisfying' *Heat*

'Darkly funny and sexy – literary escapism at its very finest'
Sunday Independent

'The novel's likeable central characters are so well painted that
you feel not only that you know them, but that you know
how right they are for each other'
Daily Telegraph

'North charts the emotional turmoil with a sexy exactitude'
Marie Claire

home truths:

'An eye-poppingly sexy start leads into a family reunion laced with secrets. Tangled mother/daughter relationships unravel and tantalising family riddles keep you glued to the end' *Cosmopolitan*

'You'll laugh, cry, then laugh some more' *Company*

'Freya North manages to strike a good balance between drama, comedy and romance, and has penned another winner in *Home Truths*... touching, enjoyable'
Heat

'An addictive read with a realistic view of home life, sisterhood and identity crisis' *Prima*

love rules:

'Freya North has matured to produce an emotive novel that deals with the darker side of love – these are real women, with real feelings'
She

'Tantrums, tarts, tears and text-sex... what's not to love about this cautionary tale for true romantics?' *Heat*

'A distinctive storytelling style and credible, loveable characters... an addictive read that encompasses the stuff life is made of: love, sex, fidelity and, above all, friendship' *Glamour*

'Plenty that's fresh to say about the age-old differences between men and women' *Marie Claire*

'Sassy, feel-good chick lit with a good sting in the tail'
Cosmopolitan

Also by Freya North:

Freya North
chances

HARPER

Harper
An imprint of HarperCollins*Publishers*
77–85 Fulham Palace Road,
Hammersmith, London W6 8JB

www.harpercollins.co.uk

This paperback edition 2011
2

First published in Great Britain by
HarperCollins*Publishers* 2011

Copyright © Freya North 2011

Freya North asserts the moral right to
be identified as the author of this work

A catalogue record for this book
is available from the British Library

ISBN: 978 0 00 732666 2

Typeset in Sabon by Palimpsest Book Production Limited,
Falkirk, Stirlingshire

Printed and bound in Great Britain by
Clays Ltd, St Ives plc

Mixed Sources
Product group from well-managed
forests and other controlled sources
www.fsc.org Cert no. SW-COC-001806
© 1996 Forest Stewardship Council

FSC is a non-profit international organization established
to promote the responsible management of the world's forests.
Products carrying the FSC label are independently certified
to assure consumers that they come from forests that are managed
to meet the social, economic and ecological needs
of present and future generations.

Find out more about HarperCollins and the environment at
www.harpercollins.co.uk/green

For Mummy
Lovely, funny, beautiful – and so very very brave.
A woman of worth, indeed.
With love,
Your Chief Sherpa

All discarded lovers should be given a second chance
– but with somebody else

MAE WEST

That Shop

Sitting in her shop, That Shop, on the stool behind the counter (an old console table which was for sale and had been since she opened three years ago), Vita kept her head down, nose buried in her book, yet managed surreptitiously to watch the elderly lady whilst wondering what she'd allow her to nick today. A fortnight ago, it had been a small jar of pastel-coloured guest soaps in the shapes of seashells. Prior to that, an ashtray, brass, in the shape of a Moroccan slipper. Vita didn't think the old lady smoked, she thought her vice might be little more than the occasional sherry and shoplifting. Fascinating. And why had she stolen that tin of mini sparklers with 'Wedding Wishes' embossed on the lid? Not that Vita had minded – they were on offer anyway. The most expensive thing the lady had swiped had been the small pewter noughts and crosses set – but there again, no one had expressed any interest in it.

Sometimes, Vita could anticipate which object would be pilfered; at other times, she knew something had gone but it took her a couple of days to figure out quite what. She liked the fact that what was taken was dictated not by its value but by its desirability. Those sparklers had been cheap as chips but the little tin was so pretty.

Vita watched and tried to guess. The Gardener's Handcream? The light-pull in the shape of a black cat? The old lady was currently admiring the candy-coloured dustpan set. Vita thought, She'll never get that under her jacket. A couple of months ago, perhaps, when spring was late and it was still cold and the woman was swamped by a shabby old coat in Prince of Wales check. Today, she wore a light blouson a shade darker than her lilac rinse. What would she be able to squirrel away when true summer came? Did she choose her summer clothes on account of capaciousness of pockets? It was only June but the weathermen were predicting a heatwave for this summer. The shopkeepers of Wynford hoped so. Vita thought back to last summer and all that rain that had been so bad for business. It seemed such a long time ago now.

It was one of the animals! Vita detected a sudden lift in the old lady's energy from near the rack at the back of the shop on which the plastic animals stood as if lining up waiting to board the wooden ark on the neighbouring table. Which, though? Which had gone?

Gazelle. Vita reckoned it had to be the gazelle. There were plenty of them left. In her experience, the children always made a beeline for the carnivores.

'Nothing today, lassie,' the woman said diplomatically as if, on some future occasion, with new stock, or just what she was looking for, she might be happy to part with her money.

When I was at school, Vita mused once the tinkle of the shop's bell had subsided and she had the place to herself again, I stole for a little old lady just like you.

Tim thought, If she's reading a bloody book – if she's reading a bloody bloody book . . .

His business philosophy was that his shop, That Shop, needed to make money, notwithstanding the average item price being around £10. Vita's personal philosophy was that her shop, That Shop, should simply be somewhere people loved to go, to be heartened by lovely things.

She *is* bloody reading a bloody book.

'Hi.'

Tim jerks his head at her book and raises an eyebrow.

'*Robinson Crusoe*,' Vita says, as if it vindicates any objection. 'I read this fantastic novel about a young girl who was obsessed with Robinson Crusoe – so when I finished it, I started this straight away. Have you read it? I can't believe I hadn't.'

I'm gabbling. *Still* nervous around him – madness. 'It's a classic. Did you know Daniel Defoe is credited with inventing the novel? I even wonder whether "cruise" comes from "Crusoe".'

'This isn't a desert island, Vita, it's a deserted shop.'

He approaches the till and prints off a balance. 'Christ alive.'

'I know,' Vita says gravely, 'it's been slow.'

'I saw that mad old woman coming out,' he says.

'I don't think she's mad – just, you know, eccentric.'

'She's a thief, that's what she is,' Tim says. 'Watch her like a hawk.' He had caught the woman shoplifting last Easter. A small papier mâché rabbit. Not expensive – but a key seller at a time when they were shifting loads. He'd made her put it back. He'd done it tactfully and authoritatively. As though he was talking to a child. Vita hadn't liked that at all. It was just a little Easter bunny.

She won't be doing *that* again, he'd said to Vita.

Just now, Vita muses how it wouldn't cross Tim's mind

5

that the old lady had been doing precisely that, on a regular basis, ever since. With Vita's unspoken blessing.

She glances at Tim. Experiences a pang. Wonders how that could be, after so long. After everything.

'Hey, Tim.' It isn't a question and, though she says it softly, she knows she shouldn't have said it at all. He just looks at her. There's nothing behind his eyes. It's the neutrality that hurts the most.

When did he buy that new shirt? It suits him, it suits his dark grey eyes, his close-cropped hair the colour of slate.

'Be in touch,' he says as he leaves.

He doesn't look back.

Tim is someone who never looks back.

Six years together, now heading towards a year since she left him. Vita looks at her watch and reprimands herself for having spent a daft amount of time lost in pointless reflection. She could have been reading. Or tidying. Or engaging with customers. Now look at the time. Sorry, Robinson, school's out and the kids will soon descend, with their exasperated mums killing time to interrupt the drag of the remainder of the day. It's Monday, though, and good for trade usually, on account of pocket money left over from the weekend.

She slips off the stool and goes to the store cupboard at the back of the shop, which is only slightly larger than the loo. She takes out a plastic antelope and a couple of other items and carries them back into the shop. Then she writes herself a Post-it note, sticking it next to the hook on which her jacket is hanging.

> *Order gorillas and lions.*
> *Think Robinson, not Tim.*

Oliver and Jonty

Oliver was washing up. He'd spilled water on himself and on the floor. His shirt had been clean and now the floor was dirty. The water was too hot and his hands were red. He needed a new washing-up sponge. There was no more room on the draining board. He'd used too much Fairy but as he still hadn't fixed the cold tap it meant the water spurted everywhere each time he rinsed something. To the right of him, the dishwasher stood empty. Top-of-the-range, still under its extended guarantee. Unused for nearly three years. His wife had loved that appliance more than any of the others.

'I could live without TV,' she'd said, 'I don't mind laundrettes. But the dishwasher? I'd sell *myself*, rather than part with it – it's the apotheosis of modern invention.'

He thought about that now; how only DeeDee could refer to something as dull as a dishwasher as the Apotheosis of Modern Invention. He thought about how she liked to say she didn't have 'hands that do dishes'. Not from any pomposity but because her hands really had been slender and soft – pale, silky, protected. She rubbed cream in as though it was a ritual. Tubes of the stuff remained. They were still there, on windowsill and bedside table, by the basin, by the phone near the front door. Some were scented with lavender, some with rose. Some were formulated for Norwegian fishermen. One was for babies' bottoms. It was called Butt Butter. Her cousin in the States used to send it at regular intervals. This was the last tub. Oliver looked at his hands, redder by the minute. He should have taken his watch off.

Of all the things to miss, it was the simple sight of a meticulously stacked dishwasher he longed for most these days. And yet, it had been one thing that had wound them both up at the time. DeeDee hated him stacking it because she said he didn't do it properly. She'd physically shove him out of the way, complaining how he didn't maximize space the way she did, even accusing him of doing this on purpose (which was true). He'd hated her tutting and huffs and the exasperation written all over her face. It had made him sling stuff in on purpose. Put a mug in the wrong way up so that it filled with the sedi, entry water. How ridiculous had that been? Both of them. Life's way too short to fall out over a stupid dishwasher.

He'd called her a fucking control freak once. She'd gone stony cold and had said, I'm doing it for *us* – it's the way I keep our home and if you want to make a mockery of *that* you can fuck off yourself. He'd said, Stop being so bloody melodramatic. Jonty, who had been about eight or nine, had said, What's melon-traumatic? And she'd said, Mel-o-dramatic, darling, it's nothing, just a silly word for a silly thing. So gently, so sweetly, so patiently that this had wound up Oliver even more. He'd stropped off to the pub. And later, when guilt had made him leave before closing time and he'd returned and unloaded the dishwasher, he'd had to concede how well she'd restacked it.

One beer too many had made him annoyed that she could be right over something so trivial, exasperated that her natural fastidiousness, the high standards she placed on family and home and perfection, necessitated this crazy rigidity to maintain them.

That night long ago – when was it? – if Jonty had been nine-ish, it must have been a good five years ago. The dishwasher before this one. That night, back then, Oliver had slept in the spare room. And DeeDee had crept in during the small hours. And they'd shuffled closer and closer together, cuddling and kissing and pressing and offering silent apologies. Jonty had gone into their empty bedroom in the morning and wondered whether aliens had abducted his parents.

DeeDee would die if she saw the state of the house now. Or, rather, she'd die again.

Today, Oliver can still feel the muddle of conflicting emotions – like washing up with water so hot it feels cold. He likes to justify that, these days, it's environmentally irresponsible to use a dishwasher. Especially since there's only him and Jonty. And mostly they eat takeaways direct from the tubs. And the food they cook at other times rarely requires many utensils. Just plates, really, for pizza or cold cuts or beans on toast. They often don't bother with knives. They use their forks – to spear, to scoop, to sever. They go through an industrial quantity of teaspoons each day.

'Remember how Mum used to always lay the table? Including a spoon for pudding even though she invariably said, Help yourselves to fresh fruit?'

'Yeah,' says Jonty.

But his father can't tell what his son's eyes are saying

behind that lank curtain of dye-dark hair. It is one of those moments when Oliver considers how a teenager's hair can hide a child's eyes. And he is not sure what he's meant to do about it.

'You can dry.'

'There's only about two plates and a hundred forks, Dad. Let it all drain.'

His son is on his way out of the kitchen, to flick on the TV in front of which he'll sit with his dad, quietly watching whatever crap might be on until they're finally tired enough for bed.

Oliver looks at the draining board.

Only two plates. And just forks. It breaks his heart all over again.

'Cup of tea, Jont?'

Bugger. No clean mugs again. He rinses out a couple with scalding water, using his thumbs to rub away the ring marks from previous brews.

I missed you today, DeeDee.

Is it OK to tell you that there are days now, almost three years on, when I don't know if I've thought about you so I remind myself to? That one day recently I merely mentioned you in passing and didn't pause after doing so? You were in and out of the conversation in a click. I was chatting to Adrian. Your name simply slid in and out of the conversation like a bird flying past.

Now I'm going to sit beside our son and watch TV till we're knackered. We don't put biscuits on a plate any more, DeeDee. We just eat them from the packet. And when Mrs Blackthorne comes – because she still comes – she has a week's worth of crumbs to deal with. Today, though – today I miss you, darling.

The Tree Houses

Where Vita lived, officially called Mill Lane, was always referred to as the Tree Houses. Not that these were eco-savvy dwellings in lofty boughs, however, but a terrace of small, plain, Victorian two-up, two-downs in red brick. Cherry Tree Cottage, Plum Tree Cottage, Walnut Tree Cottage, Damson, Apple, Hazel, Quince and Pear Tree Cottage. Apple Tree Cottage had a small, old, wizened tree in the front garden that each spring blossomed in a half-hearted manner but rarely followed through with fruit of any quality. The only blossom at Cherry Tree Cottage was garishly painted onto an elaborate name plaque. There were no eponymous trees at Walnut, Quince or Hazel. Damson Cottage had its windows and door painted the colour of the fruit but the garden itself was laid mainly to gravel. Plum Tree Cottage was by far the prettiest with roses around the front door, a lavender-bordered path and a profusion of gay bedding plants through the summer, but no plums. Pear Tree Cottage, Vita's house, was right at the end.

When she'd been house hunting, she'd felt sorry for the cottage as one might a mangy old dog at a rescue centre.

The exterior was drab and unkempt. Inside, it was dank and forlorn. The place smelt musty, in need of air, but many of the window frames had been painted over so often they no longer opened. Though the whole house needed decorating, it was actually the old wallpaper upstairs which had sold it to Vita. It was faded, but when she looked carefully she noted how it had been pretty once. Sprigs of flowers – mauve in one room, yellow in the other. She'd been told the late owner had been a bachelor who had lived there alone for over fifty years. But she'd stood in the back bedroom quietly considering that the lonely old bachelor must have had a lady friend who had advised on the wallpaper all those years ago. That, for a while, this shabby, stale house had been a home where the rooms had been tended to not just with floral paper. At some stage, love had been in this house.

Her mother, who was insisting on giving Vita her small inheritance early, had said, Darling, isn't that nice all-mod-cons, ten-year-guarantee new-build apartment overlooking the canal a better investment? But Vita said no. She wasn't looking for an investment; she was looking for a home.

What had once been Tim's house, Vita had made into their home over the four years they lived together; softening the hard edges of his statement furniture and proliferation of gadgets with a little bit of Cath Kidston here and there; making something domestic and homely of the space. But it wasn't hers to start with. When they'd split, Tim had given her an amount of money. Initially, she was resistant to his offer – not from any sense of pride or independence but because it was so brute. It felt as though Tim was quantifying the relationship, paying her off, throwing money at a problem to make her go away.

Vita's friends – who constituted a tight ring rather than a wide circle – let her stay in their spare rooms and marched her up and down local streets with estate agents' particulars in her hands. That's how she came to find herself at the Tree Houses and the down-trodden cottage right at the end of the row. The smallest of the cottages, in that no extensions had been added over the years, nor had the loft been converted, but of all the Tree Houses, Pear Tree Cottage had the biggest tree, and it was indeed a pear, dominating the back garden.

'I don't like that tree,' her mother had said. 'It looks a bit leering – like some guardian troll of the garden.'

But Vita made light of it.

'You can make me pear upside-down cake, Mum,' she had breezed deliberately. Her offer had been accepted, the surveyor had been round, the mortgage granted, and she desperately needed this to work. 'Or pear and chocolate brownies. Like you used to when I was little.'

Why doesn't she go for the canal-side flats with the gym in the basement? her friends worried behind her back.

That blimmin' great tree, the neighbours at the Tree Houses often remarked to each other over the garden fences.

* * *

Vita *thinks* she really likes the house and now that it is spring, and the blossom is stunning, she *thinks* she'll really like the garden too. But she keeps any ambivalence from her friends. She tells herself she doesn't want them to worry. Nor does she want to catch them giving each other 'that look' – which she reads as their frustration that she's still not quite cock-a-hoop about her new life. Their strategy is to enthuse, to encourage her and tell her that if she can work the wonders on the exterior that she has on the interior, then Pear Tree Cottage will reap dividends for her emotionally in the short term and financially in the long term too.

Her possessions are around her; it's her linen on the bed, her books on the shelf, her Cath Kidston oilcloth on the kitchen table. Those are her brush and roller marks on the white walls, that's her careful satinwooding on the skirting and doors that she spent weeks rubbing down. Apart from one wall of the faded wallpaper in the front bedroom upstairs, there's no longer any hint of the previous occupant. She bought a new seat for the loo, her mother gave her some ready-made curtains and the guy who fitted out the shop put in the Ikea kitchen units as a favour.

Despite all this, despite the black-and-white fact that it's Vita's name on the title deeds – the first time she's owned property – sometimes, it still feels as though she's squatting, as though she's in transit, that this can't be her destination. She's made the house very nice – but occasionally, she still feels her real home must be elsewhere. Not Tim's place, not now. Sometimes it simply feels that Pear Tree Cottage can't really be the place she's meant to live. She may well have signed the transfer papers, the mortgage, and a million other forms – but when did she sign up to living alone in her mid-thirties?

In the days just before she completed on the property, in the New Year, and just after she moved in, Vita desperately regretted the purchase. It was legal and binding and it meant that nothing could remain up in the air with Tim. He'd paid her off. She'd taken his money and invested it in the foundations of a house that in turn was apparently going to provide the foundation stone on which she'd be building her new life, or so her friends kept saying.

During those early weeks, when she was exhausted and

14

dusty and unnerved, guilt seeped in – on paper, she had her very own place, her friends had bedecked it with hope and good wishes and lovely moving-in gifts, her mother had poured money into it. How could she feel so ambivalent when she had such good fortune? She didn't want to record an answering machine message in the first person singular. She didn't want to cook for friends and then clear up on her own once they'd gone. She didn't want to stay in and watch a DVD by herself, nor, however, did she want to go out and then have to return on her own to an empty house. She was in limbo and so she didn't quite unpack. There are still a few boxes left to do, even now. Instead, she filled her time painting. White. White everywhere, apart from that one wall of faded floral paper. Coat after coat. Litres of the stuff. It wasn't a whitewash; Vita was providing herself with nothingness all around to contradict the emotions at loggerheads within.

Six months and two seasons on, she doesn't quite love her little house, but she does like it very much. What she still doesn't like is leaving and coming back during the working week. At That Shop, her link with Tim and the past remains and weekdays are comparatively unchanged. He'll come in and print off a till balance. She'll email him about an order. They'll discuss takings and promotions and what's to be done with the useless Saturday girl. The bills and statements come in, addressed to them both. There they are on paper, side by side still, in it together, partners. She doesn't see it as a stumbling block to the steady progress of moving on, she sees it as a safety net.

But Tim's made no secret of the fact that when business picks up, they should sell. Their only tie to each other is now financial. They remain bound to each other. And Tim has made it clear that it's a bind.

15

Michelle and Candy

'It's the first time she's ever missed Jakey's birthday.' Michelle nudged Candy that the traffic lights were on green. 'I know she'll be mortified when she finds out.'

'Was Jake all right about it?' Candy crunched gears and drove ahead. 'Damn, I could've taken a crafty back-double down there.'

'He's ten years old. I don't think he'll be emotionally scarred because his godmother forgot his birthday – but he'd calculated in advance how many presents he was due and he told me tonight, before I left, that he's going to sack Vita if she still hasn't remembered.'

'Scamp.'

'Bless him.'

'He'll go far.'

'He's a boy genius.'

'You would say that. You're his mother.'

'You'll be like that about Amelia.'

'Oh, I already am – she may be only nine months old but you do know she's the most beautiful child ever to have been born and staggeringly gifted too.'

'Come on, bloody traffic.'

Candy passed Michelle her phone. 'Let her know we're going to be late. Tell her it'll give her time to wrap Jake's present.'

'V, it's Mushroom – yes, late as always. Actually, it's traffic this time. Honestly! We're on our way – with wine and delectables from Marks and Sparks. See you in a mo'.'

'Is delectables a word?' Candy asked.

'It's perfect.'

'Mrs Sherlock, don't you think you're too old to be called Mushroom?'

'She couldn't pronounce Michelle when she was little. Granted, it's not the most beguiling of nicknames.'

'But you like it.'

'I do.'

'And yet you call her V, which she hates.'

'I know.'

'She gave me short shrift the one and only time I tried it.'

'I've known her my whole life – you've only known her since school, remember.'

'Ner ner!' Candy laughed. Then she paused. 'I haven't actually seen her since the Easter egg event at her shop. It'll be good to see what else she's done to the house – though I can't believe there was any more minging old carpet to rip up. And there's only so many times you can paint a wall white.'

'She'll put the colour back into her life when she's ready, Candy.'

'Or subtle shades of Farrow and Ball – I bought her a subscription to *LivingEtc* for Christmas.'

'I bought her a deckchair emblazoned with "Keep Calm and Carry On".'

For Candy and Michelle, seeing Vita barefoot was a great sight. Not that she had particularly stunning feet – just

17

that, to her closest friends, it made her look so at home, standing on her doorstep with no shoes on. It also spoke of the warm weather, that summer was truly coming, that socks wouldn't be needed for months, indoors or out.

Michelle and Candy waxed lyrical about the Victorian tiles on the front doorstep even though most were cracked or chipped, and as soon as they were over the threshold, they continued their assault of compliments, gushing about the floorboards as if Vita had sawn them herself instead of simply ripping up the old carpets. Both had been to the cottage many times and could see that she'd done little more to it since they were last there. Still, they cooed over her soft furnishings, ran their hands over windowsills and doors and told her the kitchen smelt amazing, even though she was merely heating up the finger food they'd brought with them.

Their enthusiasm was excessive – especially as neither saw her staying there indefinitely. They saw the cottage as a good, solid foothold on her road to independence, a good thing financially – she'd bought just at the right time – but ultimately wouldn't the hip-and-happening canal-side development better suit a single woman in her mid-thirties?

'Let's eat outside,' Vita said.

'Have you done much to the garden?'

'Come and see.'

Michelle and Candy brought out a kitchen chair each and Vita followed with cushions. To make room for the extra chairs, Vita scurried about moving the pots of pansies, a galvanized trough with chives and thyme doing well, a trowel and a plastic watering can. The deckchair that Michelle had bought her was positioned to catch the last of the sun that lingered on the small paved area right outside the kitchen door as if blessing it. It couldn't really be called a patio – just as the small patch of grass couldn't be called a lawn; nor could the bed which ran the short length to the back of the garden be called a herbaceous border. But Vita's friends noted the planting she'd done – just busy-lizzies and geraniums but a quick colour fix to welcome the summer nonetheless.

'I really need a table – sorry, laps'll have to do.'

'What's in the shed at the back?'

'Spiders.'

Back in midwinter, when she'd first shown them around, Vita had gone on and on about trees being the cathedrals of the natural world while Candy had described the pear tree as more like a derelict sixties tower block. The tree had seemed so dark, so overbearing and ominous with its thrust and scratch of bare branches, its dense trunk. Today, it struck Michelle and Candy as a more benign presence, like an over-the-top prop at a Hollywood wedding, billowing with blossom which wafted down gently around them like confetti, like manna, like fake snow in a department-store window display at Christmas. Soft and pretty – if you ignored the little brown bits which were surprisingly itchy. Vita, however, was grinning at it inanely.

'Who needs acreage and fancy shrubs when you have something like *that* in the garden,' she said. 'The tree *is* the garden!'

'Can you imagine the amount of pears you're going to have,' said Candy, with slight unease. She wasn't entirely sure whether each flower on Vita's tree equalled a future fruit.

'I know!' she said, ignoring the point. 'I thought I might try making chutney or something, perhaps a cordial – and I could bottle it and do labels and sell it in the shop.'

19

'Tim'll love that,' Candy said under her breath.

'I heard that,' Vita said.

'How is the charming son-of-a?' Candy asked.

The pause that ensued really should have been long enough for Candy to check in with Michelle and note a glower which said, Don't go there. But she didn't. She was picking petals from her wine.

'I miss the company but I don't miss him,' Vita announced brightly, a mantra she'd trained herself to deliver. 'It's a bugger about the business – but neither of us can afford to buy the other out.'

'You wouldn't sell to him, would you?'

'I'd rather have That Shop to myself. But I can't afford it.'

'How's his day job?'

Vita shrugged. 'I don't know how much marketing consultants are wanted – or worth – in a recession.'

'Here's to you,' said Candy, 'not him.' She chinked her glass against Vita's.

'And you.'

'May a gallant knight ride by soon and sweep you off your feet.'

'No, thanks,' said Vita.

'A bit of rough, then?'

Vita laughed. 'I think I should be on my own for a while, actually.'

'Yay! Girl power and women's lib and all that.'

Candy always had the other two giggling.

'It's warm, isn't it. I can't believe there's going to be a heatwave – when we've just raided the piggy bank to go to Florida this summer,' said Michelle.

'I'm going to have a staycation,' said Vita, 'here in my garden.'

'Gathering pears and churning chutney?' said Candy.

'How delightfully Thomas Hardy,' said Michelle.

'Oh shit! The spring rolls!' Vita darted back into the kitchen to rescue them.

'Don't tell her,' Michelle said to Candy.

'Don't tell her about what?' Candy said to Michelle.

'About Tim,' Michelle said to Candy as if she was dense.

'Don't tell me what about Tim?' Vita said to both of them, standing there with a plate of spring rolls so over-cooked they looked like cigarillos.

'Oh, nothing,' said Candy. 'I do love busy-lizzies.'

'They're called Impatiens,' said Michelle.

'Stop changing the subject,' said Vita, hiding growing unease behind a larky tone.

'Actually – you know what? It's no bad thing for her to hear,' Candy said to Michelle who turned her head and stared stubbornly at the old fence that looked as though it was staggering along at the back of the garden.

'Candy?' Vita gestured that she'd be ransoming nibbles for information.

'I had lunch at the Nags Head the other day,' Candy said. 'I hadn't been in there for ages – anyway, the landlady greeted me like a long-lost friend. She asked after all of us – you especially. Well, you know how she likes a gossip.'

'And she said –?' Vita was fixing her best carefree smile to her face.

'Oh, she just said that Tim often goes in there. Gets plastered.'

'That's nothing new.'

Candy was in her stride. 'Yes, but here's the funny part. He tends to go in there with this girl and invariably they get drunk, have flaming rows and one or other storms off.'

*

Who is she? Who *is* she?

'Anyway, last week they go in there, the pair of them,' Candy continued, 'they drink, they row – she flounces out the back door, he storms out the front then half an hour later, he *reappears with a totally different girl*! The sleaze! A couple of hours pass – then he's suddenly ushering *her* out of the *front* door before *Suzie* comes in again through the *back* door and—'

'Suzie?'

Candy stared aghast at her burnt spring roll as if looking directly at her faux pas. Michelle glanced at Vita, noted the goosebumps on her arms.

'*Suzie?*' Vita said again.

Candy shrugged. 'Does it matter?'

Vita gave herself a moment. 'No,' she said brightly, 'not a bit. You're right. He's a sleaze. It's just hard hearing *she's* still on the scene. I wish he was with someone completely different.'

'It hardly sounds like he's gone on to forge a good relationship though, does it?' Michelle said in a tone of voice Vita had heard her use to great effect with her children – when downplaying a fall or a bump, so they wouldn't be alarmed. So they would feel better.

'I'd pity *her*, if I was you,' Candy said. 'She's now lumbered with all that you shifted.' She touched Vita's knee. 'Promise you'll think of Tim even less now – and think even less of him because of what I've told you?' Candy said. 'Me and my stupid big gob?'

'Don't call yourself Big Gob,' Vita said softly. It's what the bullies had called Candy at school. A beautiful Ugandan refugee who'd arrived in their small Hertfordshire town twenty years ago.

Vita didn't want more details. She didn't want to be

22

reminded of her past or how different her present was from the future she'd taken for granted. So she encouraged Candy to run off on tangents about films she'd never get to see and frocks she still couldn't fit into. And she gave Michelle a nod every now and then to say, I'm fine, stop worrying about me.

Vita Whitbury, way past midnight, all on her own. Not that it seems that way, with the riot of Tim thoughts filling her head. Infidelity, lies, deceit. She tried to rationalize that Tim's life was the same but the cast around him had changed. And though his life sounded lairy, uncouth, unsavoury and diametrically opposed to all Vita hoped for in her own, a niggle remained to taunt her. Suzie was still on the scene. Of all the people – why had it to be her?

Vita wonders, Why do I still feel I could have done more to inspire him not to stray? Why do I still feel it's a failing, an inadequacy, on my part?

And she wonders, How does his happiness graph look these days?

And she wonders, Where has my self-esteem gone?

And how am I to get it back?

She reaches to the bedside table and takes her pad of Post-its and a pen.

Phone Tim

She reads what she's written. Then she adds *DON'T* at the start, scratching the letters down hard. She switches off the light and tucks down. She can see the pear tree, the blossom ethereal in the moonlight. It's one of the things she really likes about her house – she doesn't need to close the curtains and be surrounded by darkness at the end of the day.

23

Tinker, Spike and Boz

'Can I get a lift to school?'

Oliver raised his eyebrow at his son. 'Again, please?'

Jonty groaned and thought, Yeah, yeah, I know, Mum would make me ask again – at much the same time as his father was saying precisely that. Jonty thought, Give us a break, Dad. But he knew his father was right because his mother had been right too. He cleared his throat and gave a quick toss of his head to flick his long fringe away from his face. '*May I have* a lift to school, please?'

Oliver smiled. 'Of course.'

'What use is textbook grammar when we communicate more by text messages anyway?' Jonty murmured, shuffling into his blazer and hoicking his schoolbag over one shoulder.

'It's not about the grammar, per se,' said Oliver. 'It's about laziness, it's about apathy. That's why I hate all this texting business – not bothering with vowels because consonants will do because *y'know wha' I mean*.'

'*Innit*,' Jonty said and they laughed together. 'Language evolves, Dad. "Chav" is in the dictionary. L8R looks good – it's clever.'

'It's a fad.'

'You sound like an old fart.'

'I *am* an old fart. Believe me – you'd rather have an old fart for a dad than some divvy trying to be cool. Far more embarrassing.'

'Who the heck says "divvy"!'

'I do.'

'Don't say it again.'

'Pillock.'

'That's worse, Dad.'

'I know. It's my job to annoy you like it's your job to wind me up.'

Jonty thought, Actually, my dad is cool and he doesn't wind me up all that much.

'Come on, kiddo, let's go. Have you got money for lunch?'

'Father!' Jonty remonstrated. 'Again, please!'

Oliver coshed him softly. '*Do you have* money for lunch?'

Watching Jonty lope off towards school with his mates, all of them in skinny trousers slung low, schoolbags as beat up as possible, hair lank and long and dyed darker than necessary, Oliver thought to himself how, had DeeDee still been here, he would probably be the one coping with their son's teenagerisms the better, and it might well have caused a degree of antagonism between them. She'd have been much more *You can't go out looking like that* at Jonty. She'd have said, Oliver! You speak to him! Oliver might have been caught in the crossfire. It gave him a lift to know he was doing all right as a dad to a teenage son. He liked to sense DeeDee's approval. It was very odd to feel that these days Dead DeeDee possibly liked him more than DeeDee Living might have done.

25

Oh, but what I'd give for a little healthy real-life snippiness, Oliver thought as he headed off for his yard. What I'd give to hear her mutter, For God's sake, Ols.

How he longed to argue over the finer points of managing a teenager, instead of muddling through it all on his own, albeit now doing things his way all the time without prior discussion. So, though he wasn't the stickler for homework she had been, and although bed-time had become a movable feast and supper was now very movable indeed – usually in foil trays eaten off laps and sometimes left on the coffee table overnight – keeping up DeeDee's obsession with grammar was a baton he'd gladly taken from her. He knew he and Jonty would run with it their whole lives.

At the yard, Boz and Spike, the two Aussies working for him, were loading the truck.

'Tinker?' Oliver asked.

'Making a brew,' said Spike. Oliver often reflected how he only seemed to employ youngsters from the Commonwealth – but there again, home-grown interest in arboriculture appeared to be sparse. And he did wonder why he gravitated towards those with names like Tinker and Boz and Spike – but he had to concede there were few applications arriving on his desk from Tom, Dick or Harry. He had a great team though – hardworking and sweet-natured. He enjoyed having them under his wing and his clients responded well. He felt paternal towards them – their own fathers being back home, time zones away. He also felt a keen duty to his trade – to hone their technical abilities as well as to train their eyes to *feel* a tree. Having a licence to use a chainsaw up a tree was one thing, but to sense innately how each individual tree ought to look was another. Two to four places on every branch where cuts could be made while balancing the resultant shape for the good of the tree – that was where art met science and technical ability met intuition. That's where Oliver felt an aboriculturalist's true skill lay. To make a tree look more like a tree, to return some hacked-about old giant, or some mangy neglected specimen, to the sculptural beauty that was its birthright. Every tree he'd ever worked on, Oliver aimed to leave as an archetype, as if Gainsborough or Poussin or Constable, Cézanne even, might have chosen it as the prime example of its genus to grace their art.

Just as Oliver chose his branches with care, so too did he select his workforce. Boz had a degree in Art History. Spike had exhibited as a sculptor before retraining in Arboriculture. Tinker grew up in Canada, in Jasper, surrounded by trees.

Oliver checked the diary.

'You two – take the ash near Much Hadham we saw last week. You need to offer the wood to Mrs Cadogan first – if she doesn't want it, don't chip it. Bring it back and it can go on the first wood pile there – because?'

'Because you can burn it green,' said Boz mechanically, an answer he'd given many times.

'Good lad. Tinker – you can come with me. It's the cherry near Hatfield you took the call about.'

'Laters!' called Tinker to the other two.

And Oliver thought, Good God, kid – if DeeDee had heard that.

A village green, a single-track road all around it, cottages encircling it with swathes of grass in front of their boundaries. A gathering of oaks to one side, two grand sweet chestnuts on the other side. Small trees – apple, magnolia – in front gardens. A weeping willow in front of the cottages on the far side. And here, on the common ground by two cottages, was the tree Oliver had come to see. It was a breathtaking sight. A magnificent holly-leaved cherry still in full bloom in June.

'When I have a garden of my own, I'll plant every type of prunus and have flowers from November to now,' said Tinker.

'You'll never have that garden on the wages I pay you,' Oliver said with a gentle regret.

They sat in the truck and regarded the tree. People were crossing the green expressly to see it. A mother and two toddlers. An elderly couple. A youth with a fierce-looking hound. Two female pensioners. It was singing out, its blossom festooning the boughs and drifting gently down and around like sugar petals. Catching the sun, caught on the breeze, captivating. A man, with hands on hips, stood at the bottom of one of the cottage driveways.

'Come on,' said Oliver, striding off, followed by Tinker. 'Mr Macintosh?'

'Do you see?' called the man from the driveway, long before they were near. 'Can you see?'

'It's some sight,' said Oliver, '*Prunus ilicifolia*.'

'It's new!' said Mr Macintosh.

'Sorry?'

'My jag – it's *new*. And look at it!'

Oliver glanced at the new car on the driveway. 'Very nice,' he said politely.

'Look at it!'

'I was looking at the tree,' said Oliver.

'But look at my Jag. Look at what that wretched tree's done to it. Weeks now. Weeks of this – this *stuff*.'

Oliver and Tinker dragged their eyes from the tree to observe the car, covered with petals as if it had been decorated for a bridal couple.

'It's got to go.'

'That's a shame,' said Tinker. 'I'd love a Jag.'

'Couldn't you park it in your garage?' Oliver asked.

'Not the car, man – the tree! I'm not putting the car in the garage – I want to see it every time I look out of my window. I worked my whole life to have a car like that. And I want to see it in British Racing Green – not flaming white bloody mess.'

'The blossom will only last another week,' said Oliver, 'a week or so.'

'I want that tree gone – it's a hazard, a menace. It's dangerous. If it rained, all that blossom underfoot would be slippery. I might fall. I might do my other hip.'

Oliver looked around. Cars had parked along the green, visitors were coming into this village precisely to see the tree and the heavenly blossom. Furthermore, it was set to be a very dry July.

'Can you take it down now?'

'No, I can't.'

'Well, when can you? I'll pay now.'

'I'm not going to take the tree down.'

'Well, chop off all the branches on this side, then.'

'That's not possible. It would damage the tree.'

'It's criminal damage! It's affecting my property.'

'It's blossom.'

'It's *litter* – natural litter. That's what it is. I want the damn tree down.'

DeeDee would say, I want doesn't get.

'It's a healthy tree, it's a superb specimen and it is not affecting your house.'

'Well, I'll tell the council, I will. It's their bloody thing. It's on their land. I pay my council tax. They can cut it down. I'll sue. That's what.'

And Oliver thought, As soon as we're back in the car,

29

I'll phone Martin in planning and I'll tell him this tree mustn't come down. That'll save him a journey.

'What are you doing?'

'I'm photographing the tree,' said Oliver.

'I don't give permission for you to take my picture.'

'You're not in the picture.'

'Why are you photographing that tree? For the council? Yes! Show it to them. They'll see what I mean.'

'Not for the council – for my own archives. I'm photographing it because it's stunning,' said Oliver. 'Goodbye, Mr Macintosh. There's a hand car wash on the way to Asda.'

'Are you not going to do anything today? Can't you give it a *trim*?'

'No, I can't, I'm afraid. Paperwork.'

'Good God! How long will that take?'

'Difficult to tell,' Oliver shrugged and walked back to his truck. He and Tinker sat and marvelled a little longer.

'What a jerk,' said Tinker.

'It's not just extraordinary trees you meet in this job,' Oliver told him.

Back at the yard later that afternoon, ash branches cut, split and added to the pile of seasoned wood, the team shared tea and anecdotes. Oliver looked around. There was a little clearing up to do, a couple of calls to make, some paperwork.

'Call it a day, chaps,' said Oliver. 'See you at eight tomorrow.'

'You sure?'

'I'm sure – Jonty's playing cricket so I'll finish off here and then collect him. It's a strange sight, moochiness and Goth-dark hair – in cricket whites.'

'Is he good?'

'He's not bad at all.'

'Cool. How's he doing?'

'He's doing well, Boz – thanks for asking.'

'Is he going to hang out here in the vacation? He was useful last time.'

'I hope so – though he'll probably want to renegotiate pay and working conditions.'

'Good on him.'

'Don't put ideas in his head, Spike. Go on, all of you, off you go.'

'Cheers, boss.'

'See you tomorrow.'

'Laters.'

Good God.

But Oliver smiled as they walked off. He could hear them chatting and they weren't talking about beer and birds. They were talking about cherry trees and gifts.

'I need to send home a present for my sis. Any ideas?'

'Go online and do the whole Amazon dot com thing.'

'Nah. She's going to be ten. Requires something special.'

'Gap? Topshop?'

'I can't go in there on my own.'

'Twat.'

'Cheers, mate.'

'Try that shop in town? You know the one – That Shop? All the trinketty things in the window?' Tinker was often teased for the way he made every sentence a question.

'Oh yeah.'

'We can go past that way – come on.'

* * *

To Vita, the three young men with a good day's manual work written all over their tired faces, dusty boots and forearms, were far more incongruous customers than her notorious little old lady, currently rifling through the fruit-shaped scented soaps. When she started the business, Vita swore never to utter the four words sure to dampen the ardour of any unsure shopper, *May I help you?* She'd researched it – listening in other shops, trying it herself. May I help you? Nine times out of ten, four words sprang an automatic reply. *No thanks, just looking.* Vita, therefore, devised other techniques, discovering how casual asides worked best. She assessed the posse and tried to work out which one was buying. The tallest one, she reckoned, the one with the curly dark hair and the smudge of something or other on his neck. Yes, the other two appeared to be looking on his behalf while he stood still and scanned the wares as a whole. She put down her book as if it was high time she had a little tidy of the table with the notecards and scented lip balms. As she neared, one of them – the one with the closely cropped hair and goatee – picked up the linen-and-patchwork beanbag mouse.

'Lovely for a baby,' she mentioned as she passed by. 'Organic cotton – and nothing that can be pulled off or swallowed.'

The lad looked at her, jiggled the mouse, put it back down. 'Oh, it's not for a baby?' he said. 'It's for his kid sister?'

Aha!

'How old is his kid sister?' Vita asked.

'Boz – she's ten, isn't she? Ten, ma'am?'

Vita, who'd never been called ma'am before, was suddenly quite taken with it. 'Ten, hey? Ten-year-old girls have secrets – and they need places to hide them.'

The other two had gravitated towards her and their mate.

'Well – I don't sell secrets, I'm afraid,' said Vita. They all laughed. 'But I do have – *these*.' She guided them towards the back of the shop, smiling sweetly at the old lady who was pocketing something. 'Here.'

She showed them the balsa-wood boxes made to look like miniature wardrobes. Each had a drawer under a door, with a proper keyhole and brass key that was ornate and looked old. They were about the size of a shoebox, deceptively light, in paint washes that suggested they'd been found on a sand dune.

'Yeah!' said the brother of the birthday girl who she thought was called Bruiser or something. 'That'll hit the spot.' Australian, Vita thought.

'Ma'am?' said the American or Canadian who'd first spoken to her. He was talking quietly but urgently. 'That old woman? She's – I think – well, she's kinda taken something? I don't know what. Would you like me to – you know?'

Vita brushed the air quickly. 'No, no – she's fine. I know her.' She was much more interested in matchmaking a ten-year-old with a gift.

The three young men looked towards the door where the old lady was headed – and then earnestly back at Vita.

'But she's—?'

'Please,' Vita said, 'it's fine. Honestly. Now – about your sister?'

'It's awesome, miss,' said the Bruiser brother. Vita thought she preferred *miss* to *ma'am*. 'I'll take it. The bluish one, I reckon. What do you think, Tink?'

'If I was your sis? I'd think you were damn cool, Boz.'

'Boz,' said Vita, to herself but out loud.

'Yeah?'

Vita reddened. 'It's just the male customers I usually

33

have are mostly called Felix and Ted and Blaise – names like that. And they're usually holding their mums' hands.'

'It's short for Robert,' Boz told her, which he could hear didn't make any sense so he chuckled.

'Spike's short for Michael,' Boz continued, motioning to the one who had yet to speak. 'And Tinker – what the fuck is your name, mate?'

Vita thought, I'll let the swearing go – there's no one else in the shop and the boxes are quite pricey.

'Taylor,' said Tinker and everyone simply nodded.

'When do you need this for?' Vita asked. 'It's just that I could put your sister's name on it – hand stencil it – look, like the one in the window.'

The boys murmured their approval.

'I could have it ready for tomorrow morning And I could gift-wrap it too. After you've seen it, of course.'

'Thanks, miss, that would be awesome.'

'Excellent. What's her name?' And Vita hoped it was something pretty and not a daft nickname.

'Megan.'

'Excellent.'

'Shall I pay now?'

'Would you mind?'

Boz looked at her as if she was mad. 'Of course I don't mind. This is *awesome*.'

'See you tomorrow,' Vita said as she handed back his credit card and receipt.

'I've read that book,' said Spike, the quiet one, another Aussie, motioning towards *Robinson Crusoe*. 'Couldn't get to grips with *Moll Flanders*, though.'

After they'd gone, and once the school rush had abated, Vita started stencilling Megan's name. She'd felt so dis-orientated after that night recently with Candy and Michelle – but today she felt as though she'd been sent

34

three rugged guardian angels, one of whom was paying her to do something other than think about Tim and Suzie. She rifled through her stencil collection.

'I'll add a pattern,' she said. 'Free of charge.' Her evening was sorted. She was relieved. She wrote on a Post-it and stuck it to the box.

Megan
Butterflies?
Vines?

Something for the Weekend

'I remember this shop,' Oliver told Boz as they drove past That Shop towards the end of that week. 'Not that I've ever been in. But when my wife – but when my late wife and I – used to come into town, she'd always say, I'm just going to pop into That Shop. And ten hours later she'd always bought some tutt or other.'

'Tutt!' Boz liked the word. Then he looked worried. 'The box – thing – I've bought Megan, it's not tutt. It's nicely made – it's not cheap. Value, I'd say. She'll love it.'

Oliver smiled as he scouted for a parking place in the multi-storey. 'By *tutt*, I don't mean the quality, I don't mean *tat* – I mean *girl stuff*. The bits and bobs females never grow too old to fawn over and buy. Yet more photo frames, vases, candles, strange holders for wooden spoons, retro tea towels, bowls that are pretty but shaped too oddly to actually be useful. Heart-shaped stuff. Cushions. Bloody cushions – to be arranged daily, meticulously, on the bed or sofa yet always chucked off.' He raised an eyebrow at Boz. 'I'll stay in the car, thanks.'

'Might be a trinket that tickles your fancy, boss?'

'I'll stay in the car.'

'I'll be quick.'

Boz thought, Poor fucker. Boz and the boys always gave each other a look on Oliver's behalf which said, Poor fucker, whenever he referred to DeeDee as if she was an old pal who had simply moved away from the area temporarily instead of being the victim of a tragic road accident three years previously.

I'll stay in the car.

I'll make a couple of calls.

No signal.

I'll stay in the car.

Christ, this car park is a hellhole.

I'll listen to the radio.

No signal.

I'll stay in the car.

Boz won't be long.

There's only so much tutt even a young bloke can take, surely.

Vita heard the door open and read fast to just near the end of the page where there was a convenient line-break before she looked up.

'Ah! I was wondering when you'd be along.' She presented Boz with the wooden box. 'I hope you like it. And, of course, your sister Megan.'

Boz was delighted as he inspected it from all angles. 'It's cool. It's very very cool.'

'I did her name, as you see – but I also added this little design. I was going to do a grapevine but I chose hops. They're native to Kent, tell her. Which is known as the "Garden of England", tell her – not that I've ever been. Tell her, we make beer from hops.'

Boz looked at her quizzically. He wanted to say, Like

37

we don't have beer in Oz? But though there was an engaging artlessness to this woman, there was a fragility too – and she was so serious about this box and the extra design – and he thought perhaps a tease might be heard as sarcasm. So he nodded and thanked her. She wrapped it in pretty paper, swathed it in bubble wrap and parcelled it up in heavy-duty brown paper. And then he saw a photo frame. It was in a soft padded faded floral fabric and it reminded him of the dress that Jessie had worn to her sister's wedding.

'I'll have this too,' he said. 'It's for my girlfriend, Jessie.'

'That's nice,' Vita smiled.

'She's back home.'

'You must miss her.'

'Yeah – but you know what? We've been together ages – we're cool.'

'I could unwrap this lot, then you could put it inside your sister's box and tell her to deliver it for you – save on two packages.'

Boz thought this was quite the most brilliant plan and told the lady so as she unwrapped and rewrapped the goods. If he was still in the UK at Christmas-time, he told her, he'd do all his gift shopping right here.

I'll take some fresh air, I think.

I'll wander down in the vague direction of That Shop.

Oliver looked at the window display, glanced beyond it, noted the sales assistant sitting on a stool, reading, absent-mindedly tucking her hair behind her ears as it fell forward again and again. Stuff. Everywhere. Tables and shelves of stuff.

Oh God, DeeDee, he would groan when they used to meet back at the car after one of her forays. Not more *stuff*.

38

But I love That Shop, she'd protest with a pout that turned into a smile. And Oliver would unlock the car and say, Get in, Mrs Bourne, we're going home.

He wasn't about to break the habit of a lifetime ago, today. But he did pop his head around the corner of the door and immediately felt he should raise his voice a little – as if the colliding fragrances from all the candles and soaps were a sound as much as a scent.

'Come on, Boz. Back to work.'

'Scented drawer liners for you, boss?' said Boz, holding up a pack.

Oliver laughed. The sales assistant looked up momentarily before returning her attention to her book.

* * *

'You are coming to a party!' Michelle breezed into the shop, moments later, fresh from the hairdresser; her chestnut hair glossy and well cut, her eyes glinting at Vita who looked up from her book, a little confused.

'Am I?' She wracked her memory but could only conjure an image of all the empty boxes for June on the calendar on the back of the kitchen door at Pear Tree Cottage.

'You *are* coming to a party,' Michelle said again, this time in a fairy-godmother tone as if telling Vita, You shall go to the ball. 'It's on Saturday. You remember Mel and Des? It's their party – they're having it at the George and Dragon. They said to invite you. They said they haven't seen you for ages. They said for me to tell you that there are a couple of other single women going.'

Vita was just about to dwell on this fact being an anathema to someone who'd so liked being half of a couple when Michelle told her to hurry up, grab her bag and put the *Back After Lunch* sign up in the shop door.

'My treat,' said Michelle, linking arms with Vita and heading off towards the brasserie.

'Two for One,' Vita read the offer emblazoned over the lunchtime menu. 'Cheapskate!'

'Shut up and eat,' said Michelle. 'You look like you've lost half a stone since I saw you last – and that's not a compliment.' She pushed the bread basket towards Vita and poured a little olive oil into a saucer. 'It's quiet in here, isn't it? The weather's glorious, there's no World Cup or Olympics – where is everyone?'

'I ask myself the same question,' Vita said. 'The shop's been dead today.'

'Mind you,' said Michelle, 'I saw some strapping young bloke with a big package coming out of your shop.'

'You ought to rephrase that,' said Vita and Michelle laughed before noticing that Vita was miles away, staring into the middle distance and pulling little pinches of bread off the slice.

'Earth to Vita?'

Vita gave Michelle an unconvincing smile before masticating excessively over a small crust. Michelle tipped her head to one side and dunked her foccaccia thoughtfully in the oil. She never needed to say anything for Vita to feel she could offload; no invitation required, no subtle extraction of information necessary.

'Having a bit of a wobble?' Michelle simply said.

Vita stopped chewing. 'A bit,' she nodded. 'Been feeling a little thrown off balance this last week.' She shrugged. 'Stupid, really.'

'What does it boil down to?' Michelle asked, shooing away the waiter with a *two minutes, please* gesture.

Vita took a moment. Then she placed her hands palms down on the table as if laying her proverbial cards out. 'I wasn't doing too badly recently,' she said at length. 'The weird thing is, while I have no regrets – I do still hurt. I do. I'm sorry. I know it frustrates you. I know you all hate him. But I find myself at thirty-three on my own, alone, when all I wanted was to be part of a pair.'

'Tim was the rotten part of the pair,' Michelle said carefully. 'And if I was Candy I'd be able to think of some pithy allusion to the plentiful pears on your ridiculously big tree.'

Vita looked at Michelle and shrugged. 'We were together six years. We lived together for almost five.'

'I know,' said Michelle. 'But you wouldn't want to go back.'

'No,' Vita said quietly. She paused. 'You'll be mad at me for saying this – and I know it's probably irrational – but last week, finding out he's still with this bloody Suzie woman, it's knocked me sideways. I've been feeling – Christ! – *insecure*. It now feels like it diminishes what we ever had, as if *he* left *me* – for her.' She gave Michelle an embarrassed smile.

Michelle wanted very much to call her crazy but she resisted. 'You don't want to be her and you don't want what she has.'

Vita shrugged. 'It's. Just. Hard. It's tough knowing there's a woman placing her head in the crook of his shoulder where mine used to fit so nicely; that he's spooning up to her at night. There they are, watching telly, side by side, while here's me who can't see the point of watching TV any more – how can you watch *The Apprentice* without someone with whom to marvel at the atrociousness of the contestants?' Vita paused. 'Then there's the sex. And Sundays. And the domesticity of a shopping list. And something as stupid and enjoyable as compiling future rentals on Lovefilm dot com.'

Michelle nodded as she thought of her husband and

41

the domesticity and the closeness and the lists on Lovefilm dot com. The safety and the pleasure.

'I've been doing a lot of what-if thinking,' Vita confessed as if it was a crime.

'Let me guess,' Michelle interrupted. 'What if he's changed! What if he's turned over a new leaf! What if you gave him one more second chance – which would, over the years, probably amount to, let's see, his third second chance? What if love means never having to say you're sorry!'

'What if I hadn't been driven to check his messages and I hadn't found "Sxxx" all over them like a rash – would it have run its course? Would we still be together? What if we'd set the date for the wedding – would he have been less tempted?'

Michelle looked at her levelly. 'What if there's a fantastic new breed of leopard that can miraculously change its spots! What if it's all your fault – what if it's you who made a stupid mistake in leaving him!' It was as ridiculous as it was challenging.

Vita stared down at her uneaten goat's cheese tartlet. 'What if she's the new me?' she shrugged. 'A new version, with improved features and a lifetime guarantee?'

'What if it's not about you,' Michelle countered, 'and it's not even about her. Just him.' Her tone softened. 'Look, lady – you wanted what was wholesome but you were doomed, V, from the start – not from any failing on your part, but due to inadequacies on his. Please don't fret about floozy Suzie. If Candy was here, she'd be banging on about her Laws of Karma – for the person who behaves badly, worse things await them. For those who behave well, rewards will be reaped. You're entitled to something good now. I just can't tell you when. Probably not this Saturday night at Mel and Des's party – but you never know.'

Vita smiled and took a forkful of tart. 'For all his faults, I did love him, you know.'

'I do know,' Michelle said, 'and you'll take all that love forward with you.'

'Closure doesn't come with one slam of the door,' Vita told her. 'Moving on isn't a continuous forward momentum. It's a process and this last week, it's been a bit demoralizing for me to realize I'm not as near the end of it as I thought.'

'It's a journey, V – and you're well on your way. Don't dwell on all the crap that made you so sad – let's welcome summer and all things new. Go home tonight and sort out what you'll wear on Saturday – or borrow something of mine – and start gearing yourself up to enjoy yourself. It's party time. It's summertime. Look around you – everything is bursting with colour and warmth and vitality. The evenings are long. The days are gorgeous. Lie out in your deckchair on the patch of grass which that flipping tree doesn't cast into shade – and get yourself a little bit of a tan before Saturday night.'

Vita tried to look convinced. Michelle could see she was trying and that was good enough for her. She'd be all right, her best and oldest friend. She'd get her bounce back. This was Vita – and her name meant life and it suited her very well.

'Saturday, then?' Michelle kissed her on each cheek, having walked her back to That Shop.

'Saturday indeed,' said Vita, not with reluctance but with a little trepidation.

She phoned her mother later, when she was home. She was sitting in the 'Keep Calm and Carry On' deckchair, her T-shirt sleeves rolled up and over her shoulders, her skirt pulled right up to her knickers. Fortunately, Mr Brewster next door was very short-sighted. He was very

43

short, full stop. And polite too – he'd never think of looking over the fence. Not that he'd be able to.

Vita was about to tell her mum about the party; she thought it would make her happy, relieved. But suddenly there was something far more exciting to tell her because, from her deckchair, when she looked up, she could see that pears were just beginning to form. Small, misshapen and bitter green. But growing. Lots of them. Look at them all!

*   *   *

Jonty was doing homework when Oliver logged into his email account, the Hotmail one, the private one, the one his son couldn't possibly know about. As a family, DeeDee had set them up with their own web address, all of them at Bourne three dot com: *deedee@bournethree.com, jont@ bournethree.com, oliver@bournethree.com.*

From the start, Oliver had rarely used it, entrusting DeeDee to check his inbox, to physically drag him to the computer, when absolutely necessary, to read some missive of merit. He told her he was always happy for her to respond on his behalf. She often did, signing off as Ols and sometimes having the last laugh by adding an inappropriate x or two. Nowadays, he logs in and deletes most of the messages, making a note on a pad of paper who's been in touch so he can call them at some later date if he can remember. That evening, the inbox was crowded but he deleted most of them, still unread. Then he checked DeeDee's account. New emails still arrived. Today, there were offers from Johnnie Boden and Jo Malone – as if they were personal friends. Ocado was trying to coax her back with discounts and free delivery if she could order before Friday. It was comforting that out there, she was still seen as alive.

Mostly, for email, Oliver used his work account *bourne@arbor-vitae.co.uk*, but actually, he preferred the phone. A man in his mid-forties doesn't really do the whole email thing as a social communication tool. Nine months after DeeDee died, however, he set up the Hotmail account, realizing there was a useful distinction between communication and contact. This account he does check regularly – not obsessively, but regularly and very privately. Furtively, rather than privately. A secret account, really, rather than simply a private one.

He logged on. There was an email in the inbox. He opened it. It was an invitation for that weekend. He thought he'd better respond straight away.

Saturday is good, he wrote. *Let me know where and when.*

The George and Dragon

'And you're here with—?'

This was the third time Vita had been asked the question, as if a girl like her couldn't possibly be at a party like this on her own. Or be on her own, full stop.

The first time, she'd faltered and blurted out, Oh, I'm here on my own – because, because I'm not with anyone. Not any more. Just me – I'm on my own, you see. Which is why I'm here – er, on my own but it's a nice party, isn't it. And the woman had given her a kindly nod contradicted by a slightly startled look about the eyes. So after that, Vita had taken to saying, I'm here with Michelle and Chris. Because everybody there knew Michelle and Chris.

'I'm so glad you're here.' Michelle came up behind Vita and gave her a squeeze. 'And you look good enough to eat.'

She'd been with Vita when she'd bought that frock this time last year, a shift dress in soft raspberry hemmed in velvet the colour of blueberry. 'You look like summer pudding.'

'Better than Eton mess,' Vita said, thinking back to the first outfit she'd tried on – a cream top with a skirt of splodgy reds. God, the trauma of changing time and again, earlier that evening. How she cursed Tim for not being there – completely overlooking how she'd cursed him when, on occasion, he'd given her a look just before they went out which said, Honey – I'm not sure about the frock. It had hurt like crazy and such evenings had been marred because of it. But he'd loved the dress she was wearing tonight. She'd given herself a twirl in her bedroom and she'd stopped and stared straight at herself. *Amazing how he could both raise my self-confidence and dash it.* And yet she did long for him just then, to hear him say, Come on, woman! We're late already – nice frock, by the way. Instead she called out Bye! to the emptiness of the house, locked the door and made small talk with the cab driver.

Michelle hugged her, Mel did too. Their husbands brought her drinks and food. Then they made a really sweet, attentive job of introducing her to anyone they were talking to. And Vita worked hard to join in breezily, to laugh alongside them and nod or frown at appropriate moments. She raised her glass in a nonchalant way when they drifted away naturally to socialize elsewhere while she dealt with the excruciating intervals when she found herself alone, standing like a lemon with a casual smile fixed to her face while she gazed vaguely around the room. What she wanted to do was go home and watch TV in her jimjams. And it was hard work when Michelle so sweetly passed by every now and then with a fresh drink for her and a really genuine, Are you OK? Isn't this fun! The only reply possible was to nod and grin some more and say, Yeah! It's great! because it wasn't the place to say, Mushroom this is *torture*.

'*He's* single,' Michelle whispered, bringing Vita a cosmopolitan. She was nodding towards an oaf of a man with a laugh as bad as his shoes, who already had food and drink splattered over his taut shirt like bad graffiti.

Momentarily, Vita looked at Michelle in horror until she saw the sly smile. 'Cow.'

'Moo,' said Michelle, matter-of-factly. She scouted around the room. 'I don't think you're going to pull tonight.'

'I'm not here to pull,' Vita said levelly, 'I'm here because you told me to come.'

Michelle looked at her gravely. 'Well, I'm glad you came.' She looked over Vita's shoulder, smiled and raised her glass. 'Come and talk to Annie. She's lovely. She's single. She went out with a real shit – he'd disappear without warning on drunken benders which lasted days on end. And Corinne – her ex gambled away all his money and then started on hers, but she's picked herself up and dusted herself down. Di over there found out her husband went dogging. Radiant, all of them – don't you think?'

As Vita let herself be led over, she thought, Why do I want to make small talk with strangers when all we have in common is the thing I hate most? I am reluctantly single. No doubt I am now known as Vita, the one whose fiancé couldn't keep it in his trousers. I don't want to spend my evening alternately slagging off men and then raucously talking of pulling them too.

When she was introduced, she knew in an instant that they knew who she was – as if they'd been briefed, as if her misfortune was manifested physically in the form of an unsightly blemish and they mustn't stare. Talk about anything else. Steer clear. Don't mention the scar. It was burdensome to realize that, for the time being, she was spoken about, albeit with affection, as Poor Vita who's been through a Really Tough Time.

But actually, Corinne was sweet-natured and Annie was

funny and Vita was heartened by their normalness; their self-confidence and good humour were compelling. Had their bad experiences made them stronger? Hers had made her feel feeble. Perhaps their poise and vivacity came from the passing of time. Give it time, dear – that's what her mother had said. Everything passes, love, everything passes – she remembered still her late father's mantra.

But the women were funny and spirited and bright and, as Vita listened and laughed, she wondered whether they had made a fundamental decision that at some point, introversion had to stop and a life apart was to be embraced. Did they close the door on their past one day, padlock it and seal it shut with a massive sign saying *CLOSURE*? Had they read the prescribed quota of self-help books? How many therapy sessions had they attended? (Vita hadn't gone down that route.) Had they worn an elastic band around their wrist to ping hard when negative feelings surfaced? Did they take a physical step to the side when confronted by destructive reflection? Did they resort to evening classes to keep the loneliness at bay for just one night a week? A little voice whispered to Vita, See, this could be me.

Actually, the women didn't bond merely because they were all single; it wasn't weighty issues which attracted them to each other, it was discovering that they shared much softer common ground. They soon found out they all preferred vodka to gin and George Clooney to Brad Pitt. They all wanted Nadal to win Wimbledon. They'd all been to Lanzarote. They all loved loved *loved* the new Mark Ronson. They chinked glasses not because the aim was to knock the drink back, but because there was simply great geniality between them. And when they shared a puerile snigger at the expense of the bad-shoe lousy-laugh man Michelle had first singled out, it wasn't because they'd been scouting the room for talent or that they were man-haters, it was because his shirt now had even more detritus stuck to it and he'd spilt his drink on his trousers which made him look as though he'd wet himself.

And at some point an opportunity arose for Annie to quietly say, 'My ex used to get so hammered he'd piss in the kitchen sink and for some stupid reason, I felt too intimidated to confront him.' And then she smiled sweetly at Vita. 'You'll be OK, chook,' she said. 'You need a distraction. I did pottery evening classes, joined a running group and bought myself a Wii.'

'Like you needed any more wee in the house,' Corinne laughed.

'*Mais oui!*' said Annie.

'Bugger evening classes – though I have to admit I went to a macramé one,' Corinne said to Vita. 'What you ought to do is have a fling.'

'That's what Michelle says.'

'Well, she's right. Don't look so appalled!'

'I just can't imagine it. I don't think I'm interested. And anyway, how will he find me?'

'He won't,' Corinne said. 'You'll come across him – and that, my dear, will be that.'

Annie looked at Vita. 'You don't believe her, do you?'

'Nope,' said Vita, 'but I'm just going to nod – like I do when friends like Michelle say, You'll so be OK, babe. Nodding's good.'

'How about the sappy half-smile I fix on my face at the start of an evening like this?' said Annie. 'When you're not actually talking to anyone and you feel like a beacon but you don't want people homing in on you and thinking, Aw, poor woman, all on her own, better go and talk to her.'

Corinne drained her glass thoughtfully. 'It's not easy,' she said quietly, 'but it's OK. It always turns out OK.'

Though Vita thought, I don't think I'll bother with evening classes and flings and things, she was comforted that these women had been through much that she was going through. Their lexicon was so similar, they understood each other perfectly, despite very different circumstances. Best of all, they'd come through the other side without turning into boorish man-eating harpies or bitter man-hating harridans. And, for the first time, Vita thought that perhaps the task of getting over it was not so much an uphill struggle with no visible summit within reach, as some sort of crazy ride which, if she just held on tight, would be worth it.

Sipping Coca-Cola and taking a couple of Nurofen before bed to ward off a hangover, Vita thought to herself that, actually, none of this felt like a game. To see it as such demeaned the enormity of the journey, the rigours of the process. She thought about how she felt but she balanced it with what she'd thought about Corinne and Annie.

Actually, it wasn't a game. It was a storm. A mighty one.

She heard her Dad's words again. It'll pass, sweetface.

'Perhaps I'm currently passing through the eye of the storm. I'm like a scrap of torn paper being carried along and there's nothing I can do about it. Corinne and Annie – they were once like me but they weathered it, they made it through. They emerged the other side, no longer scraps of plain paper – but colourful and vibrant now.'

It was OK to let a tear drop.

'I'd like that to be me.'

She reached for pen and Post-it.

Calm after the storm

51

The Thorpe Arms

Vita had only had to travel twenty-five minutes to the George and Dragon. For Oliver, however, although the Thorpe Arms was over an hour's drive, in the next county, he wouldn't have wanted it closer.

'Jonty – this party –?'

'Told you, it's at Mark's. His mum's going to be there – us downstairs, the olds upstairs.'

Oliver knew Mark's mum. Much younger than him, so if the kids considered her old, they must think him positively ancient.

'Would you like a lift then, Jont?'

'Er – sure. Thanks, Dad.'

'We'll leave in half an hour?'

'But it's only three o'clock? Actually, that's cool – I can help him set up. I'll just give him a call.'

Oliver heard his son talking to Mark in a weird language of abbreviations and odd inflection.

'Cool!' said Jonty to his father which Oliver took to mean, Yes, please, I'll have a lift in half an hour.

'OK. Oh – and no smoking.'

'I know, Dad. I don't – you know I don't – and I haven't, not since I puked.'

'OK – and no booze. Alcopops included.'

'OK!' Jonty was gently exasperated. There'd be contraband – they both knew it. But since the time that Jonty threw up his guts after half a litre of cider and five cigarettes, they both knew he wasn't impressed by the effects of either.

Would DeeDee have let him go? Of course she would. If anything, Oliver was more disparaging of Mark's mother than she'd ever been. A single mum, cool and sassy, with a tattoo on her arm and a nose ring and a groovy job in the music industry – all the kids loved her open-house policy and MP3 players in every room. She's a really sweet girl, DeeDee had told him. Oliver had argued with her about suitable environments for Jonty to hang out in. And DeeDee had argued back that a rather nice home, not too far away, of a mother she knew from the occasional mums' night out was a preferable location to some dodgy bus shelter or chippy.

As Oliver locked up and watched Jonty ambling over to the car, plastic bag containing his clothes and things slung over his shoulder like a nonchalant Dick Whittington, he thought how sometimes, co-parenting and the heated debates it incurred had been more fraught than setting the boundaries, establishing the ground rules and doing all the worrying solo.

'Will you be all right then, Dad?'

'Me?'

'I don't have to stay over. I could come back?'

'Nonsense! It's a party, it's not a school night. And anyway – I have, well, not plans exactly but I'm off to meet someone about some work ideas. And then I have plenty of stuff I've been putting off which I'll do. Including hoovering.'

Usually, Jonty would help without being asked. And he never minded evenings in with his dad. But recently, it had occurred to father and son that Saturday nights oughtn't to be spent with one's dad. So Jonty felt equally grateful to Mark's mum and to his own father.

'I'll be back tomorrow then.'

'OK. Maybe we'll do something in the afternoon. I don't know – bowling? Cinema?'

'OK, Dad. Cool.'

'Do you have your phone?'

'Yep.'

'And it has enough battery?'

'Yes, Dad. Yes.'

'Have a great time, then.'

'Thanks.'

'Enjoy.'

'You too.'

It had been an unspoken request, initiated a couple of months ago, not to be dropped off outside a friend's house. So Oliver had pulled up at the end of Mark's street and though he didn't wait until Jonty had disappeared from sight, he did turn the car very slowly so he could surreptitiously check his son's whereabouts in the rear-view mirror. He watched him lope off and turn up the path to Mark's.

Have fun, he thought quietly. Don't smoke, kiddo – though a little booze won't kill you. Have a laugh and party.

Oliver couldn't listen to the radio. Every station had a presenter who sounded inane and the news was so depressing not even Radio 4 would do. He had a Springsteen CD in the glove compartment and he racked it up loud, singing along badly. He didn't dwell on what lay ahead but he did want to get there. The road map was open on the passenger seat, his scribbled directions were on a piece of paper. Certain journeys were not for the sat nav. A motorway services neared. He glanced at the clock and decided to stop and buy a sandwich. He hadn't had lunch. He ate it off his lap in the car. It was disgusting but it filled a hole. He washed it down with a can of Coke which tasted too sweet, the bubbles too large, sharp almost.

He arrived in plenty of time. It was a small market town whose high street was depressingly generic with the token Starbucks and McDonald's, and discount book-shops, video games stores and cheap clothing emporiums from which incessant music poured out like the teenagers who shopped there. Woolworth's remained derelict. The letters had been pulled away, but a dirty imprint spelled out the name like a grubby shroud. Oliver felt like turning around and driving away but the hotel itself was a little way further on out of the town. It was an unassuming building, old but with no immediate architectural value. However, it was spruce, freshly painted and the window boxes and pair of bay trees flanking the entrance were well tended. A girl in a white shirt and black blazer smiled from reception as he walked in.

'Can I help you, sir?'

May I, Oliver corrected her silently. 'I'm meeting someone,' he said. 'I'm a little early.'

'Very good, sir,' she said and Oliver thought, This is her Saturday job – she's probably only a couple of years older than Jonty. And then Oliver thought no more of Jonty or home or of being one of the Bourne Three or that the Bourne Three were down to two and that was why he was here. Nor did he ponder what all this was about. He wiped his mind clean, took a seat in the lounge, chided himself when he saw the very nice sandwich and light snacks menu served all day, ordered a sparkling mineral water, unfolded the Saturday *Times*. And waited. Every now and then, he glanced around. No one new had arrived. This had happened once before and had been the most soul-destroying thing. He decided to give it perhaps ten more minutes, time enough to finish the water and the paper.

'Pete?'

It takes Oliver a moment to click, then he looks up, smiles, stands.

'Hi,' he says, offering his hand, 'Pete. You must be Louise?' The woman nods. 'A drink?'

'Cup of tea,' she says. 'I'll order it – don't worry. Do you want anything else?'

'No, thanks.' He watches her go over to the bar. She's tall, quite masculine really, her hair is thick and blonde and probably looks better tied back. She doesn't look as though she's dressed for a Saturday, she looks as though she's wearing office clothes. And then Oliver thinks this is catty. She probably works somewhere during the week where she has to tie her hair back and wear flat shoes and slacks and thus it feels good for her to slip into court shoes and a tight skirt and wear her hair loose for a change.

She walks back to him and smiles. Very red lipstick. Nice eyes. She flicks her hair over her shoulder. It falls back. Long nails. Similar shade to her lips. She matches her description well. God knows if Louise is her real name. It doesn't matter to him just as no doubt it doesn't matter to her whether he is Pete or Oliver or Lord Bastard Montague-Caruthers.

As she sips her tea, they talk politely if cautiously about

their journeys and the weather and one or two current affairs items. And then there's no tea left, and the ice has melted in Oliver's glass and he's drained that too.

'Shall we?' she says.

'Sure,' he said.

'I've checked in,' she says.

'Please,' says Oliver, standing and gesturing for Louise to lead the way.

She doesn't take the lift, she opts for the stairs but Oliver won't be able to recall that the staircase is rather fine, wide and sweeping with a lovely newel post and a banister of polished mahogany. With Louise walking ahead of him, he is focusing now only on her, on her rear, her tight skirt causing her arse to swing seductively as she climbs. He doesn't notice the length of the corridor, he's staring instead at her bra visible beneath her silky shirt. Ankles. Long hair, loose. Shoulders quite broad. She slides the key card into the door, opens it, her hand lingering on it as she walks into the room. Long nails. Red. The type that might grab, scratch, trace patterns over his chest. He closes the door and stares, without reading, at the emergency instructions posted on it. He turns and walks on in. She's closing the curtains. The bed is between them. A trouser press in the corner, a tray on the desk with kettle, cups, sachets – all are noted subliminally, all will remain untouched.

They stare at each other, no awkwardness – not like the first time when he'd said to whatever her name was in that hotel in Manchester that he liked her necklace. Anyway, Louise isn't wearing a necklace. She's unbuttoned her shirt, her bra is lacy and semi-transparent and he can see her large dark nipples through it. He pulls his top over his head as she lets her skirt fall away and then she walks to him, in her matching underwear either bought specially

57

for today or else kept specially for such days. She has kept her shoes on. And just then he thinks how he wants her to keep her shoes on and so he tells her so.

She's in front of him, those red talon nails doing what they ought to do, tracing a lascivious path up and down, from his neck to his stomach to the top of his trousers, up his torso again, up his neck, over his chin to his lips. He sucks her finger into his mouth while she deftly unbuckles his belt, unzips him and slips her hand down his trousers, fast and urgently, locating his cock now bulging awkwardly in his boxers.

She squats, pulling his trousers down as she goes. She's licking his knee – a first for him and more ticklish than erotic. She doesn't stay there long, using her mouth and her breath over the surface of his thighs until she's level with his groin. She pulls down his boxers and his cock springs out as if it had been gasping for air. No preamble, he's in her mouth, all the way and at this point he is neither Pete nor Oliver, he is simply a forty-six-year-old widower who needs to fuck and doesn't want any emotion in the way. He just needs to get rid of this basic carnal desire which goads and tortures him, he needs to empty his balls and feel the velvet comfort of a real cunt.

'Pull my hair.' She's standing now, one hand around his cock, the other between her legs. 'Be rough with me.'

He pushes her onto the bed, fumbles with a condom. Missionary would have been fine for him but she's up on all fours with her arse bucking at him. Eyes tight shut, he rams into her from behind while she spews out a quite shocking litany of filth. He blocks it out. He might be fulfilling her fantasy – she's probably snuck here away from some sexless marriage and her husband is probably farting in front of the footie none the wiser – but she isn't the stuff of any fantasy of Oliver's. All he wants from her is the consensual go-ahead to shag. Let her holler that he is to take her like the dog-bitch slut she is – he doesn't listen. It is about his cock, his balls and a fortnight's cache of spunk.

She's on her back now with her great tits just begging to be fondled and sucked. She's looped her arms under her thighs, spreading her legs wide. It's a great view – it's all on show, it's just what he needs to see. He stares and stares, gorging on the sight before plunging right in. She's bellowing. Five thrusts. Then three. Two. One.

'Fuck,' he says, repeating it again and again as he comes. His body feels as though it's peeled inside out, he feels sucked into the depths of her, he can feel those talons fixed into his buttocks. She's still writhing and humping and she's roaring at him to make her come again. But he doesn't want to, he just wants to go. She's not letting him. She's bucking and twisting and screwing herself onto his spent cock and now, thank God, she's making coming noises. His face is buried in the pillow, turned away from her and he wants her to let go of his ear with her teeth.

'God, that was good,' she's purring, dragging her nails up and down his back, through his hair. 'I needed that.'

But Oliver can't reply because actually, he could weep. He could sob and howl. It's always the same these days – as soon as his balls are empty he is subsumed with an all-encompassing hollowness, a dreadful terrifying emptiness that sex without love causes. It's a hateful situation – to need to fuck so badly, to need human touch though he knows now the utter wretchedness its aftermath brings.

But Oliver is a good man, a lovely man. He has manners and innate kindness and a sense of decorum. So he won't run to the bathroom, change and get the hell out of there as soon as he can. He could, but he won't. He gives himself a moment, a long moment, then he slides out of her, lies on his back, lets her lie on his chest, lets her run her hands in that post-coital languor over his torso. But he can't feel it. His spent body is numb now, there's nothing left inside or outside. And he can hear her talking but he's not really listening.

'My husband had an accident at work. We don't have sex. He has depression – impotence. Don't get me wrong, he's a lovely man. But I need sex, you know? I'm almost fifty. I love my husband – don't get me wrong. But I don't want to leave him and I don't want to find myself drawn to having an affair. So that's why I do the websites – because they're discreet, aren't they? People like me – like you – good people who have *needs*. It's saved my marriage. Do you know that? It's *saved* it.' She pauses for breath. Oliver hopes she'll start up again with, Well, anyway, I'd better go now. Thanks a lot and good luck!

But no.

'So Pete – tell me. Shall we meet again? I work part-time. I could be here Wednesday.'

'I can't.'

'Home? Wife?'

'Something like that,' he says.

'You told me your wife isn't around?'

'That's right.'

'You just don't want another relationship?'

'That's right.'

'Well, nor do I. That suits me. I could do this time next week, then, if you can't do Wednesday.'

'I'll check – and I'll email you.' He smiles at her. 'I'll email you if I can do this time next week.'

And he hates it that her eyes light up. She no longer looks or sounds like the horny vixen who'd screwed him senseless minutes ago. She looks, now, on the plain side of normal but her eyes don't sparkle, they have a dullness,

60

a sadness. Everything about her expression points to too much hope at the thought of being able to escape home again this time next week. Her make-up has smudged. Oliver wonders if at some point during sex, she'd wept silently too.

She'd paid for the room in advance. She won't take any contribution from him.

'You can pay next time – if you might be able to do this time next week,' she says. 'Email me, won't you – either way.'

'Of course.'

And he will. That was the beauty of these websites; that's the etiquette – no embarrassment emailing to say, Actually, it was bloody great but I'm not into seeing the same person more than once. He could be as honest as that. It didn't matter. There were plenty of other willing one-off bunk-ups online. A whole society. It wasn't about relationships for any of them. For Louise it wasn't about this Pete man at all – it was purely about being able to have good sex, fantasy sex, sex full stop, without cruising some dreadful bar on a Friday night and bullshitting her way through a loud evening of overpriced drinks and inane chatting-up in the hope that she might pull at the end. She'd never do that – what, with her husband at home? What kind of a Friday night would that be for him? She wouldn't do that. Ever. But she could tell him she was off shopping on a Saturday afternoon, have someone clean, sober and like-minded fuck her brains out and restore her to the good wife she still really wanted to be.

Oliver Bourne. Forty-six. Lost his beautiful wife not quite three years ago in a tragic road accident. She was forty-three. No age. They'd been together since they were both twenty-one. And he'd loved her and she'd loved him. He'd been faithful to her and it had been easy. And now she was gone and he was mortal and every now and then his physical needs were overwhelming. And websites like the one which had brought him into contact with Louise today were the way forward for him to survive as a man on earth who had a wife once, but no more, and never wanted a relationship again. Louise and an alarming number of others just like her, able to replace something missing in their lives. For Oliver though, something was missing which he believed could never be replaced. Because it hadn't been lost, it had gone. DeeDee had gone and life would go on; it just wouldn't be the same and it could never, ever, be as good as it had been.

Suzie Vs Candy

'How's Vita, then?' Suzie asked, trying to be casual by using a vague but light tone of voice while flipping through a magazine.

'Vita?'

'Yeah – you know. Just wondered, that's all. You know – how things *are*. With – the shop? And stuff.'

'Stuff?'

Suzie didn't like it when Tim was like this. Unhelpful. Sharp. All she really needed – and surely he could fathom this – was an answer along the lines of, Oh, Vita's fine, I think – haven't had to speak to her much at all recently, thank God. But Tim wasn't saying that. He wasn't saying much and his tone was flat, guarded. Suzie couldn't leave it at that, now. She needed more information but also to bring back his focus to the brilliant fun beauty that she spent so much effort hoping he'd see. She walked over to him, slipping her hand into the back pocket of his jeans and giving a squeeze. She took the plates from him and took over loading the dishwasher. He went and sat down at his kitchen table; she glanced over her shoulder hoping to catch his eye. He was reading the paper. Yesterday's.

Breezy. Be breezy. 'Because you were saying that it's been – what did you say – *stressy*.'

Tim shrugged. 'Only in terms of the business – it's not making what we'd forecasted. It's now practically July.'

'Only in terms of the business.' She needed that phrase to be repeated out loud, as if she was quoting his statement of intent. 'So you're getting on well outside of that?'

'I hardly see or speak to her!' Tim paused, irritated, and looked over to her. 'You know all this – why do you ask? Nothing's changed.'

'I'm just interested.' Smile. Sweet sweet smile. 'I care. What I mean is, I care about *you* and I hope she's not giving you a hard time or stressing you out. With texts and stuff.'

You're paranoid, Tim thought to himself. You sound like Vita started to. Just then, to him, it seemed an annoying coincidence that the women he chose seemed to exhibit similar traits.

'So you don't speak to her socially then? Much? At all?'

Tim looked at Suzie as if he didn't quite understand the question. She came and sat at the table, flipped through a magazine. Lingered a while and then started up again, as if momentarily she'd forgotten she was halfway through a conversation because it was so unimportant.

'She doesn't – you know – *bother* you with late-night texts? She leaves you alone now, does she?'

'Jesus – I'm with *you*. Why would I socialize with her? If it wasn't for the business, there'd probably be no contact. Texts bypass the need to talk.'

Suzie nodded slowly as if it was no issue and she understood completely, as if she was only half aware of the conversation because mostly she was engrossed in the magazine. But actually she was on the horoscope page and, as was her habit, she was reading her star sign. And Tim's.

But also Vita's too. She was drawn to doing so in any magazine or newspaper no matter how trashy; to read and cross-reference the three star signs. Today, Vita's and Tim's reports – though different – had a worrying synergy. The astrologer was prophesying that communication could vanquish a difficult period, understanding could deepen and dreams which had seemed impossible could be within reach. A new, rejuvenated period of domestic happiness was forecast. Suzie shuddered. Hers simply said to trust her instincts and be prepared to relinquish foundering projects with dignity.

'Actually, I'm seeing Vita today,' Tim said and, though faint, there was a confrontational edge to his voice.

'At the shop?'

'Yes. There's a trade show coming up – we need to discuss logistics.'

'Why not just call her?' Suzie eyed his phone, lying on the table just in front of him, as if it was a black box stuffed with secrets and information. 'Does it need both of you to go? Who'll look after the shop?'

'Only one of us need go,' Tim said, knowing he was going to Edinburgh for a meeting but deciding not to tell Suzie just yet.

'Cool,' said Suzie, but she wasn't cool at all. She felt heated and tetchy, wishing she'd been born in July or November.

Tim was gathering his stuff together.

'Tonight?' Suzie said. 'Shall we do something?'

'Cool,' said Tim, kissing her on the forehead in the perfunctory way Suzie had seen a hundred bored husbands kiss their annoying wives.

Suzie thought, I'm always instigating the plans. And then she thought, it seems to mostly be me initiating sex too, these days.

It was hard work, all of this and she was tired. She didn't feel quite so effortlessly sassy these days. She had to turn it on. She did really, really want Tim to really, really want her, though. She'd set herself the challenge of being the one he desired more than any other he'd had. Especially Vita. Especially annoying old Vita. For Suzie, Vita actually stirred up more emotions in her than Tim and frequently she swung from triumph to insecurity, superiority to jealousy, from loathing to fear. She thought about her a lot and tried to be better at the things she knew Vita did well while trying not to do the things she knew had pissed Tim off about her. It was a constant guessing game and sneaking a look at texts and call logs assisted her. She'd spent much time analysing the photos in the box under Tim's bed and many evenings with friends – on the phone, out in a bar – evaluating and dissecting Tim's relationship with Vita and now hers with Tim. He's with you, hon, not *her*, they all said. But he was with Vita for *years* and he loved her enough to want to marry her! she'd counter. If he loved her that much, why aren't they still together? they'd bat back.

He's. With. Me.

She had to keep remembering that. But sometimes it just didn't feel that way. At those times it was easier for her to hate Vita rather than doubt Tim.

Vita was in deep discussion with a customer about the merits of the cream enamelware pitcher and tray, as opposed to the same items in white edged in blue.

'The cream is more contemporary, modern Shaker you could say – perfect for the Farrow and Ball type interior,' she was saying when Tim walked in. 'Anyway, they're the same price – whichever you choose.'

'It's for an American friend of mine.'

'Oh,' said Vita, as if solving a riddle, 'well then, I'd definitely go for the white – it's more traditional. More Englishy cottagey oldie worldie.' Tim smiled. It was a very Vita thing to say. It was also a good sales tactic. The white set was bought. The customer looked thoughtful and all it took was a collusory prompt, sotto voce, from Vita.

'You love the cream set,' she said. 'Why not treat *your*self?'

The customer glanced back at it.

'I'll knock a little off, if you have both.'

'Really?'

'Five pounds.'

The customer paused and then grinned guiltily. 'Go on then.' And while Vita was wrapping and packing, the lady handed over four packets of quirky paper napkins that were displayed near the till. They cost more than the discount.

'She'd have bought both without the discount,' was Tim's opening gambit when they had the shop to themselves.

'She wouldn't have bought the napkins though. It's the feel-good factor. She'll be back. She'll always come here for gifts. And sometimes I'll give her a discount and other times I won't. And that means she'll come back even more often.'

'Whatever you say,' Tim said. He'd never really figured out Vita's business strategies.

Vita looked at him. They were standing next to each other, both of them with hands on hips, looking at the table with the little creatures made from teasels and pine cones, as if observing naughty children.

'Are these popular?'

'No, not really,' Vita said. 'The kids all want them, but

the mums worry they'll make a mess or have creepy crawlies hibernating in them.'

Creepy crawlies. A Vita-ism. Tim smiled.

'How's things?' he asked. She looked good today. He'd stopped noticing. A long time ago.

She shrugged. 'June's not been a good month – but not a bad month either, all things considering. A little down on last year.'

'And outside of the shop? Work and play?'

She shrugged again. 'Not a good month, not a bad month. A little down on last year. All things considered.' The allusion was lost on him. 'And you?'

He shrugged too.

Tell me about Suzie, Tim. Own up. No, don't.

An awkward silence during which, standing there, side by side, elbows almost touching, she could sense his body heat. They were close but too close for comfort. Vita stepped away. 'So!'

'So,' said Tim, 'about the trade fair.'

'Yes,' said Vita, 'what do you think?'

'I'm meant to be in Edinburgh,' Tim said. 'I can't cancel it – they're a new client for the consultancy.'

'But what about the shop?'

'Could Jodie come in? The show's only at Alexandra Palace. You don't need to stay over. One day would probably be enough anyway.'

'I thought you said Jodie's beyond useless?'

'As a Saturday girl, yes,' said Tim, 'but midweek – she'll probably be flattered, she may even rise to the challenge. She's an impoverished student – she'll probably relish the chance to skip some boring lecture.'

'I'll ask her. But what if she can't?'

'God, Vita, why don't you just ask her first – and depending on her answer, then worry about a plan B?'

And Vita thought to herself, Remember that? The way he turns? The way you think you're pals and suddenly you wonder if he really dislikes you?

'I'll do that,' she said and she wanted him to leave.

'Let me know,' he said, on his way out. And then he paused. 'Nice dress. By the way.'

It gave her a lift. And she was angry with herself for letting it.

Before she rang Jodie, Vita did the sensible thing and allowed herself a few minutes to think about Tim. To really think about him. Wondered why he didn't use his relationship with Suzie against her when that really would be a very Tim thing to do. Shove it in her face, brandish it about. What meaning could Vita find in this? Was it that he didn't want to hurt her? If so, did that then imply he had feelings for her still? Or did it mean Suzie meant nothing and wasn't worth mentioning because in the course of his life she simply wasn't important? If so, then she really wasn't the new Vita, she was an opportune distraction. A bed warmer. A drinking buddy. An ego boost. Cheaper than a Porsche but with the same penis-extension factor.

I hope it's that she simply doesn't figure large enough in his life to be worth mentioning, Vita thought.

And then she thought, if that was the case, it was therefore rather pathetic that Suzie loomed larger for her than for Tim, that Suzie was in some ways a more real presence in her life than in his. What she thought it boiled down to was that she just really didn't want the woman he left her for to be the true, profound love of his life.

I auditioned for that role, I put so much effort into it, I loved it. I'm not ready to let it go to someone else.

But you keep forgetting he didn't leave you, Vita – you left him.

69

And then she thought, is this a skewed version of *Aesop*'s dog in the manger? I don't want Tim – but I don't want him wanting anyone else?

And then she thought, For God's sake, shut up! This is doing me no good at all. All this thinking and wondering that I do isn't going to change him or the past. What a waste of quarter of an hour – sitting, staring into the middle distance, sifting through all that emotional *junk*. She knew there was nothing of value in it – she'd been through it with a fine toothcomb over and again.

Go to London! Go to the trade show! Do something different.

Vita phoned Jodie.

Tim was at the bar when his phone rang. Suzie heard it, reached into his jacket pocket for it, saw it was Vita and answered it before she really thought about the ramifications.

'Hullo? Tim's phone.' Purr, she told herself, purr. 'Who is this?' Just let her think that Tim no longer puts a name to her number!

Vita felt the adrenalin rise in her throat and dry it out immediately. 'It's Vita.'

'Well, this is Suzie.'

There was silence while Vita scurried through thoughts about what to do in this situation; the pressure of having just a few seconds to frantically sort through a mental filing cabinet for a missing page of instructions of what to do in an emergency.

'Why do you phone?' Suzie was suddenly asking. She was outside now. Tim would just think she'd gone out for a smoke. Say he came out? And if he didn't, how would she return the phone to him without him knowing? It was dangerous, mad, exciting – to be on his phone to his annoying ex. But this opportunity was too good. She'd figure it out later. Seen my phone? No. Wonder where it is? I don't know. Weird. Oh look, Tim, your phone's in my bag – you must have put it in there on our way here. Later, later – all that could wait. In the here and now she had Vita, cornered.

'Why do you phone in the evenings?'

'Sorry?'

'You heard. Could you *not* phone *us* in the evenings. Tim's got a life, you know, outside of *work*. It gets on *our* nerves.'

'Sorry?'

'Oh, come on, Vita – I'm Suzie. *The* Suzie. We're together – so back off.'

Vita was shaking, not just because Suzie had hung up on her, but because the level of aggression had been horrible. People were usually nice to Vita – probably because her line of work was to provide lovely items to gladden the heart. Even the mad old shoplifting lady went about her crime with a genuinely sweet smile and a warm, Hullo, lassie. Vita tried to tell herself to judge a person by the company they keep – so what did this say about Tim and Suzie? And yet part of her felt unnerved, undermined and small. Embarrassed too – because a sappy sorry was all she'd managed and it really was the wrong word to use when what she'd meant by it was *pardon*. Her mind twisted away from the reality of the situation – that Suzie's unpleasant ownership of Tim probably came just from insecurity. Vita didn't stop to think how she obviously loomed pretty large for Suzie too. It didn't cross her mind that Tim didn't know about the call and that Suzie had deleted it from the list, slipped the phone into her bag and smuggled it back into his jacket a little while later.

*

71

When her hands had stopped shaking and her voice didn't sound too brittle, Vita phoned Candy, relating what had happened in such a tumble that for a while Candy wasn't sure who said what and whose phone was whose. But once Vita was all talked out and was ready to listen, Candy said something that made her think.

'Where's the triumph in leaving you for someone like *that*?' she said to Vita. 'Do you see? This should make you feel good. The triumph would be if he'd progressed from you to someone superior. By that I mean more gorgeous – not that that's possible, darling – someone brighter, more successful. Has he? How does this woman measure up to you, Vita? Think about it. She doesn't! She's not the new you. She doesn't even come close. If she's the best *that* man can get – then his barre is set pretty damn low.'

Vita actually took notes, scribbling frantically on the back of an envelope no doubt to transfer some of Candy's pithiness to Post-its later.

'And don't boost his ego by mentioning it to him,' Candy said. 'Bloody men – they do love being between two women. Whether they're being fought over – or fucked.'

'Candy!'

'It's the most clichéd male fantasy, honey,' Candy said before vaulting onto her high horse. 'I absolutely guarantee you that the man you meet next will be an improvement on Tim. Do you know why?' She didn't wait for Vita to answer. 'Because you learned from your heartache, while he didn't. He ignored it. He hasn't dealt with any issues. The natural scheme of things in this universe of ours dictates that until he does, his life will be flatter, poorer and much worse than it was. Karma, honey. It's the law of karma.'

Vita did love Candy's moral indignation, her outrage, her passion – they were her trademark, they were contagious.

'There are character traits you'll no longer tolerate, basic moral coda on which you'll insist,' Candy was saying. 'I know Michelle's said the same and it's true. You are destined for a much better relationship because all you wanted and worked for was a good relationship in the first place. Meanwhile, look at what shit-for-brains has gone and done for himself – look what he's settled for.'

My lovely sweary friend, Vita thought. Michelle – sensitive and wise. Candy – a firecracker of identical unwavering support, but expressed at top volume with a potty mouth.

'I know,' said Vita, 'I do really know. I promise you.'

'Then you need to start acting like it, cupcake,' Candy said. 'Which means what he does and who he's with should hardly dent your thoughts. Certainly, it shouldn't take up an entire phone call and all my choicest fulminations at – blimey – at almost midnight.'

'OK.'

'Vita, you started to take as the norm the way he treated you, the way he behaved. You won't know what's hit you when you have the good relationship – the normal relationship – that's *so* coming to you.'

'If you say so.'

'I do. And I'm going to bloody love every moment of saying told-you-so.'

Rick

It was to be an early start on the first Thursday in July
– but not that early. On the morning of the trade show,
Vita was woken not by the alarm clock – when she reached
for it, she saw to her annoyance that there was still half
an hour to go – but by a peculiar noise. Very peculiar.
Dull but unmistakable thuds, no rhythm, no pattern, just
every now and then thud thud thud. Accompanying this
was sporadic screeching. Part car, part angry child, part
something last heard on a David Attenborough wildlife
programme. Both noises kept her paralysed in bed for a
while. What the hell was that? And that? Who's out there?
What on earth is going on? Gingerly, she crept to the
window, stooping low and peeking out as if expecting to
confront some hideous monster direct from Roald Dahl.

Even at that early hour, a fine day was in the making;
wisps of coral-coloured clouds were already filtering off a
pale blue sky like dreams drifting away in one's reverie. There
was no one out there. The garden was still. Vita straightened
a little, craned her neck, tried to see over the tangle of Mr
Brewster's hedge into his garden. Thud. Where was it coming
from? There it was again. This time, she looked down to

see a small, unripe pear fall to the ground. Then the screeching again, a dreadful noise, irate and threatening. Then silence. She looked up and, staring back at her from the branches of her pear tree, was a most peculiar bird with virulent green plumage. Vita thought, I must be dreaming, you don't get parrots in Hertfordshire. But high up in the pear tree were two – wait! Three! Four! All of them clashing with the peaceful morning, clashing with the subtle hues of the foliage and the vibrant green of the young pears, clashing with what should be a delicate dawn chorus at this hour, clashing with all that was meant to be natural and normal to a small back garden in the home counties.

Had they seen her? If they had, they didn't care. If they had, they'd have seen her start to grin, fascinated to see them peck at the unripe pears whilst posturing to each other like rock stars mid-act; looking just as exotic and incongruous as if a band had been perched in the branches. They worked at the pears quite viciously until they fell, then they moved on to another fruit. Well, what a sight! A smorgasbord for parrots! Vita praised the munificence of her very own pear tree as she dressed. She went quietly into the garden but by that time, though still early, the birds had gone. Plundered fruit lay around the ground like delicacies spoilt children had taken just a bite of. Would they come again – and if so, perhaps at just a slightly more civilized hour, please? There were plenty of pears, plenty!

Vita enjoyed trade shows. There were two a year that were essential to attend. Mostly, Tim had gone, justifying that she was a liability because she ordered far too much merchandise purely because she liked chatting to the traders. Then he softened this by saying he was rubbish in the shop. The truth was, he wasn't rubbish. He just found it boring. He didn't like customers and he didn't much like the stuff the shop sold, but that's why he mastered the trade shows early on – he could select objectively. And he didn't fall for schmooze partly because it was a tool he used himself to such great advantage. He knew never to buy whilst there but always to show interest, to talk numbers, to take cards and give out his own. He would bring Vita pictures and information, the occasional sample and then he'd sit her down and show her spreadsheets of their stock, their sales, their forecasts. He'd tell her to think about Easter or Christmas or Halloween or Valentine's. Then Tim would place the orders. He liked hearing the supplier's surprise – Well! What do you know! That good-looking guy who we spoke to at the show, who wouldn't commit, whom we swapped cards with? He's placing an order and a good one at that! This strategy always enabled Tim to secure the lowest unit price.

Double-checking and double-locking, Vita left the house with mixed feelings. She was looking forward to the show – but a text from Tim reminding her not to buy a thing made her wonder if she should go at all.

'Stapler.'

Living on your own can make you introverted – yet instead of talking to yourself, you say things out loud.

'Stapler,' she said again, going back into the house and delving into kitchen drawers, the shoebox in the cupboard under the stairs on which she'd nicely stencilled *Bits 'n' Bobs*. No stapler. And then she wondered if she had a stapler of her own, whether the one she'd been using for the last few years had been Tim's all along and, as such, would have been in a drawer or box at his place bearing a Post-it note saying *LEAVE*. Momentarily she thought back to those strange dark days of moving out – how, when she'd come to remove her belongings, she'd read those Post-its as notices hounding her to go, rather than marking the items of his which were to stay.

She locked up again and gave herself a quiet talking-to. All of that was last year, remember, and, after Candy's talk the other night, Vita decided to perform a mental sidestep any time she felt her mind drift off to time gone by, or Tim Gone – Bye! as she was calling it, emblazoning it on Post-its.

Stapler. She needed a stapler before going to London. She went via the shop and left a note for Jodie who'd be opening up in a couple of hours. It was still early.

> *Jodie – don't hesitate to call if there's a prob. I have borrowed one of the caterpillar staplers – have taken a red one as they're the least popular. Good luck and enjoy, Vita.*
>
> *PS: Tim says no discounts for friends and family. Sorry.*

* * *

Alexandra Palace; that Victorian pantheon of glass domes and grand halls and giant potted palms, straddling an elevated position with far-reaching views over parkland, over the ladders of streets crawling up and down Haringey like zips, to London beyond. The radio mast, rocket-like, proclaiming this place a summit and, as the plaque attests, an apotheosis of communication, with the BBC's first public television transmissions made from here in 1936. Vita loved the view. She'd never lived in London, had no desire to and hadn't spent much time there at all but she'd been to this part a few times and when she stood outside the Palace (she'd heard other people call it Ally Pally but she liked to call it the Palace) and soaked in the view, she felt a surge of excitement. Yonder lies my capital city!

The trade show was humming already. The stands were

colourful and varied and at odds with the standardized cubicles provided. Most had bowls of sweets, or free biros or useless fluffy things to give away. The scent of stewed coffee and batches of slightly dried-out croissants permeated. Vita couldn't remember the last time she'd been at a show. And this one was very large and she was suddenly looking forward to her day very much indeed.

'The beauty of these – Mouse in a House, Ted in a Bed, Mole in a Hole – is that it's a collection, of course.' Rick Edwards looked at Vita levelly. 'Kids love them – and parents do too, because it makes buying birthday presents for other kids so easy.'

'I see,' said Vita, wanting to order loads of each but trying to sound like Tim.

'Look at this little fellow: Dog in a Clog. Isn't he a superstar?'

'Adorable,' said Vita. And then she cleared her throat and said, 'Interesting.'

'I did ask the manufacturer if they'd consider Ants in Pants.'

'I like that,' said Vita.

'I was joking – Mrs?'

'Vita.'

'Mrs Vita.'

'No – Vita – Whitbury. Miss.'

'Richard Edwards. Rick.' They shook hands. 'Here.' He gave her the small plastic house whose hinged roof revealed an open-plan living area with fixed plastic furniture and a small, removable mouse.

'Thank you!' Vita inspected it. 'I will think about it.'

'Oh, come on,' Rick said, 'you love it! How many can I put you down for? Buy at the show and they'll be in your shop by the weekend. If you're not reordering by early next week, I'll give you your next batch at fifty per cent off.'

This made a lot of sense to Vita. She thought, This is the way that Tim does business, surely. She felt slightly flushed, she'd only been in the show for an hour or so and had taken lots of cards and information, using her stapler often.

'Miss Vita,' Rick said sternly, 'you look concerned.'

'I should pass this by my – business partner.'

'Bring them over!'

'He's not here.'

'Not here?' Rick baulked and Vita suddenly thought how Tim was really more of an investor than a partner.

She looked at Rick, she liked his open smile, his dark eyes which were looking at her enquiringly. She liked the way he had a Mole in a Hole in one hand, and a Ted in a Bed in the other. 'OK,' she said.

'Good girl,' he said and she liked that, she liked it because actually, he looked a fair bit younger than her. He rattled off unit prices and discount bundles and she nodded carefully and tried to do mental maths.

'I'll start with ten of each.'

Rick shook his head. 'That won't see you through Saturday.'

She wasn't sure what increments she should advance with. 'Twenty?'

'Good.'

'But I want a good price.'

'It's an excellent price,' said Rick, 'with my special guarantee too.'

'I wanted a better price still,' said Vita, getting into a stride she didn't know she had. 'Times are hard – pocket money is frozen.'

Rick laughed loudly. 'Miss Vita – you're a horror. OK.'

He thought about it. 'I'll give you twenty-five of each. How's that.'

'That is – acceptable.' It was difficult for Vita not to laugh at herself and the incongruous sound of her chosen words and businesslike tone.

'Lovely,' Rick was saying, filling out an order form. 'Sign.'

She signed. And only then did she read back through the order. Yes. Yes. Yes. He'd even written down his guarantee. And under that, she suddenly saw he'd written something else. '*Payment on ordering. Delivery conditional on drinks after the show this evening.*' She read it again.

'I can pay now,' she said, with the company cheque book in her hand. 'I can't do the drinks, though. I'm not staying over.'

'I can't deliver, then.'

She was startled but he was smiling that unnerving, open, attractive smile. Lovely teeth. 'I have to get back tonight.'

'Husband?'

'No – but—'

'Boyf?'

'No. No. It's just—'

'Cat? Dog? Mouse in your house?'

'No! But—'

'But?'

'I hadn't planned to.'

He looked at the shop address. 'You're hardly the back of beyond,' he said. 'It'll be fun! Do it! It's a two-day show! Just open up later tomorrow.'

'I could call Jodie –'

Rick hadn't a clue who Jodie was. 'Great idea! Call Jodie.'

And Vita stood and let a barrage of thoughts scramble around. A drink. A night out. Freedom. Something new. Handsome boy with lovely teeth. Better discounts. And perhaps – just perhaps – fun.

'I'll phone Jodie,' she said.

Rick nodded. There was a lovely pub in Muswell Hill that he knew. He'd take her there, perhaps. They'd start off at the exhibitors' post-show drinks, and then end up at the John Baird, a pleasant stroll away in Muswell Hill. And then – well. Whatever. The drink would be nice – he liked her, she was pretty in a slightly careless way, her fringe a little too long, her top just verging on old enough to have gone a little shapeless but still promising nice breasts beneath, cropped jeans that were cool, perhaps a little incongruous for the show but still made her bum look good, sandals that would have looked better if she'd painted her toenails. But it was all natural, there seemed no artifice, no act at all and he liked that. He never really understood the attraction of power-dressed women. And of all the women who'd come to his stand that morning, Vita was the youngest by at least two decades.

She wasn't quite sure how to slope away. 'Bye and thanks.'

'I'll meet you in the main entrance at six – that's where the drinks are.'

She nodded.

'Phone Jodie,' he said.

'I'm going to.'

She did. Jodie was fine about it. And then Vita wondered if she should tell Tim. And then she thought why should she? And then she remembered the times when he'd spontaneously decided to stay over after some show or some meeting and how his phone would be off, off all evening and the following morning, how he'd look bleary and slightly self-conscious when he returned. A lingering whiff of stale booze. Times gone by she'd dwell and fret but right now, she's sidestepping the memory, chanting, *Tim Gone – Bye!* as she wanders from stand to stand.

At lunch-time, she took a walk to Muswell Hill, buying a small travel pack from Boots, wondering what to do about a room. And then she felt embarrassed, ridiculous. What if the drinks were boring? What if she felt uncomfortable? What if he forgot? What if he didn't really mean it? What if, actually, Rick was a prick with all this Ted in a Bed stuff. And talking of ants in pants – she hadn't a spare pair on her. Was there somewhere in Muswell Hill she could buy pants? The charming high street with its boutiques and organic food stores and artisan bakeries and aspirational homewares stores – would she be able to find simple white knickers?

No. Stop it.

She turned her gaze downwards and walked on, looking at the pavement, having to suddenly skirt around a man lying prostrate who turned out not to be drunk but to be painting tiny jewel-like designs on the splodges of old, dried-out chewing gum. How very Muswell Hill. How very un-Wynford. The shops, the pedestrians, the cars, the buggies, the kids in their bedecked Crocs – everything rather alarmingly hip and gorgeous. These weren't just yummy mummies – these folk were direct from the pages of the Boden catalogue. In comparison, Vita, provincial at best, downright dowdy at worst. Suddenly she felt tipped right out onto the ledge of her comfort zone.

No. No staying the night.

For goodness' sake, she said to herself, trains run late and indulging in taxis to and from the stations would still be cheaper than a hotel room. And Jodie, who'd be expecting to work now? Vita would simply swap the Saturday with her, therefore avoid having to pay her extra. And Rick? It was probably just client relations and there'd be all the other new stockists of Teds in Beds and Bugs in Rugs at the drinks.

A text arrived from Tim asking how it was going.

And that's when a litany of his nights out, nights away, disappearing acts, hit her like a freak downpour. And suddenly, in the sunshine and warmth and busy brightness of North London, for the first time she didn't allow the memories to soak her and chill her to the bone. Instead, she said to herself, Vita! You shall go to the ball! Do something different. Just see what life may have in store for you – you never know, you might really enjoy yourself.

To bolster her resolve, she sent a text to both Candy and Michelle.

Bloke at show asked me for drink!!!

There. She'd done it. They'd kill her if she opted out now. She sensed them in the background, jumping for joy. She anticipated the barrage of What what what????!!!! and Go girl!!! texts. And when they arrived on her phone she smiled and switched it off and felt happy to be all on her own, feeling her way. Now she was liking her time in a new place, a sunny day, out and about in Muswell Hill with the pedestrians who bustled that little bit more than at home, cars that took a few more liberties, people noticeably trendier, younger, more savvy. The energy was more lively than at home, and yet somehow more anonymous too. And that was a good thing. People weren't unfriendly, they were just in their own bubbles. City versus market town, Vita supposed. She'd never trade her home patch for this – but it was nice to be a visitor because you were welcomed without actually being noticed. Vita could blend and partake and no one really acknowledged her; thus she could relax and enjoy the novelty of it all. Returning to the show, she checked her phone quickly. A deluge of hyper-enthusiastic texts from Michelle and Candy. And another from Tim, asking again how it was going. Great! was all she needed to say to that. Then she switched off her phone, and went inside to browse and chat amongst the stands with a confident smile and her stapler and instincts at the ready.

North London

Rick and Vita started off sipping complimentary white wine and talking shop. He'd left his stall and gone to find her, finally tracking her down at the Heaven Scent stand, sniffing candles.

'Loo cleaner with top notes of joss sticks?' He peered over her shoulder.

She didn't miss a beat. 'I'd say it's more bubble gum underscored with grass cuttings.'

He took the candle from her and made a show of inhaling with eyes closed as if it was fine wine. Actually, Vita wasn't far off the mark.

'I'm going to be in the foyer in twenty minutes,' he said. 'I like to get there promptly and take advantage of the free booze. I shall be the bloke in the corner, who's decanted warm white wine on the irritating side of sweet into a pint pot. I shall pilfer you one too.'

When she located him, however, she was pleased to find him holding two wineglasses of chilled, quite decent white. He chinked her glass and she wasn't sure what to say so she took a steadying glug, conscious that he was looking at her intently. She knew if she described the sensation she experienced, Michelle would say butterflies and Candy would call it a frisson. Whatever it was, it was giving her a buzz and she felt lively, chatty and chuffed.

'Had a good show today?'

Vita nodded. 'Excellent,' she said, looking around for nibbles to balance the booze, the adrenalin; but complimentary canapés were apparently beyond the sponsors' budget. 'It's been great. Loads of ideas.'

'Orders? Have you bought much?'

She reddened a little as if she'd done it all wrong but then she thought, That's only by Tim's rules. 'I have,' she said. 'Candles and diffusers. Some really nice little planters – tin, embossed. Some amazing bookmarks – they're made from laser-cut ply, so thin they're like lace. Some china too – milk jugs in the shape of cardboard milk cartons, butter dishes which look like margarine tubs, sugar bowls resembling a crinkled open packet of sugar, espresso mugs like crumpled paper cups – but all in white glossy stoneware.'

'Quirky,' said Rick.

'That's my shop! Oh, and some Dogs in Clogs and Mice in Hice.'

Rick laughed.

'How was the show for you?'

'It was great,' he said, 'a really good day. If tomorrow is the same, it'll be fantastic.'

Politely, she asked him about his business, when he formed it, what gave him the idea, how hard it had been to set up and keep going in these challenging times. He responded with ease and threw in extra details as if they were bonus discounts. His age (twenty-nine), his back-ground (Hampshire, older sister married with kids, parents still in his childhood home), his current situation (owner of small modern house in Milton Keynes, drives an Audi, plays five-a-side), his work (serviced offices he can walk to as well as travelling to clients a couple of days a week). And then he mentioned an ex, just in passing, just so the information was out there (four years together, split in the new year, bit of a mad woman so good riddance).

'And you?'

'Me?'

She told him about the shop, her mum, the Tree Houses, and then she told him about Tim, surprising herself how easy it was to mirror Rick, to mention her ex casually.

'How is it sharing the business?'

'Not ideal.'

'I'll bet,' said Rick. 'I admire you.'

Vita shrugged. 'We'll see.'

He raised his glass to her. 'Shall we get out of here? Or do you want to butter up traders?' She looked around the hall and thought, If we leave here, where might it lead? Simply up to Muswell Hill? Or beyond?

'What do you think?' he asked. 'I feel quite hungry,' he added.

Did she feel hungry?

'What do you think?' He said it in an American accent this time.

How much thinking should she do about whether it was a good idea? She glanced at Rick who smiled easily at her. Friendly, easygoing, nice-looking bloke.

'Let's go and have a quick drink somewhere else,' he said. 'What do you think?' His regular voice now.

'I think –' said Vita. And then she decided not to think, just to act. 'That would be great.'

They circumnavigated the Palace, pointing out landmark buildings hazy in the distance. When he located them, he tucked his head close to hers, his outstretched arm against her, guiding her gaze. It sent a tremor through her body which mixed with the adrenalin and dried her mouth and in all, it was a fantastic sensation. They crossed a rather dingy car park and walked along a path by the children's playground, strolling up Dukes Avenue making small talk about the Edwardian splendour of the area. When they crossed roads, he put a hand on her shoulder, at her elbow, in the small of her back, and she felt herself all but float along the pavement.

'Look at these,' she said, pointing out the paintings on chewing gum, and she liked it that he simply marvelled at them, with no need for clever quips. She liked him. She liked the feeling of liking him. She felt light and smiley and too full of excitement to think about her friends, both of whom were desperate for updates, haranguing her phone which was deliberately on silent. She felt bolder than she had done in months, and this had a momentum of its own. She had no need of her support network. Pretty soon, she was nudging Rick teasingly when he said something intentionally daft or corny.

'Age before beauty,' he said, opening the door to the John Baird pub.

'Fuck off!' she laughed and as she went in ahead of him, she thought to herself, Have I just added a nonchalant wiggle to my walk?

It was a nice pub in that it was very un-Muswell Hill. It hadn't been converted into a gastro eatery, nor was it in any way indulgently stylish. It was traditional, down to earth; the clientele from various walks of life across the age groups, the staff friendly and with an obvious landlord and landlady at the helm who were most welcoming. Refreshing, really. A proper boozer. Oh! And with a small Thai restaurant within it to one side. Perhaps

Vita would find her appetite later, after all. They took their drinks out to the small patio area at the back, the conversation between them now larky and flirty. They sat side by side and Vita consciously serpentined her body close to Rick's. She thought to herself, Look at me! And then she thought if Michelle had been here, she'd have called her coquettish. Candy would probably call her foxy. She felt both. In fact, her senses were heightened and she felt everything: the breeze that changes with the arrival of evening, the tang of the vodka and cranberry, the light intrusion of somebody else's cigarette smoke, the contagion of other people's high spirits, the warmth coming through Rick's body.

They drank.

Eventually they ate.

He forked tasters of his dishes into her mouth. She hand-fed him a bite of her Thai spring rolls. They did the whole lingering-gaze thing, following it with the glancing-away, smiling-knowingly routine. Vita felt vivacious, a feeling she remembered, enjoying the self-confidence, the larkiness. And then it was last orders and that bell set off the one that Vita naturally carried in her subconscious. It wasn't so much a warning note, it was a checkpoint, a reminder to be sensible, at all times. And then she thought about trains and tomorrow and she thought she'd really better go. As they left the pub – her in front, doing the wiggle again – Rick put his hands lightly on her shoulders and the tingle it sent through her made her think, Why don't I just throw caution to the wind for once and see where it takes me?

But she couldn't. Not yet, not tonight.

'I ought to go – last trains, and all that.'

He regarded her for a long moment, assessing whether to push it tonight or pursue it tomorrow. Ultimately, he shrugged and then nodded. 'OK. I understand. Let's find you a cab.'

His conceding made her waver – so different from Tim always pushing for what he wanted, Vita eroding her own wishes in order to please.

'It was fun,' Rick said. 'Here's a cab.' He whistled through his fingers.

'I'd love to be able to do that,' Vita said, blowing hopelessly on hers. Suddenly Rick took her fingers between his lips, kissing the tips of them before filling Vita's mouth with his. Oh God, the feeling!

Rick cleared his throat and shoved his hands in his pockets, leaning forwards to speak to the driver. 'King's Cross.'

Straightening, he grinned at Vita and despite the din of the cab engine and a waft of diesel, they stood motionless on the pavement for a suspended moment and she thought, Oh, sod the cab and the train – come on, Vita, come on!

But it was only a thought and though she'd opened her mouth, she just couldn't chance words out loud. Again, though, Rick made use of her parted lips, leaning towards her, his hands lightly on her waist, kissing her mouth slowly with unmistakable intent. Just as Vita started to kiss him back, he pulled away.

'Hop in, lady – your carriage awaits.'

'Let it wait,' she said, her hands at his neck, tilting her face towards his, kissing him back. Her lips and his, both wet with the torrent of kisses they were trying to hold at bay because they couldn't help but be aware that they were in the middle of the pavement on Fortis Green, the taxi's meter was ticking, she wasn't going to stay with Rick, she was going home and trains were waiting. Oh, but just to kiss him for a little longer!

'Safe journey,' he winked at her. 'Goodnight.'

'Sleep tight,' she winked back.

'Like a Bug in a Rug,' he laughed, leaning into the cab, kissing her again.

And then the taxi drove off.

You really can't call that a dawn chorus, Vita thought, wide awake at just gone five with the parrots attacking her sleep much as they were pillaging the pears on her tree. She lay there, listening to their screeching, unsure whether they were cheering or berating the pears for falling. She'd been to the window and counted five birds this morning. Though she'd gone back to bed, sleep was impossible but she didn't need to be up for at least another two hours and she happily lay there, indulging in playing back all the fun of the fair. Would she see him again? Was it just schmooze? She didn't think herself a particularly good judge of character but Rick did seem genuine. Perhaps he'd ring her next week and see if she was happy with her order. Or she could email him, couldn't she? Did the Rules – those stupid, contrived, dating-etiquette stipulations she'd read about in her twenties – also define dating in one's thirties? Did she have to wait for him to make contact? Was she allowed to send an email then? A friendly one, a little larky, perhaps to say, Oi, you! I want my further discount! She'd wait until after the weekend, she decided, plenty of time to muse and practise.

When Vita opened the shop the next morning, she imagined all the traders setting up their stands in Ally Pally and the high street in Muswell Hill starting to hum with activity. Tables and chairs on the pavement outside the cafés; perhaps the chewing-gum man would be searching for the perfect blobs for that day's work. Maybe the day staff at the John Baird were hoovering and polishing and spritzing away the linger of last night's spilt beer. Then she dragged herself back to Wynford and the first thing she did was look for the best spot for Rick's wares which would be arriving by courier sometime the next day. Time for the teasel figurines to go, she thought. Bless them – they really hadn't been popular and they did look a little forlorn and dusty.

Jodie had been fine about not coming in because no matter how strapped she was, that girl liked working even less. Vita checked the ledger. Not much business had been done yesterday – but actually, it was about average for this time of year with the schools not yet on summer holidays. A text came through to her phone. It was Tim. How did it go?

She stared at the message and then she thought, You know what, I actually don't want to correspond with you just yet. So she didn't. Mid-morning, he sent the same text again, following that with another half an hour later which just said, U ok? Tx. It was his fallback text – the one he'd sent her over and over again, not for the last three or four months but frequently prior to that. It always used to give her a lift, that text. He's thinking about me. Today, though, she saw it for what it was – him checking in, needing to know he was still alpha, not liking to be ignored, wanting to assume that she might not be OK, that she might be needy, down, just where he liked her to be. It was like his Night Babe, Txx texts – those had stopped too and initially she pined for them but now she saw them as equally manipulative. How could he send those to her when his new girlfriend was no doubt waiting for him in bed? And did that mean that when Vita was still with him, he was sneaking out the same text behind her back too? Today she felt a novel nothing about this contact from Tim. A non-feeling that was a great feeling. No surge in her stomach, no intrusion into her thinking, no need to text back in the way she would have done not so very long ago.

Lunch-time was quiet so she continued with the notes she'd been making about ideas for window display, about rotating stock, even rearranging the layout of the shop altogether. She was standing in the centre of the floor, trying to envisage the tables over there, moving the trunk out of which the throws and cushions were displayed to over here, shifting the baskets to the side wall and the console over that side, when the shop phone rang.

'That Shop – can I help you?' she answered.

'Hullo. I'm looking for this great new toy I've heard about called Dog on the Bog or something?'

Vita couldn't believe it – her first solo trade show and she'd pinpointed the new must-have! The caller was American or Canadian or perhaps even Australian.

'Clog!' she said. 'The *dog* is *in* a *clog*.'

'That's the one.'

'My stock is due in tomorrow – I'd be happy to put one on one side for you?'

'Actually, I wanted to buy the one that's the Kit on a Shit.'

Pardon? The *what*?

Silence.

'Miss Vita?'

It's him! The sod, *the sod*!

Quick! Be wacky! Be clever!

But she couldn't think of a thing to say.

'Vita?'

'I'm—' I'm what? 'I'm trying to think of something really clever and wacky to say. Mister Rick the Dick.'

Laughter. She'd made him laugh. She felt very pleased with herself. And then all of a sudden she was saying, Yes, OK, yes – a drink tonight? Sure, why not! And that

93

was when Tim came in. Vita turned away from him to have a moment to properly end the conversation, and Tim thought, Has she just turned her back on me? Then he thought, Who's she on the phone to? She's gone all furtive. And when Vita ended the call and turned to him, he saw her face was quite flushed.

'Who was that?'

'That?'

'On the phone, Vita.'

'Oh, no one. No one. Just someone, actually, from the show yesterday. I might pop back into London tonight. For another – another meeting. A meeting-type drinks thing.'

'Who was it?'

'Oh, a new supplier.'

'Called?'

'Mouse in a House.'

'The person?'

'Oh, er, Rick Edwards?' She said it as if she wasn't entirely sure she had the right surname. And then she thought, Why on earth am I doing that? Michelle would kill me and Candy would say, Be loud be proud, or something.

'And what does Rick Edwards want tonight that he couldn't get yesterday?'

And Vita heard every word and she absolutely knew the answer and she couldn't possibly say, Well, he probably wants to kiss with tongues tonight and who knows where that might lead.

'Vita?'

And then she thought, Why not just tell Tim the truth. It's all I ever did when we were together and as Candy would say, it's good for my funds in the Bank of Karma. 'He asked me out on a date.'

Tim had to take a moment to absorb the words but he couldn't do anything about the fleeting look of shock that swiped over his face like a slap. Eventually, he nodded and changed the subject to how the show had gone in terms of business. And when Vita found she could tell him quite assertively about what she'd ordered, she also found no need to justify her actions. It felt as though she'd acquired some kind of coating, an emotional Teflon. Because when Tim tried to berate her, when he tried to ridicule what she'd ordered, the way she'd ordered and the deals she'd struck, his words slipped off her and slithered down between the gaps in the floorboards.

All the while, when Tim was talking, he was shouting inside his head, Some fucker is taking Vita on a date! Some trumped-up sod wants to bang my girl! And then he thought, But she's not my girl. And then he thought, Oh God. And then he thought, I should have gone to the show, I knew I should have gone to the show. And then he knew the angry tone he was using at Vita was not allied in the slightest to his criticism of how she'd handled the show. The tone he was using was directed purely at the bewilderment he felt about someone else approaching her. Vita Whitbury, he thought, thirty-three years old. Pretty and funny. And single.

Location Location Location

'You do *not* go to a hotel – it's seedy,' said Candy.

'I wouldn't dream of it,' Vita said. 'I'm going in to meet him for a drink. And that's it.'

'Well, good for you. You need to see yourself as a virgin all over again.'

'Good God, woman, I'm just looking forward to a little harmless flirting.'

'The *frisson*,' Candy said, rolling the word around her tongue as if it were delicious, 'works wonders on self-esteem.'

'A stomach full of butterflies.'

'Call it what you will – and, if you're not in too much of a jitter, can you try and sneak a photo of him onto your phone? Or record his voice? There's bugger all on TV tonight.'

'Candy!'

'Seriously though – you have to promise to keep me updated. I need to know you're OK.'

'OK. I promise.'

'Just a yum or a yuk or an omg will do.'

*

Michelle, however, texted Vita in capitals with no exclamation marks.

DO NOT GO BACK TO HIS - AND NOT JUST COS IT'S MILTON KEYNES.

It made Vita laugh.

Don't worry - just a drink, Mush. U know me!

Michelle then requested Vita simply a ☺ or a ☹ or even a ☺ at some point during the evening.

'How cute do you look!'

For Vita, Rick's warm smile, the sparkle in his eyes, the compliment, the hand in the hollow of her back while he kissed her on the cheek close to her mouth, justified everything. Closing early – even though a customer was just about to come in. Not stopping to chat with elderly neighbours keen to do so. Ransacking her wardrobe and changing three times before settling on the shortish flippy skirt, a fitted white T-shirt, denim jacket for later on and cowboy boots. Candy called it her girly rock 'n' roll look and Vita always felt upbeat in it.

The Flask pub in Highgate had been an easy Tube journey from King's Cross. She felt relaxed, much more so than yesterday. Actually, she felt buoyant. It was a balmy early evening with just the minor irritation of a few arrogant wasps until dusk saw them vanish. Vita liked everything; she liked the chatting, she liked her drink, the snacks, and she liked the look of herself each time she checked her reflection in the loo. She also liked Rick. He was charming and flattering and easy to flirt along with. She pinched him smartly as he went over the details of his trick phone call that morning, repeating it all, laughing, mimicking her. There was an easy intimacy, eye contact she didn't feel shy about, an air of anticipation that caused her no chill.

'So tell me about your ex,' he said with no preamble.

And suddenly Vita didn't want Tim anywhere near any of this, she didn't want talk of him to taint her feeling of lightness, to intrude on the time she was having, to flatten the vivaciousness she felt. 'Oh, you know,' she said, 'it was just one of those things. We just grew apart, it just fizzled out. It's cool.' She shrugged.

'God, Kathy turned into the ex-from-hell,' Rick said, surprisingly darkly. 'Mind you, she was a nightmare girlfriend as it was, so I had it coming.'

Vita's vodka and cranberry suddenly tasted a little sour. 'Breaking up isn't easy,' she said, wanting to sound genuinely magnanimous and not hackneyed.

'Certainly isn't,' Rick said, 'especially when she's taking so long to get the message. Move on, woman! Get a life!'

Vita took a thoughtful sip. It wasn't just the details which she didn't want to hear, it was the disparaging tone of voice. Really, she should have listened hard to both. But tonight had a purpose: a preset objective she was determined to fulfil even at the expense of niggling common sense. She needed him to be nice Rick, attractive smiling teasing Rick, so she hauled the conversation back round to their industry and indulged him in talking about himself until their own pasts no longer featured. She was a little tipsy and he told her that her giggle was sexy and it was so cute the way her nose crinkled when she laughed. And she said to him, You're just saying that to get me into bed. And before she could ask herself whether she'd really said that out loud, Rick was answering her.

'You're not wrong there,' he was saying, running his hand along her thigh. 'Actually, I'm hoping to shag you senseless – but I do genuinely like the way your nose crinkles up when you smile.'

What do you say to that?

98

Where do you go from there?

It was out, in the open, and for Vita words were as seductive as physical foreplay.

'And you? Do you want to?' he asked her, with a nudge, his hand on her inner thigh now, partly on her flesh, partly on her skirt. 'Hey?'

She took a sip of her drink, sucking hard through the straw, the glass very cold against her hand. She swallowed. Looked at him. Nodded. Drank again. Can you be relaxed about all this and yet feel so very nervous at the same time? she wondered. Was that OK?

'I like your nose too,' she said.

'Your place or mine then?' he asked.

Now, neither Michelle nor Candy had mentioned Pear Tree Cottage, had they? They'd just forbidden her from going to Milton Keynes or a hotel. And, sitting there in Highgate, denim jacket on because it was just on the intrusive side of chilly now, Vita thought of her little house waiting for her to return; a small patient old building which really had looked after her these past few months, a resolutely benign place despite her ambivalence towards it, protective walls providing space, peace and refuge despite her reluctance to embrace it as home.

'Mine,' she said. 'Let's go back to mine.'

And So to Bed

The journey back had been a little awkward in that sex was a foregone conclusion which meant that spontaneity was now precluded. The frisson and the feistiness were somewhat redundant. The butterfly wings were stilled by the slightly self-conscious hand-holding on the crowded carriage of the late-night train.

'Night bus?' she suggested, when they'd arrived.

'Are you joking?' Rick pinched her bottom. They headed for the neon-drenched mini-cab office, waiting in a queue until a slightly smelly car took them the few miles to Vita's home.

'Nice,' said Rick, at nothing in particular as she showed him in and led the way through to the kitchen.

'Would you like a drink?'

'What do you have?'

And then Vita realized she only had tea, coffee, milk and half a carton of orange juice or two miniatures Michelle had swiped from some mini-bar or other. Michelle always brought the little bottles for Vita: booze, shampoo, bath foam.

'Well, that's some choice!' Rick assessed Malibu or Tia Maria. 'You choose.'

'No – you,' said Vita, 'you're my guest.'

'No, honestly, I insist.'

This was all a little awkward.

'OK,' she said and she plumped for the Malibu.

Rick sniffed the Tia Maria and then took a bold swig as though it was medicine. 'God, woman – that's gross!'

'Would you like tea then? Or coffee?'

'No, honestly, I'm fine.' He was looking around. It was only a small house but how the hell would he get her from here to up there, to bed. Meanwhile, Vita cursed herself for having no ability to play music, for having lights that didn't dim, for not having candles strategically placed. She thought about offering to share her earphones with him but whereas such an offer might have been wacky and well received earlier in the evening when spirits were high and the chase was in full pursuit, she thought it might fall a little flat now. She put the radio on, but it was Radio 4 and sensible voices discussing world news were not conducive to imminent seduction. She fiddled with the tuner, rejecting all the music she found until Rick was behind her, his hand stilling her, his lips at the nape of her neck, kissing, kissing, kissing.

And Vita thought to herself, Oh my God, any minute now. And she let her hand drop away from the radio and she didn't think about how ridiculously coconutty her mouth must taste and she didn't stop to think back on the stiltedness of the last couple of hours. The fact that there was a man not just in her kitchen but close up against her body, desiring her, desperate to take her to bed, swept all her reservations out of the room, out of the house, like light dust. Pubs and palaces in Muswell Hill and Highgate were one thing – a kind of stage on which both she and Rick had been able to act, to play, to posture; but journeying home and now being here and on the verge of going to bed, was another thing altogether. But Vita put it all to one side because her body felt great, really great. It wasn't about opening her mind, it was about closing down the racket of thoughts and opening up her body. She was tingling and throbbing and hot, not so much from her desire specifically for Rick, as from a very physical yearning for human touch, to be wanted and ravished by another person after such a long period without. His attention, his hunger, was the thrill; it was an ego massage which in itself felt even better than her breasts being fondled.

'Where's your bedroom?'

'Upstairs.'

'Lead on.'

So she did. Halfway up the stairs, his hand was suddenly up between her legs, making her stop. She let him fondle her for a moment without turning, his hand rubbing at the gusset of her underwear, his fingers probing at the elastic but snagging a little. No, let's not do it on the stairs, it's all a bit clumsy. This has to be just right.

She moved away and led on to her bedroom. The curtains were still open and he looked lovely in the moonlight. The shadows of his cheekbones, his eyes dark, his mouth a little open, searching for hers. He was grasping her against him, his tongue leaping inside her mouth, the first deep kiss she'd had in months, the first deep kiss she'd had in over a decade with someone other than Tim. She lapped him up, the excitement of the newness, the relief of the differentness from Tim's taste or Tim's technique. The smell of Rick. The feel of his back through his shirt. The unmistakable mound of a hard-on straining behind denim, the thrill of that.

'Come on, baby.'

He eased her top off, put his hands on her waist and

sunk his face into her modest cleavage while he unhooked her bra.

'Oh, yes!' he murmured approvingly and she wanted to giggle. It sounded a bit silly, but he said it again as he took first one nipple to his mouth, then the other. Alternating over and over again as if they were children who just must have absolutely equal attention.

'Come on, baby.'

Come on what, Vita thought for a moment. She unbuckled his belt but then decided she ought to do his shirt first. She swept it away from his body, revealing a very smooth torso: slim, nice. She put her lips against his collarbone, just leaving them pressing lightly along its length as she continued with his trousers. Crisp boxers. Suddenly she felt surprisingly nervous about seeing the cock behind them. Before she could dither, he'd pulled them down and it sprang out, reassuringly normal and satisfyingly hard. Funny that she should be surprised that actually, it wasn't much different from Tim's, or those of the boyfriends she'd had before him. All much of a muchness, the penises of the world. The same to be said for the steps of this mating dance that people do. No big deal, really.

Being naked had taken Rick up a gear; his hands were all over her and Vita just let herself be felt, fondled and grasped. He pushed her down on to her bed, his hand gently at her throat, his fingers up inside her knickers working her wetness, easing between the lips and straight up inside her. She gasped. He pulled her knickers down hard, nudged her legs apart, knelt between them and she watched as he faffed with the condom before grabbing the base of his cock and brushing the tip up against her sex, over and over until she grabbed his arms and pulled him down on top of her, into her, deeper and deeper.

103

I. Am. Having. Sex. With. Someone. New.

And it felt really good.

I want to come. I want to come.

She was so close, twisting against him, screwing herself down on him screwing her.

And then she suddenly thought, *What was that?*

What the heck was *that?*

The orgasm subsided.

What's he *doing?*

She didn't want to think, Tim never sounded like that.

And she didn't want to think, I don't like it.

And she really didn't want think, Is this the real Rick?

Not after spending all day, since his phone call that morning, imagining the real Rick to be an intense and skilled lover.

Right now she was aware that she shouldn't be thinking anything at all. She should just be feeling. So she writhed and closed her eyes and concentrated on the sensation, ran her hands along his body, turned on by the weight of him on top of her, the saltiness on his skin when she sucked his neck, the sound and the feel of the slap of his balls against her buttocks. She sought out his mouth, slipped her tongue in and entwined it with his, bit at his lips, breathed against his ear, sipped his ear lobes. He was humping hard, bucking into her, her right nipple in a pinch that blurred the pain-pleasure boundary. He was hot, hard, sweaty. God, she could come. She really could.

And she was about to – but then there it was again!

What on earth?

Why is he *doing* that?

And as her orgasm wilted and ebbed away, his came and though she took some titillating satisfaction from feeling

104

the intensity of his spurts she just couldn't prevent herself from feeling deflated, from thinking, Oh stop it stop it please hurry up and shut up.

Please please hurry up.

Ultimately, it was like eating out – and having a seriously disappointing meal while your partner is happily licking their plate clean.

*   *   *

'Jesus Christ, what the fuck is that?'

Rick sat bolt upright a few hours later.

'It'll be my parrots,' Vita said sleepily. He'd turned out to be a snorer. Vita felt as if she'd finally drifted off only five minutes ago after hours trying to nudge him and poke him subtly before hissing out a sharp shh! Hours lying there wondering how on earth she was going to recount it all to the hopeful Michelle and Candy.

'Your *what*?'

I'm going to have to wake up.

'Some people have partridges in their pear tree, but it seems I have parrots in mine,' she said.

Rick scrambled from the bed and looked out of the window. 'Christ alive,' he said. 'They're not parrots though, they're parakeets, but what the fuck are they doing in your garden at this time? What are they doing here at all?'

'I don't know.' Vita propped herself up, taking her other hand to her head, smoothing her hair and hoping it wasn't in as much disarray as Rick's, which was positively bouffant. 'They only recently arrived. They seem to like the unripe pears.'

'That's the craziest thing,' he said, coming back to bed.

And Vita thought, Not half so crazy as the concept that

there's a new man in my bed. Crazier still that, actually, I'd rather have it back to myself.

The new man was starting to kiss her, not remotely self-conscious about morning breath. She closed her eyes. His hands were lovely and soft and his skin so smooth, he was pleasingly muscled and his cock was hard again, and hopeful. And Vita thought, Let's give him a chance. Let's not fixate about the first time. Perhaps it was nerves. Perhaps the Tia Maria didn't agree with him. And she welcomed him back inside her.

Good sex, she soon realized, was as much about good aural compatibility as it was good oral. However, the sound of him overruled everything else that was going on. He might be a sight for sore eyes but God he was an earache. She thought momentarily about moaning and gasping loudly to drown him out but then she had to bite his shoulder to stop herself from giggling. Ultimately, she decided just to give up, to go through the motions – and to put it all down to experience.

'Did you come?' he asked, panting as he flopped away from her and onto his back.

'Did you feel me?' Vita didn't want to lie outright.

'Yeah – yeah, I did. That was fantastic. You're one horny bitch, you are.' And then he laughed. 'Joke.' He started kissing her tenderly, all over her face. 'You're so lovely.'

Vita, though, cringed. You can't experience a true level of tenderness after two days, she said silently. The kisses felt empty and annoying. Then she felt mean. And then she felt annoyed. And then she felt a bit depressed.

The parrots or parakeets, whatever they were, were still shrieking outside. Rick put a pillow over his head and did that boy-thing of falling promptly back to sleep. Vita lay there, sticky and unfulfilled. She was cross with herself, cross with him. For a moment she thought, I bet Tim has been having better sex than this. Then she thought, That really was crap sex. And then she thought, how could she be cross with Rick? Simply because he didn't make love in the same way as the Rick of her imaginings? That wasn't his fault. She was cross that sex with Tim had been much better. And that wasn't Rick's fault either.

But his bizarre, dodgy French accent?

She'd never heard anything like it.

She didn't think it was an affectation but God how it had grated on her ears and turned her off. And she felt really deflated because she wanted to really like Rick and to fancy him rotten but, though the last two days had been so liberating, so intoxicating, such fun, she felt neither. She just felt teary and very, very tired. And then she told herself off, told herself to give the man a chance, for God's sake. But disappointment dropped down through her heavily just like the falling pears outside. She hadn't been in this situation before and she just wasn't sure what to do next.

Sting

'He sounded – *French*.'

'French?' Michelle paused. French in a *"ma cherie"* way? That's quite sweet!'

But Vita shook her head. There was something just slightly humiliating in having had bad sex on her first opportunity to have any sex at all after a long-term monogamous relationship. 'No – more in a comedy French way. He didn't *speak* French – he just grunted and moaned and made weird noises with an exaggerated Gallic accent.'

'You're joking!' Michelle tried to sound appalled and though she bit her lip to subdue laughter, she couldn't help her eyes watering with mirth.

'Stop laughing.'

Michelle composed herself, momentarily. But it was short-lived. 'What, was he all, *"Allo allo mademoiselle you zexy leetle poosy chat"?*'

'Mushroom – stop it! It was dreadful. Honestly. He didn't say stuff – he just did these stupid throaty noises. *In French.*'

But both she and Michelle were now giggling.

'What do you mean?'

'*Haw haw haw,*' Vita mimicked, deep and gravelly, '*haw hee haw hee haw.*'

Michelle thought her coffee was going to come out of her nose. 'No!'

'Yes,' Vita said forlornly. '*Haw hee haw. H-h-hmmm! H-h-hmmm!*' She thought about it. 'Dirty old man noises,' she said.

'But *en Francais*?'

'*Exactement.*'

Michelle banged her fist on the coffee-shop table, tears coursing as she laughed.

'It's not funny!' Vita protested. But it was. It was actually very funny. And somehow, the post-mortem with her closest friend now managed to make light of the disappointment at the time. Now Michelle was doing an impersonation and the two of them sat there, snorting and tittering like teenagers.

'I tell you something, V – in some ways I'm pleased. By that, I mean it's a good job that it wasn't mind-blowing sex. It means you won't do something idiotic like fall head over heels. Look on it as getting-over-it sex, and in that respect it was good – great. It might not have been good sex – but it was sex nonetheless. With someone new. And that puts important physical distance between you and Tim. It's a marker. It's symbolic. It's a milestone.'

Vita nodded. 'I know.'

'But it is also very funny.'

Vita stopped to consider how the recounting of it all was actually more enjoyable than the act itself had been.

'Candy is going to have a field day with it.'

'She'll make you feel better still,' said Michelle.

'We shouldn't laugh at his expense. Poor bloke.'

'Bollocks!' said Michelle. 'Of course we should.' She paused. 'Might sex improve? How about you confide some

109

fantasy you have of making love with a mute. Or a Russian. Whatever floats your boat.'

Vita thought about having sex again with Rick. 'What it did do was obliterate the mystique of it all for me. And that was a good thing. Sex was so important to me with Tim – I used to judge myself on how often we did it, on how often he instigated it, how long it lasted, how good it was. It could affect my self-esteem. I loved Tim – and for me sex was a way of expressing that love.'

'Wanker.'

'Mrs Sherlock!'

'Sorry.'

'The point I'm trying to make is that last night I had sex without love. That's a revelation to me. Boom – it can be done. But do you know something – even without Inspector Clouseau demolishing my mojo, I'm not sure a casual shag's my thing.'

'But what about if you had a few more dates with Rick – not necessarily ending in bed – to see if you develop feelings for him?'

Vita thought about it. 'Perhaps.' She scraped the froth from the inside rim of the cup. 'I really liked the flirting and the build-up. I loved all that. I absolutely revelled in what Candy calls the frisson. The element of anticipation. The whole mating dance, if you like.'

'Is he just a bit dull, then?'

Vita thought about it. She could say yes and just end the conversation easily. 'Sometimes he was very funny, but sometimes he was a bit—'

'A bit arrogant?'

Vita shook her head. 'He was a little sharp when he spoke about his ex. A little unkind, perhaps.'

'Might've been nerves. What if he calls?'

Vita shrugged. 'I won't answer?'

Michelle shook her head. 'Wait and see how you feel. That's what dating's all about – playing it by ear. Or perhaps not, in your case. *Haw hee haw*.'

'Stop it! I bet you if he doesn't call I'll feel strangely rejected!'

'Oh, he'll call,' said Michelle. 'I'll bet you anything. Anyway, you ought to give him another chance – and yourself. Don't look for the deep-and-meaningful. Just have a bit of fun, girl. You may decide a bionic dick is worth a weird accent.'

Vita nodded. She liked the way Michelle simultaneously made light of the situation and yet cast great clarity on it. It came down to Vita having something different to think about – and some things to not think about at all. She looked at her watch – she was ten minutes later than she'd told Jodie. Still half a day at work to go, with all the Bats in their Hats or Dogs in their Clogs to unpack and display.

'I'll get this,' Michelle said, settling the bill. The two-for-one lunch offer wasn't on this week.

'You sure?'

'I'd rather you spent your money on kinky knickers or Mac make-up. Treat yourself!'

*   *   *

Vita hadn't been out in the garden for days. Not since before the trade show and that was well over a week ago. It was not on account of the parakeets or whatever they were – they were still coming each morning with their cacophonous capacity for a violent breakfast and there were plenty more pears on the tree. It was that she simply hadn't had time. She'd gone round to Candy's one night and had recounted the shenanigans to much mirth. Candy's

111

French accent was almost as good as Rick's and she was now texting Vita at regular intervals, haw hee haw hee haw. She'd gone to her mother's another night and had stayed over, feeling cosseted in her childhood bedroom, remembering when the walls were bedecked with posters of pop stars, when real men had seemed an exotic species she couldn't believe she'd ever really meet. On other nights, she'd so enjoyed luxuriating in the Jo Malone *Pomegranate Noir* bath oil she'd splashed out on, that she'd gone straight to bed to stockpile sleep until the parakeets' rude awakening. Rick had texted her – just larkily – so she'd responded in a friendly way. But today he'd called and she'd let it go to voicemail and his message said, Call me, I want to see you, I'm around tomorrow in your area, call me. So tonight her only plan was to return Rick's call. She felt she'd know how to play it once she heard his voice. She poured some juice into a glass and took her phone out into the garden. The busy-lizzies needed dead-heading and the chives needed watering. A pecked-at pear, now browning, had fallen into the middle of the deckchair. Lots to do, Vita saw. But first, Rick.

Walking barefoot onto the grass, she sipped her juice. She looked at her phone and started to compose how to say hullo. Hi. Hey there. Good evening. She sipped again. And, finally, she dialled. Almost immediately, she felt a stab of hot, hard pain on her thumb so sharp it took her breath away. Then another, on her arm. She was under her pear tree, under attack. Wasps were suddenly everywhere, their battle cries deafening. She threw the juice down in a panic and waved her arms wildly. The juice was dripping down her leg. The wasps were coming at her. Her ankle. In her hair. She bolted the short distance to the back of the garden wondering all the while why the hell she hadn't run inside. She

112

could see the wasps now swarming around the glass that had held the juice.

Her heart was pounding, the stings were excruciating, she was in turmoil. In a split second, from the relative safety of the creosoted fence, she assessed what was happening. All around her tree, the detritus of the parakeets' breakfast buffet now lay in a mushy, decaying, rank mess. On each plundered fruit, wasps were gathering. Now she'd added apple juice to the mix. How had she not seen? Had she been that preoccupied with nerves about making a Dear John phone call to bloody Rick?

Oh God! The phone. She'd dropped that too. She could see it now, amongst the pears, amongst the wasps.

She felt ridiculous but she was in pain, in shock, and the only thing she felt she could do just then was cry. It hurt. It was shocking. She'd been stung in childhood but didn't remember it hurting this much. She didn't know what to do. She wanted to be back in the house, away from this stupid garden and these bastard bastard wasps. She could hear them. She could actually hear them from where she was: an arrogant drone as they wriggled and humped over the half-eaten fruit and writhed inside the glass. They were a few metres away, terrifyingly close, really. Why hadn't she stayed calm and stock-still, as her father had trained her so fastidiously to do on a number of childhood picnics? She considered climbing over the fence into Mr Brewster's garden but if he didn't drop dead of heart failure and if he did let her through his house, what use would that be? Her front door was shut anyway. The only way in from the garden was through the kitchen door and the only way back there was to pass the pear tree.

The stings, the pain. It was horrible. She didn't dare move. She felt quite sick. She thought back to the pub in

113

Highgate, to the wasps that had buggered off at dusk. She'd just have to wait it out.

And she did.

Two hours more, she stood at the back of her garden, her limbs throbbing, her thumb swelling, pain on the left side of her face. Then she ran for it. She left the phone where it was; her only concern was to be inside.

That sodding tree with its parrots and pears and wasps. And remember all that brown mulchy stuff that the blossom became? The estate agents didn't make mention of all of that on the particulars, did they? The local authority searches didn't pass comment at all, did they?

Negligent!

What to do? She'd been stung four times. She tried cold water but it seemed to burn, and lukewarm water seemed too hot. She remembered walks on the beach with her father and him always imparting the same advice. If you are stung by a jellyfish, pee on it. On the jellyfish? she'd asked, as a child. On the sting, sweetface! her dad had laughed. Why wee? she'd asked, a little older, when hearing the same story again. You can use vinegar too, he'd said, but you may not have a bottle on you, on account of being in a bathing suit, darling. Pee, he'd said, was an excellent alternative.

Vinegar. She had an unopened bottle of balsamic in the cupboard which Michelle had given her along with fancy oils and fine herbs, as a house-moving present. She dripped a little onto her arm. It looked like iodine. Or treacle. It didn't smell good on flesh. And it didn't help.

'It doesn't help, Dad,' she said sadly. And then she remembered how he also told her that if cows chase you, run towards them yelling like a madwoman. The left-field advice that so summed him up. She missed him now, missed him dreadfully. And her mum, whose first-aid box

114

had everything in it. And Tim, who'd swat wasps and remove spiders from the bath with his bare hands and tease her and call her Miss Muffet.

What do I do now?

Vita wished she wasn't on her own. She hated it. She hated the fact that she had to deal with things she didn't want to, didn't know how to. Everything was so lopsided being only one instead of two. Yin and yang were not possible if the one had not the other. She just didn't want to have to cope with everything all on her own, she was fed up with her Brave Face. She looked at the house phone and then cursed her mobile phone for holding all the numbers she needed and, in doing so, for having taken away any need to remember numbers by rote. She didn't even know Michelle's number. Or Candy's. The only numbers she knew by heart were her mum's home number and Tim's. But what would her mum be able to do anyway? She'd worry. And Tim? What would be the point of phoning him? It wasn't his job to look after her any more, even if she'd walked into a hornets' nest. Anyway, say Suzie picked up?

So Vita stood in the kitchen shuddering, rifling through the local phone directory, choosing Pest Off because it implored her to Fone Any Time. But not, it seemed, on a Thursday evening. Instead, she searched the bathroom for some Savlon and daubed her cheek, her thumb, her ankle, her arm. She wasn't in the mood for Jo Malone. Jo Home Alone. She went to bed feeling sore, silly and acutely aware of her on-her-ownness.

Those bloody birds.

The next morning, she yelled out the window at them but they ignored her. She felt ridiculously intimidated by them. Though she was sure it was too early in the day

115

for wasps, what if the parakeets dive-bombed her? Or pecked off pears to hit her like cannonballs? Her mobile would have to stay where it was, alongside the discarded glass from which she decided never to drink again. She went to work with the stings looking like boils and her thumb unable to bend. She called Pest Off as soon as she arrived.

'I've been attacked by wasps.'

'Have you seen a nest?'

'I have a huge pear tree.'

'Is the nest in the tree?'

'I have been stung a million times. I just don't dare go outside.'

Three o'clock that afternoon was the earliest he could do. Jodie couldn't cover for her. She didn't want to phone Tim. It all sounded so pathetic. I've been stung, I'm scared of the wasps, can you watch the shop for me?

She'd just have to close up early.

Mr Pest Off was young and larky and arrived in a T-shirt. He looked silently at the tree from the kitchen window before going out into the garden for closer inspection. Vita made him tea. She always felt compelled to make tea for tradesmen, somehow believing that if she was nice to them, they'd like her and be good to her and go the extra mile, do a proper job and not rip her off. It hadn't really worked so far – previously, the plumber, the electrician and the carpenter who she'd asked to make the warped doors close again had all drunk her tea, eaten her biscuits, spent an awful lot of time chatting and never quite finished the jobs. But here she was, feeling beholden to Pest Off Man, making tea and rooting around for digestives.

'There ain't no nest, love.'

'Oh.'

'There's a lot of wasps – you're right there.'

'Can you – get rid of them anyway? Is there anything you can spray on them?'

He laughed. 'Not with so many pears about. They'll be back in the morning.'

'There are parrots who eat the pears – then they fall down and go mushy.' This isn't relevant. Just focus on the wasps.

'Pears fall down – then my little friends come.'

'Do you seriously like wasps enough to call them little friends?' Stop talking to him, just make him do something.

'I don't mind them, really. Bit misunderstood, really.' He was standing in the open kitchen doorway. Vita was standing well back.

'Look,' she said and she showed him her arm, her thumb – the stings had now settled into what looked like old carbuncles.

'That's wasp stings all right.'

'I know,' Vita said, trying to sound plaintive. 'Is there nothing you can do?'

'Not really. You can keep on top of the pears – keep clearing them away, wash it all down. Prevention, you know.'

'I'm not going out there – not till the winter.'

He laughed. But she was really quite serious. 'Do you think you could pick up my phone for me?'

He glanced over his shoulder to the tree, sauntered over and retrieved the phone, returning to find Vita even further back in the kitchen.

'You don't need pest control, love,' he said, handing her the phone which she took between finger and thumb as if it was contaminated. 'What you need is a tree surgeon. It's a big old brute – close to the house, too. Get someone to chop it down.'

That tree. Her tree. The magnificent bare winter branches making monochrome stained-glass designs against a sky, the bride-beautiful blossom in late spring. But now the pears, the parrots, the wasps. She mustn't be sentimental. That tree was not a cathedral of the natural world, it was a hellish place of killer wasps and mad birds. She could do the karma thing and just plant something else in its place, something fruitless and small.

'Can you recommend anyone?'

'I have a brother-in-law what'll do it,' he said. 'He's not a tree surgeon by trade. But he's good.' He scribbled down a number. Then he charged her an extortionate call-out fee and helped himself to two more biscuits on his way out. Vita thought to herself, Your brother is the last person I'll be calling.

* * *

'Can you take it?' Oliver called down to Spike who retrieved his mobile.

Spike cleared his voice and tried to sound official. 'Good afternoon, Arbor Vitae?'

'I have a dangerous pear tree in my garden which needs to come down.'

'Dangerous?'

'Extremely.'

'Hold on.' Spike pressed the mute button on Oliver's phone – Oliver didn't know it had such a function. 'Boss? Some woman – sounds mad – says she has a dangerous pear tree.'

Oliver abseiled down from the oak and took the phone from Spike.

'This is Oliver Bourne.'

'Well, this is Vita Whitbury and I have a dangerous

118

pear tree that really needs to come down as soon as possible.'

'I see.'

'Can you come soon?'

'I can come soon to assess it, certainly.'

'Today, though – can you come *today*? I've taken the rest of the day off work. Can you come please, as soon as possible?'

Oliver looked at his watch. No, not really – by the time they finished here it would be clocking-off time. He offered tomorrow but she heaved out such a distressed sigh.

'Off all the tree companies, I picked yours because your name is like mine.'

Oliver didn't think she'd said her name was Olivia.

'I'm Vita, and Arbor Vitae means tree of life – but my tree is killing me. Please come.'

'Look, where are you?'

'I live in the Tree Houses – well, it's called Mill Lane and I'm at the end.' She started to impart an extraordinary amount of detail as if directing someone with low intelligence, poor eyesight and no sense of direction.

'I know where you are,' Oliver said patiently. And he did. In fact, from the yard he passed by quite close on his way home. 'I'll swing by and assess your *Pyrus periculum*.'

'Thank you,' Vita said, taking comfort from the Latin though all Oliver had said was *dangerous pear*. 'Thank you so much.'

Flower Man and Tree Fella

Suzie liked it when Tim sounded pissed off with Vita. Even though it made him fractious and distracted, in general she much preferred it to when he checked his phone intently and went out of his way not to mention his ex.

'How the fuck does she think we're ever going to make enough when she fucks off early the whole time?'

Suzie was just going to open her mouth to give her twopence worth when she realized he wasn't actually asking her opinion. Just like when he'd said who the fuck did Vita think she was. Suzie was absolutely ready to say, I know, why can't she leave us alone – but Tim had bulldozed on with further grievances.

'Seriously. I swung by the shop at tea-time – the busiest time – and it's all shut up! She didn't even put one of her flowery handwritten signs in the door!'

Suzie felt momentary alarm. Why was he swinging by there? Just to drop in? Or had he already prearranged to? He hadn't made that clear. She felt anxious.

'And she's not answering her phone.'

And Suzie wondered, Does he have Vita on speed dial? If so, is she higher up than my number?

'I've a good mind to go over to her place – see what the hell's going on.'

'Don't do that!' Suzie leapt at the notion. He'd said he'd never been. Why start now – even if it was to have an argument?

Tim looked surprised. Suzie quickly backtracked. 'She's probably not there anyway – you'll just waste a journey. And you haven't been there before anyway, have you.' She hadn't made that sound enough like a question. 'Have you?' She made sure it now sounded as if she was wracking her own brains over something so irrelevant she hadn't bothered to commit it to memory. 'She's probably gone to get her nails done or something.'

Tim laughed. Not at Suzie, but at the concept of Vita taking herself off to have her nails done. She always kept them filed short and never varnished them. He'd never really thought about it until then. And then he glanced at Suzie's acrylics with the squared-off white tips and he thought how he really didn't find them that attractive but how he hadn't really noticed them either, until now. They were part of the package; the look, the type. You couldn't have the legs and the boobs and the fawning over him without the rest of it. It was the deal. And, at the moment, with his ridiculous ex behaving like a total idiot, Suzie was the better option.

'Just phone her again,' Suzie said, making out the shape of his phone in his trousers. A pocketful of secrets.

'I told you – I have. Her phone's off.'

'Sorry,' Suzie huffed petulantly and flounced down on the sofa, flicking crossly through a magazine.

The doorbell went. Tree man, thought Vita, rushing to open it. Rick was the last person on her mind but there he was, standing on the doorstep with a cockily raised eyebrow and a bunch of supermarket flowers with the 20%-extra-free label facing her.

'Now, lady,' he said, inviting himself in, 'I did leave messages. And then you half-phoned me before it cut out. Like I said, I was in the area – but when I went to your shop, it was closed. So I reckoned I'd swing by – and see if everything is all right.'

Vita didn't look good. She looked messy, tired, and agitated. Her eyes were red and darting and she had a dreadful red thing on her cheek.

'I have a wasp problem,' she said, cupping her hand protectively over her jaw, 'and I'm expecting this guy any minute now.'

'Yuk,' said Rick, inspecting her stings and not liking the look of them. 'Do you want a drink later? Or would you like to go straight to bed, do not pass Go, do not collect two hundred pounds?'

Just then, Vita didn't want to smile politely or laugh awkwardly; in fact, she was so preoccupied she didn't even get his allusion to Monopoly. None of this was a game to her. She wanted the wasps gone and, just then, she wanted Rick gone too. 'Another time?' She didn't have the energy for the soliloquy she'd practised; vagueness would have to do even if it complicated things in the long run.

'I can see you're a little distracted. How about later? Thing is, I'm avoiding Witch Woman who apparently *needs* to come over this evening to search for yet more non-existent items she's convinced she's left.'

And then Vita thought of Witch Woman, whose name she might not even know but for whom, just then, she felt great empathy. 'Perhaps she's lonely,' she found herself saying, 'perhaps she's sad, perhaps she wants to be near all the elements of her old life. Perhaps she just wants to see you. Because she misses you. Because she's sad.'

Rick looked at Vita as if her theory was the most crackpot one he'd ever heard. 'Er, she's sad all right. Anyway, call me later,' he said, 'let me know.' He was about to clarify that he meant about the drink, as well as the wasps, but Vita was already looking over his shoulder. He turned and regarded a truck pulling up on the other side of the road. 'Look, call me when the Tree Fella has gone,' he said, laughing at his wit and taking the flowers with him.

They passed each other along the path. The tree man thought he heard the flower man mutter, They're not for her, as he used the bunch of flowers to swat at a wasp.

'I'm looking for Miss Whitbury?'

'I am – *Miss Whitbury*,' Vita replied, suddenly deciding if she kept things nice and formal, and didn't offer tea and biscuits and larky chatter, then this man could knuckle down to the job. His truck looked the part, certainly. He could chop the tree down and then chip it with that big machine.

'Oliver Bourne,' he said, extending his hand. Everything about him was warm: his smile, his voice, his hand and his handshake, the sandy colour of his hair, the deep brown of his eyes. She felt immediately confident that he'd look after things. She liked his rugged work trousers, the dark green well-worn T-shirt with the company motif in gold. She liked the motif – a sort of abstract tree of knowledge or tree of life and again, she thought, Here's a bloke who knows.

'Show me the problem, then.'

'Here,' said Vita, showing him her arms, pointing at her ankle, turning her face to show him the other cheek, then giving him a sore and slightly swollen thumbs-up. He looked at her, and politely regarded the stings whilst

123

quietly wondering if she was waiting for a doctor and had somehow mistaken him.

'The tree?' he said.

'Oh God, yes, of course. The tree did this anyway, that's why it must go.'

'The tree. Did this to you,' Oliver said quietly. What a case to end a day's work. He stooped to untie his boots.

'Oh, don't worry about those,' Vita said, leading the way into her house. 'I would, normally – but these are exceptional circumstances and there's no time to lose.'

The smells in the house accosted Oliver at once: woman's things like candles and drying laundry. It was a comforting fragrance. She wasn't as he'd imagined; he'd thought she'd be wild-haired and odd, older, surrounded by cats and wall-hangings – but this Miss Whitbury looked very normal, even with an angry sting on her cheek. Her place was homely and she was leading him through to the kitchen, pointing out the small garden beyond, as if some rabid dog was lurking at large.

'It's out there,' she said.

Oliver thought, That's a beautiful tree.

Even now, all these years on, seeing a new tree was such an uplifting sight.

'Can you cut it down now, do you think?'

'Cut it down?' He started to laugh. 'That tree?'

'You have to. It's a danger.' Oliver looked at her. She was obviously dead serious. Her eyes appeared to have turned navy with graveness – he'd thought they were green when she was on her doorstep showing him her stings. 'If not now – when, then?'

He looked at the tree and then back to her again, standing there all fiery and indignant. 'Clarify danger,' he said. He could do with a cup of tea.

'It's a *constant* danger,' said Vita.

And one of those chocolate digestives he could see on the worktop.

'Throughout the year,' she was saying. 'Apart from midwinter, I suppose.'

She was too young to be batty. It was all a bit odd really, yet quietly amusing and a little intriguing. 'Could I trouble you for a cup of tea?'

Vita glanced at the kettle. Then at Oliver Bourne, standing in her kitchen, broad-shouldered and softly spoken. A tanned friendly face and strong brown forearms. The company logo on his sweatshirt – *his* company. A specialist. Approved. Registered. She thought, I'd better not piss him off. She thought, I'll bet it's hard work, chopping down a tree. No biscuits, though. And no irrelevant chat.

'Milk?' she asked. 'Sugar?'

'Yes and two. Milk in first, please – makes such a difference. And a chocolate digestive too, if you can spare one.'

She couldn't now not offer him a biscuit, could she. He'd thrown her off balance and yet she felt strangely comforted by him, by his calmness, his experience, his gentle strength.

'Are you not having one?' It was the way he said it, as if to say, Come on, Miss Whitbury, take a load off. Have a cuppa. I'm here now. So she made herself a cup too.

He had sat himself down, right there at her rickety kitchen table. She was bemused more than indignant. She thought back to Tim telling her once about people skills, about how to deflect confrontation, about how to diffuse tension. She was always aware when he was using them on her – so patronizing that she'd felt trapped, beaten into submission, denied the ability to vent, to express herself, even to simply say, But.

Oliver Bourne, however, sitting in her kitchen with his tan and his sun-tipped hair, was different. He seemed – natural. He probably hadn't thought, Silly cow, calm down. He was probably just dying for tea and a sugar rush after a full day's work chopping wood or whatever he'd been doing. Vita leant against the sink, cupping her mug for a long moment, feeling calmer with the first sip.

'It's good to have a hot drink on a warm day – it actually cools the blood, sends the capillaries closer to the surface, tricks the body into cooling itself down,' he said.

'Tea calms me down, rather than cools me down,' Vita said, 'though I only ever drink half a cup. Even if I make half a cup, I just drink half of that. For me, it's the process, I'd be happy enough just making the tea and holding the cup.'

Oliver smiled. 'My staff are mainly in their twenties – brawny, beefy guys who strip off their shirts and work up a sweat and can't figure out why, when they down can after can of ice-cold drinks, they're still hot and I'm there fully clothed, drinking tea and not breaking a sweat.'

Vita thought, I like hearing this man talk – his voice is as soothing as a cup of tea. She felt herself unwinding. She thought about offering another biscuit. But then she thought, I can't bear another day with that bloody tree. She placed the bottom of the hot mug over the sting on her forearm. The immediate discomfort subsided into numbness and relief and the soothing cool when the mug was lifted away.

'You said the tree did that?'

She nodded. Showed him her non-bending thumb,

tipped her face back so he could see the sting on her jaw and those on her ankle, shin, elbow. He winced sympathetically. 'The wasps did that,' she said.

He could see they were wasp stings. 'And the wasps are –'

'In the tree,' Vita said. 'All over the place.'

'That'll be the pears.'

'Exactly.'

Stings weren't much fun – it was an occupational hazard of his job. They could make a person as agitated as the wasp had been to sting in the first place. He'd go softly with this girl. 'I might not be the right person – you may need pest control.'

'Pest Off.'

'I would be too.'

Vita smiled. 'No, I mean I called a company called Pest Off – they've been already.'

'And?'

'Told me to call a tree man.' She looked at Oliver. 'Is that what you are?'

'I'm an arboricultural consultant,' he said. She liked the word consultant – it implied top of the – well – *tree*. 'But you can call me a tree man, if you like. I think of myself as a tree geek, really.' He finished his tea. 'Come on then, Miss Whitbury, let's take a look, shall we?'

'I'm staying in here, thank you very much.'

She watched from the kitchen window, watched as he walked calmly all around the tree, looking up, down, coming in close and sitting on his heels to inspect the base of the trunk. He walked to the back of the garden and then back to the tree, did the same from the kitchen, saluting Vita when he caught her eye which made her smile and salute back. He picked up a fallen pear. She saw a wasp fly from it and back to it. He put it back down, slowly. How was

127

he not stung? He stood for a while longer, hands on hips. Then he came back in.

'Are you OK?' she asked.

'I'm fine,' he said, 'thank you.'

'Do you see what I mean?'

'There are a lot of wasps,' he agreed. 'A lot of fallen pears. You really need to clear them daily – you're not helping the problem.'

'You can't seriously expect me to go out there daily?' she said, as if he was telling her to take her life in her hands.

'Husband?' She shook her head. 'Boyfriend? Brother? Dad?'

'I'm an only child, my dad died when I was fourteen and I don't have – I'm not –. I'm single.'

She appeared to be close to tears. He spoke quietly, almost apologetically. 'I can't chop down a tree because wasps are eating its fruit.'

'But it's *dangerous*!'

'The tree itself isn't – it's in good health.'

'But the *parrots*!'

'The – what?'

'Every morning, at the crack of dawn, these *parrots* come. Hundreds of them.'

'Hundreds?'

'About six. Or five.'

'Are they green?'

'Yes. And they scream and attack the pears and then the pears fall. Donk. Donk. Donk. At the crack of dawn. Then they go and the wasps come. Till dusk. It's a dreadful, dangerous cycle.'

'It's a bizarre ecosystem for Hertfordshire, I'll grant you.'

'But it's my first summer here – in this house. And

it's turning into a nightmare. That's why you need to do something. Please! Isn't it obvious? No tree – no parrots. No parrots – no fallen pears. No fallen pears – no wasps. No danger.'

'I can't chop the tree down because of wasps and parrots.'

'I need you to – it's, it's . . .' But suddenly she felt acutely self-conscious.

'It's what?'

That gentle voice of his, the level gaze with the soft brown eyes.

'Ruining my life.' It sounded ridiculously melodramatic.

'Are you sure?'

Now his calmness, his control, irked her.

'Yes, I'm bloody sure – I moved here because I had to. Because I needed a fresh start. It hasn't been easy. It's been bloody difficult. Still is, sometimes. And this tree is now seriously affecting my life. My happiness, my sense of security and well-being are all under threat.'

Don't laugh, Oliver. Poor girl. She's in a right old state.

He had an urge to make *her* another cup of tea, just to hold or to place over the sting. To sit her down for a while and cheer her up. Then he thought, What am I thinking! Procedure! Think procedure! In itself, it should leave her with a little bit of hope, for the time being at least.

'Look, I will see what I can do. But I can't do anything tonight. I can put in an application for you, if you like. It's the steps you have to go through, I'm afraid. I know the officer who oversees tree planning at the council very well. I will make the case for you.'

'You can't cut it down today?' She was desolate.

'Not today. Let's see what Martin says. He'll call round soon. He's good like that.'

'In the meantime?' Her voice wasn't rising, it was cracking.

'Earplugs? Long sleeves? You have to try and work *with* what's going on here, not against it.'

'I haven't slept properly for days.'

'I'm sorry.' And he genuinely sounded it. 'They're not parrots, they're parakeets.'

'What are they doing in my garden? Why are they even here? Shouldn't they be somewhere tropical?'

Oliver smiled. 'They're from the Wynfordbury Estate.'

'I don't know what that is.'

'Wynfordbury Hall? Just near here – it's still owned by the Earls of Seddon. The Victorian earl had an aviary – as was fashionable at the time. And some of the birds escaped – and liked the surroundings and have stayed ever since. I see them up Flamford way too – there's an orchard I maintain there. The poor owner only ever harvests half the fruit that grows – the rest is rotten. You should see *his* wasps. Makes yours seem as innocuous as butterflies.'

'No, thanks. Can't we call – the zoo?'

Oliver laughed. 'Parakeets are common now. Anyway, they've made this their habitat. They've become indigenous.'

'Sods.'

'It's like the wallabies in Derbyshire.'

'Sorry?'

'They escaped from Chatsworth or somewhere – and now leap around the dales.'

'But wallabies are cute and quiet,' Vita said sulkily. 'These bastard parrots are anything but.'

'Those wallabies wreak a fair amount of havoc,' Oliver countered. He considered how crestfallen she looked. 'Wait a moment.' He left, leaving the front door open and when he came back into the kitchen, for a moment Vita wondered whether he'd have a chainsaw with him. No.

Just paper. Official-looking forms. He took down her details; his writing bold, rhythmic, neat. 'I'll send this to Martin first thing – OK?'

He glanced at his watch. Vita glanced at the kitchen clock. Couldn't believe the time, either of them.

Tim and Vita and Rick

'Vita, it's Tim.'

'Hey.'

'Where were you today?'

'Today? In the shop, of course.'

'Not at four o'bloody clock, you weren't.'

The words, spoken seethingly quiet, were squeezed through clenched teeth like pressurized steam.

'I had to shut up early,' Vita said. 'I had an appointment.'

'At peak time? Well, that's just excellent planning, isn't it! *I need to make an appointment – I know! I'll book one for four o' clock.*' Sarcasm now; abrasive and harsh.

'Tim – I had to. It was an emergency.'

'An emergency – oh! An *emergency*!'

'I have problems at home. I had to see a man about a tree. Two men, actually.' She could hear that it all sounded stupid, so feeble.

'Well, while you were entertaining Robin Bloody Hood and his Merry Dickheads, did it not cross your mind that we're losing money hand over fist? Jesus, Vita – why the

132

hell didn't you call someone? Christ! I'd've stepped in for a couple of hours.'

'It was only an hour or so early. Today only. You hate working in the shop.'

'That's not the point. It's my business and if you can't be arsed to run it responsibly, I suggest you back out and we'll employ a professional manager.' The sarcasm had gone, in its place rock-hard nastiness dressed convincingly as common sense.

'Tim?' She hated it, *hated* it when he was mean. And the strangest thing was that it didn't make her feel vindicated for leaving him, it didn't even make her feel relieved she was no longer in a relationship with him and bearing the brunt of it; she didn't feel justifiably indignant nor did she defend herself. It made her feel feeble. It made her feel that she had to earn back his tenderness because somehow it had been lost for skewed reasons which she felt compelled to justify. 'I have an – epidemic – of wasps. At mine. I've been badly stung.'

Tim was quiet. He knew well enough how she hated wasps. In the early days, he'd gallantly swipe them away. Later on, it infuriated him and he accused her of over-reacting. Just sit still, Vita – for Christ's sake, stop all the flapping. Chill out. Grow up. 'You should have phoned me. You do *not* make decisions concerning the business without consulting me.'

'I'm sorry.'

'What's happening tomorrow? An anthill giving you grief? A spider's web a bit too near the front door?'

'Everything will be back to normal tomorrow,' she said, subdued.

'It better be,' Tim said, hanging up.

*

133

And then Rick phoned just minutes later and, though she'd have been just as pleased to have an early night, by the end of the short call, she'd agreed to meet him for what he kept calling *A Quickie*. Vita laughed politely at his euphemism, but clarified quite clearly that she was coming for A Quick Drink.

He was already at the Bull and Last, a small pub nearby she'd been to only on a couple of occasions. Rarely had Vita heard herself say, God, I need a drink – but that evening the phrase seemed totally justified. Rick beamed at her, stood and kissed her when she arrived; a bottle of red wine open and two glasses already filled. He was gregarious and attentive and handsome and a distraction and soon enough she was thinking, Maybe I will take him home, maybe sex isn't everything. Perhaps it'll be better this time anyway. Maybe it was just nerves or booze or a head cold. Mediocre sex she could tolerate, she thought, for the company it would afford her. Maybe I could just close my ears and stare at the ceiling.

But she couldn't close her ears in the pub and the asides Rick wrought against his ex were enough in themselves not to warrant him coming back, never mind his French alter ego.

'So, Miss Vita – that's a bottle of wine gone and the question is, do we drink another here – or do we go back to yours and sip miniatures your mate nicked from some mini-bar or other?'

'I'm out of those,' Vita said. 'And really, I could do with calling it a night now, and going to bed.'

Rick gave a throaty growl and raised an eyebrow – all very comic but obviously with intent.

'Alone?' Vita ventured.

'You can't throw me out –'

'– I haven't invited you in.'

He wasn't smiling now. 'What I mean is – you can't not let me come. I need refuge from the Witch!' He ran his hand up the front of Vita's thigh as he spoke.

She put her hand on his wrist and stilled him. 'Why do you call her the Witch?'

'If you'd met her – you'd know why.'

She tightened her grip. 'Is she evil? Nasty? Unpleasant?'

'She's just mad,' Rick laughed. 'The Ex From Hell.'

'But in what way?'

He looked at her as if he really didn't know why details were relevant when surely a statement like that was enough. Anyway, hadn't he told Vita enough already? 'She didn't want to split up and she's just gone a bit – you know, psycho – ever since.' It was as if he thought insults had some great comedy value.

'Define psycho.'

'You know – the waterworks, the late-night messages, the long – oh my God – long *long* emails, snail mail. Not taking *au revoir! auf wiedersehen!* vamoosh! for an answer.'

'She didn't want to split up?'

'It's been *months* and she's still moping and pleading and sobbing and promising.'

'And you left her – why?'

Rick shrugged. 'It had just run its course. I needed a change. I wasn't in love with her anyway. Sex was crap. She was annoying – always talking about getting married, having kids. She became really needy.'

Vita finally removed her hand from Rick's wrist. He started rubbing her thigh again. Quickly, she crossed her leg away from his touch. 'You know, Rick, to me it sounds like she's in pain. It sounds like she really loved you and planned a future and now that's been denied her, she's mourning, she's finding it hard to cope – her hopes have

135

been dashed, the future she dreamed about has gone and she's scared about that. There's nothing in its place. She wants you back. She doesn't want to let go of everything it meant to her.'

'Jesus, tell me about it! Why can't she just move on!'

'Because the world seems horribly big and empty. Because the future is a very frightening concept when you'd previously planned on sharing it with someone. Because she's a girl, she's a romantic and she fears that if she lets go of her dream, she'll live a nightmare. Because she has hope and she fears if she lets her hope go, who will she be?'

'Pathetic.'

'No, it's not!' Vita's emphatic tone made Rick jerk to attention. 'Listen here – I *know* that pain. I know that panic. The least you can do is to be gentle on her. She's suffering because she obviously cared deeply and she's hurting desperately and she feels she must cling on to all she hoped for because if she lets go, she might plummet. The effort, the pain of clinging on is preferable to the wide-open fear of letting go.'

'It's such a waste of time!' Rick saw the whole thing as ludicrous.

'It's a process. It needs to take the time it takes.'

He considered this for a moment. 'Why can't she see it's pointless? It's madness! Why can't she just do what all the agony aunts would no doubt say – and Move On? It's certainly a pain – it's a pain in the neck.'

'God, you're a sod,' Vita muttered. She turned to him. 'Let her talk, Rick. Allow her the pain. It's very real – though the only real madness I'd say she's exhibiting is being hung up on you.'

'Whose side are you on!' he laughed.

'Hers.' Vita was emphatic. She stood. 'I'm going back home now. Goodbye, Rick.'

He stood too. 'Oh, come on, Vita – chill! God, why do all you women catastrophize the whole time?' He was making light of it all, brushing the air dismissively and then resting his hand on her arm.

Vita looked at him, took his hand in hers and squeezed it. 'We don't. You men just interpret it that way. To make you feel better, superior, to absolve yourselves of any responsibility in the matter. Us silly girls – we're too emotional, aren't we?' He wasn't meant to nod at that. In some ways, Vita was pleased that he did. 'Just – be – *nice*. Please be kind. Help set the poor girl free of you. She'll be so much the better off.'

'So is a shag out of the question?' He was pulling a soppy face, as if to say, Get over your hump, woman, and let's get humping.

Vita thought, God, I could so easily adopt a phoney French accent at this point and say, *Pardon, monsieur, haw hee haw*. But then she thought of Candy's karma and Michelle's down-to-earth wisdom and she even thought of the man she'd met that afternoon, Oliver Bourne, and his sound, steady demeanour. So she smiled at Rick and added a little meekness to it for the benefit of his ego.

'Look, I'm sorry. I'll have your Teds in Beds but I'll be sleeping alone in mine.'

He shrugged. 'I'm just talking about sex,' he said, as if she'd overblown the situation, 'not love and marriage, for God's sake.'

'Actually,' said Vita, 'that's precisely what I'm talking about too.'

She felt surprisingly light, leaving; even happy to turn at the door and give Rick a conciliatory wave which he didn't see as he was staring into a pint. It was just growing dark, she'd be back home in time for an early night. The wasp stings were still sore but the swelling was finally subsiding and her limbs felt more her own again. And, with Oliver Bourne promising to send the forms off first thing (and to Vita, he seemed like a man whose word was his bond), what had been a problem now had a solution. She'd have her garden back to herself too. Even more of the garden, with the tree soon to be gone. So, no more parrots and therefore good nights' sleep. No more wasps and nicer summer days. Just a little red tape, perhaps some noise and mess, in the interim.

This has been a good evening, Vita thought to herself. I've done well.

*   *   *

Vita and Tim were like an old-fashioned mechanical weathervane. One coming out as the other went back in. Rain versus shine. Dark versus light. Cold versus warm. They lived on opposite sides of town. There was no reason for their paths to cross anywhere other than by the till in That Shop.

'I can't believe my mum said that thing – you know, of when you're going to make an honest woman of me.' Suzie was fidgeting in the passenger seat; she'd been quiet on the way out, a bit excitable once there and was now gabbling on their homeward journey.

'She was just joshing,' said Tim, wondering whether to go for the winding short cut or keep on the main roads. He opted for the latter.

'But – I mean – we haven't spoken about this – but maybe we might start thinking at some point – you know, about moving in together?'

Suzie didn't know how to read the sudden glance Tim gave her, but she sensed she should change the subject.

'Did I tell you Hel's having a party this weekend?'

'You did. Bastard lights.'

'Sorry? Oh! The traffic lights. Yeah. Anyway – we've been asked. Of course. Shall we go?'

'Sure.'

'Are you sure?'

'I just said "Sure", Suzie.'

'OK – it's just, we can do something else if you prefer. I know you think a couple of the blokes are knobs.'

'They are.'

'But it might be good.'

'Look, we'll go, OK? We'll go.'

Suzie turned her head and looked out of the car window, feeling a little bruised that he should snap. She only wanted him to know she was cool with whatever he wanted to do at the weekend. And the moving-in thing? He could have said something instead of just *that look*. She hadn't known how to read it – it was in a language she was only just getting to grips with.

Why doesn't she just shut up for five minutes? Come on, lights, come on. At last. Thank you.

Turn left. More lights. Amber to green. Thank you.

Left again. Green lights.

And more green lights.

And a zebra crossing. Slow down, someone's about to cross.

Vita was aware of a car slowing sufficiently so she stepped out onto the crossing. It was only a step later that she came out of her thoughts and glanced at the car. And the first thing she saw was the registration plate which of course she knew off by heart. But it was out of place, out of context, like seeing a celebrity in the supermarket and thinking, Oh, I know you, wondering if they were an old school mate or friend of a friend. And then the penny drops.

But it wasn't a penny that dropped for Vita just then, it felt more like an anvil falling from a height right onto her.

Tim's car. That's Tim's car. Oh God – and she's there, next to him, where I once sat.

Vita couldn't help but stop and though she prayed for it, the ground didn't open up and swallow her nor did time speed up – in fact, it stood still. She was trapped, staring at him and Tim was staring back and Suzie was fiddling with her nails thinking she wouldn't use that nail bar again because the white tips had gone a bit yellow already.

It was a split second, but it was loaded as Tim and Vita looked at each other. Then the car on the other side of the crossing tooted and now Suzie looked up and Suzie saw the woman in the road looking at Tim who was looking at her.

'What's *she* doing here?'

And, without diverting his gaze, Tim said, 'She's crossing the road.'

'I can see that,' Suzie said, 'but why's she doing it in front of our car?'

And in an instant, both she and Tim were acutely aware what a ridiculous thing that was to say.

Vita kept on walking, concentrating on a steady straight path on all this black and white. And she kept walking, briskly, straight ahead, not glancing over her shoulder, just walking forwards in the direction of home.

Helpful Unhelpful Thoughts

The parakeets were noisier and earlier than ever. The wasps Vita could sometimes hear bickering beyond the glass of the kitchen window which she was keeping resolutely shut until the tree was down. Though she could see honeysuckle starting to rampage over the shed at the back and though it was one of her favourite scents, she didn't dare go out. The plundered, festering pears lay where they fell and there was no way Vita was venturing over to clear them away. The heatwave was coming and she was discovering that Pear Tree Cottage was a place that both mimicked and magnified the weather outside. In the winter, it had been bone-chillingly cold, necessitating layer upon layer of clothing and toilet paper stuffed into the gaps of the old window frames. Summer, the house transformed into a sauna. The windows, ironically, let no air in and were warped tight in their frames to the same extent that they had rattled and moved during winter. Not that Vita would have opened them anyway, too afraid was she of the vindictive wasp community outside. Now she was peeling off clothing, often resorting to doing her chores in just her bra and knickers. In the evenings, if she was reading or watching television, she'd taken to sitting with her feet in a washing-up bowl of lukewarm water, a damp cool flannel at the back of her neck. Despite the discomfort, she was starting to feel less like a lodger at Pear Tree Cottage.

One week on from meeting Oliver Bourne, the tree still stood and the post brought no word from the council. One week on, after ignoring a text sent by Tim late on the night of the zebra crossing (U ok?? Txx), Vita was into a new regime to deflect any need for him to phone or visit, by texting him pre-emptively.

New stock flying out. V

  Have ordered more beeswax candles, also bubble wrap. V.

   Jodie in tomorrow a.m. V

    Will email balance Fri pm. V

At strategic locations at home and at work, she'd stuck Post-its with the same two words. *Unhelpful Thoughts.* And, so far, it was helping. She'd put one on the mug rack, to prevent her brooding that she was only making tea for one. Another on the bathroom mirror, to steel herself before she went to bed and to bolster her for the new day when she woke. Another she used as a bookmark (currently, she was midway through a bittersweet David Nicholls novel that might well have made her self-indulgently reflective otherwise). One was in the spare compartment of the cash register at work. Jodie never read the notes she left her, so she certainly wouldn't bother with this one. Vita even placed one on the top right-hand corner of the television. The one she placed inside the door of the store cupboard at work still managed to sing out to her from all the others whose subjects ran the gamut from *Use less wrapping* to *Double-check bottom lock* and *Christmas starts in October* and *Marmite & de-caff*. The patchwork of small squares of paper, slightly curled, resembled a shingle roof in need of attention. But it worked for Vita, she always paid note. Jodie ignored them all and Tim had never bothered to read any.

As she headed into the weekend (tea with her mum, babysitting for Candy, a barbeque at Michelle and Chris's) after a good week at work, the call from Martin the tree officer in the planning department was the cherry on an already nicely iced cake.

'Miss Whitbury?'

'Yes?'

'Martin Standon here, TPO department.'

'Hullo! Brilliant!' Vita thought her tone was possibly inappropriate, but she couldn't help it. She didn't know if the letters stood for Tree Planning or Tree Protection but the process was now underway and that's what mattered.

'I have your forms – and wonder if I could come and take a look at the tree.'

'Now? Today?' It was nearing closing time on Friday. What better way to start the weekend. 'I could be home in about twenty minutes?'

'No, my dear. Not today. Would Monday at ten suit you?'

'Absolutely! Not a moment too soon, Mr Martin. I'm sure Oliver Bourne has impressed upon you the utter nightmare that tree is causing.'

There was silence. 'I shall see you on Monday at ten, then, Miss Whitbury.'

'Okeydoke, Mr Martin. Many thanks – and hey! have a great weekend.'

Standon! Martin Standon! Not Mr Martin but Mr Standon. Oh well, thought Vita. Whatever he's called, he's still coming on Monday and by next weekend hopefully it'll be me hosting a barbeque with the heady scent of honeysuckle charming my guests. She phoned Jodie to book her in for Monday morning and the part-timer was astounded that recently she was being paid so much to do so little. Then Vita texted Tim. `Have appt Mon a.m. Jodie working.` Then she cashed up, set the intruder alarm, double-checked the double lock and headed home. There was no need to even skim-read the Post-it on her purse. She wasn't having any unhelpful thoughts at all.

Suzie Vs Vita

In the early months after they split, Tim had relished his weekends. No Vita hopping out from bed at ridiculous-o'clock on a Saturday morning, full of enthusiasm for the day and brimming with plans about how to spend it. Walks in the country, painting the kitchen, visiting farmers' markets, oiling the garden furniture – something, always something. He'd loved it at first, her energy, her joie de vivre – but soon enough he tired of it; it grated, it annoyed him. He went from gently teasing her – Sit still, woman, just relax would you! – to berating her – For fuck's sake, Vita, I don't want to traipse across the sodding woods, I just want to read the paper. He didn't want to rub down a teak bench on a Saturday, he wanted to slob out on the sofa. He didn't want to spend Sundays at some village fête or other, he wanted to fall asleep in front of the grand prix.

After they split, began a most refreshing period for Tim where stultifying snuggling in front of Friday-night telly with a takeaway curry was replaced with drinking until closing time, having messy sex and then sleeping off the hangover until Saturday lunch-time. Suzie tended to outsleep him, even. Marvellous. He could have as long as he wanted with the papers. He needn't acknowledge if it was Walking Weather, he was blissfully unaware of what craft shows were on and Homebase could have all the twenty-per-cent-off promotions possible – he wouldn't be going. Suzie and friends, younger by a good decade, hung on his every word or else set the conversation at a level so banal that it became strangely addictive. Switch your brain off, get an ego massage, get wasted, get laid, get up late. And do it all again on Saturday night.

Back when Vita had left and there was no longer any need to snatch furtive hours with Suzie, Tim was temporarily hounded by a small voice asking him whether this way of living was a bit unseemly and actually far poorer than the mundane domesticity he'd engineered with Vita over the years. But he quickly justified, what sane-minded bloke would turn down a good-looking girlfriend many years his junior and a bunch of new people with whom he could unwind and take the piss out of the drudge of everyday life by partying? He didn't regard Suzie as the rebound, or consider his current lifestyle as a midlife crisis. She really, really liked him and Tim really, really liked that. He was enjoying the flimsiness of everything. He saw it all as a timely lightweight alternative to everything he'd grown to hate about the last couple of years with Vita. An antidote to heading for forty. A cure, even if temporary, for the headaches at work. A suitably mind-numbing substitute for having to spend all bloody evening and most weekends going over and over subjects like marriage vows and garden furniture sales.

Life was OK. It really was. Until that Friday evening, just over a week on from the Night of the Zebra Crossing, when he found himself saying to Suzie, You know what, I fancy just staying in with a curry and a DVD.

*

146

Suzie was happy enough with Tim's suggestion. The more Tim wanted evenings in, the sooner she could bring up again the moving-in-together issue. The curry had been delivered and eaten out of the foil containers. The DVD was halfway through and not a bad film really. Good old Matt Damon. The action-packed chase was in full swing: motorbikes, speedboats, and a whole lot of bionic base-jumping. Tim's brain was pleasingly on go-slow.

But then he'd caught sight of Suzie's feet.

And while Matt Damon was blowing the world up and Suzie was shrieking, Oh my God! Fucking hell! Tim's world came crashing down.

What have I done? Oh God – what have I done?

I am between two women.

I thought I'd gone from one to the other pretty bloody well, only I haven't, I'm caught between them but there's been a mistake.

It was Suzie's feet.

I suddenly saw her feet – really saw them. And now all I can think about is Vita's feet. The difference between them. I remember how I'd marvel at Vita's. Sweet Petite Feet – and all the other corny rhymes I once used for various bits of her. She used to giggle and twitch her toes and I'd tickle them and we'd laugh. Then I stopped noticing them until at some point they became merely these cold annoying things she'd press up against me in bed.

Suzie's feet are big. I never noticed. They're not ugly – they're just really big. So different to Vita's. Suzie is not in Vita's league but it's Suzie here on my sofa beside me, dropping hints about moving in. Tomorrow we'll get hammered and shag each other senseless and for a milli-second it'll all seem so preferable to the day-to-day grown-upness that was Vita and Me – that I ran away from and have now forfeited.

But the truth is I miss her and maybe life is meant to be a little boring and maybe that's meant to be better. Maybe it shouldn't have been about taking chances on getting away with it – perhaps I should have taken the chance Vita was giving me. I would never have left her.

I haven't really given any of it much serious thought. Until tonight. Matt Damon, a chicken jalfrezi and Suzie's feet. Would I have kept on with Suzie had Vita not found out? It probably would have fizzled, really. I would never have left Vita – never. Not for Suzie, not for anyone. But would I have abstained from all future Suzies? I'm a hedonist. I'm self-centred. I'm scared of growing old.

Suzie is now unbuttoning my jeans.
And she's taken off her top and her bra.
And her hands are easing down my jeans, my boxers.
I can't see her feet.
I can't think of anything else.

T.P.O

Vita woke excited on Monday morning. Martin Standon was due in two hours and she wondered whether to phone Oliver Bourne straight away and book him in for as soon as possible. Or maybe that would be something Mr Standon would do just as soon as he'd seen the size of the problem. So she walked to the corner shop instead and stocked up on digestive biscuits, plain and chocolate as, in this case, she was happy to make the man a nice cuppa with extras. She boiled the kettle every now and then so that it wouldn't take long once he arrived. She checked outside. Pears, wasps, nothing had changed. The parakeets had been even earlier this morning, bickering amongst themselves and taking their tempers out on the pears. She waited, she phoned Jodie who was late opening the shop because apparently she needed a latte and the instant coffee at the shop wouldn't do. Vita didn't wonder or worry whether Tim might see that the shop was still shut, because he was far from her mind. To her, just then, this mid-July Monday seemed a most auspicious day. The summer, from this day on, would be a good one, because she'd be able to enjoy the garden pain free, pear free and parakeet free too.

He arrived on the dot of ten. As soon as the doorbell rang, Vita boiled the kettle, hurried to rearrange the fan of biscuits on the plate and then welcomed him in.

'Hullo!' she said. 'It's so nice to meet you!'

'Good morning, Miss Whitbury.'

He had a clipboard. And a pen in his shirt pocket. All the better to tick boxes and sign it all off. She had scissors in the kitchen drawer, if he wanted to cut through any red tape.

'Cup of tea?'

'No, thank you.'

'Coffee, then?'

'No, thank you, I'm fine.'

'Oh. A soft drink? Apple juice?'

'No, really.'

'Water?'

'Nothing. I'm fine.'

She'd offer him a biscuit in a while then.

'The tree?' he asked, still standing in the hallway.

'Of course!' she said. 'This way. Did Mr Bourne fill you in?'

'Yes.'

'Oh, good! This way, Mr Martin. Standon. This way!'

He looked at the tree through the window in the kitchen door, then he looked at Vita. 'And do you have a key for this door?'

She thought, Ought I to advise him against going out there just in shirtsleeves?

'A key, Miss Whitbury?'

'Oh – yes, of course. Here. I must advise you there is a catastrophic wasp situation out there. You may want to

150

cover up a bit.' She was putting on a sludge-green voluminous ancient cagoule, hood up, tucking her jeans into wellington boots before pulling her hands far up inside the sleeves, clutching the elasticated wrists tight shut. Mr Standon was unlocking the door, having declined her father's old fishing anorak that she'd offered him.

They went out into the garden. At ten o'clock, it was already hot. Vita dressed as if having to venture out into a monsoon, Martin Standon dressed according to a record-breaking hot July. Martin thought to himself, How on earth can I have a serious conversation with a woman who looks like her face is poking out of a tent? Vita though, stood back, hovering close to the kitchen door, just in case the wasps started attacking. She watched the man assessing the tree. He didn't grin at it the way Oliver Bourne had. A good sign. Not long, she thought. Not long before I can go back inside. Not long before this sorry episode is put to rest.

He was making notes. Taking measurements. Using something camera-like from different distances. He was standing still, looking hard, seemingly not bothered by the wasps. Vita started to wonder whether that was a bad thing – and maybe if he was stung – even if just the once – it might hasten the outcome. He could fill in his forms at her kitchen table, over a refreshing cup of tea and a couple of nice biscuits and balsamic vinegar on cotton wool for the sting. But he was coming back towards her and before she could offer him a drink, he gave his verdict.

'Miss Whitbury, this is a very fine pear tree. Very fine indeed. I understand your discontent with the seasonal issues which arise, specifically the parakeets and wasps that share your fruit – but I have to advise you that I am compelled to place a Tree Preservation Order on this tree.'

Standing there, in her kitchen, still dressed like a

151

mannequin in a camping shop, Vita was unsure what all this meant.

'Any questions?'

He wasn't asking her to sign anything.

'Will Oliver Bourne be able to chop it down then?'

'Gracious, no – I am placing this tree under protection. You will be obliged to care for it, to tend to it, to have it professionally pruned regularly and strictly according to the stipulations set out in the TPO. I must advise you, Miss Whitbury, that failure to do so can result in a hefty fine, prosecution even. I firmly believe that the trees of this borough must be accorded a status commensurate with national monuments.'

Who the hell speaks like this nowadays, Vita wondered, as reality began to sink in.

'I am aware that this outcome is not as you hoped. But I ask that you learn to live alongside this tree harmoniously.' He looked at her. And then he added, 'It's been around a lot longer than you and it will outlive you too. It deserves a little respect.' And at that point, Vita wanted the man out of her kitchen, out of her life.

'Mr Bourne is one of our most highly skilled and highly respected aboricultural consultants – not just in the county but nationwide. When it comes to pruning, he's your man and he'll be most fastidious when it comes to the paperwork,' Mr Standon said, making his way along Vita's corridor, out her front door, down her path and into his car while she just stood there, mouth agape and horrified.

Protection? Not allowed to touch it without permission? Obliged to care for it, to *respect* it? Hefty fines? For heaven's sake! Bloody stupid jobsworth tree hugger. Vita slammed the door and paced up and down the corridor.

On her third march, she noticed a Post-it on the floor. Assuming it was one of her *Unhelpful Thoughts* notes, she picked it up, about to restick it by the front door when she noticed that one was still there.

She looked at this one. It wasn't her writing. And they weren't her words. And the words she read stopped her dead. After a moment's silent disbelief, she gave out a roar of indignation. It must have fallen from Mr Standon's clipboard. It must have been attached to the forms Oliver Bloody Bourne had sent in on her behalf.

> *Martin,*
> *I don't want this tree taken down.*
> *Oliver.*

* * *

'Come on, kiddo, you had a lie-in yesterday, you'll have another tomorrow – but today you're up with me.' Oliver opened the curtains of his son's bedroom and gave the teenage lump under the duvet a gentle nudge. How easy it would be to sit on the edge of the bed and hug the slumbering boy, the way he had for all those years until he suddenly wasn't sure quite when. He still kissed his son, but when did he stop the all-out hugging? He couldn't remember. Would DeeDee have been cuddling him at this age? If so, was Jonty being in any way deprived of parental affection? Christ, he hoped not. What a mess. He looked around the room.

'What a mess,' he said.

'Dad,' came a muffled objection, 'I'll clear up later.'

Oliver didn't correct him. 'Come on, Jont,' he said instead. 'Rise and shine, kiddo. Tell you what – we seem to be out of anything breakfasty so what do you say we start the day with a fry-up at the café? The lads will probably be there anyway.'

Jonty was out of bed and stumbling into clothes before Oliver had left his room.

Boz, Tinker and Spike thought Jonty a good little worker. He never minded how menial the jobs were that they gave him and never took any offence at the gentle ribbing they gave his dad behind his back. Jonty liked being with them. They were cool. One played in a band. One had amazing tattoos. They all spoke entertainingly about lairy nights out and yet also about all the amazing places they'd been to on their travels. They cracked great jokes. They were interested in him too. Jonty also really liked the work; the hoicking of branches, the splitting of logs, the smell of freshly spliced wood, the hard hat and goggles, the long shower at the end of the day, the calluses he'd earn on his hands by the end of the summer.

And his dad paid him. On top of his monthly allowance.

And it was nice seeing his dad in action. He had more confidence outdoors than in. He seemed happy at work.

At the yard, having discussed not just the day ahead but what was booked in for the week, Boz and Spike were checking equipment, Tinker was loading the van, Oliver was inside returning a phone call and Jonty was outside helping anyone who needed it. And then everyone stopped what they were doing because stomping into the yard in her wellies, still encased in the cagoule, came Vita. Her face, red from heat and malcontent, was just about visible – which was more than could be said for her hands which were still up her sleeves.

Oliver, on the phone in his office, was distracted by the sight. He could only see the person from behind and, from

154

this angle, cloaked and hooded in some kind of voluminous tarpaulin, he or she looked like a mad hobgoblin from a schlock horror film, or some kind of crazed amputee.

'I'm so sorry, Miss Maybridge – would you mind if I phoned you back?'

'But you've only just phoned me back!' Miss Maybridge protested. 'I don't like the espaliers! They're all wrong! They look like people on a cross! They won't do! It's disturbing. Bugger the fruit, they simply won't do!'

'I'll have to phone you back *again*, I'm afraid. I have to go – some rather odd wildlife has just come into the yard. I must see to it. I won't be a moment.'

He came down the steps of his office just as Vita announced, in a breathless bellow of sorts, 'Where? Is? Oliver? Bourne?'

It sounded like a battle cry and it was accompanied by a stamp of a wellington-booted foot. No one could see her fists scrunched angrily up her sleeves. Just then, no one was sure whether she had hands at all.

Boz thought, I think I know that face – or what I can see of it.

Tinker thought, Oliver, you crafty old fox – good for you, mate.

Spike thought, You don't see this every day.

Jonty thought, Top start to my holidays.

Oliver thought, Who is it and why does it want *me*?

And all of them wondered, Why is this person dressed like that in this heat – and who would dress like that anyway?

Oliver stood where he was, observing. He hadn't yet been seen.

She was asking where he was, demanding to see him.

'Is there a problem?' Spike asked.

155

'I'm his son?' Jonty said, helpfully.

'You tell your dad there is a huge problem.' She gestured with her arms in a mighty circle and suddenly her hands appeared which was a relief to the others.

'Dad?' Jonty looked over to behind Vita. 'There's a lady here who has a huge problem.'

Vita spun.

'Oliver Bourne,' she said, 'this is *your* writing!' She brandished the Post-it note at him.

He approached calmly, knowing in an instant what it was, who this was and understanding immediately why she was here. Nevertheless, he walked to her, took the Post-it and read it carefully. 'Ah,' he said, 'Martin must have been.'

'He's just gone,' Vita said, strangely quietened by Oliver's steadiness. 'He's slapped some stupid bloody Protection Preservation Anti-Cruelty thing on the bloody stupid tree because *you* told him *you* didn't want it chopped down.'

Oliver regarded her slowly. 'That's right.'

'But you said you'd help me!'

Oh God, she's not going to cry, is she? He glanced over her shoulder, to where his son and his workers were all riveted.

'Would you like a cup of tea?'

'No!'

'Coffee?'

'No!'

'A drink of water? A biscuit?'

'No! No! I don't want anything. I just want – You! You!'

Boz and Spike loved that bit. Jonty was gobsmacked but it was only Oliver's startled expression which made Vita realize that she hadn't finished her sentence and she was feeling very, very hot.

156

'I just wanted you to cut down my sodding tree,' she concluded, crestfallen.

'Would you like to take off your jacket?' Oliver said tactfully. She'd gone puce coloured and looked a little unsteady. It was hot already. It was going to be scorching. It was going to be a gorgeous day.

He put his hand gently on her arm, peering into the cavern of green waterproofness that half-hid her face. And it was then that Vita realized what she must look like, that she'd stomped out of the house and all the way to his yard, almost two miles away, without realizing she was still in her Wasp Protection Gear. She was mortified. She looked behind her. Four young men had gathered in a crescent, ears peeled, eyes popping.

'Why are you dressed like that?' Oliver asked with no edge.

'Because you won't cut down that tree and it's the only way I dare go into the garden.'

He remembered the stings.

With as much grace as she could muster, she unzipped the cagoule, tucked back the hood and slipped out of it, handing it to Oliver who was offering to take it. Now she stood there, in a plain white T-shirt, realizing she was so hot that even a whisper of breeze was bliss against her sweaty skin. She'd like very much to just stand there awhile, cool down, then start up again. But now someone else was interrupting her plan, someone else was deflecting the heat, being really friendly. It was thoroughly disconcerting.

'I know you!' one of them was saying. 'You're the lady from that shop.'

He'd come to stand beside her; they'd all gathered around. Oliver still standing there, holding her anorak, the others now close.

Usually, it was the little children in the shop who referred to her as a lady. Mummy, ask That Lady if there's a *green* one. Now a young man was calling her a lady and it was all so soothing; the quiet yard, the gentle breeze, concerned yet friendly faces. It was all such a tonic to the rage and indignation that had propelled her here in her ridiculous get-up. Suddenly, she felt enormously tired, the outside of her head felt very very heavy, the inside of it unnervingly light; she was boiling hot so why did she just shudder?

'Steady there,' said Oliver. 'Come and sit down.'

He guided her a pace or so away to a section of tree-trunk that had had a large wedge cut out of it to make a chair. They all gathered round.

'You made that beautiful box for my sister – do you remember?' But she couldn't see who was talking. Oliver had eased her head forwards and down to her knees, his hand still between her shoulder blades.

'Yes,' she managed to mumble, relating the Aussie accent, the rugged work boots that she could see in front of her, to the item sold. 'Megan,' she said.

'You got it!' He sounded thrilled.

'Stencils,' she whispered.

They let her sit there, Oliver now talking to them quietly about the day's workload, going through a checklist, asking someone to answer the phone which had started to ring. 'Can you fetch a glass of water, Jonty darling?'

That sounded odd to Vita. Gay tree surgeons, or lovey lumberjacks or something. But she didn't dwell on it. Just then she really did want a drink of water.

'Here you go, Miss,' said Jonty darling, pushing the glass into her hands. 'Here you go, Dad.'

Ah. A son, not a lover.

'Thanks,' she mumbled, not daring to look up just yet.

158

She still felt discombobulated. Focusing on the sets of boots was steadying. She didn't want anyone to move.

'Guys – you head off. I'll just –' Oliver thought about it. Mad Miss Maybridge to phone back, and mad Miss Whitbury right here in his yard. 'I'll just – tidy up here. Jonty, go with Tinker. Boz and Spike – you know where you're going. I'll follow on in a little while.'

The Cagoule

Vita felt revived enough to feel riled again. Oliver had shown her into his office where she'd been sitting quietly sipping water, while he made a phone call to a woman whose voice came through the telephone tinny and irate. Perhaps he does this daily, she thought, imagining the caller to have a killer pear tree too. She looked around her. The office itself was just a prefab though from the interior it was well disguised. Two of the walls were given to shelves crammed with books and files on trees. The third wall was papered almost entirely with a giant map of the immediate region and neighbouring counties. A large window took up most of the fourth wall, looking out over the yard. Oliver's desk, spanning almost the entire width, was a mighty slab of some wood or other – a longitudinal slice of what appeared to be an entire trunk. The surface undulated subtly and conveniently, providing a flat area where the computer sat stable while another section dipped and rose providing an ergonomic angle for writing or reading. There were two circular dints just the right depth and diameter to keep mugs steady; also a long slim furrow in which various pens and pencils nestled. As

160

Oliver spoke on the phone, he subconsciously stroked the wood. It was amber in colour, with striations and whorls the colour of burnt toffee. It was perfectly balanced on four chunks of tree, of varying heights and breadths. It was beautiful. But Vita stopped herself being seduced, thinking instead, Well, here's a tree he was certainly happy to chop down. The room was quiet and she realized with a jolt that the phone call had already ended and Oliver was observing her thoughtfully.

'Well, Miss Whitbury, how are you feeling now?'

With Oliver being genuinely friendly, it was difficult for Vita to sharpen the edge she'd intended for her voice.

'I'm cooler,' she said, 'thank you.'

'Good,' he said. 'Can I give you a lift anywhere? I need to set off.'

'No, thank you.'

He stood and stretched. 'Well, thanks for dropping by – I'm glad you're OK.' And then he was ushering her out of the office. Hang on a tick, she thought, I might have come here to say what I wanted – but where's my answer? Oliver, however, was already locking the office door.

'Excuse me!' she said. 'Thank you for the water and the sit-down and everything – but I came here to ask about my tree.' She felt suddenly tired. A little defeated. Her voice wasn't as strong as she'd've liked.

He turned and faced her and looked directly at her and, without warning, Vita felt as though she was being lifted by a wave. It was instant, beautiful, unnerving, confusing. In a split second she had to think, Don't look at his face. And then she had to think, Don't look at his arms. And then she had to think, Not the eyes. Concentrate on the logo on his T-shirt instead.

What just happened? What *was* that?

Hate him, remember! Get angry!

161

'What would you like to know?'

Do. Not. Look. At. His. Face.

Remember why you're here!

She pressed down on the sting on her thumb, as if it was a trigger point.

'My tree,' she said. 'Why did you do that?'

'I was doing my job,' he shrugged. 'I was doing the right thing.'

'But why did you make it seem that you were on my side? When you came to my house and did all that chatting and ate my biscuits and seemed sorry for my wasp stings and told me about wallabies and parrots and God knows what?' She'd intended to sound justifiably indignant but she could hear she sounded feeble, even whiny.

'I sympathized,' he said carefully, 'but I have a duty. And I had to advise the council as I see best, according to my expertise. I have an obligation – professional, legal, moral. I'm sorry. I know it's not the outcome you were looking for – but I hope you might find a way to tolerate the seasonal inconveniences that come with the tree.'

'You sound like you're reading from a script.'

He laughed, though he could see Vita didn't think it remotely funny. 'I've been protecting trees all my working life – some phrases just trip off the tongue.'

'Then it was a load of old bullshit you delivered at mine the other week.'

'I'm sorry you see it that way.'

'What *can* I do?'

'When it's the right time, I'll come and prune it for you.'

'And what if I get someone else?'

'With a TPO on the tree, there are restrictions and procedures.'

162

'And what if I ignore them? What if, accidentally on purpose, the tree is chopped down by someone else?'

'I know someone who was taken to court – and fined twenty thousand pounds. Good God, woman – you sound faintly ridiculous. It's a tree. For a couple of months a year, you'll have parrots and pears and pests.'

In the time she'd been in the yard, she'd been called a lady, a miss and a woman. And yet there was something in Oliver's inflection – *Good God, woman*. It was exasperation, certainly, but what else? Was it amusement? No. His tone was softened by something else, by a tiny hint of tenderness. Just then, Oliver was unaware of it and, just then, Vita couldn't countenance it so she swiftly reinterpreted it as patronizing.

'And do you have a pear tree in your garden?' she asked.

He looked at her as if it was a stupid question.

'And if you did, I'll bet your back garden is so huge you wouldn't notice.'

What a ridiculous thing to say.

'The size of my back garden is somewhat irrelevant,' Oliver said, wondering where on earth this conversation was going and why he was choosing to have it instead of going directly to where he was late for already. What was it with this woman that was keeping him standing here, arguing the toss over goodness knows what? The pear tree stays! Get over it!

'It's ruining my life!'

'That's a little melodramatic,' he said, thankful she wasn't wearing her tent as, with her temper rising, he really didn't have time for her to wilt again.

'That's easy for you to say,' Vita said. 'You haven't had the year I've had – I didn't want to live there in the first place, I was perfectly happy in the home I shared with

163

my ex-boyfriend. Before it all went pear-shaped.' She paused. Of all the inappropriate puns to choose. 'I had to ask my mum for money – at the age of thirty-three.' That sounded pathetic. 'I've been sleep deprived and stung to death and now I am going to be a prisoner in my home all sodding summer.' That was downright histrionic, but she was past caring.

Sounds a breeze – my wife died. I've rarely been out in our garden since her funeral almost three years ago.

But Oliver said nothing. He just looked at Vita levelly before walking to his Land Rover and climbing in. He started the engine, moved off slowly, stopping just near her. The window was down and he leant out to speak to her.

'Poison it,' he said nonchalantly.

'What?'

'A hefty dose of sodium chlorate should do it. Or bank up a heap of sharp sand against it – it'll take longer, but it'll kill it. Alternatively, saw right through the bark all the way around the base of the trunk – that will stop the tree being able to absorb enough water. Certain death.'

She couldn't answer, partly because she was ashamed that, in the first instance, she had actually embraced his advice as plausible; initially deaf to the tone in which it had been said.

He watched her in his rear-view mirror as she stropped away from the yard in the opposite direction from him. Madwoman, he thought. But he started smiling too. And when he then said, *Madwoman* out loud, he laughed a little.

He didn't comment much when the others later joshed about the antics at the yard that morning. He just told them that the world was full of peculiar people – and most of them appeared to live in the vicinity. But he did think about Vita that afternoon; she came into his mind without invitation yet he didn't see her off. They weren't thoughts, really. Just images and replay which drifted into his mind and floated out again so he didn't have to catch them and take a closer look.

'Thanks Jodie,' Vita said. It was after lunch by the time she made it in to the shop.

'You're really late – do I get overtime for these hours then?'

'No, you don't!' Vita said. 'You can come in an hour late on Saturday or leave an hour early. I don't care.'

'What's wrong with you?' Jodie always jumped narkily to the defensive.

'I've had a shit morning, all right? Go, just go.'

'Stroppy,' Jodie said under her breath. She'd always been faintly disrespectful to Vita yet rather obsequious to Tim and just today Vita wondered why she put up with it. Jodie went without another word. Vita checked the till. Jodie had sold two candles and a packet of paper napkins. And she hadn't bloody tidied the back bloody shelves that Vita had reminded her about this morning, having first asked her to do it last Saturday. And there were crumbs on the table. And the paper coffee cup was in the bin with a dribble of liquid seeping out into the wicker. And when the door opened half an hour later, the customer who came in was the septuagenarian kleptomaniac.

Vita watched her surreptitiously for a few moments but the woman seemed slower today, a little distracted, so while she stared at the silk flowers, Vita returned to her book. She'd never read Evelyn Waugh but she was loving *A Handful of Dust*, finding it so involving that, when her phone rang, she answered it without seeing who was calling.

'Vita.'

Oh God, Tim. Not Tim. Not today.

'Vita?'

'Yes.'

'How are things?'

'Fine.'

'At the shop?'

'Yes, I'm at the shop. Checking up on me?'

'Sorry – I meant how are things *at the shop.*'

Tim? Saying sorry?

'The shop's fine.'

'Cool.' He sounded out of sorts. Nervous, almost.

'It's busy – I should go.'

'And you?'

'Me what?'

'Are you fine?'

'What? I'm fine, I'm fine. Everything's fine, Tim. I should go.'

'Wait! I just – Vita. Just a moment.'

She waited. It was a heavy moment.

'Look – what are you doing – tonight? Or tomorrow? Or whenever?'

Vita was now very unsettled. 'Sorry?'

'I just wondered – whether we could meet. For a drink. Or a meal. Or a walk.'

A walk? *Tim?*

'Why?' It had to be a trick question.

'I just want to talk?'

'To talk?' Oh shit. She anticipated the dreaded declaration about Suzie. 'What about? Say it now.' What's a bit more shit shovelled onto the pile of it that's been my day so far.

'I wanted to talk. To you. I've been thinking about you recently.'

Just a couple of months ago, such words would have filled Vita's heart and swelled her head with hope. Now she was bemused and she let him know it. With the residual anger from the morning still spiking her blood, she found her voice. 'Well, you shouldn't be thinking about me – you should be thinking about your girlfriend. You shouldn't be thinking about me at all – Suzie should be in your head if she's the one in your bed. Suzie's your girlfriend, not me. Think about *her*.' There. She'd said the name out loud.

'Suzie?' It was unnerving, hearing her name spoken by Vita.

'Yes,' said Vita, 'Suzie. The same Suzie, Tim. The one with the job promotion from secret shag to girlfriend. The one who answers your phone and gives me a bollocking.'

'Who – she did *what*?'

Oh shit, Vita thought. Bang goes my healthy deposit in Candy's Bank of Karma.

'Fuck Suzie!'

'It was precisely that,' Vita said darkly, 'which made me leave you.'

'OK, OK,' he said, 'enough.' He paused. Started again with the soft and tender voice. A little hoarse – a paleness she hadn't heard before. 'Vita. Vita.' He paused again. 'I just want to talk. Babes, I miss you.'

And that was when Vita saw the old woman pocketing the bird.

'Oh for God's sake will you just stop it!'

For a moment, Tim thought this was directed at him. The old woman had no reason to believe it was directed at her – not after the years in which she'd been all but invited to filch. 'Tim, I have to go.'

167

Vita leapt down from the stool. 'You! Yes, *you!*' She marched over to the old woman. 'I'm having a horrible day and this just about takes the biscuit. Just put it back. Put it back – now.' She held out her hand. The woman turned away but Vita caught her arm. God, it felt thin, brittle, under the blouse.

'Lassie – I haven't a thing.'

Vita rarely heard her voice. It was soft, light. There was an accent. But she wasn't going to let it fool her.

'You have plenty of my things,' Vita said, 'and you've just put one in your bag.'

'I haven't a thing,' the woman sounded bereft.

'I turn a blind eye,' Vita said, loosening her grip but not letting go. 'I let you pilfer and purloin and you don't just take and take my stuff, you take *me* totally for granted. Now put the bloody thing back and just buzz off.'

The old woman looked shocked, as if there'd been some terrible mistake, but Vita wasn't having it. 'It's in your bag,' she said. 'I saw you put it there.'

Slowly, meekly, the woman opened her bag and held it out towards Vita. 'It's so pretty,' she said sorrowfully, by way of an explanation.

Amongst scrunched-up paper tissues, opened tubes of Polo mints with the foil in long frayed twists, tattered shop receipts, an old pair of spectacles with black-winged frames and a bulging purse, nestled one of the hand-painted stoneware blue tits. They were expensive; so delicately sculpted, such attention to detail and more popular than the chaffinches and sparrows in the series.

'Dear little thing,' the lady said, placing it gently in the centre of Vita's palm, stroking the head with her forefinger, her skin so papery it seemed semi-transparent. And then she left the shop a little more stooped than when she'd entered; smaller than Vita had thought.

Why should I feel so damned guilty now? Vita wondered and the feeling haunted her for the rest of the working day.

'Tinker – just lock this stuff in the second shed. It needs a clean tomorrow morning. Thanks, Spike – that's great. Yes – just there. Jonty – whoa! Whoa! You need two people for that – cheers, Boz.'

It was the end of a hot day for Oliver and his lads. They gathered in the office where, from the small fridge, Oliver under-armed each of them a can of Coke.

'Beautiful!' Spike said after a long drink, while Boz burped quietly and appreciatively.

'Here, guys – good work today. Go and have a pint on me.' Oliver handed twenty pounds to Spike, who was closest.

'Oi, Dad!' Jonty protested.

'We'll have takeaway fish and chips, Jont.'

Jonty pulled a face as if it was a poor alternative though actually he loved fish and chips. They'd have it off the paper and watch crap on TV; the sitting room would permeate with the sweet-sharp tang of vinegar and the lingering scent would be strangely pleasant still the next morning.

'Isn't that –?' Tinker gestured with his can of Coke to the corner of the office.

And they all regarded Vita's monstrous cagoule.

'I could drop it off at that shop she works in,' Boz offered.

Oliver considered it for a long time. 'It's fine,' he said eventually. 'We'll take it in on our way home.' He could feel Jonty staring at him. He glanced at his son, who nodded.

'Laters!' called out Boz and Spike.

Tinker saluted Jonty. 'Tomorrow, dude.'

169

'Come on, kiddo, let's go.' Oliver headed to the car with Vita's cagoule over his arm.

Jonty followed, aching but content.

Oliver slung the cagoule onto the back seat.

'You know that shop is actually called That Shop,' Jonty said.

'Yes. I did. Actually, we pass by pretty near to her house – we'll leave it on the doorstep there. Or something.'

Jonty was quiet. His father thought he must be starving and exhausted. Actually, Jonty was unravelling a knot of thoughts that had been hurled to the forefront of his mind from goodness knows where.

'Dad,' he said, 'don't let's do that tonight. Why don't you take it back yourself sometime. To That Shop. Or to Her House.'

Oliver thought, My son's obsessed with fish and chips. 'OK,' he said, 'no problem.'

And Jonty thought, It's not a problem, is it, Mum? Was I out of order to say that to Dad? She's nothing like you. She's probably nothing at all. It's just that it seemed to suit Dad, putting his hand out to steady her while she was having a meltdown. And when she was all pissed off and pretty, his eyes were – I don't know – just not the dull eyes they usually are. They changed a bit.

And then Oliver parked up at the chippy.

And Jonty let him sling an arm casually around his shoulder as they walked over to buy their fish supper.

His dad entered the shop and Jonty followed him in, aching but content.

The Wretched Cagoule

The cagoule stayed in the car a further two days. Oliver had put it in a canvas Tesco shopper. He didn't want to see it because it brought Vita to mind and that was unsettling. Perhaps he would give it to Boz after all, to drop into the shop in town. At first, Vita didn't realize she'd left it because she had no intention of going out into the garden anyway and therefore had no use for it. But then Michelle invited her over for dinner and while she was there, Vita relayed the whole sorry saga. Even Chris came in to hear the last half, having heard his wife helpless with laughter, begging for mercy, threatening to wet herself.

'This isn't for your amusement,' Vita said, though she was at pains now not to see the funny side. 'It's a serious matter. It's ruining my summer in the short term – and in the long term, surely it will jeopardize the resale factor of my house?'

'Not if you include the wellies and cagoule with the sale price,' said Chris.

'Oh, sod off!'

'He's joking,' said Michelle.

'I know,' said Vita, 'and it's funny and it's not funny and what am I going to do?'

Chris wandered off.

'What *am* I going to do?' Vita used her finger to trace lines over the condensation on her wineglass.

'You're not going to poison the poor tree, are you?'

'Of course I'm not going to poison the tree.'

'Or cut the bark like he told you.'

'No, Michelle, I'm not going to touch the bloody –' Oh shit, thought Vita, oh shitting shitsville. 'My cagoule,' she groaned.

Michelle didn't understand.

'I've left it,' Vita said, 'there. At the yard.'

'Oh dear,' said Michelle. And then she thought about it. 'And are you emotionally attached to that cagoule? Or can you just go to Millets and buy another?'

'It was one of Dad's,' Vita said. 'It didn't really fit. But.'

'But?'

'Should I leave it, then?'

'I would!'

'Or should I go and get it?'

'I wouldn't bother.'

'Right,' said Vita, slowly. She trusted Michelle's advice whenever she asked for it. But she was quietly aware that the advice she sought hadn't actually been asked for.

'So,' she said, 'so I shouldn't go back to the yard to pick it up?'

'Nah,' said Michelle.

'Or phone.'

Michelle started to shake her head. Then she stopped. She looked at Vita squarely, thought to herself, I've seen that expression before. She thought, Vita's eyes are scanning, flitting, sparkling. She thought, V's head is full of something she's not saying.

'Vita?'

'I hate him for not being able to cut down my tree.'

172

'Vita?'

'He's quite a lot older, anyway.'

'Vita?' Michelle was warning her to continue, as if to say, I have a half-smile – make it a full one.

'He has a lovely – manner.'

'And?'

'Oh shit! Oh shit – OK!' Vita put her hands over her face and spoke quickly, groaning as she did. 'He has lovely forearms too, OK? And he's handsome in that rugged, I-manhandle-trees-for-a-living kind of way.'

'Vita!' Michelle pointed her finger at her. 'You go back there! In a flippy flippy skirt and your cowboy boots and a bit of lippy!'

'Mushroom!' But Vita's face was out from behind her hands and her cheeks bloomed pink with delight.

'And you say, Oh deary me! I left my jacket and there's white wine in my fridge and would you like to come over after work to have a glass! That's what you say.'

'Stop it!' But Vita didn't want Michelle to stop; her eyes were dancing and she was grinning.

'And then you say, Oh and please could you wear your nice T-shirt and don't wash your hunky forearms.'

Vita giggled into her glass. Michelle hadn't heard that larky, joyous sound for a long, long time. She held out her glass and Vita chinked hers against it. But then her smile vanished and she took a long, thoughtful sip.

'Vita?'

'What am I thinking?' She shook her head vigorously at herself. 'What am I saying!' She looked at Michelle and shrugged helplessly. 'I forgot. He has a son. And you don't get one of those without a wife, partner, girlfriend, whatever. He's probably blissfully ensconced.'

'If that's the case – don't go there,' said Michelle.

*

173

Jonty was out at the cinema. Oliver was trying to settle in front of the television with a nondescript ready meal. He'd really wanted to watch this programme, part of a series on the coastal landscape of Britain. But he couldn't concentrate and not just because the food was revolting.

'Oh, for Christ's sake.'

He switched off the TV, chucked the foil tray in the bin and left the house.

'I can't believe I'm doing this.'

The residential areas of Wynford gathered in three sections, forming a triangle around the town centre. The Tree Houses were at one apex, Tim's place was at another and Oliver's home was at the other. He climbed into his car and drove to Vita's without wondering what he'd say when he arrived. He just drove. Bruce Springsteen sang out about jungleland and Oliver joined in, not listening to the words. He pulled up outside and left the car quickly, striding up the path as if a pace any slower would allow thoughts to seep in.

But she wasn't there.

She was at Michelle's.

It would have been very easy to have left the Tesco bag containing the cagoule on her front doorstep. Right there, under the small porch. He could easily leave a note, just pop a Post-it on the door, couldn't he. It was obvious what it was and who'd returned it – he could just leave the cagoule, in the bag or not, and not bother with a note. Who'd nick the contents, anyway? And look – there's a little old lady noseying around her front garden a couple of houses up. He could give it to her, and say, Excuse me, but would you mind taking this in for the young lady who lives at the end house?

And then he thought, Young lady is it now? And he thought, Didn't I call her a madwoman on Monday? And he said to himself, with some reluctance, I like her – that's all, I just quite like her. And then he realized he hadn't thought about DeeDee all day but she was in his soul now and seemed to calm his mind, out of the blue. Two more different women you couldn't hope to meet. Perhaps, thought Oliver, just perhaps, that's no bad thing. What would his wife advise? She'd laugh at him, tell him not to be such a lummox. She'd see it all very rationally: there's no one there, Ols – so there's no point staying and no point leaving the mac because it defeats the object. Go home. Watch the TV. Make sure you record *Skins* for Jonty. Go and eat some proper food. Hang out the washing. It's the recycling tomorrow – go and sort that. Just stop standing on that doorstep as if you're trying to figure out the world's biggest conundrum.

That's what DeeDee would say.

She'd probably throw something at him too – like a cushion, which she'd then tut at him for not putting back nicely with the others on the bed.

That was DeeDee.

Feeling strangely comforted, Oliver drove away with the cagoule as it was, still in the bag on the back seat. Jonty would never know he'd been gone.

Jonty was having a lie-in the next day. It was Thursday and his dad had told him at the start of the summer break that he didn't need to work on the days beginning with a T or an S. At the yard, Oliver and the lads discussed the schedule for the day, loaded the trucks and set off. Boz was joining Oliver.

'One moment,' his boss said, going to his car and coming back to the truck with a canvas bag from the supermarket.

'All set,' he said, 'let's go.'

They'd finished the first job by lunch-time and the next appointment was on the other side of town.

'Sausage roll?' Oliver suggested.

'Cool,' said Boz, who ate anything.

'I think I'll just – pop into That Shop.' Oliver had started the sentence slowly and then scrambled to the end.

'Oh yeah?'

'Return that ridiculous waterproof,' Oliver said. 'To that – girl. The mad one – who works. In That Shop. Who came. Into the yard.'

Oliver's manner of speech was very odd. Boz thought to himself, Calm down, mate, it's only a coat, it's only a shop. He remembered how, when Oliver had given him a lift there just a few weeks ago, he wouldn't come in. He'd eventually just loitered outside. His wife, his late wife, had loved the place, hadn't she.

'I'll pop in too, then,' Boz said supportively. 'My sister loved her present. Might find something for my mum – it's her birthday next. The big Five Oh.'

'Oh,' said Oliver, 'OK.'

But then Oliver went very quiet and started to take a circuitous route to town. 'Actually, you know what,' he said, slowing down when approaching green lights as if willing them to change, 'I don't think I will go just now. Parking can be a bit of a nightmare.'

Can it? thought Boz.

'And it's lunch-time – and we have a busy afternoon. And I don't want to eat into your break. No, it's fine. We'll just pick up sausage rolls and head back to the yard.'

'No worries,' said Boz. 'You can give me the mac – I'll drop it in myself over the next day or so.'

Oliver went quiet. Boz now had the bag on his lap.

It took Oliver until they'd arrived back at the yard to

speak again. 'Actually, you know what, it's fine. I'll drop it in on my way home.'

And while Boz ate his sausage roll and ham-and-cheese toastie which, by the time they were back at the yard, had stuck to the white paper bag, he thought to himself, This isn't about Oliver's late wife at all. He munched through two packets of crisps. It's about that lady – the one in the mac, the one in That Shop. And as he washed down his lunch with half a litre of Coke, he glanced at his boss and he thought, Good on you, mate – it's time.

Though there was no need for it, Vita had set up Thursdays as housework days and she stuck rigidly to it. She was hoovering that evening after work when she thought she heard the doorbell. She switched off the vacuum cleaner. Listened. Nothing. Started the machine again. Thought she heard the bell once more. Stilled the hoover. Listened. And yes – there it was. Someone *was* at the door. It could well be Mr Brewster wanting his spare keys. He usually locked himself out of his house at least once a week. She went to open it.

'Coming, Mr B!' she called out. 'Coming!' She picked up his spare set and made for the door.

It wasn't the Mr B she was expecting. It was a different Mr B altogether.

'Oh!'

'Mr B, eh?' said Oliver. 'Preferable to the other names you were no doubt calling me earlier in the week.'

Seeing Vita so flustered put him at his ease. Her eyes were navy again today. Her hair scrunched haphazardly away from her face. She was wearing a tatty man's shirt and flip-flops.

'I –' she said. 'My neighbour. Mr Brewster. B for Brewster. He's a little forgetful when it comes to his keys.'

'A good Samaritan,' said Oliver, 'who nevertheless wants to kill her pear tree.'

He's wearing the T-shirt. He's in shorts today. I don't know where to look.

'I'm not going to kill the tree,' said Vita.

'I know you're not.'

'If I had twenty thousand pounds, I might.'

'I don't think you would.'

Pause. Whose go to speak next? What to say?

'Er, I have this.' Oliver gave her the bag with the cagoule. 'You left it. At the yard.'

'Oh,' said Vita, peering into the bag for a long time. 'Thank you.'

'Does that mean you haven't been outside?'

'Well, I walk to my shop every day.'

'I meant outside – in your garden.'

'Oh! Doh! Yes – I mean no. I'm not going out there until there's not a leaf, let alone a pear, on the tree.'

'That's a shame. The weather's beautiful at the moment.'

'That's what *I* told *you*. That's the whole flipping problem.'

Flipping. He liked her choice of word. 'I know.' He hoped he sounded sympathetic.

Pause.

'Well –' said Oliver, as if he would be following that with, I must be going now.

'Oh, OK,' said Vita, as if he'd completed the sentence.

Pause. Awkward. Both of them. How daft they both felt. How daft she felt she must look. She made a vague attempt at smoothing her hair. They both wanted to prolong this chat, however stilted it was, but neither knew how.

'Well – if you like, I don't mind popping in – to clear away the pears? Put them at the back of the garden – try to lure the wasps away?'

178

Vita looked at him. His head tipped to one side, his face open, honest, genuine, kind. Oh God, all right, rugged and handsome too.

The son! There's probably a wife, remember!

Vita saw the wedding ring. 'No – it's fine.'

'I was passing anyway,' said Oliver. 'It won't take me ten minutes.'

And Vita thought, For goodness' sake, stop over-analysing – he's just a nice bloke. He just wants to help. He probably feels a bit bad. He's on his way home. He probably phoned his wife first anyway.

'Thank you,' said Vita, 'that's very kind.'

So Oliver went into Vita's garden a second time.

She watched from the window. Once or twice he swatted at the air and she thought to herself, See! Those wasps are everywhere, aren't they!

There was a bottle of wine in the fridge. White. Chilled.

No. No. It wasn't appropriate.

She knocked on the kitchen window and made a C shape with her hand and then a T shape with both. He smiled and gave her the thumbs-up and made the T sign back at her. And then the V sign which she took to mean Two Sugars rather than Fuck Off. And, while the kettle boiled, she watched intermittently as he toiled. She noted the T-shirt stretch across his shoulder blades, his calf muscles tauten, the glisten to his forearms, the way he pushed his hair back from his forehead as he cleared up the rotten pears. And then he was walking over, taking a slight bow at which she was clapping. The tea was made. She wasn't sure what to do about biscuits.

'Bastards got me,' he said, and above his elbow just below his bicep, Vita could see he'd been stung. She felt gently vindicated.

179

'Ouch,' she said. How come he didn't go hopping mad in the garden?

'I'm still not cutting down your pear tree,' he said.

'I know,' she shrugged. Hand him his tea, Vita, he's earned it. 'Here you go.' She would have liked to dab the sting on his arm. Don't look at his arm.

They stood; him with his back to the kitchen door, her with her back to the stove, blowing into the mugs, sipping.

'Well, I'd better push off,' he said.

'Would you like a biscuit?'

'Thank you very much.'

They ate biscuits, two each. They kept glancing out of the window as if the pear tree was trying to say something.

'I hope that helps,' he said.

'Me too.'

'Right. Right – I'd better be off, then.'

'OK,' said Vita, wondering about the wine, the wife.

'Good luck,' he said.

'Hope your sting is OK,' said Vita.

'Occupational hazard,' he said and they both laughed a bit too much.

'Thanks very much,' said Vita, opening the front door.

'Goodnight, Miss W.'

And, when it came, Vita's voice was both shy yet playful. 'Goodnight, Mr B.'

But, when he'd gone, she felt contemplative and a little melancholy.

Will his wife use vinegar on his sting?

All those *Unhelpful Thoughts* Post-its had a new purpose now.

Oliver woke in the soft silent hours, jolted out of dreamless nothingness by a single word.

Wasps.

He lay there, sensing how his heartbeat had quickened.

It wasn't his voice that had said it. It had sounded like DeeDee.

The sting on his arm throbbed, so he put on the light and inspected it. Just a regular wasp sting, really. Christ, the little fuckers could be spiteful. Was it purely the discomfort that had woken him? He sat up for a while, read a few pages of some book about vampires that Jonty had told him was wicked. It was relatively raunchy in places. He started wondering whether this was entirely suitable reading for his boy. And then he remembered back being fourteen, fifteen. It wasn't books he'd read to get off on, it was top-shelf magazines smuggled into school and hired out at 50p for two nights.

Wasps.

That word had been so emphatic, so out loud.

He went for a pee, rifled around the medicine cabinet and dobbed on antiseptic cream he knew wouldn't really help. Poor Girl With The Pear Tree, he thought. She'd been stung all over. He went back to bed. It was stupid o'clock and he'd be knackered tomorrow. He switched off the light and waited and waited for sleep.

It was hopeless.

'What did you mean – *wasps*?' he said into the lonely darkness of the room.

The answer swept over him suddenly, like a chill. He sat up again, flicked on the light.

No?

Really?

Those?

Oliver sat a while longer, thinking he'd think about it in the morning. But it was useless. He'd have to go and

181

check, otherwise he'd never get to sleep. He pulled on a sweatshirt, tucked his pyjama bottoms into socks and padded out of his bedroom. Down the stairs he went, to the back door, taking a torch from the kitchen drawer on the way. He eased his feet into boots, slipped on a jacket, flicked the torch on and went out into the garden.

It was a large garden and he really hadn't been out there for a long time. This was the second summer. It had always been DeeDee's domain and since she'd been gone, he simply hadn't known what to do with it. When she was alive, he'd come out and everything would be just so – the borders rolling with health all year round. The lawn, sweeping in gentle curves around the beds. Garden furniture in which they'd while away long, chatty evenings and entire weekends. Bonfires in the autumn. Fireworks on New Year's Eve. Pots on the patio fragrant with herbs throughout the seasons, troughs hosting a fanfare of spring bulbs and later, a tumble of summer colour, a festive display of white and red at Christmas. Show Oliver any leaf, a slither of bark and he will name that tree in Latin in an instant. Plants and flowers, though, were a foreign language, one in which DeeDee had been fluent. How she'd teased him for his clumsy descriptions – Small pink one, he'd say. The blueish stuff over there. The red droopy whatsit. The one that smells like chocolate. That tall thing with purple spiky bits. That'll be lavender, DeeDee would say, as if to an imbecile. They both knew he did it on purpose, year in year out. But it had been part of their dance, their harmony, over the seasons.

And here he is, in the garden for the first time in a long, long while. It's very late. Or very early. He feels like a bit of an idiot. Surely it could have waited until morning? But here he is, all the same.

Even through boots, the lawn feels terrible, all divots

and dinks, the grass unkempt and thatchy. He's grateful it's so dark – no doubt the state of the herbaceous borders would be utterly depressing. He walks to the back of the garden where, between two larch trees, it opens out again. It was this area that had sold the house to DeeDee. It's a secret garden, she'd said to Oliver. It's a mangy old orchard, he'd said to her. But he'd tended it and the trees had fruited well. Apples and plums and damsons. But my God, the wasps! And that's why Oliver is out there now, because in the middle of the night he'd remembered his own wasps, and what his wife had done about them.

He walks to the trees, there are only eight of them. The torch spins a ghostly hue over the trunks and boughs. He ricks his ankle as his foot slides over a fallen apple. The torchlight picks out the scatter of windfall fruit on the ground. He directs the beam up into the branches. There they are. He's found what he'd forgotten about. There they are, glinting in the light. He reaches up high and takes one down, inspects it with the torch. It is absolutely disgusting. Really vile. The clean-up, though, can wait until the morning. For now, he'll just collect them up – six, seven, eight of them – and leave them by the back door.

Suzie

Suzie was beside herself. She was literally pulling her hair out; twisting frond after frond around and between her fingers, tugging anxiously until strands broke free, some with the follicles intact, littering her lap. Where was Tim? Where in holy God's name was he? He wasn't at home, he wasn't answering his mobile. Why hadn't he called? Why wasn't he here? Why was his phone off? Where was he? It had been on, late afternoon – it had rung and rung and then gone through to voicemail, but at least it had been *on*. She'd left a larky message or two, she'd sent a couple of funny texts, but she'd heard nothing. Now she'd left an arsey message – and followed that with a conciliatory one saying, Tim, supper's ready, I'm the dessert and you can provide the creamy topping.

He was meant to be here. He was meant to be coming over. He'd said he'd be here when she'd reminded him this morning, when she'd left his place. They'd spoken at lunch-time when he said his meeting in London was wrapping up. And since then – nothing. Her housemate was out – Suzie had cajoled her into staying elsewhere tonight. The meal was cooked – proper posh steak and lots of trimmings. She'd preened herself really nicely, had her nails done in her lunch hour, bought a new top, changed her bed linen, put flowers on the table. Recently, she'd been working on developing the domestic side to their relationship; suggesting nights in and trips to the cinema to balance out the dehydration of all those evenings in the pub drinking too much and talking shite. But now he was over an hour late. Where the hell was he? And why was his phone *off*? He wouldn't be with Vita, would he?

By eleven o'clock, Suzie wasn't so much angry as utterly deflated. There'd been no word from Tim and she'd given up trying to reach him.

And then she thought, What if I phone Vita? Just to put my mind at rest?

She'd made a note of Vita's number – at the time, she hadn't known why it felt so important to do so. But tonight, it seemed to make sense. She withheld her number and dialled.

'Hullo?' Vita's voice was sleepy and sober and as Suzie pressed her ear hard against the handset, she was able to detect that Vita really did sound alone. There was no background noise. There was no need for this phone call. Suzie felt humiliated to have had to make it. Vita had long since hung up. Suzie listened for a while to the tone on the dead line and thought back to those nights when Tim had been out with her before Vita had left him; when he didn't phone home, when he'd choose to stay with her. Suzie had experienced some skewed ego boost back then – interpreting the way he acted as a sign of him being *so* into her that his home life didn't cross his mind. This evening, she hadn't thought to worry whether he was all right, whether he'd had an accident, whether something was wrong. Deep down, her dominant vibe was that Tim was up to something. Just then, Suzie wondered whether this was her comeuppance, whether this was payback. For an even more ephemeral split second, she wondered whether it was sympathy she now felt for Vita. But she cancelled all such thoughts, tried Tim one final time and then went to bed in full make-up, desperately upset.

Suzie slept fitfully, jolting awake to check her phone, to listen to every car she heard driving up the street, wondering if it was a cab with Tim in it. She felt very cold when it was time to rise, though outside the sky was already cloudless. She took the bus to work, hopping off two or three stops early, compelled to make a specific detour, to walk a route she'd normally avoid. She scanned all the cars she passed – moving or parked in the side streets – in case Tim's should be one of them. Where the shops started, she slowed right down. She crossed the road though her eyes were fixed over to the other side. But it wasn't Tim's car parked outside That Shop, just a small delivery van with hazards flashing, a couple of scooters in the designated bay. Suzie walked on. Then she crossed the road, retraced the route and walked right past the shop, glancing in. She was in such a dither she couldn't actually see what or who was in there. She kept walking, turned and walked back past again. This time she stopped right outside and stared hard into That Shop.

Vita was reading. She was about to finish the Waugh and start another. She could sense someone was looking at the window display but until they came into the shop, it wasn't worth her while interrupting the flow of the chapter. But gosh, they were standing there a long time. She put her finger over her place and looked up and knew, in that split second of eye contact, that it was Suzie staring straight at her. This was the closest they'd ever been. They

186

held each other's gaze for a moment, a slew of thoughts racketing through each of their minds. Then Suzie walked away, her head down and her shoulders hunched, and Vita wondered what on earth had just happened. But then she thought, I know that deportment. And she thought, That was me – Tim's girlfriend distraught. And for a little while her emotions conflicted between Serves you right, to You poor old thing, what's he been up to? She remembered the soliloquies she'd rehearsed when she'd first found out about Suzie – some had been diatribes against Tim as if to enlighten Suzie just what she was taking on. Others were lyrical declarations, somewhat exaggerated, of all the loveliness Tim had ever bestowed upon her. Both were intended to see Suzie off. Neither type had been thought about, let alone practised, for a long while. She wasn't going to start now. There was a very different Waugh to hand and Vita was going to absorb herself in those vile bodies instead.

The Wasp Catchers

'Oh my God – Dad, that is *beyond* gross.' Jonty made an extravagant display of fake vomiting the next morning.

'Not a pretty sight, I'll grant you,' Oliver said.

He and Jonty were looking at the eight wasp catchers. They were made of glass, transparent but with a greenish tinge, with metal loops from which they'd hang. A cork in the neck. They resembled old-fashioned honey pots. But, currently, the bodies of the traps were filled with two summers' worth of dead wasps and some kind of noxious slime.

'What are you going to do with them?' Jonty asked, still retching theatrically but helpless not to be fascinated and thus inspecting them closely. 'I don't think you can put them in the recycling like that!'

'No,' said Oliver, 'no. But I'll clean them out – it's not a pleasant task, but it's easy enough. And then I thought I would indeed recycle them.'

'I'd just chuck them, if I were you.'

Oliver smiled. 'No. I am going to recycle them.' He paused, wanting to be able to judge his son's expression when he said what he was to say next. 'I thought I'd give them to – that lady.' That's how Jonty had referred to her, wasn't it. *Dad, there's a lady here who has a huge problem.*

Jonty looked at his father and then back at the wasp traps. Then he nodded. 'I think that would be – most chivalrous.'

And then they went to work and spoke of it no more.

'It's chemical, V; fancying him is purely chemical,' Michelle said on the phone. 'It's intoxicating – the frisson, the attraction – it's intoxicating because it's purely chemical. But you'll just have to remember that wedding ring – divorcees don't wear wedding rings. This Oliver guy has his own Vita at home. You're his potential Suzie. Is that who you want to be? Do you want the next man in your life to have Tim's principles?'

'You're right. I know,' said Vita, deflated. 'And no – I don't.'

'On the plus side – whatever Tim did do to you, he didn't damage you because you haven't become a bitter and twisted man-hater. You know right from wrong. So, while I know you're disappointed – and those chemicals are surging – you'll just have to let them abate.'

'I am a terrible judge of character,' said Vita. 'Useless.'

'I don't think so. You just need to take note of *facts* from the outset, not feelings.'

I must put that on a Post-it. *Facts, not feelings.*

'So any man I now meet, I have to say, Are you married and what's your position on infidelity?'

'Er, no – you'll have them running for the hills,' Michelle laughed. 'You'll learn to look for the signs, V, you'll listen to your intuition.'

Vita went quiet. 'But my intuition told me Oliver is a genuinely good guy. See – I *can't* trust my intuition and I *am* a poor judge of character.'

189

'You need to train yourself to be a good judge of poor characters.'

Vita would be writing that one on a Post-it too.

Oliver found it odd. He found it very, very strange. He didn't wonder if it was a good sign or not, he didn't read into possible reasons, he just decided it was odd, full stop. There had been two or three emails in the secret account for Pete Yorke, with offers of unbridled shagging and the fantastic contradiction of 'no-strings bondage'. Jonty was out with his mates all day and it would certainly be easy for Oliver. But no, he chose to forgo the option of mind-numbing sex for the revolting job of removing the dead wasps from the traps. He took the jars onto the driveway, uncorked them, rigged up the hose, set the nozzle to the high-pressured jet and blasted the detritus out. What a way to while away a Saturday, he thought as he balanced them on the grass to dry out. They looked as good as new, though. They'd make a great gift.

He decided to take them to That Shop. He even parked and bought a pay-and-display ticket for an hour. But he didn't leave the car park. He sat in the car for a while, giving himself a hundred reasons why not to go in, finally choosing the fact that it was Saturday and the shop would be very busy and she might not be there anyway. He returned home. He felt stupid, deluded and low. Then he pulled himself together, sat down at the computer, went to the Hotmail inbox and emailed saucysam69 to say if it's not too short notice, how about tonight.

On Sunday afternoon, Oliver went out. He drove to Vita's house and walked up the path with the wasp catchers in a cardboard box. She's probably not in, he thought to himself, but I may as well ring the bell.

190

Vita had seen him pull up and had been flattening herself against the wall since then, as if hiding from a gun-toting madman. The doorbell went. And, after an interval, went again. And Vita thought to herself, I won't let him in but I do need to tell him what's what because he oughtn't to come here again. As she went to the door, she did wonder why he wasn't at home having Sunday lunch with his family. Then she thought about her own mum and felt very bad indeed. But she qualified this – if she wasn't being a very good daughter, he was being a dreadful husband and father.

She opened the door. He was walking away.

'Sorry,' she said, wondering at her choice of word.

He turned and smiled and came towards her. She was in shorts and a Ramones T-shirt and Oliver thought how nice her knees were. She noted that he was in normal clothes: soft khaki trousers and a white button-down shirt, sleeves rolled up. She told herself to stare either between his eyebrows or at the small button on one of the collar tips.

'Hi,' he said, 'I wasn't sure if you were in.'

It was obvious she was in so there was nothing either of them could add to that.

'I brought these for you,' he said, and they both looked into the cardboard box. 'They're wasp catchers. They work really well. You just fill them with a mixture of sweet stuff – I recommend jam and beer – and the wasps are lured to a sticky end.'

Vita looked at the eight glass jars. What on earth was she meant to say now?

'It's very kind,' she said, 'but I think you ought to keep them.'

'No – really – they're for you.'

'I don't want them, though.' Vita sounded suddenly

191

strident and they both looked up from the box and straight at each other.

'No?' Oliver looked a little hurt. And lovely at the same time.

'No. Thank you,' said Vita, looking away. She wasn't happy, but reluctantly, she summonsed images of Michelle and Candy, imagining them standing behind her, arms crossed like bodyguards.

'They work,' Oliver said, not having expected this response, 'honestly.'

Vita stared hard at the little button on his collar tip. He shifted the box a little and the sun caught on his wedding band, shooting a glint straight to Vita. 'Thank you for coming and for the trap things but I don't think you should come to my house again and don't worry I'll find someone else to do the tree when it's time but I ask you not to come here again thanks.' She hadn't paused for breath and she then stood there, regretting everything she'd just said but knowing reluctantly that it all had to be said.

He just stood there, with his box of tricks.

She backed into her house. 'Sorry,' she said. 'Anyway – bye.'

Vita shut the door and sloped into the kitchen, sat at the table with her head in her hands and thought, Oh for God's sake, can't I just have a bloody break.

How can doing the right thing feel so soul destroying?

Don't I deserve a knight in shining armour by now?

This had not been a good weekend for Oliver. He returned home embarrassed and pissed off with the world at large. He thought he'd been ready – ready to give wasp traps to a girl he liked. He thought, subsequently, that he was an idiot. He thought of how he'd girded his widower's courage – of what had been wholesome intent, but also of the battle of wills he'd fought to do the right thing, at a time that finally seemed right for him, for DeeDee, for Vita. And he thought, now, how wrong he'd been. He also thought he'd have the house to himself when he returned. He wasn't expecting Jonty back until supper-time but his son was home already, watching his dad come up the drive carrying a cardboard box.

'Jont?'

'I twisted my ankle playing cricket.'

'Crikey – you want some frozen peas on that.' Thank God for something else to think about. 'Sit yourself down, keep your leg up. Flick on the telly – I'll bring them in to you.'

'You OK, Dad?'

'Yes?'

'You seem—'

'I'm fine. I'm fine. Let's watch – something.'

'What's in the box?'

'What box?'

'The one you were carrying in from the car.'

'Oh. That box. Just those – wasp traps.'

'Did you take them, then? To that lady?'

Oliver thought, I could lie to my son to save my own face. And then he thought, What's the point of that?

'I did.'

'She wasn't in?'

They was no way out of this conversation. 'She didn't want them. I don't know why. Women are strange.'

'That's what Mum used to say to you – when she wanted something or had done something or didn't want to do something.'

'She did, didn't she?' Oliver laughed gently at the memory.

Jonty watched his father fiddling absent-mindedly with his wedding ring. 'Anyway, it was a wasted journey. She told me to buzz off.'

Jonty rearranged the pack of peas pensively on his ankle. 'Dad – did you tell her? That the wasp catchers are ours?'

'No. They look good as new, now.'

'I don't mean that. You didn't tell her they were Mum's?'

'No, Jonty, I certainly did not.'

'But Dad – I think. Can't you see? I can.'

'Jonty, you're not making sense. Can we just drop it now? Oh look, a *Mr Bean* is on.'

'But Dad – it's sort of down to me. It's sort of my fault.'

'*Sort of* is lazy language.'

'She knows you have a son, right? She met me at the yard, right?'

Oliver looked at his boy blankly.

'So – if I was her, I'd assume I have a mum, then. If you see what I mean. What I'm saying is – she probably assumes you have a wife as well as a son.'

Oliver stopped looking at the television and cast his gaze outside to the garden he never went out in.

Jonty, you'll always always have that mum of yours. As long as you live.

'You wear your wedding ring, Dad, when you're not at work. She probably thinks you're some weird perv,' Jonty said.

Oliver thought about it. He looked at his left hand, the band of gold with no beginning, no end. And then he thought, How on earth could his teenage son be so astute, so right?

'Weird perv,' Oliver said quietly. 'Charming.'

'I could have said weird *old* perv, Dad,' said Jonty, 'so there.'

'Can we watch *Mr Bean* now?'

194

'Yeah.'

'*Yes*.'

'Yes. But you should take them again, the wasp catchers – and just tell her.'

Beer and Jam

Really, Vita could have done with a full and busy day but Mondays were always slow. She'd decided to compare the frightfully British charleston with F. Scott Fitzgerald's version on the other side of the Atlantic and was currently happily involved with *The Great Gatsby*. Candy, who wanted to pull her friend into the real world, had sent her a book entitled *The Men I've Loved to Hate*. Apparently it was fiction and fantastically funny, but it didn't appeal to Vita at all and she had about as much desire to read it as to attend a blindfolded speed-dating session – another of Candy's ideas. At least with Evelyn Waugh, the vile bodies were the antithesis to her, with their double-barrelled surnames and wealth and flapper dresses and shiny bobbed hair and everything. Escapism, that's what she needed and she gladly drifted off into another world, another time, and didn't look up when the customer came in at lunch-time.

'Hullo.'

Oh good God, it's Oliver Bourne.

In his work clothes. With that box again. No wedding ring today, Vita noted with some disdain.

'Hullo,' he said again, now that he had her attention.

'Oh,' she said, 'hi.' Back to the book.

But he remained standing in the middle of the shop, looking around – not at her wares, but as if scouting for a flat surface on which to put the box. He approached.

'I—' she started.

'I look like a salesman trying to flog you wasp catchers,' he said.

Vita wasn't sure how to answer that because actually, it was an apposite image, an amusing one, and she fought a smile.

'Look,' he said.

'I've seen them already,' she said.

'No – not *look*,' he said, 'but – *listen*.'

He bent down and placed the cardboard box at his feet. Just the console table behind which Vita sat was between them. He was in his work clothes. He was slightly grubby. He had sawdust or something in his hair. She could actually smell it. Warm, fresh. Vita wished she hadn't noticed.

'About the other day – about yesterday,' he said.

'I told you – yesterday – that I don't want the wasp catchers and I didn't want you coming over.'

'Semantically speaking, yes, you told me not to come to your house. Ever again. But this is your workplace.'

'But why are you here? What is it that you want?' She'd intended to sound nonplussed but she could hear she sounded confused.

'Oh,' said Oliver lightly, 'oh – nothing really.' He wondered how he could sound so stupid. How could he feel just like an awkward teenager? If it wasn't so pathetic, it would be funny. Richard Curtis could make it very funny. Hugh Grant would do a marvellous job, acting out this scene.

Vita was starting to look cross, he thought. Then he

thought of Jonty. He looked around the shop, thought of the many times his late wife would have been in here, sniffing candles and admiring all the pretty frippery.

'Actually,' Oliver said, 'I didn't make it clear to you. I didn't *buy* you the wasp catchers – I should have said so and for that, I apologise.' It was a sentence, certainly, but it didn't explain much. Vita had put her book down, though, and was looking at him – a little suspiciously, but he had her attention all the same. 'You see – what I should have told you was – the wasp catchers are my wife's.'

Vita's shoulders slumped a little and her displeasure was an audible squeezed sigh.

'Why, then, are you trying to give them to *me*?' She was accusatory, but her tone wasn't hostile. It was just thoroughly deflated.

'They – *were* – my wife's.'

Oliver paused. He looked down, in every sense of the word. When he lifted his eyes, he caught Vita's. They weren't so navy today. Her hair was tidy. He hadn't noticed the light spatter of freckles before. Then he steeled himself to stop looking and to start talking. But he hated these words out loud, really despised hearing them, having to say them.

'My wife died.'

Vita's intake of breath was sharp.

He shrugged, raised his arms and let them fall. 'My wife died – almost three years ago. She used these wasp catchers in the garden – to great effect. And you're right – I do have a big garden, not that I go out there much. At all really. Anyway, the wasp catchers were still there, filled with the little fuckers. I cleaned them out and thought you might like them and I have been talking way too much because, because—'

'Your wife *died*?'

He nodded. 'She was killed. In a road accident.'

Vita felt tears prick sharply. 'I am *so* sorry.'

The depth of her emotion somehow calmed him. 'Thank you.'

'Would you like a cup of tea?'

'Thank you.'

And while she was busy out the back, making tea, Oliver looked around the shop and said thank you under his breath a number of times.

'Thank you.'

'Two sugars,' she said, flicking a V sign at him.

'That's right.'

'I did have biscuits here – but the Saturday girl is a greedy pig.'

Greedy pig. Oliver liked her terminology. Other people might have said *Fat Cow* or something. It was funny, it was gentle. It was quirky. It reminded him of when she'd said *flipping* – about the wasps being a flipping problem.

They made much of sipping their tea because it helped to mask the emotions churning. Vita felt almost high, Oliver felt exhausted.

'Anyway,' Oliver said, 'I was just wondering whether you might like the wasp catchers now? Now that you know a little of their background?'

'I would like them very much indeed,' said Vita.

'My wife had a great recipe,' he said. 'She honed it over the years.'

'Beer and jam, I think you said?'

'That's right,' he said, flattered that she'd remembered. He paused. 'Would you like me to – put them up for you?'

Vita tipped her head and then nodded, hoping it was OK that a gentle smile was now a grin even though the man had just told her his wife had died.

Oliver nodded. 'You provide the beer and jam, then,' he said. 'I think DeeDee used to use bottled French lager.'

'DeeDee,' Vita said the name.

'Her full name was Danielle – but no one called her that.'

'They're both pretty names.'

Oliver nodded. 'Yes.' Then he looked at Vita. 'May I ask – did you think, when I came over –' He paused. 'I'm not sure how to phrase this – but if you thought I was married, did you think I – well –?'

Vita looked a little embarrassed. 'Well –'

'I'm not sure how to phrase this either – but for what it's worth, I was never like that, when I *was* married. I was very happy to be married.'

'If DeeDee was alive, you'd never have brought me wasp catchers?'

Oliver laughed. 'Exactly.'

'OK,' Vita said, 'I'm happy to hear it.' Oh God, that sounded wrong. But Oliver's raised eyebrow put her at her ease and there was no need to backtrack. Vita thought of Michelle, of Candy. She thought of the nerve it must have taken for Oliver to bring the wasp catchers to her house yesterday, to the shop today. She had to do something for all of them. 'Would you like to come over, then? Would you like to come over – perhaps even this evening? I don't know. Or a different evening? Or a daytime?'

'This evening would be fine,' Oliver said. 'I could come on my way back from work.'

'Great,' said Vita. And then she thought about it very quickly. Much as he looked a treat in his work clothes, with all the visible signs of his toil, perhaps it would be nicer if— She stopped thinking. 'Or,' she said, 'you could come along later on?'

200

He thought about that. It was a much better idea. 'OK,' he said, 'I'll be along later on. I'll have supper with Jonty – and come along afterwards. Jonty's my boy.'

'I think he was at your yard. When I came in, doing my unhinged hobo impression.'

'He was indeed.'

Vita hid her head in her hands.

'Tonight, then?'

She nodded and they shared a quick grin before awkwardly wondering how Oliver was going to take his leave. In the end, he raised his hand and said bye a couple of times, backing away for a few strides before turning, saying bye again, and going.

Vita wouldn't know of the utter relief he felt as he walked briskly back to the car. Thank God, he thought to himself, thank God. And luckily Oliver was already driving out of town and thus had no idea of the jubilation Vita felt; that she was excitedly dialling her best friend because she had just heard the best news in the world.

'His wife died!' she said in an excited whisper as soon as Michelle picked up the phone. 'His wife's *dead*!' Vita stopped and groaned. 'I didn't mean it like that. Oh God – is negative karma possible?'

'Stop,' said Michelle, 'just stop. Whoa. Backtrack. Whose wife has died? That's terrible.'

'Oliver,' Vita said. 'He's a widower, not a philanderer.'

'You're joking.' It had never crossed Michelle's mind. People their age didn't lose partners their age. The concept was hideous. 'How do you know?'

'He came yesterday – to my house. With a box. And a wedding ring – so, obviously, I assumed he really wasn't divorced but married.' She paused – that sounded wrong. She'd explain another time. 'I thought of you – I wouldn't let him in. I told him I didn't want him coming around. I told him I'd find someone else to do the pear tree. He'd brought these glass bottles you kill wasps with – that was what was in the box. I told him to buzz off.'

'He didn't mention the wife,' Michelle said, almost to herself.

'No – but he's just come in to the shop – with the box of wasp whatsits. And he told me. She died almost three years ago. Her name was DeeDee.'

'DeeDee.'

'DeeDee – short for Danielle.'

Vita and Michelle said her name with gentle reverence. They allowed for a dignified pause.

'And now?'

'He's coming over tonight,' Vita said, unable to keep an excited squeak from her voice, 'with the trap things.'

'Yes!' Michelle was thrilled and not merely excited but relieved too. 'Tell me properly what he's like?' So Vita indulged them both.

'You know, Michelle – even when we thought he was a philandering sod, there was something about him that, to me, just seemed genuinely *nice*.'

'I remember,' said Michelle. 'So speaks a true judge of good characters.'

Oliver had left the wasp catchers at the shop. It would have been more convenient if he'd taken them with him and brought them over later, but neither he nor Vita had thought of it at the time. So, after locking up, she headed for home, carrying the cardboard box. It wasn't heavy, it was just a little awkward, but every time she shifted it up, or an edge caught her arm or stomach, she'd glance down at the contents and feel bolstered. She was in her own little world and the car horn was just a faint background detail, really. But then Tim's voice calling her name corrupted her peace. It had been his car horn, it was his car crawling along beside her. The passenger window was down.

'Want a lift?'

She kept on walking. 'Oh – no, thanks.' She put a cheery lift to her voice so he wouldn't think she was being awkward.

'Don't be so stubborn, just hop in,' he said and the passenger door was suddenly flung open, encroaching on her passage forwards. She thought how, sometimes, it was just easier to do what Tim wanted than to make her case to the contrary. So, giving in, she sat herself in the car and clung to the box.

'Seatbelt, Vita,' he said. 'What's in the box?'

'Wasp catchers,' she held one up. 'You put jam and beer in them and then the wasps are trapped.'

'And come to a *sticky end*?'

He was being charming, funny, friendly. It was more unnerving than when he was being a grumpy sod.

'Where do you want me to take you?' he asked. Suddenly, Vita didn't want to be in his car at all. She didn't want to see that a hair scrunchy was around the gearstick. It was as blatant as Suzie's hand encircling his cock. But, most of all, she didn't want Tim anywhere near her house.

'Just drop me on Durham Road,' she said. 'That would be great.'

'You don't want me to take you – to your home?'

'No, no, thanks – I have to post a letter,' she lied.

They drove on.

'How's life?' he asked.

'Good,' Vita said, 'very good. And you?'

'Fine – you know. As ever.' He swore at another car.

'Vita – I've been meaning to ask you something. It's awkward – but you said you'd spoken to Suzie? That she picked up when you called?'

Vita looked out of the window. They were approaching Hereford Street. In the British Isles, Hereford was right the other side of the country from Durham but in Wynford, Hereford and Durham were neighbouring roads.

'What did she say?'

'Why don't you ask her?'

'I'm asking you,' he said softly.

Vita recalled Suzie's haunted look the other week. 'Look – it was some time ago. I phoned – she picked up. I think you were in a pub or somewhere.'

'What did she say?'

Vita thought back; a memory of how she had felt that evening spliced through her. She could go for it, really go for it. She was sure Candy would say, Oh, sod the Bank of Karma, let rip, baby! But a sudden rattle from the wasp catchers as Tim took a speed bump too fast jolted Vita back to how her week was unfolding. No. Be bigger. Just leave it all behind. 'She just said *Tim's phone*.'

'That was it?'

'How is Suzie, then?' Vita asked, a strong instinct telling her not to inform Tim about her silent visit to the shop's window. Tim made much of shrugging with a nonplussed look on his face.

'It's not what you think,' he said.

'I try not to think of it at all,' she countered.

'I mean, she's – not *you*. She's *so* not you.'

'I know,' said Vita.

'It's not what you think, you know,' he said again, all ambiguous and in a serious voice.

'What I do know is quite enough,' she replied.

'I regret everything,' he said hoarsely, having to jostle

204

under the box to put his hand on her thigh. 'I miss Us. I want you back.'

'I want to get out,' she said. 'Here's fine.'

'You said Durham Road – this is Hereford Street.'

'It's fine, it's fine. Please, Tim – I just want to get out.'

'Vita – can't I just –? Please – can we –?'

'No!' She was agitated

He took his hands from the steering wheel in mock surrender. 'Vita, if we could just *talk*?'

'No! No!'

'Babe – I lie awake and think of you. When I'm with *her* – I fantasize it's with *you*.'

'Enough!'

'I miss your beautiful little toes.' His voice was hoarse.

'My toes? You hated my feet – you didn't want them anywhere near you!'

He stopped the car and took his hands from the steering wheel, throwing them into the air. 'Jesus wept, Vita – just come off your high bloody horse, will you? Just listen to me – you owe me that, surely?'

'I owe you nothing,' she mumbled, faffing with the seatbelt.

'Here,' he lifted the box to help her. He looked at the traps. 'Are these samples? They're a good idea for the shop. What's the unit price? What do they retail at?'

She stared at him in disbelief. He was brilliant at this – a master of hurling her from the jagged peaks of acute emotions back down onto some kind of bouncy mundanity. It always caught her out.

'They're mine,' was all she could think to say.

'We should sell them.'

'They're *mine*,' she said. 'I'm keeping them.'

'Where else is selling them?'

'I don't know. These are a gift.'

She was scrambling out of the car, leaning in to take the box, feeling that however durable the glass appeared, in Tim's hands they could surely shatter in a moment.

He handed her the box.

'Vita,' he said while his mind was whirring over who was buying her gifts.

'Thanks for the lift, Tim. Go home.'

'Vita,' his tone of voice pulled her gaze reluctantly back to the car. 'Can we talk? Sometime? Meet for a drink? Something?'

She just stared, wanting to swear, to shout, to run.

'Life's too short,' he was saying. 'This isn't a dress rehearsal, you know. We won't get this time back. Life's too short.'

And Vita felt very still as suddenly she thought of DeeDee. She nodded vigorously at Tim. 'You're so right.'

'Please?' he said.

She looked at him. 'Check with Suzie first,' she said, thinking that would be the end of it.

It didn't spoil a thing. Vita refused to let it. She strode along with marching mantras adapted from phrases on her Post-its. For the first time ever, once she reached the beginning of the Tree Houses, she felt happy to be back. Pleased to be back. Pleased and happy to be – home. She'd stayed late at work because she knew she'd be in a dither waiting and waiting if she left too early. Now she had only an hour before Oliver was due. She took the box inside and then raced back out to the corner shop.

Jam and Lager, Jam and Lager. She marched to the words.

Was it French jam? Or French beer? What kind of jam? She couldn't remember if Oliver had specified. The shop had fancy conserve and bog-standard jam. She went for the cheaper option but bought strawberry, raspberry and apricot – in case wasps had a preference – and then she stood and pontificated on how much beer it took for a wasp to drink itself to death. There were six-packs on offer. But they were cans and Oliver had said bottles so she forked out before clanking her way home, the bags bashing her legs in her haste.

'*Simpsons*, Dad,' Jonty called as Oliver swilled plates and cutlery under the hot tap. He'd made supper, eschewing the selection of frozen meals filling their freezer, for chops, rice and peas which he'd cooked from scratch. He knew he was compensating and he knew he was an idiot. It had been Jonty's idea, after all. He'd had his son's blessing without even asking for it. He should go, he didn't like being late.

'Dad – it's starting.'

He should go.

'Coming.'

He sat down next to his son. *The Simpsons* was a ritual. *The Simpsons* was genius. *The Simpsons* was about family and *The Simpsons* was religion for him and his son. He hoped Vita would understand. He'd only be half an hour late. But when Homer cracked open his Duff beer, Oliver couldn't concentrate. He could only think of Vita's rickety kitchen table, imagining jam and beer and DeeDee's wasp traps set out on it. He turned to Jonty.

'Jont,' he said, and he put his hand on his arm. 'I'm – if it's OK with you – I said. I would. But – you know – not if it isn't.'

'That makes a lot of sense, Dad. *Not*,' Jonty laughed, not taking his eyes from the screen.

Oliver took a deep breath. 'I said I'd go and help – the Vita lady – with the. With Mum's wasp traps.'

His son looked at him. 'Did you take them, then?'

'Yes,' Oliver said.

'Today?'

'Yes – today. That's where I went at lunch-time.'

'Ah – so it wasn't just about sausage rolls.'

'No.'

'You told her – about Mum?'

Oliver nodded. Then Jonty nodded. Then Oliver asked his son if he was cool about him popping over there. Just for an hour. And Jonty thought, When has my dad ever used the word *cool* in a sentence? Suddenly Oliver really didn't want to leave his boy at home.

'Do you want to come with me?' he asked. 'Why don't you come with me?'

'Er,' said Jonty. '*Der!*' He really stretched the word.

'Shall I just pop over then?'

'Der!' Jonty said again.

'OK,' said Oliver, but he sat just as he was.

'Dad!' Jonty protested. 'Just *go.*'

'Yep,' said Oliver.

'*Go!*'

'OK,' said Oliver.

Jonty knew the one failsafe method to see his dad off the sofa and out of the room in an instant. He flicked channels to MTV.

* * *

And so here he is, driving up the Tree Houses as slowly as he can without stalling. And, in the cottage at the end of the street, Vita is trying not to glance at the clock, at her watch, at the time on her mobile phone, every two seconds. It hasn't crossed her mind that she might be stood up – Oliver just doesn't strike her as that kind of man.

But he is late. Not very, but late all the same. She's pinched her cheekbones for a healthy glow because she remembers an actress doing so in a film. She has boiled the kettle a dozen times, she's checked on the wine in the fridge and the whereabouts of the corkscrew. There's been a slight breeze today so the cottage isn't as stifling as it has been recently. She has put the jam and beer on the kitchen table. She has taken the wasp catchers out of the box, arranged them in a semicircle and then rearranged them in an arbitrary configuration. She hasn't even looked outside to the pear tree. But she has looked outside to the front intermittently, from the safe distance at the back of the small room upstairs, to see if he's here. Now she can hear a car. She can hear that the engine has stilled. Footsteps up her path. Oh God – he really is here.

And Oliver rings the bell saying under his breath, Here goes.

'Hullo,' he says. A skirt. Cowboy boots. Those nice knees again – and she's all flushed.

'Hey,' she says. 'Come on in.'

'Sorry I'm late.'

'Late? Are you? Come on in. Tea? Coffee?' she pauses. 'Wine?'

'I'm driving,' he says.

'Oh. Yes. Tea, then?'

'Just a small glass, perhaps – of wine, that is. Not tea.'

And they smile at each other, a little awkwardly.

He follows her into the kitchen. While she pours wine and curses herself silently for having no nibbles and thinking it would be ridiculous to offer chocolate digestives with wine, he is making himself very busy inspecting her shopping.

'I'd suggest strawberry jam for starters,' he says. Then he assesses the beer. 'This is rather posh.'

209

'You said bottled French lager. It was that – or Stella. They only had cans on offer.' Vita pauses. Then she tells herself, He was honest with you – he was open. Do the same, woman. Do the same. 'I couldn't bring myself to buy Stella. My ex used to drink it.'

'Stella can have quite an unpleasant effect on some people,' Oliver says.

'I'll second that,' Vita says.

'Say no more,' Oliver shrugs sympathetically. 'Oh – unless you want to say more?'

'Suffice it to say San Miguel was his lager of choice at the start of an evening – and Stella was his poison by the end of the night.'

She gives Oliver a glass of wine and he chinks it thoughtfully against hers. They say, Cheers! and beam a bit and take a good sip or two to calm their nerves.

'I'm sorry,' he says.

'Sorry?'

'If you had a hard time – with your ex.'

Vita nods.

'How long ago?'

Come on. 'I left him last autumn.'

'Did he leave you for Stella?' Oliver's humour was gentle.

Vita smiles. 'No – for Suzie. But Stella will always be a part of his scene.'

'And a thousand other Suzies – no doubt.'

Vita shrugs. 'He cheated on me before – early on.' She pauses. 'Love is blind.'

He pauses. 'Love is a very good thing.'

'Hopeless romantic, me,' Vita says as if she's ashamed.

'Hope is a very good thing too.' Oliver pauses again. 'His loss, how careless,' he says, chinking her glass again. 'Here's to you, Vita – and your future happiness.'

'Thank you,' she says, 'thanks.' She thinks how she's told Oliver more truth in two minutes than she ever told Rick. She wants to ask him more about his wife – it all seems unfathomably tragic. But this isn't a situation of 'you tell me your sad story, I'll tell you mine'. It's an evening for being tentatively positive, for feeling light, an evening for beer and jam and wasps and wine.

'Right,' says Oliver. 'Let's get cooking. Do you have a jug?' He mixes the jam and the beer and pours a dose into each trap. 'Come and see. The funnel in the base of each lures the wasps up – but then they can't fly out.'

'I suppose, if you're a wasp and you have to die it's not a bad way to go.'

'Such equanimity for a woman who thinks wasps are agents of the devil.'

'My friend Candy bangs on about karma.'

Oliver laughs.

'Be careful out there,' Vita says as he goes into the garden with the stepladder. She watches him climb up and position the jars, not just in the pear tree but at the back of the garden too, as well as in the branches of Mr Brewster's ash which bends over into Vita's garden like a neighbourly handshake.

'There,' he says, back inside, washing his hands at the kitchen sink. 'Let's see how that goes. I'll come back in a week and sluice them out.'

I want to see you before then. Vita wonders what to say. 'Tea?'

He looks at his watch. He'd love to stay. 'I said to Jonty – I'm sure he'd be fine – but I said to him I wouldn't be long.'

Vita is looking out at the garden but it's dusk now, and difficult to see if the wasps are out there. She turns back to Oliver. In her head she can hear how Michelle and Candy – even her mum – would be begging her to do *something*. There's no awkwardness, there's just shyness. They can detect each other's body heat. They don't dart away from eye contact. But they're tentative. It's both silly and yet a mark of the people that they are and the pasts they've had.

'So,' he says and he's moving away from the kitchen. 'Thanks for the wine.'

'Thanks for the company,' she says, 'and the present.' And she was going to end it there. He's already opening her front door and then it'll be too easy to round it all off with a cheery goodbye. So Vita leaps in. And she surfaces just fine; no need for a deep breath. 'Oliver – would you like to, I don't know, perhaps we could – do this again? Not the wasps and jam and mediocre wine from my fridge – but something else?'

'Something else?' Is he musing over her phrase or the concept?

'Yes.'

They both pause.

'I don't know what,' Vita shrugs.

'I'd like to see you again,' says Oliver, finding that Vita's obvious nervousness has taken the edge off his. She smiles, reddening a little.

'Like a date?' she says shyly.

'Daft word, isn't it,' Oliver says, picking at some loose mortar near her front door.

'Perhaps before next week? Before you come back to empty the traps? Maybe we could – well, anything really. Have a meal. Climb a tree.'

Oliver stops fiddling with his words and Vita's masonry and he laughs. A big proper laugh, open and natural. It is such a great sound, ringing out after the tiptoeing voices

212

they'd been using. '*Climb a tree*. I love that.' He looks at her for a moment. 'I know where we could go.'

'Where?'

'You'll see. Are you free – on Friday, perhaps?'

'I am,' she says.

'It's a date,' he says.

'A date,' Vita says and he likes the coy lift to her voice.

'I'll pick you up – early, though. Say six-ish?'

'OK. Where are we going?'

'You'll *see*. Oh – and don't wear high heels.' He looks again at her boots and at her knees. Very nice knees.

She likes the idea of *you'll see*.

'Bye, Vita.'

'Bye Mr B.'

Roots

Vita liked the way that when she thought of Oliver, she didn't construct scenarios or veer off into fanciful imaginings, she simply enjoyed playing back the real scenes, the actual conversations, between them. She found she could physically conjure both the feel of his hand between her shoulder blades when she'd had a funny turn at the yard, and the feeling in her stomach that his prolonged gaze could cause. It was the real Oliver firmly in Vita's here and now. And they had a date at the weekend, and that was exciting.

'It really is a *date* date – we both said so!' she effervesced to Michelle.

'What'll you wear?' Michelle asked. 'I'll lend you my Stella McCartney top if you like? It would look amazing with your hair colour. Talking of which, you should treat yourself to a cut, lady – it's a bit nothingy at the moment.'

Vita touched her hair self-consciously. She couldn't remember the last time she'd had it cut because she'd told herself she was growing it. But Michelle was right, it was no longer an outgrown bob, it was just shapeless and dreary.

214

'I'll bring it over, I'll bring Stella McCartney to the shop.'

Vita laughed. 'Michelle, it sounded like he's taking me to the great outdoors – I was thinking jeans and trainers!'

'Don't you dare!'

'We're going for a *walk*. If you ask me, he seems to be the type of man who walks with purpose over fields and through woods – I need to be suitably attired.'

'Well – *which* jeans then? And say it's as sweltering as it is today? You'll end up walking like John Wayne! What about your soft grey cropped trousers?'

'That's an idea. But I'm comfortable in jeans.'

'Well, your trainers are awful – haven't you some cute walking boots?'

'That's surely a contradiction in terms?'

'What about my Belstaff boots? Just slip in an inner sole. I'm telling you, trainers are a no-no.'

'You forget, he's seen me in wellies and Dad's old cagoule – and he still wants to take me on a date.'

'What time's he picking you up? Right – I'm going to phone you an hour before and, depending on the weather, we'll make the final decision then.'

'Whose date is it!' Vita laughed.

'Yours,' said Michelle. 'That's the point. And I'm not having you scupper your chances in inappropriate clothing.'

Oliver was going to tell Jonty he might be home a little late and he was half hoping his son would ask why so he could tell him, but as it was Friday night and the school holidays, his son already had plans of his own, including staying over at Mark's. So Oliver said nothing and the only thing Jonty asked about was whether his dad could pick him up sometime tomorrow.

The house seemed very quiet, very calm, to Oliver yet

the silence felt loaded. He busied himself making tea, putting a wash on, opening post; whistling all the while so he didn't have to listen. When he showered, he found it was easier to hum than whistle. He talked to himself as he dried and changed, just meandering over neutral subjects like the clients he'd seen that week and that the weather really was glorious even for this, the most temperate period of the season. Then he regarded his reflection in the mirror and said, Oh God, do I really want to be doing all this? And suddenly DeeDee was looking at him from the photo on the chest of drawers, and Oliver was desperate to sense her saying, Don't go, I'm not ready, Ols, please don't do this just yet. But there was simply unequivocal silence. It wasn't even heavy any more, it was just a quiet house because he was the only person in it.

He picked up the photo and traced his finger gently over her image. She didn't come to life, she said nothing to him, just stared out beyond him. He remembered vividly the day that photo was taken – she hadn't been looking at the camera, she'd been preoccupied with looking over Oliver's shoulder while he told her to say cheese, because she'd been watching Jonty climbing the rope ladder in the adventure playground behind him. Sometimes he hated photographs – the caught moment, the person frozen in time and place. The realism of the lie.

He put the photo back and sat on the edge of his bed, feeling caught between the past and the present, between two women, wishing there were guidelines on timing, wishing the feeling of limbo would abate yet not wanting to be any further from the time when DeeDee was alive and life was just simple. Back then, the days just passed gently and the concept of the future wasn't onerous, indeed it wasn't analysed much beyond when they'd change the car or whether they'd holiday in Europe or blow the budget

216

and go to the States. Last Tuesday, when he'd suggested today to Vita, it had all seemed so far in the future. Now it was upon him, Oliver wondered if he really felt ready. Wouldn't it just be easier to carry on as Pete Yorke at weekends? Keep mind and body separate, not try to take a chance with his heart again?

'Look – I'll just see how I feel. When she opens the door.' But though he said it out loud, he was aware that he was saying it to himself now, not to DeeDee. She was locked back in the photo of a brilliant morning seven years ago. He was here, on his own, this late July Friday afternoon. He knew, too, sensible as he was, that wondering about Vita had nothing to do with how he felt about DeeDee, just how he felt – might feel – about Vita. And however he felt about Vita – about seeing her in half an hour – did not, would not, negate how he would always feel about DeeDee. He left the house and, as he drove to Vita's, he considered how all those grief counsellors and bereavement books would declare all this a marker of progress. Though he felt no triumph, he did note that he felt calm. And nerves, those fantastic first-night nerves.

Vita told herself, I bet he doesn't turn up, I bet he cries off, I bet he's changed his mind, I bet it will be all awkward. Oh well, she thought, my hair needed a cut anyway. And she thought, I bet I needn't have dug out my walking boots and brushed off the old mud and given them a good polish. But then her doorbell rang and she caught sight of herself and she said to herself, See! And she spoke to herself as Candy or Michelle might: You have a lovely time, woman. Just be yourself and enjoy.

'Ready?' There he was, a step or so away from the doorstep, hands loosely on hips, squinting slightly in the late-afternoon sun. He was wearing a shirt softly striped mint and white, sleeves rolled midway up his forearms. And jeans. Hurrah for jeans!

Vita looked down at his feet. He was in lovely well-worn docksiders. 'I've been dithering about what I should wear – on my feet,' she told him. He regarded her socks. They were navy blue trainer socks, with pink parts over the heel and toes. 'I have walking boots? Cowboy boots?'

'I'd say a pair of trainers would do fine.'

'Michelle will kill me!' Vita said happily.

'She sounds – charming,' Oliver laughed.

'If you meet her – never tell her about them. Or the jeans.'

'Scout's honour,' said Oliver, with a three-fingered salute. 'Shall I take a quick look at your traps?'

'Be my guest.'

And while Vita walked ahead, chucking her walking boots into the cupboard under the stairs and retrieving her trainers as if they were ruby slippers, Oliver carried on out into her garden. He came back through to find her sitting on the second stair up, lacing her shoes.

'There are a fair few wasps, you'll be pleased to know,' he said, liking the way she was doing double bows. 'Very dead.'

Vita pulled a face of revulsion.

'Nice,' Oliver laughed and he thought it really was nice – to meet someone at ease enough in his company to pull a silly face, rather than obsess about painting it pretty. 'You've had a haircut,' he noticed. She looked immediately self-conscious. 'Was that on my account?' She mumbled in obvious embarrassment but Oliver felt flattered.

'It suits you,' he said.

'Michelle,' Vita said.

'Is this Michelle woman your own personal stylist?'

Vita laughed. 'She's my very best friend and she has no

compunction telling me what not to wear, what my bum looks big in and when my hair looks like rats' tails. She'd much rather I was in a Stella McCartney top.'

'But then what would poor Stella wear?' Oliver said as Vita locked the door, giggling. And, as she walked ahead of him down the front path, liking her shiny hair and the new flicky bits, he thought, Your bum looks pretty good to me. Her lightweight jeans and fitted white T-shirt were fine by Oliver.

'Oh! A *car*.'

He laughed. 'The truck – like the green shirts with the logo – is strictly for work.' He held the door open for her.

'Where are we off to?'

'Wynfordbury Hall.'

It rang a bell. Then she remembered. 'Where the parakeets escaped from?'

From where they escaped. 'Exactly.'

'I thought you said it's privately owned?'

'It is – by the umpteenth Lord Seddon. But the gardens are open to the public Thursday to Monday, from July to September, dawn to dusk.' He reached behind to the back seat and retrieved a clipboard which he placed on Vita's lap. It had a blank sheet of paper attached. 'I'm part of the team running a nationwide project to identify, record and protect our ancient trees. We have more ancient trees than any other country in Europe and our historic trees will be accorded the same respect as works of art – given the same status and protection as public monuments. They're one of our greatest natural assets and I'm estimating there are a hundred thousand of them. There is a wonderful arboretum at Wynfordbury. Though we're actually going to verify the yew.'

'Am I your assistant?'

Oliver had pulled away and was driving up the Tree Houses when he looked at her.

'No,' he said, 'you're my date.'

There.

Unequivocal.

Crystal clear.

'I chose a career in which I can mix work and pleasure,' he shrugged, 'but I just think you might really like this place.' He reached across her, to the glove compartment, and retrieved a circular tin of old-fashioned travel sweets – hard and square and dusted in powdered sugar.

'Thank you,' she said, digging around for a red one.

Vita looked out the window as he drove. She'd never been on a date like this before. She could imagine Candy's reaction: *he gave you a sweet and took you to see some crunky old tree?* She could almost hear Michelle: *thank God I didn't lend you my Stella McCartney.* But Vita knew how they'd both coo a bit too; they already liked the sound of Oliver, they were happy for her and hopeful. She knew they were waiting in the wings, their mobiles at the ready, excited for her, rooting for her. Vita, though, had left her phone at home. She didn't want the distraction of three thousand texts.

'*This* is Wynfordbury Hall!' Vita marvelled. 'I'm ashamed to say I must have been up this way a million times.' They were driving past a grand old stone wall fringed with ivy, which ran almost the entire length of the long road. 'I assumed it was a golf course or something.'

Oliver pulled up to towering iron gates; the rust somehow adding to the drama of the flamboyant curlicues and the lichen-scorched stone supports. One side was open and they drove through, continuing up a long drive, sheep grazing on perfectly manicured parkland to either side. The house was not yet visible.

220

'The whole estate is landscaped – every rise and fall you see was planned to perfection. The vistas, the proportions – it's all sublime.'

'Wow.'

'Very wow.'

'Is it Calamity Brown?'

'No,' he said, not correcting her, 'it's the Indigo Jones school.'

'Did I just say Calamity not Capability?'

'You did.'

'And did you just say Indigo and not Inigo?'

'I did.'

'So I wouldn't feel such a numpty?' she asked quietly. Michelle and Candy might not appreciate just how much that meant to her.

They drove on and on. A curving lake came up on their right; an ornamental bridge white and delicate, spanning the central narrowed section. The drive swept around it and suddenly, there was the house. The Hall wasn't huge but the details were imposing – from the chimney stacks to the tall windows, the intricate brick-work, the grand entrance portal. But what took Vita's breath away was the mantle of wisteria softening the lines and swaying just perceptibly in the early-evening breeze.

'Chinese wisteria twists anticlockwise. Japanese twists clockwise,' Oliver said as he carried on driving, past what must once have been a carriage house and stables, finally parking just beyond them. There were other cars there, visitors arriving and leaving.

'Clipboard and pen?' he asked.

'Roger,' she said.

'Another sweet?' he said. 'And don't call me Roger.'

They set off, Oliver having to practically drag her in

221

his direction when Vita wanted to veer off to the Knot Garden.

'As a nation, we're doing a great job protesting about rainforests,' he said, as they strolled away from the house, 'but we're guilty of taking our own trees for granted. Then, when they die, we feel bereft.' His voice and his words were compelling, and when she snuck a long look at him as he spoke, she experienced a surge of adrenalin as she wondered what were the chances that at some point that evening they might kiss.

She had assumed the arboretum would be some kind of organized system of planting, as if the trees would be standing formally like obedient schoolchildren lining up in the playground. But actually, it had been designed to look informal and natural. Oliver pointed out the different species, greeting many as if they were old family friends.

'Oh, look at that one!' Vita tugged at Oliver's shirtsleeve.

'*Davidia involucrata*,' he said, 'known as the handkerchief or dove tree after those exquisite, ghostly white bracts.'

'It's so –' Vita stood still. 'Not ghostly – heavenly. Ethereal.'

Oliver smiled at her as she looked up and around, the bracts fluttering silently as if made of the finest silk. 'This one was one of the first in the country – brought over from Indochina in the mid-nineteenth century.' He let her marvel for a couple of minutes, then he cupped his hand around her elbow. 'Come on – there's so much more.' He led her on, kicking himself for taking his hand from her arm so quickly, missing the chance of taking her hand in a natural way.

'I know that one!' Vita pointed to her right. 'That's a

222

cedar.' Now it was Vita leading the way. 'My dad used to tell me to close my eyes and just breathe in.'

'Do you know which type this is?'

Vita stopped, turned to Oliver and made much of putting a thinking-cap expression on her face. She looked over to the tree. It was vast, the foliage spreading out in flat plates, appearing stable enough for one to sit upon, lie down on, use to climb up and up. '*Cedus maximus*?' she tried.

Oliver laughed. 'That's *Cedrus Libani* – cedar of Lebanon. If in doubt, look at the angle of the branches and think of the first letter of the tree's name. Lebanon – they're level. Deodar – they droop. Atlas – the branches are ascending.'

They walked over to the tree. 'He's an old boy, this one – you can tell because the bark is now dark brown, rather than grey.' He looked at Vita who was doing what her father had told her, eyes closed, inhaling deeply. He looked at her for a moment longer. Pretty girl – how he wanted to kiss her. Her lips, raised a little into a gentle smile. Might she want to be kissed? Right now? A little later? It was so long since he'd had to read the signs.

Vita's eyes opened. Oliver glanced away, looked up through the boughs. 'This time of day, this time of year, I think the fragrance is like boot polish, don't you think?' he said.

Vita closed her eyes again and took a deep sniff. When she opened them, Oliver's were still closed. She snuck a long look at him. If she stood on tiptoes, she could reach his mouth, she could plant a small kiss there – something light – then skip away over to that strange tree over there. She could. She really could. But she was overwhelmed with butterflies so she shut her eyes again and tried to concentrate on boot polish. When she opened them after a few more deep breaths, he was looking directly at her

223

and she gazed back, feeling as light as the bracts on the handkerchief tree. Oh, to be kissed under those boughs, the scent of the neighbouring cedar. But no, not yet.

'Come and see the *Sequoia*,' and Oliver's hand was at her elbow again, just briefly before his fingertips were whispering down the inside of her bare arm until her hand was encircled by his. Just a few steps hand in hand until he placed the flat of her palm against a giant redwood. '*Wellingtonia*,' he said. 'Look up! *Sequoiadendron giganteum*.'

'That's putting it mildly,' Vita marvelled. 'Feels like the sky's going to fall!'

'Tallest *Sequoia* I've seen makes this look like a sapling,' he told her. 'In California.' Vita went up close to the ridged, fluted base. She loved feeling so small. Oliver picked a sprig of fallen foliage; it was so delicate compared to the immensity of the tree. He crushed it between his fingers and held them to Vita. She took his wrist in her hands and smelt.

'I know that smell!' She couldn't place it. Oliver laughed. 'It's – it's—?'

'Aniseed?'

'Yes!'

He folded Vita's hand into a fist and punched it against the bark. It was a peculiar sensation – something that surely should be hard and abrasive was so soft and giving. It was like a sponge. 'Does it hurt the tree?'

Oliver laughed. 'Genius!' he said. 'From the mouth of the girl who wants to inflict a grisly death on her pear tree!' That mouth.

She stuck her tongue out at him and pouted a little but he just kept laughing. And so did she. And then the laughter ebbed away until they stopped and just stood there, smiling at each other, slightly breathless, eyes glinting. Vita's hand was still in Oliver's and it felt as though some inner forces were at work, unfurling her fingers and interlacing them with his. Then he was slowly, intoxicatingly slowly, pulling her towards him while the butterflies swarming in her stomach helped her float there. They were sharing the same thought and it was overwhelming: I am going to be kissed. As Oliver lowered his face Vita raised hers and they fought to keep their eyes open until their lips made contact. Then they could have been anywhere in the world at any time of the day during any season of the year. They could have been on a highway or a clifftop or the middle of Marble Arch roundabout. They could have been by a redwood or a telegraph pole. For Vita, her surroundings became irrelevant. Oliver was kissing her and she felt warm, hot, shivering, alight and so overjoyed to be kissing him back. His hands were in her hair, cupping her head, his tongue tip darting along her lips. She was clutching at his back, his neck. His arms were now encircling her. He tasted wonderful – warm, fresh and oh my, how he kissed! She had no idea how long they stayed like that, but when they broke off she was surprised to see the world was exactly the same as when she'd closed her eyes and drifted away from it.

When they stopped, they gazed at each other all flushed, eyes glinting, lips parted and moist. The kiss had been a perfect profound silent conversation – but what on earth were they meant to say now? Vita didn't think, actually, she had to say a thing. She was soaring, she felt overjoyed. It was the right kiss at the right time with the right person in a magical place. She laughed, she couldn't help it, she laughed and she laughed and then she came close to Oliver and put her arms around him and held him there saying, Oh blimey! Oh blimey!

His nose buried in her neck, Oliver simply felt good.

Thank you, he said silently over and again though he had absolutely no idea to whom his gratitude was directed. He held her close. She smelt divine, better than the *Sequoia*, better than any cedar. He kissed the top of her head and lifted her chin so he could look at her. She was beaming and he grinned back.

'The yew?' he said, rubbing his nose against hers.

'The *you*,' she said, lifting her face to kiss him again.

Hand in hand they walked; the trees now their silent and supportive audience as much as the focus of their attention. The yew was some way off, not part of the arboretum, predating all the Earls of Seddon and any mark of man on the land.

'Yews, like oaks, are considered ancient at five hundred years old. But they say an oak grows for three hundred years, lives for three hundred, then takes three hundred more to die – whereas yews count their age in millennia.'

Vita liked it now she could hang on his arm and his every word.

'The Fortingall Yew, near Aberfeldy, at five thousand years old is possibly the oldest living thing in Europe,' he said. Then he stopped. 'Am I boring you? I am a bit of a tree geek.'

'Not at all,' she assured him. 'I'm loving it! I could just about tell my horse chestnut from my oak,' she said. 'If you're a tree geek, I'm a tree dunce.'

'I would say the Wynfordbury Yew is a baby in comparison. Around fifteen hundred years, perhaps.' They'd arrived.

'That's a *tree*?' It didn't look like a tree at all. There was barely any trunk on display. 'It looks like a copse!' It looked a right old mess.

But it was a tree; its great boughs bending and stretching,

heavy with the weight of having lived so long. They formed a tunnel of sorts into which Oliver and Vita ducked and stooped and shuffled. The tunnel gave way into a chamber almost twenty feet high. Vita had no words.

'Doesn't cease to amaze me,' said Oliver, 'and I've seen it dozens of times. Most trees look older than they are – but yews are even older than they look.'

'What should I write down? On my clipboard?'

Oliver laughed and tucked a lock of hair behind her ear. 'The clipboard was an ice-breaker. I know this tree off by heart.'

'Was this some kind of test?'

Oliver laughed again. There'd been more laughter in the last hour than in the last month. God, that felt good. 'I had a hunch you'd react the way you have. However, if you'd've said, very nice, Mr B, but where's the gift shop – I'd've made you write pages and pages.' She thwacked his thigh with the clipboard and he jostled her for it and though she tried to prevent him, she didn't try very hard because she knew that he'd pull her to him and press his mouth against hers again. And so, under the boughs, in the secret space the yew provided, they kissed and kissed and kissed.

'You should have brought a nice picnic rug,' she murmured. 'I wouldn't mind the prickly bits – I'm not in my Sunday best.'

They heard voices. Oliver winked at her. 'We're not the only ones here, missy.' Two small children came scampering into the yew's den. Oliver asked them to guess how old the tree was. They said a million-trillion-gazillion years old, which spoiled his point but was funny in itself.

Back out in the open, Oliver looked thoughtfully ahead, towards the horizon, but then started to head back.

'Where are they going?' Vita watched a young couple

heading away from them, up the swathe of green to a distant tree where Oliver had been looking.

'Oh,' said Oliver as if it was of no interest, 'just having a mooch, I suppose. It's a lovely evening, after all.' He made to walk off but Vita stood stock-still, frowning a little. Her eyes were fixed on another visitor who had just passed that couple and was now walking towards them.

Her?

Here?

What was *she* doing *here*?

'That's my old lady,' Vita said in disbelief.

Oliver looked. 'Your what?'

'I mean – she comes into my shop.' Vita realized she hadn't seen her since the day she'd told her to give up the goods and go. 'I let her steal stuff.'

'You *what*?'

'Can I have a moment? She's shy – she's odd. But I'd like to speak to her.'

As Oliver watched Vita making her way towards the elderly woman he thought, I like this girl, I really like her. He thought, I feel good. And he thought, I feel horny too. He thought about the fact that Jonty was at Mark's tonight. And then he thought, No – not on a first date. He felt sure that chances were there would be more dates to come and the concept was heartening and exciting for him.

'Hello, lassie.' The woman's reaction was little different than if they'd passed in the street.

Vita, though, was thoroughly disconcerted.

'It's *you*. You're here!'

'I am. Oh, indeed I am.'

'I'm sorry,' Vita put her hand out to the woman's arm, 'I'm sorry.'

'You're sorry?'

228

'I mean, about the other week. About asking you to leave my shop. To put back what you'd – borrowed.'

'I wasn't borrowing it, dear,' the lady said straight, 'I was having it. Such pretty things. So many pretty pretty things. I look after them, you know? I take great care. Extra special care.'

'I'd had a bad day,' Vita wondered why she felt compelled to justify, to apologize, 'and the bird – it's expensive.'

'I understand. I don't read the prices. I am drawn to the prettiness of a thing, not the value.'

'But will you come back? Come back to the shop?'

'I will. Thank you for asking.'

Then Vita stopped and gave herself a little shake as if to jolt herself back to the incongruity of it all.

'Why are you *here*? What a coincidence!'

'I always come,' the woman said, 'each and every year. I always come – just to check.'

'Just to check – what?'

'To check that I – we – are still here.'

Vita had no idea whether she was talking metaphors or madness but Oliver was now sauntering over to her side.

'This is Oliver,' Vita introduced him.

The lady tipped her head. 'Very good.' She looked at Vita levelly. 'I didn't like the other one. *At all.*'

Oliver accepted the compliment graciously.

'Are you here for the tree?' She posed the question to them both.

'Yes,' said Vita, looking over her shoulder back at the mighty yew. 'It's fifteen hundred years old, it's the Wynfordbury Yew. It's a national monument.'

Again, the woman tipped her head to one side and regarded Vita quizzically. 'Not the yew!' She looked to

229

the horizon but Vita could see no other people, just a solitary tree.

'Anyway, we should go,' Oliver was saying while the old lady was muttering on about someone called Tristan.

'Without paying a visit?' the woman said again, looking from Vita to Oliver. She shrugged, took her leave and walked away from them.

'I wonder who Tristan is?' said Vita but Oliver had put his arm around her waist and she was happy for him to lead her slowly back in the direction of the car. 'It's odd – to see her here. I've only ever seen her in the shop. I wouldn't have said trees were her thing.'

'And I reckon you've seen so many trees tonight – soon you won't be able to see the wood for them.'

'I don't mind,' Vita said brightly. She would have been happy to go back inside the yew, or within the magical space of the arboretum where kissing came so naturally.

'Another time, hey?' he said.

Another time – so much more to come. Vita experienced a gentle whoosh of anticipation. It was only just becoming true evening. What would they do now? Who was to suggest what to do next, where to go? She didn't want the date to be over.

'Is there somewhere we can get a cup of tea?'

'Not here,' said Oliver. 'This really is a private estate save for these few open evenings. Vita looked disappointed. 'Sometimes there's an ice-cream van parked outside the gates,' he said.

'A Mr Whippy?'

'With a chocolate flake in it.'

Oliver led the way back to the car and then drove through the grounds and away from Wynfordbury Hall in search of ice cream.

Mr Whippy

Vita insisted on the ice creams being her treat. Her purse was full of change and Oliver liked the way she used up as many coins as possible. DeeDee used to do that. Oliver could never be bothered – easier just to pull out a note and then empty his pockets into the change bowl at home. They strolled along the roadside, keeping close to the great wall of Wynfordbury Hall. As they walked and licked, Vita told him all about the old woman, how she let her steal goods and about how, the other week, she'd let rip.

'When I was at school,' Vita told him, stopping, 'I stole for a lady just like her.'

'How very Dickensian that sounds.'

'I was expelled because of it.'

This he hadn't expected.

'I was sixteen.'

Pretty much Jonty's age.

'I had a weekend job at the supermarket. They weren't hyper-huge supermarkets back then – it was a local one, an independent one. One day I saw an old lady nick some biscuits. She saw that I saw. Her face – her eyes. She just wanted the biscuits. I didn't tell on her. And then, week after week, whenever she came in, I sort of shielded her. Of course, we didn't have CCTV so I was free to mooch around the aisles with her – a little ahead, a little behind. She didn't take much – usually sweet stuff. A malt loaf. Biscuits. A packet of fondant fancies. Just one item per visit. Then I was promoted to the tills. And she'd always choose my line. And I'd slip things from the conveyor belt into her bag without ringing them through. But you don't need Big Brother watching you – you get caught anyway. Other members of staff had noticed – and they told on me. And they watched and waited and logged it all down and eventually – they swooped.'

'It's heart-rendingly Robin Hood, though,' Oliver said kindly.

Vita shrugged. 'I never saw her again.'

'Did they cart her off?'

'They phoned – for *police cars*,' Vita said, forlorn.

'And do you have a criminal record?' Oliver asked, deadpan, and Vita looked at him and felt OK – about what she'd done, about telling him about what she'd done. About letting this other elderly lady purloin goods from the shop, even if it was her own shop and their turnover really couldn't justify altruism on such a regular basis. Criminal record? Funny man.

'And do you have fur-lined handcuffs?' she batted back.

Oliver looked at her as if momentarily unsure whether he'd heard correctly. Look at this girl, giggling and reddening! She's funny, she's – different. Really just refreshingly *different*. And she's finished her ice cream already, despite doing all the talking.

Oliver broke off the bottom of his cornet and used it to scoop up a blob of ice cream. He handed it to Vita. He might as well have presented her with a dozen long-stemmed roses.

'Cheers!' she said, knocking the miniature cone against his.

'Cheers,' he said.

Vita said to herself, Go on! Ask him for a drink after this! But she found herself overcome by sudden timidity and started asking him banal questions about his own schooldays instead. It was lovely, though, hearing details to flesh out the person at her side. She asked him about what training as a tree surgeon had entailed and soon enough she was riveted about the rungs and hierarchy of qualifications. She couldn't wait to tell Michelle that, actually, he was an arboricultural consultant.

'Did you study?' he asked her.

She nodded. 'History of art.'

'And the appreciation of fine things has assisted you in your chosen career?' he mused. 'Surrounding yourself on a daily basis with what we chaps like to call "tutt"?' He waited for that to sink in and loved it that she thwacked his arm and said, Oi, you!

They walked on. 'My late wife loved your shop,' he said and Vita wondered about the best way to reply.

'Oliver,' she said and she stopped. 'DeeDee – your wife.' She paused. Wasn't this slightly crazy – she'd felt too shy to ask him for a drink and yet wasn't reticent about enquiring about his late wife?

'Yes?'

'I just don't know anyone of my generation – who's lost someone of my generation.'

Oliver shrugged and nodded. 'That's the way it should be.'

There was a tumbledown section of wall and Vita headed over to it and sat. 'I'm sorry. For – your loss.' Her words felt awkward and clumsy to her, but there was a sweetness to the sound of them for Oliver.

'Thank you,' he said. His voice was normal, conversational, and it put Vita at her ease. 'That's my situation. My wife died. In a car crash. She was a pedestrian. I was at work. Jonty was at school.' He looked at Vita who was very pensive. 'Do you need to know if I'm OK about seeing other people?'

Yes, that was precisely what Vita wanted to know but she felt embarrassed to admit it. Was it voyeuristic in some way?

'It took a long time. You can't rush it. It's a process – well, it has been for me. It has to take the time it takes. But now – yes – I reckon I'm ready.'

Vita nodded. She felt shy again. The ice cream had gone. It was easier to talk and lick than just talk and listen.

'I feel good about – this – though.' He nudged her.

She nudged him back. 'Me too.'

'Don't think I'll chop down your tree or even give you a discount on the pruning in the autumn,' he said, nudging her again.

Vita calculated the tone perfectly. She grinned, stood up, looked at him with mock distaste. 'Well, that's me gone, then.'

He laughed, reached for her, pulled her onto his knee and swiftly they were kissing again. His hands running up her bare arms which, combined with the evening's breeze, scattered goosebumps over her skin. In a swift movement, he'd cupped her breasts fleetingly but the desire it sparked in her was profound and now, thoroughly light-headed between her legs, she kissed him ravenously.

'We are going to have to make a move,' he said. 'This wall wasn't made for ravishing – and my backside's numb.'

She didn't want the date to be over. She was high – on ice cream and information and lips. She wanted to eat and chat and laugh and kiss and plan another date soon. 'Shall we go and have a pizza or something?' There!

'Good idea,' said Oliver. 'I know a great place.'

'I do too.'

'Cipollini's?'

'I'm so glad you said that,' said Vita, 'because the date would have been over if you'd said Pizza Hut.'

'Come on then,' said Oliver and Vita slipped her hand into his and responded in kind when he gave hers a little squeeze.

'Your boy?' she asked, buckling her seatbelt.

'Jonty?'

'Yes – Jonty. How is he?'

'He's an amazing kid,' Oliver said.

'Will he mind you – dating?'

'He won't mind.' Oliver paused. Then he laughed. 'He'll think it's gross, probably.'

'I was fourteen when my dad died,' Vita said.

'I remember you telling me – when I was in your kitchen.' Oliver paused. 'Do you miss him still?'

'Often.'

'But do you remember him? Truly *remember* him?' He looked at her, searchingly.

Vita put her hand on Oliver's arm. 'I do – I really do.'

Off they drove. Oliver realized that releasing information had freed up space for his own curiosity. This lovely girl beside him – what had she been through? His significant other was dead – Vita's was down the road.

'Your ex?' he said, whilst he indicated right and turned, his tone casual. 'This Tim bloke?'

Vita thought, Where do I begin? Then she thought, How much detail ought I to impart? And she wondered, Will what I tell him make a difference – will he think I'm

235

a screwed-up madwoman on the rebound? And then she thought, Take his lead, be honest, let him know.

'I'm not prying, am I?' he said. 'I just gather that you had a tough old time.'

Vita nodded. 'Tim's charismatic – one of those people you're never quite sure where you stand with, so you work very hard to win their attention, doubly so to inspire their love.'

'One has to work at relationships,' Oliver said, 'but they shouldn't be hard work.'

Vita nodded again. 'He does flings and excitement very well,' she said. She paused. 'We were together six years. He cheated early on – I gave him another chance. A one-night stand – a one-off, he promised. Then there was another, but I found that I had another chance to give. However, last year, I found out he was seeing someone else. It was horrible.'

'Not nice.'

'No. Not nice at all. It was all the more horrible because it came at a time in my life when my thoughts should have been about marriage and babies – not splitting up and dismantling what I'd built. All the hopes – the chances I'd taken, the chances I'd given. For a time, I felt I'd failed at what for me is the most important thing to get right in life.'

'It wasn't your fault.'

'I know. I know that now. It was tough – I had a rubbish time of it, really.

'And now?'

'It's taken a while – it's taken a while even to like Pear Tree Cottage, my very own place, for goodness' sake.'

'And now – with Tim?'

'It's awkward.' Should she tell him about Suzie? About Suzie then and Suzie now? No. Suzie was part of Vita's

236

past. 'He can be – unpleasant. But we have the business together, out of necessity. I can't afford to buy him out.'

'Well, he's a fool to have let you go,' said Oliver with a kind lightness now. He was pulling up near to Cipollini's. 'But his fuck-up is my gain. So I must shake his hand and thank him.' It made Vita giggle. She could imagine Oliver doing something like that, wryly but with good grace.

'Am I your rebound then, missy?' he asked her casually as they crossed the road.

Vita looked horrified. And then she reddened. 'Actually, I've had one of those.'

Oliver laughed. 'Tart. Come on, I'll buy you a pizza.'

Post-Mortem

'Oh Michelle!' And Vita said her friend's name over and over again. And Michelle repeated, What! What! at the other end of the phone line. The excitement in Vita's voice was contagious. 'I *really* like him.'

'Yes, yes – but you're skipping the details. So, you left the posh park place, had a licky ice cream, went for a pizza and then *what*?'

'We came back here – to mine.'

'And?'

'I made coffee and we had a chat – the heart-to-heart we'd had earlier had formed this really lovely surface, secure but soft, on which we could just natter. I can't tell you how exciting it is, learning about someone you know you click with – hearing about their lives, discovering all the funny things that make them tick. The things you share.'

'Yes, yes, yes,' said Michelle, 'enough of the questionnaire information. *And then what*?'

'What?'

'Action – not words.'

'Well, we did some more kissing.'

'And then *what*?'

'And then he went.'

'He *went*? What about coming?'

'Michelle!'

'Did you not jump his bones?'

'It's not like that! I don't want it to be like that. Not yesterday.'

'What do you mean? After all that talk of handcuffs and heart-to-hearts and all that snogging? You can't just hug trees and talk about wasps.'

'I can't wait to sleep with him. But I am going to wait – because we will. I know we will. And that thought is sexier than if we'd got deep down and dirty last night.'

'Blimey.'

'I know.'

'Well – what's next?'

'Sunday. We're seeing each other tomorrow. He said he'd pick me up at midday.'

'And?'

'Today I've booked in for a wax and polish.'

'You make yourself sound like a car.'

'Well, hopefully by tomorrow I'll be a bit of an old banger.'

'That's better, filthy cow – I do love you.'

'A wax. A pedicure.'

'I got that, dear. I *twigged*.'

'Very drole, Mrs Sherlock. You'll like him, Michelle. He's strong, he's upright.'

'Enough of the tree analogies. Let's just hope he has a great big trunk of a schlong too.'

'Michelle – you're incorrigible.'

'I'll let you go. Have you phoned Candy?'

'I'm just about to.'

* * *

239

'Candy?'

'Wait! Wait! Hang on. OK – cup of tea to hand. Sitting down in favourite chair. Plonked baby on husband. Wait – OK! I'm all ears. Did he make the earth move?'

'He made the leaves on the trees whisper and glint.'

'Good God, woman – what did you *do*? Does he live in a tree house too?'

'I'm talking metaphorically. But he did take me into this yew tunnel.'

'Is that a metaphor?'

'He kissed me under a redwood tree – a *Sequoia* something-or-other. With the scent of cedar and the flutter of the handkerchief tree in the background.'

'OK, OK – enough of the Thomas Hardy bollocks. What about *his* trunk?'

'Honestly – you and Michelle – you're dreadful.'

'Come on! We're living vicariously through you. We need details – the more gory, the more squelchy, the better.'

'No gore or squelch last night – but my God, he can kiss.'

'Tell me you went beyond First Base? You're both – you're both *grown-ups*, for God's sake.'

'Taking it slowly, Candy. The pace feels right.'

'Will I like him, Vita? If he doesn't pass muster with me and Michelle – he's out. You know that, right?'

'You'll love him. I promise.'

* * *

'Mum?'

'Darling.'

'How are you?'

'Oh, I'm very well. I had a lovely few days with Lorna – Northumberland is very beautiful if somewhat remote.'

240

'Was the hotel nice?'

'It was luxurious, darling. And I brought you back some of the toiletries.'

'Thank you.'

'And how have you been?'

'I've been fine.'

'And work?'

'It's fine.'

'And home – the cockatiels, the hornets?'

'They're fine.'

'They're *fine*?'

'They're – being looked after.'

'Oh?'

'The tree man. The tree surgeon. The arboricultural consultant.'

'The scoundrel who dobbed you in to the council?'

'He was just doing his job. And he's not a scoundrel.'

'Vita?'

'Mum?'

'Everything OK? You sound . . . *different*.'

'Mum – he took me out. We went out on a date. For a walk, and he talked to me about trees and life and love and he had proper travel sweets in his car. He made me giggle, Mum, really had me giggling. My stomach muscles can feel it today – they hadn't been used like that in a long while.'

'Bless you, darling. Why do I sense there's a "but" coming?'

'He's a widower.'

'Gosh, is he terribly old?'

'How old were you when Dad died?'

'I was forty-five – you know I was. Because you were fourteen.'

'Well, Oliver's forty-six. It's just – I want to ask you – I want to know. I mean – I am nervous. I am nervous

241

about my own heart – after Tim. And Oliver's heart – after DeeDee.'

'Darling, I would say that, for what it's worth, the heart is a very big strong muscle and if you've treated it well – and I don't mean by holding off the booze and cigs, I mean by nurturing its other more spiritual purpose – it will in turn look after you. I know you – and I would say, Don't you worry about your heart. I would say, Use your *head*. Think about things – think about how you feel and if your head tells you this feels right and you feel happy, then your heart will accompany you.'

'But while I now know I was dealt a bad card – in Tim – Oliver had the best wife. They were happily married.'

'Then she looked after his heart well. People who've loved well – and lost love, through whatever misfortune – tend to be those who go on to make other very good relationships.'

'But Mum – you? After Dad – there hasn't been anyone. And your marriage was great.'

'I practise what I preach, Vita. My heart's in good nick – thanks to your father. And I *have* met men. But my head told me not to go climbing trees with any of those I've met. Shall we have Sunday lunch together? We could go out – my treat.'

'Can we make it next Sunday? It's just Oliver's picking me up at midday tomorrow.'

'Then you can tell me all about it next week. Or the parts that won't make me blush.'

*   *   *

'Candy?'

'Michelle! Have you spoken to Vita?'

'Yes – we had a long chat.'

'Me too. So – what do we think?'

'It's a tricky one, isn't it. I'm thrilled for her, excited for her – who wouldn't want a gorgeous burly bloke with fantastic forearms and a natural tan. But – and there's a great big *but*.'

'But he has a Dead Wife.'

'And there's a teenage son too.'

'And that's a complicated enough age with or without dead mothers and new girlfriends.'

'I don't want to burst her bubble – but are widowers prone to shagging around on the rebound? Or are they just needy for someone to look after them? I don't know – we have no experience of this in our circle. It's a terrible thing, poor man. But Vita's my first concern and she's done so well so far – a shag she can laugh about, time on her own which no longer terrifies her, a cool head and padlocked heart when it comes to Shit for Brains. Now she just deserves something lovely and someone – good.'

'Do you know something, Michelle, for once I don't think this is about karma – I think it's about timing. Timing is everything – it's about time Vita met someone nice. But you're right – how do we know if it's the right time for this Oliver to meet someone as nice as Vita?'

Sunday

'Do you have a spare towel? You really should take a spare towel in a—'

'—in a plastic bag all knotted up. Dad – yes, I have one.'

'And batteries – spare batteries, for the torch.'

'Dad!' Jonty gave his father an exasperated pat on the shoulder. 'Chillax.' He knew how his dad detested the word.

'What about your mobile – is it charged?'

'Mobi – check. Towels – check. Torch and batteries – check. Dog tag with all my vitals on it – oops, don't have one of them.' Oliver raised an eyebrow. 'Dad – Ed's parents are staying at the hotel which owns the campsite.'

'And they'll tuck you up at night and read you a bedtime story?' Oliver knew he had to lighten up. But this was Jonty's first unsupervised camping trip. *That's what summers are for*, he kept telling himself. *And I camped out on my own, a hell of a lot younger than Jont. And I've spoken to Ed's parents. And actually, I think it's a brilliant idea.* 'I just want to be sure you'll – have a great time.'

'We're going to have bangers on the fire. And marshmallows. And hot chocolate. And Tom's bringing camouflage facepaint so we can play daft buggers in the woods pretending we're in a Vietnam movie.'

Oliver laughed. 'Watch it, kiddo – sounds such fun I may turn up and join you.'

His son tipped his head to one side and Oliver knew that actually, Jonty would be OK with it if he did. 'Back Monday by supper, then? Ed's parents can drop me off. Come to work with you on Tuesday this week too?'

'Sounds good to me. Oh – remember to brush your teeth. And try and wash.'

'Dad – there's a shower block.'

'In my day, I had only a freezing cold brook.'

Jonty grinned.

'But you know that already,' Oliver said. Jonty shrugged. He didn't mind his dad telling him his stories over and again. It was cool to have a dad who'd learned to skin rabbits when he was a teen, who knew how to make a fire, how to sterilize water, which mushrooms weren't poisonous.

'What are you going to do, then, the rest of this weekend?' Jonty asked.

'Oh,' Oliver said nonchalantly, 'nothing much.'

Jonty looked at him. 'Why don't you see if the Pear Tree Woman is around?' He knew her name was Vita. He didn't feel he could be so familiar just yet.

Oliver thought about it quickly. 'Actually – yes. I have already.'

'Cool,' said Jonty, not really wanting to know the details. It was enough. She was nice. He loved his dad. He didn't want to think of his dad rattling around the house on his own eating crap takeaways while he was toasting bangers on a campfire having a brilliant time. Actually, he didn't want to think of his dad with another woman – not because of his mum. But because the thought of it was a bit – well, you know, bizarre.

'Come on, kid, they'll be here any minute. Just double-check your backpack, would you. Just humour your old man.'

That evening, Oliver's mobile went. His first thought was Jonty. But it wasn't Jonty. It was Vita. And Oliver thought, Please don't cancel tomorrow. But she wasn't phoning to cancel tomorrow. She was just phoning to say hullo, it seemed. To say yes, she had a picnic rug but had he heard the weather forecast – there could be summer storms.

'Does that mean you'll be bringing *that* cagoule?'

She laughed. 'It's multi-purpose. It's a tent, it's wasp resistant, it's waterproof.'

'What are you doing? Just now?' He wanted to be able to envisage her.

'I'm just at home.'

'Where are you, at your home? Are you in the kitchen?'

'No, in my front room. I was going to watch TV but there's nothing on.'

'Have you eaten?'

'I'm going to have a baked potato. Have you eaten?'

'A microwaved ready meal.'

'That's dreadful.'

'I know. But Jonty's gone camping – there seemed no point cooking for one.'

'Have you heard from him?'

'A text.'

'Does the house seem . . .' She paused. 'Are you all right?'

Oliver smiled at the phone. 'I'm very all right, missy,' he said. 'How are you?'

'I'm fine, thank you.' She paused again. 'I had a lovely evening yesterday. I've been looking at trees today – whenever I pass one, I have a long look. I probably can't tell my elm from my ash – but none of the trees seemed *plane*. Ha ha.'

'Plenty of *Platanus*, I assure you – *hispanica, acerifolia, orientalis*.' Oliver laughed. 'Does this mean I ought to be visiting all the gift shops in the locale, and wow you with my knowledge of trinkets and tutt? Ought I to know my jasmine candles from my tuberose?'

Vita laughed back. 'You're funny.'

'So are you,' Oliver said. 'You'll like tomorrow.'

'I'm going to have an early night – because I'm looking forward it. Rain or shine.'

'Goodnight, Vita.'

'Night Oliver.'

'Ha! You silly weatherman you! You're so wrong! It's a beautiful day!' Vita was darting around the house talking to herself, making the bed, hanging out washing, eating a proper breakfast in case Oliver was planning a late lunch, washing her hair, dumping her cagoule back in the cupboard, hoovering – because for the first time she hadn't done so on Thursday. She liked her house very much today. When she woke up, the light had been beautiful and she'd felt content to just lie there, listening to the soft silence, liking the way she had her bedroom now. It was feeling homely, it really was. She'd even unpacked the box of CDs and found space for them in the living room.

Oliver could hear the hoover as he made his way to Vita's door. He thought back to when she'd been hoovering that evening he'd summoned the courage to return the cagoule. When she'd called him Mr B for the first time.

247

How odd that it should seem so long ago. Stop thinking! He rang the bell, squinting up at the cloudless sky, wondering whether he should sluice out the wasp traps before they went.

'You're early!'

'Your watch is slow, missy.'

'You're right!'

'I'm going to do your wasp traps for you, before we go. Would you like to watch and learn?'

'No, thank you.'

'Well, you can mix up the jam and beer then.'

'Roger.'

'Will you stop calling me Roger.'

'Can I call you Ollie?'

'Not if you expect me to answer.'

He pulled faces for her as she watched from the kitchen window. Inspecting the traps as if he was a mime artist handling Ming vases or grenades. It was funny. She watched him as he moved more fallen pears to the back of the garden and then he came right up to the window, goading her with a wasp trap full of its putrid gunk while she made him laugh with her extravagant fake vomiting. She thought to herself, I must change my top. This is my hoovering top. My mint-coloured halterneck is laid out on the bed.

Oliver came into the kitchen with the cleaned wasp traps.

'I've washed everything away,' he said. 'They're certainly working – but there's still a lot in the land of the living.'

'Here.' She showed him the jug in which she'd mixed the jam and beer.

He came to inspect, took the spoon from Vita and dipped it in, assessing the consistency.

'Too gloopy. You need to add a little more beer.'

She did so. He tested it.

'Too runny – add more jam.'

She sighed theatrically and, as she was dolloping in more jam, he came up behind her, resting his hands lightly on her hips, brushing his lips against the nape of her neck. She thought, Shit, I still have my hair in a pony-tail, I planned to wear it loose. She thought, Add more jam. She thought, I must change my top. She thought, Actually, I needn't think at all.

'Too gloopy again,' Oliver said, Vita against his chest and between his arms as he dipped his spoon into the jug. 'Do it again, missy.'

Vita was still holding the jammy teaspoon. Slowly, she dipped it into the jam jar. She tried to ignore him running his fingertips up her bare arms. She tried to ignore the T-shirt she didn't want to be wearing. And her hair in a messy pony-tail.

'Beer, woman – the wasps need more beer.'

The spoon was loaded with glistening, deep red jam. What else was she meant to do? She turned in a flash and flicked it straight at him. It landed in a splat on Oliver's cheek, some of it dripping off onto his shoulder. He looked at her in disbelief, not remotely enraged, just stunned. Her defiant grin. She was sparkling. He experienced a surge, as if joy was physically lifting him.

'Miss Whitbury,' he asked, deadly serious, 'did you just flick me with jam?'

'That'll teach you not to be so finicky about your effing wasp potion.'

Effing. Who the fuck says *effing*. This Vita, that's who. This Vita, whose waist his hands still encircle, whose eyes are holding his, whose hand is reaching up to his face, whose fingers are lightly wiping at the jam. This Vita, who's stupidly scared of wasps and says *effing* and *flipping*. She's putting her sticky fingers to her lips, into her mouth and she's sucking them, staring at him, with a grin that is as cheeky as it is warm. Her fingers are at his face again, stroking the jam off his skin. Now she's giving her fingers to his lips. It's raspberry. So sweet, really delicious. Her fingers touching and pressing his mouth. He holds her wrist and licks her fingers, sucking each in turn to the knuckle. It's no longer the jam he's sucking. This isn't about the effing jam.

She's pressed herself against him, standing on tiptoes, reaching her lips to his cheek, kissing away the last traces of jam, bringing her mouth to his. And it's still raspberry, just as sweet – but it really isn't about the jam. It's about her. It's the taste of her.

In the kitchen, Vita is standing with her back to the window, her body held tight up against Oliver, kissing and being kissed. The pony-tail, the T-shirt. Nothing matters. What time is it? How long have they been kissing? Who knows. His hands at her waist, pulling her in close, the fabric of her top riding up, his touch becoming tantalizing light as, for the first time, he makes contact with her bare skin. Her waist, her back. A bra strap. Back down her back to slip beneath the waistband of her cargo pants, his fingertips alighting on the elastic of her knickers. His hand travels back up; up and down the side of her body, the beautiful undulation of her waist, around to the front, up her stomach, to quickly, deftly, cup her breast. There's a bra in the way. Suddenly, there's way too much clothing in the way. He stops kissing her, keeps his face very close.

'Can I take you to bed?'

She wants to say, I want you so much you can have

me right here on the kitchen floor, splashes of beer, splatters of jam, I don't care. But actually, all she can do is nod. She takes his hand and leads him upstairs. Her curtains are open but the pear tree is their privacy screen. He pushes some green vest thing off the bed and turns to Vita and undresses her, peeling away clothes slowly, as if great care must be taken, as if there's something supremely delicate beneath. When she's naked, he takes her hand and raises her arm and twirls her slowly under his arm, like a ballerina on a jewellery box.

'God, you are gorgeous.'

She looks at him. 'And you still have all your clothes on, matey.'

Oliver strips away his clothing and Vita drinks in the sight of his broad shoulders, the smatter of chest hair inching down his belly, his delineated biceps, strong forearms. He's masculine, more than any other man she's been with. Not intimidatingly so; not the gym-induced beefiness, as was Tim's wont, not the litheness of Rick's young buck physique. Oliver is archetypally manly. It will sound so daft when she describes him thus to Michelle, to Candy. But at the moment the only thing in her mind is the man she sees before her; the man gathering her to him, the man whose hands are sweeping up and over her body, the man she's pulling down onto her bed. His hands are good, really good – and his kissing is incomparable. Her body is burning, she is overcome with a hunger for him, actually she's ravenous. They romp and roll around her bed; tenderness blending seamlessly with lust. He's so hard he almost doesn't want her to touch him in case he explodes. But her fingers are tracing up and down the length of his cock, encircling it, caressing. He props himself up, his arms either side of her and takes a look at her.

251

When did he last keep his eyes open during sex?

When he last made love.

And that was a long time ago.

Vita is gazing up at him, her lips parted and glistening. She's moving her legs so he's in between them. She smiles at him, a little shyly. Then she nods and her smile widens. Her hands in his hair, her eyes closed, her heart as open as her legs as she welcomes him in. He pushes up inside her, sinking his body down on top of hers, groaning with pleasure, with relief, with joy. He feels – everything. They don't take long to come and they come together when they do.

As Oliver lies there in post-coital reverie, Vita resting in the crook of his arm, he muses how the phrase that has always come to mind, post-orgasm, since DeeDee, was *What the hell was that all about*. But in a sweet bedroom with all the personal details, rather than some innocuous hotel, he thinks to himself, This is about a hell of a lot. Gone is the instinct to get the hell out of there. He has no compulsion to leave; quite the opposite. He's glad that she's in his arms, their legs still entwined. He likes feeling her breath warm, then cool, on his skin.

Since DeeDee, he'd always bolted from the realness of the person from the website who he'd just fucked under a fake name. He'd feel an aching hollowness after coming, a need to be on his own. Guilt. He'd feel guilt. But today, he's happy to cuddle up with the woman he's just made love with. There's no emptiness. Even his balls feel full, as though he'd love to do it all again.

Soon, Vita will wake from her doze and Oliver will be able to look into her eyes again. And chat. And plan the day. And laugh, and feel happy. And feel horny again, hungry for her. He realizes he'd be quite content spending the entire day right here in her bed just eating jam. He looks at her. Vita. That's who you are. And he thinks to himself, This is a turning point in my life.

Dermott Hogan

The elderly thief returned to That Shop the next day. She chose her time carefully. It wouldn't have done to have come in during a quiet period. The young woman would have felt obliged to chat about trees and coincidences. There couldn't be burgeoning familiarity; formal introductions were to be avoided; the customary exchanging of pleasantries would suffice. The woman knew that the girl's name was Vita – she'd heard the other man, the awful one, use it. He'd used it that day last year when he'd caught her taking a pretty thing. Vita! he'd said, I've got her! Get the door! Right, he'd said, you're coming with me – or would you rather I got the police. Such ugly words, *get* and *got*. So unnecessary. It wasn't about grammar, it was about talking *nicely*. People weren't taught so, nowadays. The man the young woman had been with on Friday evening – he was a good one. She could tell. The eyes. And she'd seen him before, right there at Wynfordbury Hall.

Tea-time, school's-out time – that was when she returned to That Shop. And though Vita felt relieved – almost joyous – when she showed up at the busiest time, she instinctively felt it would be wrong to greet her over and above the way she usually did. What she really wanted was for everything to be as it had been. And so, Vita simply said, Hullo, can I help you today? though she'd already noted that a biro in the shape of a miniature ice-cream cone was safely in the woman's bag.

Then the shop phone went anyway and the lady could slope away without the need for polite come-again-soons.

'That Shop? Hullo? Hullo?'

'Is that Vita?'

'Yes? Can I help you? Hullo?'

It had been a woman, but the line appeared to have gone dead.

'Yes. I mean, I don't know.' She was back.

'Who is this?' asked Vita. 'Hullo?'

'This is Suzie.'

Vita glanced to the window, as if she might see her standing there again. But only two small faces, squashing up pig-like against the pane, stared back while their mothers chatted.

'Vita?'

'Yes. This is Vita. What is it that you want?'

'I – I –' The voice cracked.

Is she crying?

'Hullo? Are you OK?'

'No. I don't know. I don't even know why I'm phoning you.'

'Is everything OK? Is Tim all right?' Vita suddenly thought how she hadn't heard from him at all, let alone seen him since that time in his car.

'I just – I just. I'm sorry.' In the background, Vita could hear Suzie trying to control her sobbing. 'I wanted to know if it would be OK if I met you somewhere. I just wanted to ask you – if we could talk.'

In the early weeks following her break-up with Tim, Vita used to pray for such an opportunity. That's why she'd honed those soliloquies, practised until word perfect in front of the mirror or out into the darkness of sleepless hours. There had been an acute contradiction between wanting to let this girl know that she was nothing and that Vita was everything to Tim – to telling this girl all the heinous details about him. Either way, back then, Vita's driving force was to see her off and keep the road clear of obstacles for Tim to return to her, contrite, restored and on bended knee. Back then, though she knew she'd done the right thing by telling him to go – oh, how she hoped it might instigate his epiphany, to serve as the short sharp shock to inspire him to change his ways and return to her. Today, when the call had ended, Vita had dialled for the caller's number. A load of digits were repeated back at her. Suzie hadn't withheld her number. She wasn't hiding today. Something significant had changed.

At Starbucks, faffing with the froth of a cappuccino, Vita waited for Suzie. All the old soliloquies were in a jumble. Though intensely curious and very uneasy, Vita realized that she needed to listen before she could talk. And then, hopefully, she'd know what to say.

Here she is.

Vita can't help but feel just slightly deflated by her slim shapely legs in black leggings, the handkerchief vest-top revealing toned tanned arms. Vita makes a sizeable withdrawal from her Bank of Karma account when she notes, with some satisfaction, hair that's been bleached

256

too often, an ungainly nose and not very good skin. But she also sees anxious eyes brimming with distress and a hollowness to her posture which Vita recognizes at once. It's a virus she once had. It's doing the rounds.

'Vita?' Suzie has bought herself a bottle of water.

'Did you want a coffee?' Vita asks as Suzie sits down. She shakes her head and busies herself opening the sports cap and taking urgent sips.

'Does Tim know you're here?'

Again, Suzie shakes her head.

'OK.' Vita watches how Suzie's eyes flit everywhere, anywhere, but to Vita.

'Are you OK?'

She shrugs. Sips. Flits.

'How can I help?'

Vita's voice is soft, kind. She's surprised herself in that she feels no satisfaction at this girl's obvious distress. She's partly curious – who wouldn't be – but her overriding feeling is surprising; it's empathy. She's been there, she's done it, she threw the T-shirt away.

'What's he done?' Vita asks.

Now Suzie looks up and as she checks Vita's gaze for any signs of malicious redress and finds none, her eyes brim with tears. She shrugs. 'I don't know. I have no proof,' she says. 'I just have the strongest – vibe.'

Vita sighs. How often she had used the same sentence herself, to Michelle, to Candy.

'It's hard for me to tell you this,' Suzie says.

Vita nods. 'I can imagine.'

'He says he's coming over – then doesn't show. His phone is off at odd times. He spends nights I don't know where – but not at mine and I don't think at his.'

'Oh God,' says Vita, remembering such scenarios and the acid anxiety she'd feel.

'I know he did it to you,' Suzie really can't look at her for this one. 'With me.'

The two women look at each other, eyes locked for the first time. Then Suzie hangs her head.

'And you fear he's doing it to you – with someone else?' Vita asks quietly.

Suzie nods. She lowers her voice, as if ashamed. 'I found something – on his phone. I found a text. A few actually. Between him and someone else. And at first, the name didn't alarm me – it's a man's. But there were so many texts, I just thought I'd have a quick look.' She looks at Vita. 'You know, to put my mind at rest.' Vita nods for her. 'You know, to prove to myself I was just being a silly cow.' Vita nods again for her. A tear drips down Suzie's cheek and she sniffs snottily. 'They were the kind of texts we used to send each other.'

Vita feels suddenly cold.

The women stare at each other again. On the worry lines on Suzie's forehead, Vita sees guilt and regret writ large. 'I'm sorry,' Suzie whispers and she tiptoes her fingers over the tabletop to rest lightly on Vita's. 'I'm sorry.' And then she pulls herself together, takes her hands back to her lap. She's not here for Vita, she's here for herself. 'Whoever she is, he's given her a code name,' she says, hoarsely.

'Dermott Hogan?' Vita asks.

Suzie's jaw drops. 'How did you know *that*?'

'That's the name he gave to your number too. I discovered it when I felt beside myself – like you do now – when I felt I had no option but to search for clues.'

Suzie is stilled into silence. Dermott Hogan. It's so premeditated, so underhand, deceitful, so sleazy that if Tim was to walk in right now she'd slap him across the face and yell, Fuck you. Then she slumps. Dermott Hogan exists; Tim's invented partner in crime.

'I've phoned the number,' Suzie admits, 'and it *is* a woman.' She looks at Vita. 'Do you think I should say something?'

Vita shrugs. 'I don't know how to advise you.'

'I am caught between not wanting to ever see him again – and some stupid instinct to see this Dermott Hogan woman off and win Tim back.'

Vita shudders. It's too odd – carbon-copies of all the emotions and utterly irrational theories she experienced at Tim's mistreatment; now owned by her polar opposite and, until recently, her nemesis. Vita looks at Suzie. No doubt Candy would say, Revenge is justified, go for it – this is karma paying out for you. But Vita feels, now that she herself has mended, that there's something about a fellow sufferer which makes her feel peculiarly compelled to offer only support.

'How I wanted to hate you – you don't mind me saying that, do you?'

Suzie's expression – startled, amused, ashamed – says it's OK.

'I, too, wanted you to know that you were nothing and that I was everything to Tim,' Vita says. 'But at the same time I wanted you to know how morally inept he is. I wanted you to know that he proposed to me. I wanted you to know how derogatory he was about you when I found out. I wanted to tell you that if he couldn't change for *me* – he certainly wouldn't be changing for *you*.'

They both linger over Vita's words. Strange as it seems to both of them, no offence was meant and none has been taken.

'Now Dermott Hogan is back,' Vita sighs, as if a bad penny has just turned up. 'You see, if a man shacks up with his lover, a job position becomes available.'

'But I love him!'

A tiny part of Vita still wants to automatically react, Oi! But she knows now it's just habit, past conditioning, a reflex. '*Do* you love him?' she asks Suzie. 'Or is it the idea of taming him, the challenge and chance of winning the heart of someone like Tim?'

Suzie shrugs.

'He's set in his ways,' Vita says. 'When I found out about you I just sobbed at him, *It's not about getting away with it, it's about not fucking it up in the first place.*'

Suzie thinks Vita is so right, so clever. She didn't realize how pretty, in the flesh, she is. She feels comforted – as if by a wiser, older sister. But what is she to do?

'Suzie, whether he loves you – whether he loved me – he's only capable of loving to a certain level. Which isn't enough for you or me. Or anyone in their right mind and with basic self-respect, really. No one's special to Tim, apart from Tim. He's the most self-centred person – by that, I mean he has a quite staggering lack of regard for other people's feelings. Are you content to mean only a limited amount to him?'

'If he thought he was going to lose me, he'd change!' But Suzie's battle cry was brittle and Vita remembered how she'd clung to that very belief herself.

'Suzie – what is it you want?'

'A relationship.' She answered quickly and with conviction.

'One like this?'

Suzie thinks about it. Looks embarrassed as she shakes her head. 'My mate Anna has some annoying phrase – Horses for Courses. She says you wouldn't ride the Grand National on a donkey. She says Tim's suited to the casual stuff but he isn't made for more.'

'Well, your friend Anna's a genius,' Vita says. 'She's spot on. Tim won't give you more. It is not possible for him to do so. It's in his make-up. Or not in his make-up. His ethics are very different – I think they're fundamentally skewed. That's not subjectively speaking – give anyone a list of Tim's demeanours and they would define his behaviour as categorically wrong.'

'People fuck up.'

'They do. Of course they do.' She looks at Suzie, all crumpled. 'But it's not a person's mistakes which define them – it's the way they make amends.' Vita remembers how she'd written the phrase again and again on Post-its – initially, it was for her to access the forgiveness for which Tim was begging. Later, it was to strengthen her resolve. She shrugs at Suzie. 'Tim's possibly doing to you exactly what he did to me. He hasn't changed his ways.'

Suzie is very quiet, very still, captivated by all Vita has said, knowing it's pure common sense, aware now of the path any sensible self-respecting girl should take. She's also frozen by a thought. She slumps a little. 'I wasn't going to tell you this –' Maybe she won't. Maybe she'll just make something else up. But after a pause, she shakes her head at herself. 'I wasn't going to ever tell you this, but do you know something – he keeps all the texts you send him. Even the dull-as-shit ones about till receipts and orders.' Her eyes are filling again. 'I think you're the one he really loves.'

Vita broods on this for a while. It is slightly satisfying. But it changes nothing. 'Tim's "real" love isn't sufficient for me, Suzie. I don't think anyone should settle for so little.' She thinks hard. 'It wasn't love – not in the true sense. On my part, it was neediness, insecurity, dependence, habit – desperate to feel loved by a man who was often so ambivalent towards me. I was caught in a vicious circle. But it wasn't love.' God, that feels liberating.

'I wanted to move in with him,' says Suzie, 'and the

261

less he wanted to talk about it, the more I wanted it. I wanted to feel he liked me enough to jump at the chance.'

'Listen to me, Suzie. I have never been as lonely as I was when I was living with Tim.' Vita pauses, sees how she's struck a very strong chord with Suzie. 'God – if I heard it once I heard it dozens of times from my closest friends – do not judge *yourself* by how Tim treats you. Judge *him*. You know, if my friends' husbands are out of the room when their phones ring or texts come through, they think nothing of picking up and passing on messages. What is there to hide? Nothing. In a mutually trusting and wholesome relationship, there is nothing to hide; life is shared.'

Suzie nods. And rests, head bowed. And nods some more. And finally, when she's ready, she looks up at Vita. 'Thanks,' she says. And Vita can't believe she feels like doing this – but she reaches across the table, across the sticky smudges from someone else's mochaccino foam and she lays her hand on Suzie's. 'You're young,' she smiles at her, 'and *a stunna*.' She says it in a funny accent but she says it with kindness. 'You deserve someone you can trust, whose phone holds no fear for you, who doesn't disappear, who is where he says he is. Someone who speaks respectfully about their ex. Someone who treats you well. Who's kind. Someone who doesn't know a Dermott Hogan. Ultimately, you simply deserve someone who leaps with joy at the end of each day at the thought of coming home to you.'

Suzie is half smiling, half crying, wanting to ask Vita to write it all down.

Starbucks is filling with teenagers. It's time to go. Vita feels tired – but not half as exhausted as poor Suzie looks. At the door, she offers Suzie first her hand, then a hug.

'Are *you* OK, Vita?' Suzie asks, squeezing her tight. 'You must've been through hell.'

Vita accepts the sentiment quietly. There's a flurry of activity in her mind. Oliver. Pear Tree Cottage. Her mum and the legacy of her dad. Her friends. And Oliver, again. She really likes the answer she can give. 'I'm doing OK,' she smiles. 'I'm very OK.'

Day Trippers

Time doesn't always fly when you're having fun. Sometimes, it does you the greatest favour by slowing right down so you can hold on to the hours, indulge in every passing minute, appreciate each second, sense it all with every fibre of your being, as though you're moving in zero gravity, as though you're floating. Wynfordbury Hall seemed so long ago – Oliver and Vita having seen each other often in the intervening fortnight. In some respects, with their relationship unfolding and so much newness coming into their lives, the world seemed different. In other ways, it was reassuringly the same. The weather was wonderful, business was quiet for Vita but busy for Oliver. The wasps were still as lively and as pissed off with the world as ever – but Oliver saw to the traps regularly and persuaded Vita that she really could keep her kitchen window open and let the summer air into the house.

'Hey, Mum.'

'Darling – I was going to call you later.'

'When are you off?'

'Day after tomorrow. How are you?'

'I'm well – really well.'

'And things? How are things?'

'His name's Oliver, Mum!'

'I didn't want to appear pushy, darling.'

'Well – Oliver things are great. Exciting, lovely. We had fish and chips on the Essex coast last night – sat on a bench eating it straight from the paper, it beat any fancy restaurant I've ever been to. That's why I'm phoning you – I suddenly remembered that crazy old oak tree that Dad loved. Do you remember it? I don't know where it is – even if it's still standing. But I thought I could find out about it. I thought I could take Oliver.'

'The Bowthorpe Oak.' Vita's mother went quiet. 'He did love it, your dad. I'm so glad you remember it. I'm so glad you want to go there.'

'Where is it – can you remember?'

'Lincolnshire.'

'I wonder if I can Google it.'

'No – I'd go by car. A lovely day trip. You could have lunch in Stamford. Or go for a stroll around Burghley House.'

'I think I'll make a picnic.'

'How are the pears, darling?'

'They're still everywhere.'

Oliver knew Vita had planned a picnic, but she'd harped on about keeping the location a big secret and it tickled him not to know. Of course, he'd have to know at some point because he'd be driving, but for the time being he did as he was told and turned up at Vita's early on the Sunday with a tank of fuel and travel sweets replenished.

'Hullo, missy.'

They stood at her doorstep, kissed a little clumsily, grinned – still experiencing the tingle of apprehension and

265

nerves which made the first few minutes both awkward and delicious.

'I'm just making final preparations. Come in.'

Oliver came into Pear Tree Cottage. Something smelt good.

'Chicken!' Vita told him. 'Come on through.'

He followed her. In the corridor he could hear *The Archers* on Radio 4 drifting through from the kitchen, as if familiar friends were in there, sitting at Vita's table. 'Do you want me to check the traps? Good God, Vita!'

'Sorry?'

He was gesticulating towards the garden. 'You've been out there!'

'I know!'

'With or without the Legendary Cagoule?'

'With – silly!'

'Are you hosting a village fête?' He was looking out of the kitchen window, at yards of pastel-coloured bunting which Vita had strung along the fence and across the small paved area between the kitchen and the pear tree. 'Is that the surprise?'

'It's bunting!'

'I can see that.'

'I'll probably have to take it down soon – if we run out in the shop. It's very popular, this time of year.' She paused. 'Village fête? You cheeky sod.' It felt good to be relaxed enough in his company to tease him.

He came over to her, tucked her hair behind her ear and kissed her on the forehead. 'You've been out in your garden,' he marvelled. 'I think that's brilliant.' And he felt chuffed, as if some of the credit was his.

'I know,' she said and she really looked so proud of herself. 'Vita – One. Wasps – Nil.'

In the fortnight since they'd first slept together,

tenderness had grown exponentially to the passion because, as much as they wanted to get naked, they wanted to learn about each other too. With these early dates came a sense of achievement – how nerves and an endearing artlessness at the start of a date could smooth out naturally into easy conversation and confident energy in bed. The monumental subjects weren't returned to – DeeDee and Tim had been a necessary part of the trip to Wynfordbury Hall, paving the way for Oliver and Vita to progress onwards on their own. Since then, the more they found out about each other – whether it was over a shared love of brown sauce, not ketchup, on chips; or that Oliver had a dodgy ankle from an old windsurfing injury; or that Vita loved horror films; or that they both liked Springsteen and that they never missed *Top Gear* even though neither were that interested in cars – the more that fondness and desire blended and burgeoned. It was heady – the excitement of discovering the unique facets of the person they were each growing to like so much. They loved each other's company. They fancied each other rotten.

For Vita, there was another emotion which she was experiencing – confidence. She had felt energized over this last fortnight, and that's why she could go out into the garden with the bunting, that's why she hadn't written a Post-it in two weeks. For Oliver an emotion returned which he hadn't felt for a long time – joy. He felt it when he was with her and he even felt it when the lads at work made references at his expense to 'nice pears'. For Oliver, such lightness in his life was welcome. Michelle begged to meet him, Candy too. But Vita just wanted to spend time with Oliver. They were both engrossed in their jigsaw puzzle; the various pieces slotting into place, a great picture emerging with fine details and beautiful colour.

*

'What are we doing today then? And when can we eat the picnic? It all looks great.'

Vita grinned. 'We're going to a place that's special to me because my dad loved it. I haven't been for years. It's in Lincolnshire. It's right up your street.'

He helped pack the basket, amused by her choice of Wotsits to go with the fancy bread and organic chicken drumsticks she'd roasted herself. They left Pear Tree Cottage laden.

'Where to?' Oliver asked once they were in the car, a tatty road map on his knee opened at Lincolnshire.

'Well, funnily enough – it's a place called Bourne. It's my turn to take you to see a fantastic mad old tree.'

Called the Bowthorpe Oak, Oliver said to himself. He wouldn't spoil it for Vita. He wouldn't tell her that tree was like an eccentric ancient uncle to him, nor that he'd been the one to verify it for the Woodland Trust.

'The Bowfield Oak!' she declared.

So he wouldn't correct her. He'd just drive. And they'd catch the last of *The Archers* en route. Oliver let Vita direct him all the way there, even letting her overshoot the small turning up a farm track; continuing on in the wrong direction for another mile or so, until Vita realized her mistake. Eventually, they arrived.

'We have to give a small donation, apparently,' she told him and he let her lead him to the farmhouse where, to Oliver's relief, the elderly farmer appeared not to recognize him. Vita pored over the photograph album of the tree over the decades before leading the way according to the farmer's instructions, her memory kicking in much to her delight.

'This way!' she said to Oliver. 'I remember this – it's this way.'

It was wonderfully quirky – walking around the house

and up through the farm garden, passing by a gate, going on alongside the raspberry beds until they came to a meadow in which a flock of geese paraded as if they were part of the entertainment. The tree stood at the top end. Or, rather, it squatted, gargantuan. One thousand years old, partly hollow and with a girth of over forty feet, it resembled a gnarled old cave crowned by a thick straggle of immense branches.

'In the last century, apparently, you could sit and have dinner inside the tree. And it's been used as a stable,' Vita told Oliver who had put his hand tenderly over a nodule of bark. 'Isn't it brilliant? Have you seen a tree like this on your travels?'

How was he meant to answer that?

'Don't you like it?' Vita asked. 'Is it not a thousand years old? It is an *oak*, isn't it? What?' She looked confused while he tried to prevent his face from creasing in amusement. 'What?'

So Oliver had to confess. And with mock indignation, Vita found a section where she could clamber up so she sat there and pulled her face into a theatrical pout. But she let him reach up his arms to her, to help her down and, with the massive tree affording them privacy, they kissed while the geese bickered in the background. Vita thought, Am I falling in love? She thought, Is it safe to do so with this man? She thought, I don't need to answer.

On the way home, after the picnic had been plundered and then walked off in the grounds of Burghley House, Vita felt pensive. She thought back to that first date at Wynfordbury Hall during which it had felt easy, right, to speak of the profound times they had experienced before meeting each other. She thought how, since then, she and Oliver had focused on their newly combined here-and-now, on lovely happy dates. If Tim or DeeDee were mentioned

269

it was fleetingly, conversationally, which felt natural and appropriate. But on the journey back from Lincolnshire Vita wondered whether they had consciously veered away from weighty subjects. But hadn't it been so uplifting just to explore and discover and enjoy and be happy?

As they drove back to Hertfordshire, she thought about how Jonty was staying at his friend's – yet there had been no mention of her and Oliver going back to his house that night. They'd be watching *Top Gear* at Pear Tree Cottage. Later, they'd make love in her bed. They'd wake with the parakeets, make love again, doze off until the alarm went. Then she'd bring him up a cup of tea in the morning before he left her to return home; to change into work clothes, to swap his car for his truck, to pick up Jonty on his way to work.

'How's Jonty?' she finally asked halfway down the A1, unnerved that such a simple question had taken miles and miles for her to voice.

'Having a ball,' Oliver said.

Vita couldn't let the pause last too long for fear of it turning a question into an issue. 'Does he know about me?'

'Yes,' said Oliver, 'he does.'

'I'd like to meet him,' said Vita, 'properly.' There was another pause she was quick to fill. 'At some point,' she qualified, trying to sound light.

There was only a split second of silence, but it was loaded. 'Of course,' said Oliver, wondering when.

And it crossed Vita's mind – is Oliver perhaps not as ready for this as I am?

Tim and Vita

Vita's mum went to Amsterdam with her friend Lorna.

Michelle and Chris took the kids to Disneyworld.

Candy's sister rented a house in the Lake District and the extended family all decamped there.

The shop was quiet, but it always was, this time of year. Oliver was busy, as was customary in August – as if nature was helping him to stockpile income now, in preparation for the more meagre midwinter months. He had taken to popping into That Shop occasionally during the working week. One time, he brought Vita plums from a client's overladen tree. The old lady had been in the shop that time and Oliver had offered her a handful too. She still stole the candy-coloured measuring spoons. On another occasion, he came in with Boz who bought a pair of cherubs, just on the cool side of kitsch, to send home. When Boz brought them to the counter, while Oliver was fiddling with a dog trying to put it back into its clog, he had touched Vita on the arm.

'Thanks, miss,' he said, giving a flick of his head in Oliver's direction, 'for him. Cheers.'

Vita hadn't known how to respond but she was so

271

moved, so flattered, that she gave Boz a twenty per cent discount.

Jonty continued to work with Oliver all the days not beginning with a T or an S. He knew about Vita and once or twice his dad had asked if he'd like to pop into the shop to say hullo on the way back from work. Though Jonty was cool with the concept, the beauty of a teenager's summer holiday was earning a bit of money and then hanging out with mates. So, thus far, he'd had his own plans which had clashed with his dad's suggestion. But it worked both ways now; Oliver was a little less fussed if Jonty asked to stay over at friends because it gave him a whole night asleep with Vita. At Pear Tree Cottage. Vita had shelved any previous anxiety about why her place was their sole base. It felt more and more like home now and, with the garden generally under control and blistering July replaced by a more benign late August, she was starting to love being there, inside or out, on her own or with company.

As for Tim, Vita hadn't seen him in over a month. Phone calls had been kept to a minimum, texts had all but dwindled. Their relationship was being conducted over emails focusing purely on business and Vita had stopped noticing the times when he signed off with an 'x' and the times when he didn't. When he called into the shop, unannounced, he really was the last person on Vita's mind.

'Hey.'

Vita had just discovered Laurie Graham and was galloping through the author's backlist, currently enchanted by *Gone with the Windsors*. Reluctantly, she hauled herself out of the 1930s and looked up to see Tim. She hadn't heard him at all.

'Hey,' he said again. He looked different – smaller,

somehow. Not healthy. That haircut was not good on him. And what's with the sideburns, Tim – where have they gone?

'Oh,' she said, 'hi.'

'May I?'

That was a first – asking if he could come over to the till and reach across to print off a balance. Vita stepped down from her stool and went to tidy a table that didn't really need it. Tim read through the figures and sighed heavily, staring levelly at Vita as if she was mostly responsible.

'It's on a par with this time last year,' Vita told him, 'which really isn't bad considering it's August, we're in a recession, the flower shop on the corner has shut down and Tiley's are constantly having sales and promos to shift their crap.'

Usually, Tim would have huffed off out of the shop at this juncture, with some withering aside. But he didn't go. He lingered, staring at two customers who'd just come in as if they were of a lowly caste. Vita returned to the till, took money, gift-wrapped a glass storm lantern and gave the customer a scented tea-light for free. The other bought a greetings card for £1.99 and asked for a plastic bag. All the while, Tim loitered like a useless store detective. Once the shop was empty, he spoke, tossing a froggie beanbag from hand to hand.

'It looks to be a nice evening,' he said. 'Do you fancy a quick drink?'

Vita stared at him blankly.

'A drink, Vita – tonight? With me?' Was that a little-boy-lost look he was giving her?

Vita realized she was frowning. She straightened her brow and attempted to sound as neutral as possible. 'No – Tim. Sorry.'

And then it came. She wasn't doing as she was told, she wasn't reacting as she should, as she used to, and Tim wasn't having his own way and therefore he wasn't having any of it.

'How long are you going to give me the cold shoulder?' He dropped the beanbag back on the pile as though it was contaminated. 'What's going on?'

'Sorry?'

'But are you?' Tim let it hang. 'You continually blank me these days – you're only in touch about work, and that's only by email. You never phone or text. I haven't seen you since God knows when. You just ignore me.'

'Tim?' It was as if he was midway through some imagined heated discussion between them.

'What's the point you're trying to make?' He was pleading now. 'I know I fucked up – and I regret it. But there's only so many times I can say it, Vita. So why are you still up there on your lofty Moral High Ground doing your whole Mortally Wounded act?'

Vita stared at him in disbelief. She hated his tone and she hated his deluded conviction in the nonsense he was spouting. 'I have other plans,' she kept her tone level. 'And Tim, you have a girlfriend.'

'Jesus wept,' he said, 'not *that* again.' The whole world seemed to wind him up.

'She's not a *that*,' said Vita, 'she's a Suzie.'

'We don't get this time back, Vita,' he said to her, 'these months we've lost. I made a mistake.' He was raising his voice. 'I cocked up.' Vita found she had to stifle a giggle. 'How many times do you need me to say *sorry*?' She really had no answer for that. 'Sorry, sorry, sorry.' He sounded like a kid. He could see it wasn't working. He changed tack. 'I never wanted us to be over,' he added pitifully.

Vita had heard enough. Not just today, but over the

years. And now she'd had enough. Look at that beautiful day outside, rapidly in danger of becoming tarnished. She closed her book and placed it slowly on the worktop. She had one chance to say this and, more importantly, to say it right.

'What you did to me, how you treated me, how you abused everything I tried to give you – my trust, my self-respect, my beliefs, my self esteem – I wouldn't wish what I went through on my worst enemy.' Vita thought about that. She thought of Oliver. She thought of Suzie. Even of Rick. So much had changed already. She thought, So much has happened and there's so much on the cusp of happening. And she thought, I don't want to go back in time, I want only to go forwards. And she thought, Time has been on my side after all. 'I've changed,' she told him.

He didn't like the sound of that. 'Into what? What have you changed into?'

She shrugged. 'Into someone who knows what she wants and what she won't settle for. Into someone proud of herself. Into someone – with a rosy future. Clichéd or not. My life is different now. I like it.'

He was staring at her and he looked anxious. 'Have you – are you – *seeing someone*?' His tone was one of burgeoning disbelief.

'It wouldn't make any difference if I was.'

'OK – OK, I get it – independent woman who's just fine in her own company bla bla. But are you? Vita? I just want to know. I don't want to bump into you and Prince Bloody Charming without being forewarned.'

How dare he!

Because he's Tim, that's how.

'Actually,' Vita said levelly, with no tone of malicious triumph, 'I am.'

Tim physically steadied himself. 'Who?' His voice

rasped, he seemed utterly stunned, which offended her somewhat. How little did he think of her? How much did he think of himself!

'He's called Oliver.'

'And?'

'Bourne. Oliver Bourne.'

'Not the name – I don't give a toss about the name.'

'And *what*, then, Tim?'

'Are you – do you?' He didn't look well.

'Do you know something Tim, I think I am. I think I do.' So hard to say something gently when the beautiful sound of it should be sung out.

Tim sat down on the ledge of the window display. He was quiet for a moment. When he spoke, his voice was suddenly softer. 'When did this happen?'

'Recently.'

The gentler tone went. 'You can't be in love with someone so quickly.'

And Vita thought, Oh yes, I can.

'Vita – we were together *years*.'

'This is not about us, Tim. This is about me now – I've met someone. And I love him.'

Tim was squeezing the bridge of his nose. He used to do that when Vita did something which inadvertently irked him.

'Tim – you have Suzie to think about. You've been with her, on and off, in whatever capacity, for well over a year. Longer, probably, for all I know.'

'This isn't about Suzie. I told you all along – she's nothing, compared to you. She's not relevant.'

Vita looked at him thoughtfully. 'In some ways, she's very relevant – even if you two don't last. She has great relevance to your past and the chances you have to shape your future.'

'It was just me being a wanker, an idiot. I kept telling you it meant nothing. I'd never have left you, Vita, *never*.' It sounded as though he was passing the buck.

'Then for God's sake, let her go – don't treat her badly too. If you have any respect for me, any true remorse for what happened – will you please just do it differently this time?'

'But you're the One, Vita. It's always been you. Only you.' Did he lift that from some cheesy song? And that was Tim's thought – not Vita's.

'No, Tim. No. It's always been *you*.' Then she thought about it. She thought about herself – remembering how diminished she'd felt by Tim, how worry shaped her days, how much hard work it was trying all the while to make sure he'd find no reason not to love her, to stay not stray. She thought about Suzie – how she'd recognized the haunted look about her eyes, the sorrowful tune of battered self-esteem, the details – the same details – that had tormented her when she'd been with Tim.

'You're the *One*, Vita. Please – a final second chance.'

'I gave you a couple of those – remember?'

'OK – OK – I had my chance—'

'—no, Tim, you had chances, *plural*,' Vita said. 'You took them. I gave them. You abused them.'

'OK – that's semantics. This isn't about chances – it's about forgiveness. You have the power, Vita – to forgive.'

Vita thought how not so long ago, talk like that would have seduced her. 'No,' she said, 'it's not about forgiveness. I am able to forgive. It's about trust – that's gone. And without trust, there is no relationship.'

Tim dropped his head. 'But I'd never have left you – you're the One.'

'I'm not the One – because it's *not* about me, Tim. It's always been about *you*.' She paused. And then she couldn't

277

help smiling. And Vita thought – Suzie, this is for you. 'And Dermott Hogan too, of course.'

That night, Vita lay right in the centre of her bed. She'd always favoured her side – even when she'd been single, she'd slept only on that side. Now that she had Oliver, on the nights they weren't together, she generally snuggled down into his side. But tonight she positioned herself right in the middle. It was very comfortable.

She thought, I buried Tim today.

Nailed shut the coffin.

A tear rolled an oily hot path down her face, her neck – like the swansong of final emotion which had connected her with Tim. She sensed it blot out on the pillow. What a year. Tim. Oliver. Even Suzie. Candy. Oliver. Michelle. Rick. Her mum. The memory of her dad. And Oliver.

I've done well. How well I've done for myself.

*　　*　　*

While Vita slept soundlessly, dreamlessly that night, Oliver lay awake. Something wasn't sitting easily with him and he wasn't sure quite what that was. He went downstairs and made a cup of tea, sipping it whilst absent-mindedly looking at the dishwasher, shiny, white, redundant.

'Dad?'

'Jesus Christ, Jont – you scared the life out of me.'

'Sorry – I heard something. It was only you.'

'Only me.'

'Are you OK?'

'I'm fine, kid, I'm fine. I just couldn't sleep.'

'Oh.'

'Are you all right? Why are you awake?'

'I heard you.'

278

'Go back to bed.'

'I'll have a tea too, I think.'

Jonty made himself a mug.

'Jonty.'

'Dad.'

'I think – I don't know. It really is up to you. But maybe.'

'Dad – if I spoke like that to you, you'd rip a strip off of me.'

'Off of? *Off Of*? That's abominable.'

'Off me. It's tired. I'm late.'

They laughed at that one.

'Let me try again.' Oliver took a sip of tea. 'I was wondering what you thought and how you felt about me inviting Vita *here*. For supper, perhaps. But *here*.'

Jonty stared at the floor, at their bare feet. He thought, My feet are like my dad's. I have his feet. He thought, My dad wants to bring the Pear Tree Lady to our home. He thought, I knew this was coming – but I didn't expect it now, in the middle of the night. And then he thought, Mum – is it OK that I don't have a problem with it?

'Jont?'

'I don't have a problem with it, Dad. I guess.'

'It's not just the meeting-you bit – it's that it's a woman, *here*.'

'I know. It's cool.'

'There hasn't been a woman here – since Mum.'

'Apart from Mrs Blackthorne,' said Jonty.

'And she's part of the furniture.'

'It's cool, Dad – seriously.'

'Good – that's good.' Oliver paused. 'Isn't it?'

'I do have a problem with something though,' said Jonty. 'This thing about supper. What are we going to do – give her a ready meal?'

279

How Oliver could have hugged his boy. 'Could go to the chippy?'

Jonty laughed. Then he had a quiet moment. 'Or you could do those chops?'

'Chops would be good.'

'She's not a frikkin' vegetarian, is she?'

'No,' said Oliver, 'she frikking isn't.'

'Frikkin' *so* doesn't have a "g" on the end,' said Jonty.

'The chops then? What should I do with them?'

'Chips?'

'Chops and chips?'

'It's got a ring to it.'

'It *has* a ring to it.'

'God, *Dad*!'

'Chops and chips it is.'

'Tell her to bring the dessert.'

'I can't do that!'

'I bet she'll ask – *What can I bring?* Don't you remember how Mum always used to say that, when anyone invited us over?'

Oliver had forgotten.

'If she asks what she can bring, tell her she can bring dessert.'

Oliver nodded. 'Righty-ho.'

'When's she coming then?'

Oliver shrugged. 'Are you around Saturday evening?'

'I'm meant to be playing cricket with the guys.'

'How about Sunday evening?'

'That's good.'

'I'll ask her for Sunday evening then, for chops and chips.'

'Don't tell her what we're cooking, though. Say it goes pear-shaped and we make a mercy dash to the chippy anyway?'

'Chippy's closed on a Sunday.'

'Let's hope we don't balls it up, then,' said Jonty. 'Night, Dad.'

'Night, kiddo.'

And as Oliver rinsed out the mugs with his hand and hot water, he thought, *We*. Not the Royal We but the Bourne We. He thought, Jonty said, *Don't tell her what we're cooking*. And he felt tears course up from his heart. I hope I don't balls it up, he thought. DeeDee would kill me.

Jamie Oliver Oliver

It was worth a long-distance phone call to Florida. Only Vita forgot about the time zones and Michelle's phone went straight through to voicemail. Candy's phone, it seemed, was out of signal in the Lake District and hers went through to voicemail too. Vita's mum wasn't at home and she didn't have a mobile. Why would I want one of those, she'd asked, I've managed perfectly well without one all these years – she had said the same about auto-banks, answering machines and DVD players. So, once Oliver had left on Sunday morning, Vita paced around wishing there was someone to call. She was excited, nervous – she wanted to ask Michelle, What do you think, what do you think? She wanted to ask Candy, What shall I wear – dress down for the son and up for the man? She wanted to ask her mum, What shall I take for dessert, Mum? But then she thought how it probably wasn't advice or answers she really sought – she simply wanted to share her excitement, her nerves. She was flattered to have been asked, and she was proud too. She sent texts to Candy and Michelle simply telling them that Oliver was cooking and she'd be meeting Jonty. And she knew if she asked her mum what she should take for dessert her Mum's brilliant answer would be Keep It Simple.

Right then. Lemon drizzle cake and fresh raspberries it is!

Vita took a bus to the supermarket, ashamed to find her cupboards empty of all baking ingredients. All those shop-bought biscuits lavished on workmen over the months! She wondered, if she had made lemon drizzle cake for Oliver on his first visit, might he have chopped the tree down then and there? She laughed as she picked up a basket – thank goodness for small mercies. She'd keep the parakeets, the wasps, the rank pears because Oliver came with the package.

Self-raising flour.

She didn't mind, really, that the corner shop shut at noon on Sundays – That Shop didn't open at all. But she did think it daft to go all the way to the supermarket for self-raising flour.

Oh, and baking parchment.

And where was her loaf tin? Still in one of the remaining packing boxes?

She'd treat herself to a new one.

And a rubber spatula, so that she had no excuse to lick more of the mixing bowl than was absolutely necessary.

The trip to the supermarket was now worthwhile. In fact, it was very worthwhile because, just then, she caught sight of Oliver and Jonty, standing at the meat counter, scratching their heads.

She swept herself into the toy aisle, out of their sight line. They were in deep discussion, the two of them, pointing at cuts of meat in the display cabinet, reading off a piece of paper which Jonty held in front of Oliver. They bought something, finally, and wondered off; shoppers having to duck out of their way, so engrossed were they in their list.

They oughtn't to see me. That wouldn't be fair.

But Vita watched them. She nipped behind this aisle and that, like a character in a cartoon caper. Preparing for this meal was obviously an extremely important task for the Bournes. And she felt touched. She'd make them the best cake ever. And she bought the most expensive brand of raspberries available. She wanted to take flowers too – but do you give flowers to blokes? And then she thought that their house probably hadn't had flowers in it for a long time. It was a woman's thing, wasn't it, buying a bunch just to treat the house. Selecting the vase, trimming the stems, displaying them artistically, managing to eke out a few blooms for a smaller vase for elsewhere in the house. Smiling at the display whenever they were seen. And then she thought, The last time Oliver's house had flowers in it might well have been after DeeDee's funeral. An awfully long time for a house not to have had a vaseful. But Vita sensed it wasn't for her to bustle in there with a bunch. It would be like coming in to see someone's newly laid floor and walking all over it in heels. If Oliver was preparing a new emotional pathway into the future, the least she could do was tread lightly, softly, on it. So she bought a bottle of wine. And then she thought, Jonty's not quite fifteen. So she bought him *Q* magazine and, checking that Oliver and Jonty were still embroiled in lengthy discussions by the green vegetables, she nipped to the self-service checkouts and made a swift exit home.

'Do you think we're trying to be too fancy?' Jonty wondered.

'If Jamie Oliver says it's pukka, we can do it.'

He and Jonty spent a happy hour in the kitchen, chucking in the ingredients just as the recipe instructed, adding their own mockney accents and daring dashes of tamari sauce.

Vita wore a floaty short-sleeved summer dress, soft green speckled with little white flowers; leggings and ballet pumps. She pulled up the sides of her hair and fixed them with a slide. She put on a little eyeshadow, a little mascara and a spritz of Eternity. It was a warm evening, it would take a good half-hour to walk to Oliver's side of town. She thought of the cake and the raspberries and not wanting sweat patches or a red face, so she took a cab.

She thought Oliver would live in some kind of woodsmansy cottage, with roses and a lavender path and a tree stump with an axe ready for splitting logs. The house was handsome, period and semi-detached, on a neat road lined with similar homes. Driveways with cars pulled up close to their garages, recycling bins by front doors. Oliver's house looked like any of the others on the street. She'd asked the cab to drop her at the start of the road, wanting a little time to steady herself. But she was shaking as she walked up to the front door. Ridiculous! You'll bruise the raspberries! She rang the bell and quietly, under her breath, said, Think of me – as if it would carry to Florida and the Lakes, to her mum, faster than any text or call.

'Hey.'

'Hi!'

Oliver gave her a clumsy kiss on her cheek, a better one on her lips. 'Come on in.'

'Something smells nice.'

'Domino's pizza,' he said.

'I love Domino's,' Vita said generously, ingenuously, and Oliver laughed.

'I'm teasing. I'm Jamie Oliver Oliver tonight.'

He took her through to the sitting room, too quickly

285

for her to be able to take in the details of the hallway. She noted the kitchen off to the left. Glimpsed a carpeted staircase. Laminate floors downstairs. The sitting room was surprisingly tidy and incredibly still. It reminded her of her grandmother's front room. Always a sense of stillness, just the steady tock of a mantel clock.

'Would you like a drink?'

'Oh yes, please. This is for you.' She gave him the wine. 'Oh, and this.' She gave him the cake and raspberries. 'And this is for Jonty.' She gave him the magazine and then stood there, twisting two plastic bags around and around each other.

'Thank you.' Oliver made a sensible pile of it all and carried it off into the kitchen.

'She brought cake,' he whispered to Jonty.

'Cool,' Jonty whispered back.

'Look – and a mag for you.'

'Cool.'

'Take her this glass of wine, please.'

Jonty thought, If only my dad knew how much I could do with a good glug of that.

Jonty came into the sitting room, followed by Oliver. Vita felt as though she was some kind of exotic dignitary being stared at by the People.

'Hi,' Jonty said with an awkward wave.

'Hullo,' said Vita, wondering whether she should shake hands or something. She'd never had a boyfriend with a child, let alone a teenager; in fact, she didn't actually know any teenagers currently. Jonty came over, gave her the glass of wine and stood there, as if she was a teacher and ought to be telling him what to do next. Oliver just stood behind him, sipping quickly at his own glass.

286

'Thanks for the mag,' Jonty said, with another odd wave which started at his chest and ended at his hips.

'My pleasure,' Vita said. 'I expect you'd've preferred a can of cider.' He blushed. 'But I'm on my best behaviour,' she said.

'I am too,' said Jonty. He looked back at his father.

'Shall we all sit down?' suggested Oliver.

They sat. Vita on a leather armchair, Jonty and Oliver on the sofa. On the coffee table, a little bowl of peanuts and another with olives. She saw Oliver give Jonty a just perceptible nudge.

'Olive? Peanut?'

She loved the way Jonty proffered them in the singular and, accordingly, she took one of each. Then she looked around the room, heartened by alcove shelving groaning with books and framed photographs. Sliding doors to an unkempt garden beyond. Over to one side, internal glass doors opening into the dining room. She'd finished her peanut and her olive and wondered whether she could help herself to more.

'Yummy olives,' she said.

'Thank you!' It was as if Oliver had harvested them himself. 'Right, I think it's ready. Shall we eat?' They'd been sitting down all of three minutes.

Oliver led the way to the dining room, with Jonty behind her. The table had been laid properly. Side plates. Butter knives. And folded pieces of kitchen paper in lieu of cloth napkins.

'You sit here,' Jonty said, tapping a chair opposite the one Vita was about to sit in.

'It's fine,' Oliver said to him, under his breath.

'I can move,' Vita said.

'Honestly,' said Oliver.

'Seriously,' said Vita and she moved to where Jonty was.

287

'It's just Dad said I should sit there – because then it's quicker to get to the kitchen, you see. And I was meant to pull this chair back for you.'

'Ah,' said Vita, relieved, because she'd wondered whether it had perhaps been DeeDee's place.

She let Jonty hold back the chair for her, then she sat and they disappeared. And she looked around her, at the art on the walls – mostly beautiful vast abstracted photographs of landscapes. Lovely small pottery bowls on windowsills. And, every now and then, a framed photo. Jonty at various ages. And family groupings. And one, quite near by, of DeeDee. It was angled slightly away from Vita, as if DeeDee was looking out from the dining room back into the lounge, as if DeeDee didn't know Vita was here yet. But in came Oliver, followed by Jonty, and Vita pulled her attention back to them.

'Hors d'oeuvres,' Oliver announced.

'Wow,' said Vita.

'Asparagus,' said Jonty. Then he said, Doh!

Vita laughed. 'Yup, no mistaking asparagus.'

Oliver and Jonty used knives and forks and cut the asparagus into genteel portions. Vita, however, had already picked up a spear, dipping it liberally into the hollandaise while a little of the cooking water dripped down her wrist. Jonty looked at her almost enviously. 'Did your dad say, *Knife and fork, boy*?' she asked him sotto voce.

Oliver just laughed. 'We have manners,' he said. 'But actually, you're right, I did.'

'We usually just have stuff from the microwave, on our laps in front of the box,' Jonty said.

'So I've heard,' Vita said and she looked at Oliver fondly. 'Well, thank you very much for this – it's wonderful.'

'You sit here and chat to Vita,' Oliver said to Jonty,

288

collecting the plates just as soon as Vita had finished her last spear. 'I'll bring in the next course.'

They listened to him clattering about for a moment.

'Sorry about the cagoule-madwoman incident,' Vita said to Jonty.

'It was funny,' Jonty said.

'How's your summer?'

'It's been cool. I've been helping my dad. Hanging out with my mates. I went camping.'

'I heard.'

'That was pretty cool.'

'I'll bet.'

'Yeah.'

'Do you like music, then? I didn't know whether you liked computers and stuff – I could've bought you one of those mags.' Vita had to laugh at herself for dumbing down her voice. But she wanted to bond with Jonty and was relieved to find him chatting easily.

'I totally love music. I live for music.'

'I thought you might. Who do you like then?'

Jonty listed umpteen bands whose names Vita nodded sagely at, though she was appalled at not knowing any of them. How old she suddenly felt. *You can't hear what they're singing about* – that's what her mum used to say about Vita's choice of music. She thought, God, am I old enough to be saying the same?

'My dad's not had a girlfriend before,' Jonty suddenly said. But then Oliver came back in before Vita could respond. She regarded Jonty a moment longer: his teenage gawkiness, his butch-black T-shirt emblazoned with a band's name and a skull motif but his slender arms appearing from the sleeves like young branches, his zeitgeist haircut half hiding a child's face, half revealing a young man's, and suddenly she wanted to hug him. If his

289

dad now had someone to hug, who did Jonty have? Jonty glanced back at her, all awkward eyes and a quick unsure smile.

'Blimey!' said Vita, a plate having been put before her.

'Good, eh?' said Oliver.

'Jamie Oliver Frikkin' Oliver,' Vita marvelled.

'See – told you frikkin' didn't have a "g",' a delighted Jonty said to his dad.

The plates were loaded with sticky chops, handmade chunky chips with some kind of coating (paprika and garlic, Vita was soon informed), green beans tossed with sesame seeds and tamari. And a whole tomato each, carefully cut into eighths. They all tried to eat with knives and forks – but in the end, Oliver was the first to say, Sod it as he picked a chop up in his fingers. The chips weren't quite cooked, so everyone ate the ends and left the middles on their plates like a pile of small weathered bricks. Oliver had done so many, they all had plenty.

'That was delicious,' Vita beamed, 'really amazing.' She'd only just finished and again Oliver was clearing the plates straight away. They'd sat to eat all of fifteen minutes ago.

'Jont?'

The two of them carried it all back into the kitchen and she could hear energetic whispering interspersed with the clunk and clatter of crockery.

'Can I help?' she called.

'No!'

'No!'

'OK!'

That sauce had been really lovely. She peeled her ears. It was obviously a hive of activity in the kitchen. Perhaps she should have offered to cut the cake and wash the raspberries. No, leave them to it. She left the table and

290

examined the pottery bowls on the window ledge. And then she walked over to the cabinet and looked at the photos.

Hullo, DeeDee.

Funnily enough, I imagined you looking just like this – though I thought you'd be fair not dark.

DeeDee smiled back.

Laughter lines.

A lovely smile, slightly askew and all the more attractive for it.

Vita found she didn't really spend much time looking at Jonty and Oliver, skipping over their details. She was transfixed by DeeDee, wanting to commit her face to memory, wanting to look deep into those eyes, trying to work out how tall she'd been, what clothes she liked. Lilac and navy had obviously been her colours. What her hands were like. A wedding ring and an engagement ring. Pierced ears – look at that – twice in each ear!

And then Vita turned to find Oliver and Jonty standing there, staring at her, holding plates with enormous wedges of lemon cake and mountains of raspberries. Just standing stock-still, staring at her. Vita was so shocked, she dropped the frame and it fell to the floor. It didn't break but it fell loudly and then she was stooping to pick it up, saying, Sorry! Sorry! and feeling utterly mortified. I wasn't snooping, she cried to herself, I just wanted to see what she looked like.

'I'm so sorry!'

What on earth was she meant to say now? Oh, how beautiful your late wife was, Oliver? Jonty, your mum looked so lovely? Had she even put the photo back in the right place, at the right angle? And now – how to cross the chasm from here, to her chair just there?

291

She made it back, acutely aware that her face wasn't just red, it was now prickled with sweat.

'I –' Christ, she could cry.

'Don't worry, Vita,' Oliver said, and he put his hand, his beautiful warm hand, gently on her wrist. In front of her, the great big chunk of her cake; across from her, Jonty.

'Cake looks cool,' Jonty said. He looked alarmed – as if Vita might be on the verge of one of the funny turns like the first time he met her.

'My dad,' she said to Jonty. 'He died when I was your age – well, I was fourteen at the time.'

Jonty looked at his dad. Then he looked at Vita. 'What of?'

'Leukaemia,' she said.

'Ours was a road accident,' said Jonty.

'I know,' said Vita softly, looking down reverently, 'and I'm so sorry.'

'That's OK,' said Jonty.

'Vita,' said Oliver, 'we are happy to have you here – both of us, aren't we, Jonty? We're a bit out of practice, of course. But you are welcome.'

'Shall we just eat cake?' Jonty asked.

The raspberries were sweet, so very sweet. So beautiful. So full of summer.

'Coffee?' Oliver offered, as soon as the dessert had been finished – and the cake was so good they'd scoffed it down in a matter of minutes. 'We have mints – a selection box. M&S.'

'Lovely,' said Vita, 'but I'm going to help clear up. And you must let me – or I'll take the rest of the cake home with me.'

They all walked through to the kitchen carrying the dirty dishes. The kitchen looked war torn. There were plates and bowls and all manner of utensils lying in chaos on every available surface. The oven was still on.

'Lord,' Vita said.

'The thing is, Jamie Oliver probably has legions of skivvies,' said Oliver, 'but I'm Jamie Oliver Oliver and I just have a Jonty.'

Vita laughed. 'Come on – it won't take a mo'.'

While Oliver boiled the kettle and rooted around in a cupboard for ground coffee, while Jonty half-heartedly piled things up whilst trying to read passages of *Q*, Vita made a start by swilling plates under the hot tap.

And then she flipped down the dishwasher door and started loading it.

'No!' Oliver shouted. 'Don't!'

'Seriously – I'm an expert,' and she continued to stack the racks.

'Please, Vita – just leave it.'

She laughed at his distress. Hadn't he done plenty? The host most certainly with the most. 'Honestly – I'm a whizz,' she said. 'I bet I can load every single thing in.'

'Just – STOP.'

And he was emphatic. And his voice was hoarse. And Vita was shocked to see him and Jonty looking aghast, as though they'd seen a ghost, as though Vita had committed a terrible, terrible crime.

'Please,' he said and his voice was controlled, odd. 'Just go through. Take a seat. We'll bring coffee in to you.'

She could but nod; her mind a whirl about just what she'd done. What *had* she done? She went into the sitting room as asked and sat quietly, as if in disgrace. She was too nervous to mooch over to browse the books because there were too many photos of DeeDee dotted around the shelves. She felt dreadful, with a stomach stuffed full of food from a meal that had lasted twenty-five minutes flat and a mind full of conflicting emotions and questions arising from a moment's unwitting offence. And then she saw it. Saw Oliver standing in the kitchen, head hung low. She saw Jonty walk over to him and the two of them lay a hand on each other's shoulders. And then she watched them slowly unstacking the dishwasher, taking every single item out and piling it up again, haphazardly on the worktop. And she thought, Oh God. Oh God. And it wasn't the ignominy of her unwitting faux pas. It was the realization that DeeDee was still very much in the kitchen. Not just in the kitchen; everywhere.

Vita realized that the time it had taken Oliver to invite her to his home had little to do with Jonty and everything to do with DeeDee. Vita glanced at a photo of her and whispered through smarting eyes, I didn't mean to trespass. She thought, I don't feel I should be here. This house was DeeDee's. Everything in it was hers, including Oliver and Jonty. This family was taken already. And when Oliver came back in with coffee and posh mints and his lovely smile, Vita thought to herself, This is hopeless. This is utterly, utterly without hope.

Jonty

Loss.

Loss was the key.

Vita was at a loss, not knowing what to do but having an overriding feeling that Oliver's loss – and Jonty being inextricably bound in it – was beyond any ability Vita could possibly have to counteract it.

'It would be easier, somehow, if Oliver was divorced,' she confided to Michelle who could do no more than listen and dole out tissues. 'I still don't know what I did, really. Something about helping in the kitchen – it felt as extreme as if I'd found her clothes and tried them on.'

'Did Oliver say anything? When he drove you home?'

'It was dreadful. It was awful, stilted, light chit-chat about lemon cake.'

'What did you say, though – did you say anything?'

'I didn't feel I could. It was as if the matter was closed. I didn't even feel I could apologize for whatever it was that I'd done. So I just went all light and chit-chatty back. But there was this elephant in the car, Michelle. It must've filled his rear-view mirror. Certainly it felt like it was crushing the breath out of me. It was a dark shadow cast

295

over him when he pulled up. You could see it – it was as if he was hollowed out.'

'Did you ask him in?'

Vita shook her head.

'Did you ask him anything?'

She shook her head again.

'Did you kiss?'

'In an etiquette kind of way.'

'Poor sod,' said Michelle, 'he probably felt even worse.'

They sat side by side on Vita's couch, watching her hands shred tissues.

'And it was almost a week ago?' Michelle said.

Vita nodded.

'And you haven't heard from him?'

'He phoned – the following afternoon. But he didn't leave a message.'

'And you haven't phoned him back?'

Vita shook her head.

'Perhaps he phoned to explain. Maybe he thought you don't want to hear?'

'Perhaps I don't. Perhaps it's too tangled, all of this, for me.'

'What are you going to do?'

Vita shrugged. 'I don't think it's up to me.' She thought about it. 'Is it?'

Michelle thought about it too. 'Honey, I honestly don't know. I don't know anyone else in this situation – anyone our age, having to deal with life after death. But – oughtn't you to phone him?'

Vita went very, very quiet. 'I don't want to. I don't want to hear it – I don't want to go through the being-dumped bit. I think I'll just let it fizzle.'

'Maybe dumping you is the last thing on his mind?'

'But I daren't become involved if there's no future and

296

there can be no future if he's still so happily-sadly married. The hurt – I can't put myself through it. I need to be more responsible for myself now.'

Michelle held her hand and gave it a squeeze. 'It's good to know there are good guys out there though, hey? It's good to know that you, too, can feel it all – despite the Tim crap. You *felt* it, with Oliver. It's just very unjust that the timing was skewed.'

'I've never felt anything like it,' Vita smiled forlornly. 'It was fast for me – and real. From the start.'

'I know.'

'He's special,' Vita could only whisper, 'but he's still DeeDee's.'

'I know,' Michelle whispered back. 'And as your best friend, I'm telling you that you can't let yourself fall in love with a man who's involved with another woman. Ever again. Christ – the irony. It's like Tim – but so *not* like Tim.'

'I know,' Vita wept, 'I know.'

The week passed, crawled along. It limped into the next; and soon it would be a fortnight since that supper. And Oliver was something of a nightmare to work with and a nightmare to live with and Jonty had him in both.

'Is your pa all right, mate?' Boz asked. 'I almost think he shouldn't be wielding a chainsaw at the moment.'

Jonty shrugged. 'It was that lady – the cagoule lady. Vita.'

'I thought that was a good thing?'

'Me too,' said Jonty, 'I thought she was nice. Cool, actually. Good for my dad. But she seems to have gone.'

'Has he said anything?'

'He shouted at her not to load the dishwasher.'

'You what? I meant – has he said anything, *to you*? And what's with the dishwasher?'

Jonty thought about it. And then it struck him. That dishwasher was running their lives – it had been crazy when his mum was alive and somehow, it was even crazier now she was dead. Who the fuck has a dishwasher for a shrine? Life would be so much easier if they used the frikkin' thing. And then he had a light-bulb moment. 'Boz – I know we're due at wherever we're due – but do you think we could go via town, via that shop, That Shop?'

'That's cool, mate,' said Boz and he ruffled Jonty's hair and gave him a gentle punch on the arm. 'We'll go in on the way back.'

'I need to go in on my own.'

'That's cool too, mate.'

And Jonty thought, I think I might tell Boz what's with the dishwasher. He's like an older brother. It'll be good to talk.

Although the final bank holiday weekend of the year was about to start, there was an unmistakable back-to-school feeling in Wynford, not just in the wares and window displays, but in the way that mothers now marched with their children, as though to put an efficiency back into their lives, as though there had to be a purpose to their pace between places in which items for school could be ticked off lists. Vita had put pencil boxes and satchels, personalized drinking flasks and colourful notebooks in the window display; pots crammed with pens, bowls with fruit-scented erasers and safety sharpeners by the till. The shop was now busiest mid-mornings. It was as if, to shop during what soon would be school hours, was a last nod to the freedom of the summer holidays. She had a manic trade in etching children's names onto traditional wooden pencil boxes, using a special hot iron pen for the purpose. She couldn't offer a while-you-wait service because she liked to spend time on the calligraphy. But she also found that offering a next-day personalization service for free meant that the customer came in twice and usually spent money on both visits. This time last year, Tim had insisted she charge two pounds for the service. But this year he seemed to have disappeared from the life of the shop, as well as from Vita's.

She reckoned she could finish her book by closing time. She was going to go to Michelle's tonight to help with tomorrow's BBQ. She was seeing her mum on Sunday. She hadn't thought about bank holiday Monday yet. Candy perhaps. Something – she'd have to have something organized. She hadn't had a customer since mid-afternoon and now it was tea-time. She went to the back, poured herself the last of the iced coffee, a jug of which she made each morning. She drank far more iced coffee than she ever drank hot.

Buy de-caff.

She wrote a Post-it and stuck it to the fridge door and went back into the shop to find Jonty waiting patiently by the till.

'Hiya,' he gave his awkward half-height wave. He'd had a haircut and yet his fringe appeared longer than ever. And very black. All the more so because the T-shirt emblazoned with a skeleton was incongruously yellow.

'Hi?'

'I – er.' He shuffled and mumbled and fiddled with the erasers. 'This is totally strawberryish,' he marvelled.

'Sniff the green one.'

'Wow.' He sniffed again. 'Wow – that's mega-appley.'

'Weird, aren't they.'

'How much are they?'

'Fifty pence.'

299

He started rooting around in his pocket.

'Don't be daft, Jonty – have one,' she said, 'take a couple.'

'Seriously?' She might as well have offered him free gold ingots.

'They cost me pennies.'

He chose an apple one. And a strawberry one too. Vita doubted very much whether he'd actually take them to school.

'I got my GCSEs,' he told her. And by the time she'd finally coaxed out of him that the two he had taken a year early both achieved A*, he'd turned the colour of the strawberry eraser.

'That's amazing!' she said. And she thought, Oliver must be cock-a-hoop. And then she thought, DeeDee would have been so very proud.

'Well,' he said, 'y'know. I'd better scoot.'

She looked at him. 'Nice to see you – thanks for calling in.'

And Jonty very nearly left it at that.

'Um, Vita.' His voice had changed. And so had his demeanour. He was standing tall, looking right at her. 'I just wanted to say – you weren't to know. About the dishwasher.'

'It's OK, Jonty – honestly, I understa—'

But he cut her off. He raised his hand as if stopping traffic. 'The really really stupid thing about it is that Mum and Dad used to argue the whole time about it. It used to really wind Mum up because Dad was so crap at putting things in. And it used to totally get on Dad's nerves the way Mum was obsessed with doing it her way. The *whole* time.'

He looked at Vita who was looking right back at him.

'I wish my dad would use the frikkin' thing – we both

hate bloody washing up. Did you see how many teaspoons and mugs we have? We buy loads – and pile them up for Mrs Blackthorne to do. She's our cleaner.'

Vita smiled. It was she who washed all the mugs, all the time, in the shop. She missed not having a dishwasher at Pear Tree Cottage. She'd loved stacking Tim's. She didn't remember whether they'd ever fallen out about it. At the time, she never really noticed how equally or otherwise the division of labour fell.

'Anyway,' Jonty said, 'it's just – I know this sounds bizarre – but it's just that we haven't actually used it since Mum died. Not once. Not a single time.' He gave Vita a contorted smile as if he'd just confessed the most excruciatingly embarrassing thing.

'So Dad was a bit –' He stumbled for vocabulary. 'A bit –' He paused. 'You know what, he sort of overreacted, I think. If you want my opinion. For what it's worth.'

'I wish I'd known,' Vita said regretfully.

'I wish I'd thought to tell you,' said Jonty. 'I wish we had. But in some ways it did some good. It – it –' He fumbled around for the words. And when they came he spoke them with a deep American accent. *'It, like, totally broke the spell of the dishwasher, man.'*

Vita laughed.

Jonty looked at the floor. He seemed to shrink back to teenager stature again, as if he'd been granted just a few minutes of time as an adult. 'Anyway, I wanted you to know that. And I wanted you to know that Dad's been in a crap mood. And I wanted you to know that too. In case, you know, he phones. Or in case you feel like phoning him? Or something. I dunno. I don't know how these things are done. I don't have a girlfriend – thank *God*.'

Vita was overwhelmed with the same compulsion to hug the kid that she'd experienced at his house. But the table was between them, as were all the words and sentiments with which he'd come in, all on his own, to deliver. All she could do was give him the eraser that was mega-bananary too.

*　*　*

It was the upturned mug full of sedimenty water that did it. That, and the forks still with food gunk on them. It was very late. Oliver was unloading the dishwasher which he'd used for the first time, cursing the thing for not cleaning properly. And then he thought, I should have let Vita stack it last week. She'd've known just how to do it. And then he thought, Oh God – I thought of Vita in the first instance. Vita came first, into my mind. And he went up to bed and picked up the photo of DeeDee and sat on the floor holding it in his hands as he wept. But DeeDee just kept on smiling, over his shoulder. Smiling and smiling that fantastic wonky grin of hers.

Oliver slept fitfully for an hour or two, soon wide awake in the small hours.

He dressed silently.

He left the house soundlessly, put the car into neutral and rolled down the drive without the engine on. Then he drove away as quietly as could and drove fast to Wynfordbury Hall, parking up by the great iron gates. The moon picked out the swirls and curlicues, transforming them from metal into lace. They were shut. He didn't expect them to be open, he didn't need them to be, he didn't even check. He walked alongside the wall, trailing his hand against the lichen-licked stones until he found the place he was looking for. You'd've thought, by now, all these years later, they'd've fixed it. But they hadn't. And so he climbed, a little less easily than he'd done the first time, but he made it up and over and soon enough he was walking through the trees in the moonlight.

The Cowgirl

Daylight can be harsh. Daylight can also cast shadows over what seemed a good idea at night. Oliver, therefore, made a further trip to Wynfordbury Hall on the morning of bank holiday Sunday, approaching through the gates this time, along with the other visitors. It was so hot that many folk were choosing to picnic in the shade of the arboretum rather than on the exposed swathes of grass. As he passed the Wynfordbury Yew, he could hear the squeals and scamper of children inside it – a living, mysterious, secret playground which every child should have the opportunity to experience. It was heartening to see so many people, the families in particular, enjoying the great outdoors and eschewing the tat and grime of the bank holiday funfair on the other side of town. He walked away from the yew, on towards the outer reaches of the estate. He walked with purpose. He needed to check something, from his sortie two nights ago. Check it was still as he'd intended it to be. And then he was going to call by Vita's. And if she wasn't in, he was going to phone her. And if there was no answer, he'd wait until she was home.

*

Ruth Whitbury didn't trust it when her daughter was so conscientiously upbeat, skitting over direct questions as if they were puddles on a path, smiling as if her life depended on it, breezing over how life was treating her, laughing excessively over things that warranted only a mere chuckle. They were linking arms, the two of them, strolling along the river path. They were walking out of town and along to the Swan Inn for Sunday lunch. Can't do a thing on an empty stomach, Ruth thought. She intended to feed her daughter and then, over dessert, she'd pull out of her whatever was caught so deeply inside. Just as her husband had managed the splinters when Vita was a little girl. He'd distract Vita with a choc-ice and the television and then he'd deftly needle and tweeze the splinter out without his daughter realizing.

They chose a picnic table near to the water's edge. They were lucky it was free – many people were having to loll on the grass, with their pints at precarious angles on the ground and their ploughman's lunches perched on their laps. Vita insisted on spending a long time larkily discussing whether, having ordered two – one ham, one stilton – she should have asked for plough*mens*' lunches. She was still hanging on this thread when she'd all but finished her summer pudding.

'It's like my friends the Boardmans,' Vita said. 'If I'm talking about more than one of them – should I refer to them as the Board*men*?'

Her mother thought this was a tangent too far. 'And talking of friends, darling – how's your young man? Well, I know you said he's older – but I'm ancient so he's still a whippersnapper to me.'

Vita just nodded. Nodded at the swans, at the water, at the last spoonful on her plate, at her mother.

'He's well, is he?'

305

'He's . . . It's not going to work out. What a shame!'
and Vita smiled her way through it.

'That *is* a pity,' her mother said.

'He's . . . It's not the right time for him, Mum,' Vita
said.

'Why? Did he tell you so?'

'No,' Vita said slowly, looking away from her mother's
arched eyebrow. 'Not exactly. He didn't need to. You can
tell.'

'You can? How?'

'He's still grieving.'

'He always will, darling.'

'Exactly,' Vita said quietly.

'Grief takes on a variety of different shades,' her mother
said. 'It's nothing for you to be frightened of.'

'I'm not frightened,' said Vita.

'Are you sure it's not you who has the problem with
his grief?'

Vita felt irritated. This was not the sort of conversation
to be having with one's mother and certainly not on a
gorgeous bank holiday Sunday.

'Mum – I must look after myself. I don't want to set
myself up for another fall. I don't want to be second best
to another woman ever again – living or dead.'

Her mother thought about it, thought about her
daughter. She knew her so well, far better than Vita
thought. 'I don't doubt you can look after yourself.'

'I can. So can we just drop it? It's not easy – any of
this. Talking to you about – this. I didn't think I'd be on
my own in my mid-thirties. I thought I'd be happy with
a young family of my own. So please – can we just drop
it? Oliver was lovely – really lovely. But maybe three years
isn't so long since his wife died. He's unavailable.'

'Darling, you need to accept that you will be between

306

two women for some time. You will stand there, looking over your shoulder at the woman your ex takes after you – and you will look in front of you at the woman your new man has had before you. I don't think it's the men who are your problem – it's their women. Living – or dead.' She paused. 'It's not a competition, you know. Have a little faith, darling – please.'

'Drop it, mother,' Vita muttered.

So Ruth decided to drop it. She didn't want to run the risk of doing more harm than good. She'd done so before – pleading with her daughter to take Tim back the first time Vita left him. 'Shall we move on?' Ruth stood and offered her arm for her daughter to link hers with.

I shall move on.

'Let's!' and Vita's smile, unnervingly beatific, was rigor mortised to her face once more.

Vita could hear her house phone ringing as she unlocked the door but it had stopped by the time she was inside. Then her mobile started up. It'll be Mum, checking I'm home OK.

No, it's not. It's Oliver.

Let it go through to voicemail.

Do not let this call go through to voicemail.

Vita knew precisely how many rings she had left to decide.

Her mum's voice was in her head. But so too was Jonty's. Generations apart – but strangely united.

Come on! Just answer it! If you bottle, once you've done so, just say, Oops, I have to go.

She closed her eyes, took a breath, and answered.

'Hullo?'

'Hullo, missy.'

'Hullo, Oliver.'

307

'How are you?'

'I'm well – and you?'

'I'm well. Jonty always says, "I'm good" – that is rich American, but it's poor English.'

That's so Oliver. 'Poor kid! I bet you never let him use "random", do you?' Chatting. I'm chatting. This is pointless.

Oliver laughed. 'Certainly not.'

A pause. Quick!

'Vita – I –' Bugger. He'd practised this and now he was rummaging around for the words the way he'd ferret around in the glove compartment for his house keys. He'd invested those missing words with the potential to unlock. Where the fuck were they?

'It's OK,' Vita was saying because she didn't want to hear – *stuff*. 'It's fine. I understand. Honestly. No biggie.'

'No – it's not fine. I wanted to see you – just to explain.'

'I –' Then Vita thought, No. 'No,' she said. 'You don't have to explain. It's fine. I'm fine. I understand.'

And then Oliver thought, No. He thought, No – I'm not going to let you go so easily. 'No,' he said. 'Sorry,' he said. He said, 'that just won't do.'

'Pardon?'

'Stay there – I'm coming over.'

'*Pardon?*'

'Bye.'

Moments later, he was at her door. He'd made the calls from around the corner. She was tempted to dart out of the kitchen door, wasps, pears, whatever. But then she thought of all those conversations she'd never had the chance to have with Tim, precious words which had remained trapped and ricocheting around her head, unheard, un-exorcised. It's called Closure, she thought

308

rather grandly. And then she thought, Just answer the bloody door and whatever he has to say, take it on the chin. Whatever you hear, make it useful for the long run, in the closure stakes. So she opened the door slowly, just a crack, as if he might be Jehova's Witnesses or, worse, that odd chap wanting to talk about speed bumps from the neighbourhood scheme she wished she'd never joined.

'Hullo,' Oliver said, peering in at the half a face he could see.

'Hi.'

'I don't want to come in – it's OK,' he said, 'but I want you to come with me.'

She looked at him, suspiciously.

'Please?'

'Where are we going?'

'Please.' No question mark this time.

She left him on the doorstep, went straight past her door keys and through into the kitchen where she gave herself a moment. Come on, girl, she told herself. Outside, in the branches of the pear tree, DeeDee's wasp catchers were doing their job. Outside, on her doorstep, Oliver was waiting. She retraced her steps, picked up her keys and left the house to see Oliver already walking away down the path.

He drove her directly to his home.

They didn't go in through the front door; this time, he took her around to the side gate and walked ahead of her into his back garden. There was a bowl of strawberries on the wooden table, a jug of Pimm's, a plate of shortbread biscuits. Two chairs were set, with plump floral cushions. She knew just who they were by.

'They cost silly money in comparison to the sensible

green wipeable ones from the garden centre,' he said, as if reading her mind.

'They're Cath Kidston,' Vita said. Just as DeeDee had said to him. Fait accompli. What's the problem? Men!

'Please,' he said, motioning to the chair he'd just drawn back. 'Come and sit in the lap of Cath Kidston.'

He poured her some Pimm's. He swiped away a wasp and offered her a strawberry, the biscuits. And they sat, quietly, not knowing who was meant to say what next.

A barrage of thoughts racketed through her head. If he was going to dump me, wouldn't he have done so on my doorstep? He wouldn't have done the Pimm's and the strawberries and the cushions thing, surely? She glanced at him shyly. He looked relaxed. Looking out at his garden. She followed his gaze.

'Blimey, your garden's in a bit of a state, Mr B,' she said quietly.

'I know,' he said, 'you're right. It is. But I've booked a bloke to come in for a few days this week.'

She nodded. She thought that was the end of that and wondered what to converse politely on next. But then Oliver started talking again.

'I've hardly been out here since DeeDee died. It was her territory. I haven't wanted to come out here – but then I thought of Pimm's, how I haven't had Pimm's yet this summer. And I thought about strawberries and how comfortable these second-mortgage cushions are. And I thought to myself how much I wanted to sit out here, on them, on the last bank holiday Sunday, sipping Pimm's – *with you*. So!'

Vita stirred and stirred the drink, crushing the mint against the side of the glass, sucking thoughtfully on a boozy chunk of apple.

'So there you have it,' said Oliver and he necked his

310

entire glassful down. He replenished it. 'Vita,' he said and this time he reached for her arm – his lovely way of putting his hand over her wrist – 'the other night, I couldn't believe how out of sorts I felt. The last few weeks with you – I've felt so relaxed, happy. Then, *here* – suddenly I was on a knife edge. I just didn't realize that there are still things that are a first, for me, after DeeDee. They're milestones, however bizarre or banal they might seem. Some are more logical – the first birthdays, Christmas. Some are odd – the first online delivery from Ocado, selected by me, unpacked by me. Some loom large ages in advance – you dread them, prepare for them, get through them – the change of a year, for instance. Others – like the other week – come out of the blue. I'm sorry. For shouting. For not explaining.' He let go of her wrist and stroked her forearm, covered her hand with his. 'I owe you that honesty. I've missed you.'

And I've missed you too.

So tell him.

He's speaking. He's on a roll.

So listen.

'It's not just the sex – I've been all right on that front, in that I've shagged when I've needed to,' he said and she almost choked on another piece of apple. 'But it's the *connection*, the emotional – *stuff*. The feeling *for* someone, rather than just feeling them. Well – it's both, if I'm honest. And with you, it's new. Sex with you is great – fantastic. And the connection – it's *there*. Well, it is for me. And that's great too. But new. I'm feeling my way, Vita.'

He refilled her glass.

'The other week – in the kitchen. The dishwasher. Look, it's going to sound daft, but –'

And Vita wondered whether to save him the load, whether to tell him about Jonty's visit. Would that help

311

him? Would that be kind and the right thing to do? To let him know that, in his own gawky way, his son was giving his dad the thumbs-up and an active shove in the right direction?

'I know about the dishwasher,' Vita interrupted him quickly. 'Jonty popped in to the shop – and he told me.'

'*Jonty?*'

'Yes.'

'The blighter!'

'Not at all. He's such a great kid.'

'Playing Puck, eh?'

'So let him.'

'Really?' Oliver's eyes were suddenly glinting.

'Really,' Vita nodded. And then she thought, Look at all these words he's given me. And then she thought, actions speak louder. So she walked round to Oliver and sat on his lap, held his face in her hands and kissed him with her eyes gently boring into his. There they sat for a while, holding each other, alternately gazing at each other or way out into the garden.

'By the way,' Vita said, 'where *is* Jonty? You haven't plonked him in front of the TV with a ready meal on his lap, have you?'

Oliver laughed. 'He's gone camping again – back to the same place. He's home tomorrow night.'

'So we have the house to ourselves?'

'We do.'

And they looked at each other and all the romantic gazing and tenderness was replaced by lascivious grins. The kissing changed from affectionate to lustful and, with her lips still lightly against his, Vita asked him, Well, what are you waiting for.

* * *

312

Initially, they are both acutely aware that they are in his house, in his home, his bedroom. He's let her in.

This is his marital bed.

Stop thinking about this being his marital bed.

Thankfully, Vita hasn't noticed the photo of DeeDee on the drawers over there.

Oliver is grazing the side of her neck, his hands running fast over her body, and her eyes are closing as she's melting into his arms.

*   *   *

'You're the first man I've known not to do the rolling-over-with-a-fart-and-snoozing off after sex,' Vita told him as they lay entwined some time later.

He propped himself up on one arm, lifting the sheet to take an exaggerated ravenous peek at her body. 'And have you had *many* men, then?'

He laughed at how startled she looked.

'A handful,' she shrugged. He nodded. 'You?' she asked.

'More than a handful,' he said. And then he thought, Ought I to tell her? About the website, the hotels? Do they or don't they count? And then he thought, Pete Yorke doesn't exist any more.

'Since DeeDee?' she asked.

Oliver wondered whether, if honesty was partially hidden, it became deceit? 'A fair few,' he admitted. 'It took a while – to want it again. And then it took a while not to feel I was being somehow adulterous.'

Vita looked pensive.

'It was just sex,' he said bluntly. 'Anyway, missy – what about you? Post-Tim? Been out on the pull much, love?'

Vita thought about Rick and then she started giggling. She couldn't stop. Was that really only a couple of months

313

ago? She snorted through her nose, burying her head in Oliver's chest, groaning at the memory.

'Are you going to share the joke?'

She looked at Oliver and suddenly she sensed how funny he'd find it too. Sorry, Rick, sorry to laugh at your expense.

Vita told Oliver about Rick, accent and all.

He rolled away from her. 'You shouldn't have told me that,' he said, very seriously.

'Oh – I,' Vita was alarmed. 'It's just – I thought.'

And suddenly some strange Gestapo man was in bed beside her, slipping his hand between her legs, slipping his finger up inside her. 'Ve have vays, jah? Vays to make you talk. Nein, not to talk but to *moan*. Vays to make you moan, jah? Fraulein Vitbury? Zis make you moan?'

'Stop it! You idiot man, stop it, I'll pee myself!'

In an instant, an Italian stallion was now working his way over her body, begging her for a golden shower, calling her his *bambina*, calling her his *fettuccine*, saying *mamma mia* a lot.

'Enough!'

But a cowboy with a deep voice full of high-plains dirt took his place and was now pinning her down. 'You ridden a bronco, bay-beh?' He was pushing up inside her. 'A buckin' bronco? A buckin' fuckin' bronco, honey?' He rolled her over so that she was on top.

'I can do a reverse cowgirl, if you like?' And, winking at the stupefied expression on Oliver's face, Vita lithely turned around. Then, facing away from him, she screwed herself down on his cock, giving him a great view of her bum. He slapped her buttocks and said, Ride 'em, cowgirl. And she did. She was riding him vigorously. The laughter subsided into unbridled lust. Good, wholesome, filthy sex. She was intoxicatingly close to coming. And then she caught sight of DeeDee, the photo of DeeDee on the chest

314

of drawers. And Vita was transfixed, staring at her, but all the while DeeDee was looking over Vita's shoulder to Oliver. And then Oliver was coming and as he was coming, Vita felt herself going again, deflating as if she had a tiny puncture that wouldn't cause any trouble so long as no one crushed her. Thus, as Oliver caught his breath again, marvelling post-orgasmically in an accent that was a mixture of Chinese and Welsh, Vita felt the wind being sucked out of her.

Oliver's Russian accent was very good but Vita didn't want to hear it. She wanted to talk and she needed answers spoken sensibly. She brought her face close to his; he looked sleepy, replete, happy. Was this any of her business? Was this fair? Candy had told her that there comes a point in a new relationship when it's no longer possible to probe about previous partners, you have to let it go. You can talk openly in the very early days before emotions run deep, after which it's case closed. Had she had her chances, on their first dates? Had she asked all that she needed to know?

'Oliver?'

'Hmmm.'

'Tell me more about DeeDee?'

He continued to look at Vita, his eyes now flitting a little, as if trying to ascertain what it was that she wanted.

'Please?' She stroked his arm, bringing her hand to rest on his chest.

'What do you want to know?'

'I'm a girl,' she shrugged, 'girls need details.'

Oliver thought about what to say. 'She was bright – quite feisty. Infuriating, sometimes – so stubborn and usually right. But I've told you this, haven't I?'

Vita nodded and shrugged.

'You ask me,' he said. And he answered Vita's questions on DeeDee's life; from where and when they'd met to where and when he had proposed to her, to what their wedding had been like. How had he felt when DeeDee told him she was pregnant? Was he at the birth? What was her sense of humour like? How did she dress? What were her friends like and do they keep in touch? What kind of mum was she? Where did they holiday? What was she *like*? And then he answered her questions on DeeDee's death. The brutal facts she knew already – but she wanted to know where she is buried. Oh, cremated. Her ashes? Up north. Does he still see her family? As often as ever they did – two or three times a year. And Vita wanted to know how, how on earth did he *cope*? Oliver took each question thoughtfully and in the spirit in which it had been asked. And he answered fully, sometimes with laughter, sometimes with difficulty, but he answered everything.

It was almost dark. He was all talked out. Vita's head racketed with information which was being sifted into her heart and filtered into the pit of her stomach.

'Supper?' he asked.

'What is it?'

'Beans on toast?'

He wandered downstairs, leaving Vita alone in his room. She kept her face turned resolutely away from the chest of drawers as she dressed. She was about to leave the room – the smell of hot buttered toast tantalizing – but she couldn't. She shuffled, her head down, over to the drawers. Slowly, she raised her eyes, fixing them on the base of the photo frame, inching her way up DeeDee's body until she was looking at her face. She didn't know what to say. DeeDee wouldn't look her straight in the eye.

*

316

Beans on toast never tasted so good. They sat at the kitchen counter, passing the HP sauce between them. Vita glanced at a note from Jonty, listing what they needed from the shops, signing off with a funky cartoon character.

'He's a good little artist, isn't he?' she said.

'He's very good,' said Oliver.

'Oliver – did you?' She paused. 'Would you? Did you plan to have more kids?'

'No,' said Oliver, clearing the plates. 'We only ever planned to have the one. The Bourne Three – that was us,' he said. He was smiling and relaxed.

While Oliver made coffee, Vita wandered into the sitting room. Down here, DeeDee was staring at her – wherever Vita's eyes might alight, DeeDee was looking directly at her. Even on her wedding day. Even with Jonty squirming in her lap. Even in a crowded Christmas grouping. Nothing malevolent, Vita knew that. But this beautiful dead woman was everywhere. Omnipotent. She was surrounding her; Vita felt tiny and insubstantial in her presence.

Suddenly, she had an overwhelming desire to go home. She was in love with Oliver. She knew it. Deeply. And that's what made the pain more acute. She'd spent the last few hours laughing her head off, gorged on beans on toast, talked and talked about life and death. She'd had Pimm's and strawberries and incredible sex twice. Erotic, exquisite lovemaking followed by a hot, horny, humour-filled fuck. But, with DeeDee so firmly in the picture, never mind all the photos, and with all this information about her now in Vita's head straight from Oliver's heart, she just wanted to go home. It occurred to Vita that a much-loved late wife was just so different from an ex-girlfriend. Fundamentally so. She wanted to go home. Alone. God almighty, love could be cruel.

*

How will I ever not feel that I'm stealing this man from the woman who loved him so?

How will I ever feel that he wouldn't rather be with her?

'Coffee! Jonty and I polished off those posh mints, but I found a packet of— Vita?'

He put the tray down.

'Are you OK?'

'I don't feel so good.'

'A glass of water? Paracetamol?'

'I just want to go home.'

'Have a lie-down here.'

'I just want to go home.'

Helping Hands

'Now you're just being a masochist,' Candy said. 'Actually, you're being a self-centred idiot. Oliver is taking a chance on this second chance at love – and you're going to take it away from him?' She sounded flabbergasted.

'V, you *have* to make your peace with DeeDee,' Michelle was actually quite cross. 'You can't let the opportunity you're being given for a wonderful relationship be scuppered by a ghost of your imaginings.'

Candy nodded vehemently. They were eating *matooke*, Candy's speciality – a stew of green plantains and beef in a sauce rich with tomato and peanuts. It was a taste Vita had known since schooldays, when she first met Candy. It was so nostalgic, so comforting. She thought back to how she'd smelt it before she'd tasted it, over half her lifetime ago.

'I remember,' said Vita wistfully, 'the first time I saw your parents – when I was riding my bike around the flats at the back of my house. There they were, on their brand-new doorstep, swathed in these incredible colours and fabrics – so much material. The way it was tied in a flourish around your mum's head. The way your dad was in a sort of tunic – but so exotic. I thought they were the King and Queen of Somewhere. That's why I stopped my bike, not to stare – but to curtsey. And then I smelt this smell and your mum smiled and told me it was *nyama choma*. Then your dad asked, "How old are you, young lady? We have a daughter who is fourteen." His voice was so beautiful – deep, melodious, rhythmic.'

'And why, for fuck's sake, are you reminiscing about all this now?' Candy interrupted. 'You can butter me up with your soppy memories all you like – but you're still going to answer Michelle and me.'

'I'm not the right person for Oliver,' Vita said. Christ, what more did they want?

'Last time, your excuse was that this isn't the right time for Oliver,' said Michelle. 'But it seems to me, from his point of view, it is.'

'And now you're saying you're not the right woman for him,' said Candy. 'Is that his point of view, or yours?' She pointed the serving spoon at Vita and glowered at her. 'Where does Oliver's opinion come into all of this? You're not letting him have his say on either – on timing *or* you. You're putting thoughts in his head – that the poor sod doesn't even know he's having.'

'You're not in competition with his late wife, you know.'

That was enough. How insensitive and thick *were* her friends?

'For fuck's sake, Michelle, I *am*. Can't you see? I *am*! That's the problem. He *can't* see it. That's the point. Jesus – you two!'

'You're not giving him a chance! Show him some respect!' Candy was really irritated.

'I don't even think Oliver has anything to do with it,' Michelle countered. 'It's all about you, Vita.' The three of them fell silent for a moment. 'Your point of view is actually precisely that – it's your point of *you*,' said Michelle.

'Well, why shouldn't it be about me?' Vita reacted. 'Don't I have a responsibility to myself? Why should I settle for being second best?'

Michelle knew she and Candy now ran the risk of Vita bolting out of the door so she went to her, put her hands on her shoulders, made Vita accept a hug. She softened her tone. 'I know this is a quagmire to you – but it's clear to me. To Candy. With Tim you felt in permanent competition with his dark side if you like – and you went all out battling for a man not worth keeping. With Oliver, you're tiptoeing away from someone solid and good – no edge, no agenda, nothing hidden – but it's you and only you who's dazzled by the light of the lovely but late wife.'

'Exactly!' Vita tried to flinch away from Michelle's embrace.

'*No*. You don't get it,' Michelle shook her. 'This is *your* perception, Vita. This is *your* issue. Poor Oliver. Jesus – I'd be very surprised if he gave you another chance. If you think about it, V, it's your problem – not his. It seems to me he didn't have a problem with any of it.'

'But there's another woman,' Vita wailed. 'Living, dead – it's still a *ménage à trois*, once again. But this time, I won't compete because I can't.'

'But Vita,' Michelle said, very steadily and with a gentle, wise smile. 'This was a woman who inspired Oliver to believe so steadfastly in love. You have much to be grateful to her for. He's not searching for a replacement DeeDee. He's just ready to love and be loved again. It's all he wants in life.'

Oliver was confused as to why, if Vita hadn't actually come down with some terrible lurgy, she was still adamant by midweek that she wanted to be at home, on her own. She wasn't particularly chatty on the phone and he'd called in to the shop the next day to see how she was, only she scurried about saying she was rushed off her feet though the shop had been quiet and spic and span. He'd suggested plans for the weekend but she mumbled about her mum and Michelle and so many things to do. He'd phoned her to chat about nothing in particular but got nothing at all in return.

'A woman her age wouldn't be playing hard to get, would she?'

'Sorry?' It was Tinker. Oliver realized he must have spoken aloud.

'Girl trouble,' he muttered. 'Sorry, Tinker. Forget it. Let's go.'

'They're trouble all right,' Tinker laughed, 'but they're kinda worth the trouble too.'

This heartened Oliver. He'd cut her some slack, he decided. He'd put it down to Time of the Month. Something like that. If he hadn't heard from her by tomorrow, he'd call into the shop again, perhaps with some flowers or a sticky bun. Something like that. Or maybe he'd pop by tonight, clean out the wasp traps. He knew Vita well enough to know she wasn't the type to play games. Unless, of course, it was cowboys and cowgirls. He grinned. It had put a smile on his face last Sunday – and it was doing so again right now.

'You all right boss?'

'Oh yes, Tinker,' said Oliver, 'I'm absolutely fine.'

*　*　*

'But it's not a T or an S day,' Jonty said, 'so I should be coming in to work with you.'

'Put your uniform on – we can't be late on your first

322

day back.' Oliver straightened Jonty's tie as Jonty slouched into his blazer.

'I had a great summer, Dad.'

'It's not over yet, kiddo.'

'I know – but it's back to school. And it sucks.'

'You're a star, Jont. You'll be fine.'

'I know – but I want to do what you do, so what's the point of studying frikkin' *Hamlet* and biology.'

'Biology – you'll be learning all about lady bits,' his father said. '*Hamlet* – well, we all had to read *Hamlet* at school, like we all had to have our BCGs at school too. Painful at the time – but in the long term, you'll be extremely grateful. By the way, do you really want to do what I do?'

'What – be a woodchip off the old block, Dad?' Jonty nodded and grinned. 'It's ace.'

'Well, first, you need more GSCEs, a bucketful of A levels, a gap year, three lost years at uni, not to mention four rungs of qualifications before you can even take a chainsaw up a tree – and then we'll talk family business. Oh – that'll be Mrs Blackthorne. Good – I owe her for last week.'

'Morning, Mrs Blackthorne.'

'Back to school is it, Jonty?'

'Yeah.'

'Hullo, Mr Bourne.'

'Good morning, Mrs Blackthorne – how are you?'

'Not complaining, Mr Bourne.'

'I owe you for last week.'

'When you're ready – bread and water suits me fine.'

Oliver smiled. Part of the furniture, Mrs Blackthorne.

She was already in the sitting room, gingerly picking up a takeaway carton as if handling a dead mouse by the tail.

'You've moved the photos around,' she said casually.

'What photos?'

'*All* the photos,' she said, with a broad sweep of her doughy forearm.

'I haven't touched the photos – they're always just *there*; like the books.'

'They're not in the same spots, they've been moved around.'

Oliver looked around the room. It seemed to him there was no change. All the photos were still there, on the shelves and windowsills, on the mantelpiece, the side table.

'What's up, Dad?' Jonty came into the room to see Mrs Blackthorne with hands on her hips and his Dad looking confused.

'Mrs Blackthorne says the photos have been moved around,' Oliver told him. 'Have you moved them?'

Jonty looked around. 'No?' He looked confused. 'They're always there, aren't they? All of them?'

Mrs Blackthorne huffed. 'They're all present – but they're not correct. This one should be *there*. That one is usually like *this*. Those two normally face *this* way, and that one over there – what's it doing looking out into the garden?' She rearranged the frames like so. Jonty wandered out and into the kitchen to take an apple for break-time.

'It's the sort of thing a woman would notice,' Mrs Blackthorne said and her words hung in the air like a vast banner. Black and white.

Oliver sat down heavily on the arm of the sofa. 'Shit,' he said, 'oh shit.'

Michelle and Candy's words lay so heavily on Vita that she couldn't focus on fiction and, though *A Prayer for Owen Meaney* lay open in front of her, she was unable to read a word. There was a knot of facts in a tangle in her head, conflicting with the desolation in her heart and the ache in her stomach. It was a relief when customers came in. Vita leapt at the chance to chat. All the schools were back and mothers were visiting the shop as if at a loss at what to do with their days but spend money on half-price bunting and a new mug in which to make a comforting cup of tea when they returned home alone. A steady stream of them came in and business, though not particularly lucrative, was brisk. There was a lull after lunch and then it picked up again before the school run – it was always the same at the start of term, mums killing time because they were too early for pick-up. Rick had phoned, telling Vita about a new line he'd be sending her a sample of. Food with cute little bugs in them. Lift the core out of the wooden apple, find the colourful maggot inside. No thank you, said Vita. How about a drink then, said Rick. No thank you, said Vita. So a shag's out of the question, said Rick and Vita had laughed at that one. It was all amicable now. The karma was good. Tim had texted saying he was away on business, to call if she needed him. She didn't.

When the old lady came in, Vita was just selling the last of the bunting.

'I don't suppose I shall have a chance to use this until next summer,' said the customer wistfully.

'Pop it away, then, like you do your Christmas things,' Vita said warmly. And the customer went on to buy two golden letters in the shape of an F and a G that were twice the price of the bunting. Vita waited until she'd left the shop, waited until she'd seen the old lady pocket the fizzing bath bomb (it was the mandarin one – the least popular in colour and scent) before she said hullo.

The old lady nodded and started to approach, as if

about to speak to Vita, when Oliver came in. He walked straight up to the till table and put his hands down flat.

'Please,' he said, 'I need to talk to you.'

Vita nodded. 'That's fine,' she said awkwardly.

He glanced over his shoulder, noted the old lady, now systematically looking at each and every greeting card on the carousel. He lowered his voice to a whisper.

'I'm not going to let you go, you know. I'm not going to let you think you can just *go*.'

'Oliver,' Vita looked down, saw the words swimming on the page of her book, blurring as tears gauzed her sight.

'Vita – I've been through a lot. *You've* been through a lot. We've been given a chance. For God's sake – let's take it.'

'Is it a chance?' she whispered back. 'Or is it bad timing, a bad idea? You've been through *so* much, Oliver. It's not *me* you want – you long for DeeDee. I'm not her reincarnation. I'm so sorry.'

It was excruciating having to whisper the words they wanted to give such expression to.

'Have I not expressed fully enough how I feel about you?' He was insulted. 'Who are you to judge what I'm feeling without asking me first?'

'It's just – it's just. I'm *not* DeeDee. I'm only *me*.'

'Jesus – what did that bloke do to your self-esteem? You're beautiful, Vita, and I *love* you. You. I love Jonty. I love DeeDee. I quite like myself and I certainly love *you*. You must trust again, Vita. You *must*.'

His throat was aching with the effort of containing so much in so little sound.

'You need more time,' she whispered, not daring to look him in the eye. 'I think.'

'No, I do not.'

'Say you change your mind, given time?'

326

'Say you die on me?'

His words made her catch her breath and look up at him.

'We have to take the changes and chances of this mortal life, Vita – face them head on.'

She could respond only with a nod. But, as a nod, it was a symbol of hope for Oliver and it sufficed.

'Please, Vita, try – just try and believe me.'

Another small nod.

'Will you call me?'

She looked at him, her eyes teary, her face flushed. He tipped his head to one side, his expression soft as he put a finger to her cheek to halt a tear in its tracks.

'OK,' she croaked and as he turned away from her, they both wondered when that would be.

Then he was leaving, walking away, and Vita found herself both wishing he hadn't come in at all while wishing he wasn't going; longing to have the shop to herself and yet dreading being on her own. She didn't know whether to say wait or go. So she said nothing.

But the old lady, still at the greetings cards, spoke. 'Hullo!' She greeted Oliver like a long-lost friend.

'Good afternoon,' he said, a little flummoxed about being stopped but her hand was tightly on his arm.

'It's nice to see you again,' she said, smiling all the while.

Vita could see him rummaging through a mental file of clients, not finding her there. Then she saw the fast sweep of recognition. 'You too,' he said, patting her hand. 'I'm so sorry – but I must be going.'

'Perhaps I will see you again,' she said, 'you know?'

His expression changed. He glanced at Vita, capturing her gaze for a suspended moment. Then he held the door open for the old lady and they both left.

Vita had the shop to herself, just as she thought she'd wanted.

Then something very strange happened. Ten minutes later, the old lady returned. She came in noisily and made a show of taking the bath bomb from her pocket, placing it in the bowl with all the precision of a confectioner putting the final glacé cherry garnish on a gateau. Vita was about to say, It's OK! Take it! Have a luxuriate tonight – with my compliments! but the lady was making her way over.

'I've seen him,' she pointed over her shoulder with her thumb in the vague direction of the door.

'I know,' Vita said sadly. 'At Wynfordbury Hall. With me. A couple of weeks ago.'

'At Wynfordbury, yes,' she said. 'But not with you. Just the other day.' She looked at Vita askance. 'Are you OK, lassie?'

'I fall in love with the wrong men,' Vita whispered. This woman wouldn't challenge her the way her friends did. There was something comforting about being able to speak without being judged or lectured. 'It's a bit of a pain if you ask me.'

'Well, if you are asking me, I'd say that the first one – the shouty one – you're well shot of him. But this one – you'd do well to keep this one.'

'You don't know him.'

'I know he wants to keep you.'

Vita half-smiled but she was tired of people saying things they thought she wanted to hear almost as much as she dreaded them saying the things she didn't want to listen to. She was thinking of a polite way to rebuff any further musings the woman was planning, but she spoke again before Vita had the chance.

'I saw him at Wynfordbury *again*, lassie. Just Sunday gone.' She paused. 'Tristan.'

'Actually he's called Oliver,' said Vita. 'He's an arboricultural consultant. Or a tree surgeon, to you and me. That's why he was at Wynfordbury, no doubt.'

'Surgery? I wouldn't call it that. Not when you're Tristan. Poetry, more like.'

What was this daft old bat going on about?

She was leaning in close to Vita. 'He wants to keep you,' she said again. Her breath smelt of soured milk. 'You don't have to believe me, though. Tristan Tree has your answer. The truth.'

Vita couldn't sleep that night.

Why had the old lady been so convinced that Oliver wanted to keep her?

And what's with the return trips to Wynfordbury Hall, the both of them? What else was there? Who was Tristan? Who on earth was Tristan Tree? A comedy name, if ever there was one. But Vita didn't find it remotely amusing.

Tristan Tree

It was a gamble.

But Vita rationalized that if she did it, at least she'd never be able to reproach herself for having not tried her best to understand – and if she didn't do it, she might always wonder why and what if. So, in her bid to leave no leaf unturned, she set off to find some weird chap called Tristan Tree who appeared to hang out at Wynfordbury Hall at precisely the times when Oliver and the mad old woman went to visit. It took two buses and a long walk to reach the great gates but, to her bemusement, they were closed. They were bloody closed. What's all this about dawn to dusk during the summer months? September's not autumn – nowhere near! Only the horse chestnuts were turning and that, Oliver told her, was more to do with an epidemic of leaf-miner moths this year.

The gates didn't even rattle when Vita went to shake them in frustration. She swore under her breath. What a stupid thing to do in the first place. What a complete and utter waste of time. Tristan could take his flaming tree and shove it.

There was a man. It was his country trousers the colour of butter which made her notice him because the rest of him seemed to meld with the background. She caught sight of him, loping over the grass with two black Labradors trotting at his side.

'Hullo!' she called. 'Excuse me!' She raised her voice. 'Excuse me!' She yelled. 'Hey! Hey!'

He looked over to her. He was some way off. She was clinging to the gates, her arms stuck through waving at him.

'Excuse me!'

He was walking over. As he approached, she saw he carried a gun. He stopped. The dogs didn't. 'Yes?'

'Can I come in, please?' she called. Could he not come nearer? She felt like some peasant, come to the gates to beg a favour.

'We're closed.'

'You can't be!' Vita retorted. 'It's only early September and it's not dusk yet – not for an hour or two at least.'

'We're still closed – from September, it's weekends only. Come again. Do.'

'I can't! I need to come in *now*!'

'I'm terribly sorry.'

'Please!'

'Nothing's going to be chopped down before the weekend. So come again then, do!'

'You don't understand – I have to come in now. I've made the journey – on public transport. I cancelled supper with my mum. Because I need to come in *now*.'

'Why?'

'To see someone.'

'Who?'

'I've been told to see them as soon as possible.'

'Who?'

'Tristan.'

331

'Tristan?'

'Yes.'

'There is no Tristan here. And I should damn well know.'

'I think he's known as *the* Tristan?' Vita said. Her throat was tight, why couldn't the man come closer? 'Some chap called Tristan Tree?'

The man tipped his head back and roared with laughter which, while humiliating, was better than being shot at so Vita indulged him. Anyway, laughter was obviously the key – to the gates at the very least – because he was now striding over, chortling and shouting, Get down, damned dogs! because the Labs were leaping in their own merriment.

'Tristan Tree?' he said again. Vita didn't think gun-toting men should laugh with quite so much abandon. Up close, though, his face was nicely ruddy and his eyes, watering with mirth, were a pale summer-sky blue. He had a moustache that was yellowing at the ends like a swan's feathers that have been in the water. He was staggeringly tall. His dogs were drooling, he was still chuckling and all Vita really, really wanted to know was whether her journey had been wasted or not.

He was unlocking the gates, hauling one side open and gesturing for Vita to enter.

'I'm Edward,' he said, offering his hand and she was already responding with her name at the same time that he gave his surname.

Seddon.

'Oh,' Vita blushed. 'You're the Lord?'

He tipped his head to affirm. 'Now let's see what we can do about this Tristan chap, shall we? Mr Tree.' And he was off again, guffawing.

'Thank you,' said Vita. 'I appreciate it. And could you possibly put that gun down?'

'Rabbits,' Lord Seddon said. 'Pesky buggers.'

332

They walked off, with Lord Seddon veering away from the long snaking driveway, taking Vita over the parkland instead – the crow-flies route to the lake.

'It's very beautiful,' Vita said because what else was she meant to say? He'd spent the ten-minute walk asking her question upon question about who she was, where she lived and what she did, following this with in-depth probing into the state of the gift market and the parking debacle in town.

He stopped near the house. She was momentarily unsure whether she was coming in. 'I'm terribly sorry to disappoint you,' he said, 'but there really is no Tristan chap here.'

Vita's shoulders visibly slumped.

'I think you may have confused an *it* with a *him*.'

'Pardon?'

'I think you're after our Trysting Tree.'

'Your what?'

'The Trysting Tree,' he said. 'And it really could wait until the weekend. But now you're here, off you go. Past the yew. You'll know it when you see it.'

'The Trysting Tree?'

'That's right. They've been pulling your leg, your chums. Or else you heard it wrong.'

'What's a Trysting Tree, then?'

'Another bright idea of our friends, the Romans,' he said. 'Along with sewers and concrete and grid systems for roads, they thought it would be jolly good to choose the occasional tree onto which they could carve declarations of love. And guff.'

'Romans? Here?'

'Not here, dear – we're eighteenth-century, here. But the tradition goes back to the Romans. There are a few others, dotted around the country – but they tend to be kept secret by those in the love game, if you like.'

Vita had no idea what to say and, now there was no Tristan, no idea why she was here to see yet another tree.

Lord Seddon gave a little gesture with the backs of his hands as if she was a puppy he was shooing up the garden. 'Ring the bell when you're done – I'll run you back to the gates.' And he shooed her off again.

Vita walked through the arboretum, closing her eyes to detect the fragrance of the cedars as she passed; stopping momentarily at the handkerchief tree, and again at the redwood to make satisfying indentations into the soft bark with her knuckles. She walked on to the yew, feeling strangely nervous about crawling into it on her own so she kept on walking. Over her shoulder, the house became more distant before a swell of land masked it from view completely. Ahead of her, a lone tree. A grand old beech. She couldn't tell how old but it was big; its trunk straight, the bark smooth. Only when she approached she could see that, actually, it wasn't smooth at all. Into the bark, words had been carved by many, many different hands. Vita ran her fingertips over the letters, the words, sentences, symbols, all scored into the bark over generations. As she ran her fingers into and over the lines, she could sense the love of those who had engraved them.

And then she started to read the messages.

There were simple initials inscribed bluntly above and below love hearts, there were rhyming couplets sinuously engraved. Mostly, the words were positive declarations of flourishing love.

I nor wealth nor titles bring,
But I love, and love I sing.

Some, though, spoke of broken hearts.

No colour, no warmth – all is dark since you went and
I am cold.

Of secret dreams.

AC. I wait for you still. Please come. DW

'How old are some of these?' she wondered. She was awestruck. There was something beautiful yet melancholy about it all.

Forever yours, AS x.

That one seemed to be new – the wood beneath was paler. '*Sunlight & dew & me & you,*' Vita read. 'That's beautiful. But it doesn't say who it's for!' She hoped they would have known. She wondered if perhaps they never saw it. Maybe they didn't have to – maybe they knew it was true even if they didn't know it was here, carved with love for posterity. Perhaps some were never meant to be read – entrusted only to this old tree.

And then Vita stopped. She gasped out loud.

Suddenly, she knew why Oliver had brought her to Wynfordbury. It wasn't for the yew or the handkerchief tree with the long Latin name. It wasn't for the arboretum or the privilege of visiting a private estate. It wasn't for the sublime landscaping or the lake and the bridge or the house and the wisteria. It wasn't under the auspices of the Ancient Tree Hunt. Oliver brought her here so he could see how she'd fit. He wanted to witness how she felt. And when he knew how he felt – that's when he'd returned. Recently. The second time the old woman had seen him, just a few days ago. And only after that, had he'd finally brought Vita to his home.

It was too much.

She backed away from the tree, overwhelmed. Turned her back on it and sat down on the grass, catching her breath. It took some time for her to turn again and approach the tree. Very slowly, she went up close to the bark, raising her eyes little by little. It was too much to take in all at once.

The carving was simple. The lettering was very neat; as shapely as Eric Gill or Emma Bridgewater.

DeeDee & Oliver

Over the years the bark beneath the letters had darkened down. She ran her fingers along them. The serpentine of the ampersand. Smooth. Steady. And then next to DeeDee & Oliver, right next to them, with identical spacings and lettering, another ampersand and another word. Exactly the same hand. Carved with equal care and confidence.

& Vita

There. New. Permanent.

Finally, she read it out as a whole, with her eyes, with her fingers. And out loud.

DeeDee & Oliver & Vita

It spoke more to her than any soliloquy he could ever give. It said more to her than any lecture from Candy, any heart-to-heart from Michelle, any kind wisdom from her mother. Here was Oliver, between his two women and happy in his position.

It explained everything to her – who he was and what had happened and where he had been and where he was now. Where he was happy to be. She was overwhelmed. Diamonds had nothing over wood.

But it wasn't Oliver to whom Vita spoke when she finally found her voice.

She took her fingers to the letters of DeeDee's name.

'I vow to continue to love him for you,' Vita said softly; as softly as the breeze that quivered the beech leaves and took Vita's words off into the air towards autumn.

The Wynfordbury Taxicab

At first, Vita couldn't find the doorbell. She was looking for something appropriately grand and started pressing at the carvings and corbels on the porch stonework as if the bell might be subtly contained within. And then, to her right, on the outer edge of the door jamb, she saw much the same standard modern doorbell as she herself had at Pear Tree Cottage. She could hear it, within, tinnily ringing out the dongs of Big Ben. Hers certainly couldn't do that. This was followed by a cacophony of barking and, finally, Lord Seddon came to the door, with the Labradors and various other smaller dogs in a mercurial mess around his legs.

'Well, good evening, my dear,' he said. He was wearing half-moon spectacles and he looked a little like an owl. 'Dogs! Dogs! Down!'

'Hi.'

'Successful?'

She nodded.

'Jolly good. Well, goodbye then. Come again, do – at an official opening time.'

'OK.' Vita looked over her shoulder. 'It's just – you mentioned you'd drop me off at the gates?'

He gave her a look as if she was quite the most impudent girl he'd ever met – but it transpired it was just his facial expression as he wracked his brains. 'I did? So I did. Hang on a mo'.' He shut the door and soon enough Vita was standing on the great doorstep wondering if he'd forgotten she was there. Eventually, he reappeared and brandished keys at her. 'Always takes a while to find where I've forgotten I've put them.'

'Don't you have a housekeeper? Or a chauffeur?' Vita asked, as they walked around the outside of the house to a run of garaging that must once have been for carriages.

'Housekeeper clocks off at six,' he said. Vita looked at her watch. Goodness, half past seven. 'Chauffeur? Had one of those. Nearly killed me. Literally.'

Vita liked Lord Seddon.

'Now, which one is it?' he said, pressing a button on a small contraption in his hand. One door swung slowly open to reveal a small hatchback in a cavernous space. 'Not that one. That's the granddaughter's.' He pressed another button, and another and soon all four doors were open. There was a pale blue Rolls Royce behind one, a battered old Land Rover behind another and a vintage something-or-other in the furthest space. It might be only a lift to the gates, but how Vita hoped he'd choose that one.

'I was going to take the Roller,' he said. 'Can't find the damned keys. Could only find these – so hop in.' It was the clapped-out Land Rover. Seated on the torn front seat, Vita could then smell the whisky on his breath which was a fraction stronger than the whiff of wet dog. The car sputtered into life and Lord Seddon lurched and chugged it down the drive towards the gates, while Vita shouted her answers to his constant questions above the din of the engine.

'Thank you so much,' she said, when they climbed out and approached the gates. 'For everything – I'm very grateful. I'm sorry if I inconvenienced you, sir.' Do you call a lord a sir?

He looked at her quizzically. 'A pleasure, dear.' He looked at her again, looked at the gates, the car. 'How about I run you home? You don't want to be faffing with public transport on a lovely evening.'

'I couldn't possibly.'

'No, me neither – buses? Dreadful. Just dreadful.'

'I meant – I couldn't possibly trouble you further.'

'Nonsense!' He was already heading back to the Land Rover. 'Hop in.'

He was an atrocious driver but on the public road, he stayed silent. Vita gazed out at the long great wall as they drove by. She thought of all the trees behind it; and of all the trees, her thoughts rested on the beech.

'I found my name,' she blurted when they just about stopped at a red light.

'I see!'

'On the tree,' she said quietly.

'And has that made a difference?'

She smiled. 'It's put down the roots for the rest of my life,' she said.

'*Crescunt illae, crescant amores*,' he said. 'As these letters grow, so may our love.'

The vehicle screeched and juddered a slow passage back to the Tree Houses.

'You can drop me at the end of the street, if you like. Then you can do what my dad always called a "you-ee".'

'I can barely drive in a straight line, my dear – let alone execute a U-turn.' And he drove her down the street until she said, Just here, just here's fine.

Should she ask him if he'd like a cup of tea? She hadn't hoovered yesterday, as she should have done. And there was washing hanging to dry in the sitting room. There were no biscuits, let alone a red carpet. Perhaps not, perhaps just thank him profusely again.

'Whoever carved your name,' Lord Seddon said, 'is a lucky beggar. You look after him. We men – we need our women to look after us, however able we profess ourselves to be.'

Vita smiled at him.

'That's the beauty about love,' he said. 'It's not about give-and-take – it's all about feeling safe in one's needs – wanting to be looked after as much as wanting to look after. You mark my words!'

And she did mark his words, as she walked thoughtfully up the path to her cottage.

And then she thought, Oliver!

And then she thought, Now!

She ran back to the street, saw the Land Rover zigzagging away.

'Wait!' she called, running up the middle of the road, gesticulating wildly. 'Wait! Hey! Hey! Sir! Lord! Wait up!'

At first, Lord Seddon thought she was waving him off. He thought that all the jumping and arm flailing, though a little over-the-top, was rather touching. But when he stalled near the T-junction, he could hear her yelling. Yelling at him, once more, to do as she asked.

She ran up to the car and rapped on his window.

'Please,' she said, 'please could you just give me another lift?' and before he could answer she was already running around to the passenger door.

'What the—?'

'It's not far – but it will take too long to walk. I just want to be there *now*.'

He stared at her in disbelief.

'Apologies,' she said. 'But please – drive on!'

Jonty thought this job could wait, really. It was Friday night. He'd done his homework and he just wanted to watch Friday-night shite on the TV with his dad. But his dad had put two empty boxes on the coffee table.

'Jonty,' he said, 'I think, perhaps, we should put some of the photos away.'

'The photos?'

'Yes.'

'Why?'

'It's time.'

'Time for what?'

'To make space – for Vita.'

Jonty wasn't sure what he meant. Did he have photos of her? Already?

'Metaphorically speaking,' his dad said.

'Oh.'

'I just think it must be difficult for her,' Oliver said. 'We really do have a lot of photos of Mum around.'

'You mustn't hide Mum away.'

Oliver was visibly appalled. 'I'm not hiding her away. Darling, I'll *never* hide her away. I just think it would be – respectful – to both these women, to reorganize and rearrange things a bit.'

He handed Jonty an old newspaper and, between the two of them, they began the task of agreeing which photos would be wrapped and placed gently in the box.

'Definitely that one,' Oliver said. 'She always said she looked like Yoda in that one.'

'I remember,' said Jonty, who also remembered how

he and his dad would do their Yoda voices to wind his mum up.

'At the door there is someone,' Jonty mimicked because the bell was sounding.

'Please young Jedi, to answer it you must go,' Oliver mimicked back.

Jonty opened the door to find Vita, slightly wild about the eyes, standing there with red cheeks.

'Hi,' she said, and she gave him his half-wave.

'Hi,' he said.

'Is your dad in?'

'Yes – but we're just –'

But Vita had squeezed by him and was making her way into the house.

'Dad!' he called.

'Oliver!' she called.

They arrived in the sitting room at the same time.

'Vita?' Oliver was stopped in his tracks.

Vita assessed what was happening in an instant. 'No!' She said it softly, emphatically.

'Stop,' she said. '*Please.*'

She went up to him, put her hands gently on his wrists for a change.

'It's OK,' he said and they both looked down at a photo of DeeDee grinning back. 'It's time.'

'No,' Vita shook her head, smiling at him, touching his cheek. 'It really is OK.'

She took a frame from the box and unwrapped it. She handed the photo to Oliver. 'Please, please don't. Not on my behalf.'

'But I'm ready.'

She beamed at him. 'And so am I.' She held his face in her hands and kissed him extremely slowly and ever so lightly on the lips. 'You are who you are because of that amazing woman. She's trained you well – and I have only gratitude and respect for her.' She kissed him again. 'I owe her so much – you believe in love because of her, because of what you shared.' She kissed him again. 'I would be honoured to take the baton from her – and run this race alongside you.'

Oliver's head dropped. Dear God, don't let him weep. Not in front of Jonty.

Vita's arms were around his neck and she was holding him close, swaying, whispering in his ear, I love you I love you I love you.

Oliver's voice was hoarse. 'I love you too, missy. I love you too.'

'Oh, get a room, you two,' Jonty groaned and the pair of them turned to him with elation and relief written in the same hand all over their faces.

*   *   *

But it wasn't a room they moved to; they went out into the garden instead. Vita surveyed the scene – a cricket wicket had been put up, a bat lay strewn, there was no ball in sight. Two mugs were on a tray at the edge of the patio, a plate beside them with half a pack of digestive biscuits – the empty section of wrapper tied in a twist. The lawn had been mown and the shrubbery looked less straggly. The profusion of pots had been repositioned and the ones that the time before Vita had noted had just soil in or, worse, a long-dead plant, had been emptied. Good for Oliver, she thought. And she felt strangely elated.

'You've been busy,' she said.

344

'Actually, I paid someone to do it.'

'It looks nice – more of a garden. I didn't know you played cricket.'

'Love it – so does Jonty.'

'Willow,' said Vita. 'I know that cricket bats are made of willow.'

Oliver smiled. '*Salix alba caerulea* – a straight-grained variety found in Essex and Suffolk. Ten-year-old trees can provide up to thirty bats each. And ash for the stumps. Alder for guitar necks, lime wood for piano parts, hazel for walking sticks, poplar for matches.' He paused. 'You want more?' Vita grinned. 'Did you know that willow beds are being tested as a final purification process for treated sewage before the water is returned to our rivers? Or that docetaxel – a chemotherapy drug – was first made from the needles of yew? And that recently, birch bark has been found to contain chemical compounds that can selectively kill human cancer cells with no side effects?'

'And what's gin without juniper!' Vita said. She loved hearing this man talk, she loved the job he had. His knowledge, his forearms, working in the great outdoors – all equally sexy. Trees – mighty, beautiful and so important.

'I'm a tree geek,' he said, as if confessing.

It's a quality, she thought. She tipped her head. 'Tell me about the Trysting Tree?'

He motioned to the garden chairs with the lovely cushions. Yesterday's paper was on the table, a bottle opener and a lager cap on top of it. They settled into the seats, the setting sun filtering through the leaves of the copper beech.

'We were twenty-five,' Oliver began. 'Dee and I shinned over the wall one summer's night with a bottle of wine and a chisel. And we couldn't think what to write. So I

345

just wrote our names. We came back, a few summers running. Then we stopped coming; life became so busy, my business was burgeoning, Jonty was born. About five years ago, I was invited to start verifying the trees at Wynfordbury. DeeDee and I thought it was amusing. *Is it still there*, she asked me, *our graffiti*? Yes, it's still there, I told her. Of course it's still there, I said. And I told her, It'll still be there long after we're gone.'

'I met Lord Seddon.'

'Isn't he fantastic?'

'Yes,' Vita laughed, 'he is.' And she told Oliver all about today, how an odd elderly lady and an eccentric old man had made so much possible.

'You must be exhausted, missy.'

'I am.'

'Bed?'

'Jonty?'

'Jonty? He has his own room.'

'I know – silly. I mean – I feel we ought to clear it, with him.'

'You go and speak to him. He likes you, you know. He likes you very much.'

Jonty's room is quite a revelation. One wall is red, one is black and they are both covered with posters of bands with spiky names in both meaning and calligraphy. She's knocked and he's said, Come in and she's asked if she can have a word and now she's sitting on his bed. He's on a stool, an electric guitar across his lap. He looks a little like an ironing board.

'Jonty – I just wanted to say. To ask you. Oh shit! I don't know what I'm meant to say.'

'It's cool,' he shrugs. 'It's always been cool. My dad's happy – and that's cool.'

346

'Are *you*, though? Are you OK if I were to – you know – have a sleepover?'

'A *sleepover*?' Jonty laughs. 'What – with a scary movie and a midnight feast?'

'I mean – if I stay over,' Vita is blushing. 'Stay the night. With your dad. Would that be OK? In his – you know – *room*.' She can hear how her inflection is suddenly like a teenager's. She hopes Jonty doesn't feel patronized, she hopes he still thinks she's cool.

'Cool,' he shrugs.

'Phew,' she says.

'Just one thing, though,' he says.

'Yes? Anything, Jonty – anything.'

'Please don't leave your lady stuff all around the bathroom.'

'Sorry?'

'Mum used to – I know I was younger then. But even so, I don't want to see bras and knickers and things like that.'

Vita is laughing. 'OK,' she says, 'I will make sure I don't.'

'Cool.'

'Cool.'

She slumps a little, feeling utterly exhausted. She looks around his room and then she stops.

There, over there.

Jonty follows her gaze.

'It's from your shop, isn't it?' he says.

It's a wall plaque, in plaster of Paris, made to look aged. It was stock from around four years ago. There was a whole series, carved with various maxims. Vita had always liked this one the best though.

Carpe Diem

'I kind of *carpe diem*-ed it today all right,' Vita says.

'My mum really liked your shop,' Jonty says. 'If you look around, you'll find loads of your stuff is here already.' Jonty tips his head to one side. 'I'm pleased my mum had your stuff in the house before you came,' he says. 'I suppose it's a little like she unpacked for you, a bit, before you arrived.'

'To make me feel at home.'

'*Me casa, su casa*,' Jonty says. And then he thinks, Could you go now, I want to get back to Garage Band.

'OK,' Vita says. 'Very OK.' And as she leaves his room, she gives his hair a very quick ruffle.

there is. Laughter and tears and reflection and love and hope.

Tim wasn't one for anniversaries but when autumn came, he was acutely aware that it marked a year since Vita told him it was over. And, in mid-October, while Suzie unpacked, filling his house with the accoutrements of a woman once more – scatter cushions and scented candles and hearts made out of bunched twigs – he went out, under the pretext of buying milk. Actually, he just wanted a little space to think; fresh air away from the heady scent of vanilla and jasmine or whatever it was that the candles were fragranced with. He could have gone to the pub for a quick pint, but he decided against it. He didn't feel like it. For once, he didn't want to sidetrack his thoughts or avoid his feelings, he wanted to look right at the memory and consider how he felt. He needed some space, just for a short while, to sift through all the emotions that had been in chaos since catching sight of Vita with that man earlier in the day.

Driving to Suzie's that morning, Tim had automatically used a detour that was useful when the traffic built up during the week but really, there'd been no need for it on a quiet Sunday. It took him on a quiet loop away from town and then back in. It skirted the river, where the buildings finally petered out and the long line of poplars took their place. He was stuck behind two horse riders, and yet the rhythmic sway of their horses' backsides, the leisurely pace, didn't wind him up at all – not the way a pensioner tootling along in a car might. For the eternal boy-racer, he was remarkably unfazed. The riders, the trees, the autumn light – it was all good. He was in no real rush to get to Suzie's. He had the radio on, golden oldies for a golden autumn Sunday, and he was singing along to the Kinks when he saw them on the other side of the road.

His first response was simply to smile – a nice-looking

couple strolling hand in hand, chatting. And then he realized it was Vita. And oh, how she was making this man laugh. She was animated; he could see her jabbering nineteen-to-the-dozen, speaking with her hands at the same time, not looking where she was going. So Vita. God, how that used to get on his nerves. But now look at her, jigging ahead of the man, turning to him and walking backwards whilst chatting, gesticulating crazily. And now look at *him*, see how he's laughing. See how he's lifting Vita up, his arms around her waist while he continues to walk on; carrying her, holding her close to him, and plugging shut that chatterbox mouth of hers with his kisses. Even the sun made its contribution, catching glances of gold in Vita's hair, highlighting that bastard bloke's broad bloody shoulders and cheekbones. It didn't matter what his name was. Tim knew who he was. He was the man who Vita would spend her life with, who would make her happy, keep her safe and be lucky enough to have all that Vita could give in return. The concept, as much as the sight, threw Tim, utterly.

He had to pull over.

He'd been so transfixed, gazing at the pair of them as they approached, as they passed by, as they disappeared in his rear-view mirror, that he'd become unaware of how close he was to the pair in front of him. One of the riders had sworn at him. He swerved over and pulled in; sat in his car and slumped, his forehead against the steering wheel, his heart beating painfully against his breastbone. It could've been me, it could've been me. Idiot. What a loser.

With Suzie currently unpacking back at his house, as Tim nipped out, he thought back to the morning. It had probably been to Suzie's advantage that Tim had seen Vita and the man, that he'd panicked. Had he not, he'd have been

351

most likely irritated by all the stuff she was bringing, he'd have argued the toss about what she might as well leave, he'd have shoved her belongings in the back of the car. He'd have been his usual huffy self. It wouldn't have been a good start. But, arriving at Suzie's, Tim's mind didn't focus on cushions and throws and some hideous lamp whose base was made out of blue glass pebbles. His mind wasn't even all over the place, it was miles back, down the road, down memory lane. For some reason, he remembered how, when Vita found out that Suzie was back on the scene this time last year, she'd pleaded with him, But do you love her, do you *love* her? It was as if Vita could cope with him not loving *her* – but not with the thought that he might actually love another.

He didn't love Suzie. He never would. He'd taken Vita's love for granted, taken liberties with it, taken stupid chances that she'd always love him unconditionally. Today, though, he knew he'd never need to ask Vita the question, But do you love him, do you *love* him? The love she had for this person, so clearly reciprocated and so full of joy, was as clear as the light of that morning, as strong as the branches and as deep as the roots of the trees they passed by; as bright and as beautiful as the autumn foliage surrounding them.

Now Tim walked, retracing the route he'd driven that morning. He crossed the road to the side where Vita and her man had been and, very slowly, he followed in the wake of their footsteps. He tuned his senses, listened to the crackle and crunch of the leaves underfoot, the lap of the water, the smell of moist earth and leaf mulch, the slight sharpness in his nostrils from the chill in the air, the feeling of soft warmth from the tired rays of late October's afternoon sun. As for taste, all he could taste – and all he would be able to taste for some time to come – was the caustic bitterness of profound regret.

Life could have been so sweet, but his fate was for it now to be relatively tasteless.

* * *

As she walked to That Shop in her lunch hour the following week, Suzie was not proud when she considered there had been a time when she'd have absolutely basked in what she perceived to be some kind of triumph. There was a time – not so long ago, really – when she would have gone all out to make sure Vita knew that she had moved in with Tim. However, it was no insidious emotion which compelled her to visit Vita today and Suzie knew, deep down, that rather than feeling any triumph over Tim finally agreeing to her moving in, her governing feeling was one of tired relief.

'Hullo.'

Vita looked up from her book. Goodness. 'Suzie?'

'Hi.'

'Hi there – how are you?'

'I'm fine. I was passing. I thought – you know.'

Vita noticed her hair was a bit too blonde but that, despite the orangey tan, Suzie actually looked a little wan. 'Did you want to buy something? Trick or treat?'

Suzie half-smiled and half-heartedly perused the Halloween merchandise. 'Actually – maybe a candle?'

'These are nice.' Vita hopped down from her perch and crossed the shop. She showed Suzie the candles in the tin containers. 'Smell this.'

'God, that's gorgeous.'

'Orange blossom.' There they stood, side by side, sniffing scented candles.

'How are you?'

And Vita beamed. 'I'm dandy.'

Dandy. Suzie wished wacky words like that came naturally to her.

'And you?'

'Yeah – I'm good,' Suzie said. She looked straight at Vita. 'I've thought of calling you. But—' she shrugged.

'Is everything OK?'

'Yes. It is. I wanted you to know – because he won't tell you, will he – but I didn't want you just finding out. But I moved in there – to Tim's – last weekend.'

Vita looked at Suzie and her first thought, which she knew she had to keep quiet, was, *Why?* Why on earth would you want to do that? Move in with someone who's already cheated on you? Whose track history you know and whom you are justified never to be able to trust? But she empathized with Suzie's need to give Tim a second chance. She also knew it wasn't for her to comment. It was down to Suzie's friends to express opinions and she found that she genuinely hoped Suzie's friends were good enough to do so. Suzie and Vita weren't friends, they never would be, but certainly they shared something in common and not just Tim himself. They shared what had evolved briefly that one lone late afternoon during the summer. The talk had been all about Tim and yet ultimately they'd pushed him to one side so they could pursue instead the give and take, the care, concern and confidences that exist between two women.

It made perfect sense to Vita that Suzie wouldn't have left Tim, compelled instead to struggle for his affection. 'Well!' Vita said. 'Well – I hope you'll be happy.'

Suzie nodded. 'All my mates think I'm insane. I probably am – in the long run. But do you know what, I have to give it a chance. I have to see whether I can be the one who can change him.'

Vita nodded. She knew those words off by heart. They'd

354

been her own mantra, a long time ago. Although she referred to her friends as pals rather than mates.

'I understand,' she said. Suzie shrugged. 'You'll be OK,' Vita said. 'Whatever happens, you'll be OK. Someone once said that, in life, we have to size up the chances and calculate the possible risks and our ability to deal with them – and then make our plans accordingly.'

Suzie traced an arc on the floor with her foot. 'That's deep,' she said. But she nodded and smiled. 'Thing is, I just felt I should tell you – because if I was you, I'd want to know.'

'Thank you – that's kind.'

'And you? How's life?'

'As I said – dandy.'

'Are you seeing anyone?'

Vita broke out into an expansive smile and nodded.

'Is he nice?'

'He's lovely.'

'Does he make you happy?'

'Very much so.'

'I'm dead pleased for you,' said Suzie.

'Look – please have this,' Vita said, giving her the candle. 'Have it as a secret little house-warming present from me to you. It would do Tim's head in if he found I'd been giving freebies straight back to him.'

Suzie laughed, holding the candle carefully in both hands. 'Cheers,' she said.

'Good luck,' Vita said. 'Be happy.'

At the door, Suzie turned. 'Shall I keep in touch then?'

'As and when,' Vita said. 'That's fine by me.'

'And me,' said Suzie. 'Thanks.'

Once outside, Suzie walked slowly past the shop. Vita was back behind the table, nose buried in a book. Suzie waited until she looked up, then she smiled and raised her hand. Vita mirrored her.

*   *   *

Tim and Vita sat down together on a Sunday in early November to go through the accounts. The shop wasn't open so they convened there, pushing the till to one side and stacking elsewhere the jars of pencils and erasers and the little tray with the magnets, the basket with the printed paper tissues. The accounts were straightforward. The numbers were neither bad nor good. That Shop was riding out the recession cautiously and that's what mattered.

'Is it still that Oliver bloke?' Tim suddenly asked, with no preamble.

Vita looked straight at him. 'Yes.'

'What does he do?'

'He's an arboricultural consultant.'

'You mean he's a lumberjack?'

'Sod off!' but she was laughing because Tim had said it with a reluctant smile.

'Are you happy, babe?' Tim asked gently and Vita thought how sad his eyes were when he said it. Earlier, when he'd arrived, she'd thought how shabby he looked – a bit jowly and pale, as though he wasn't eating well. She also remembered him as taller, his posture better.

'Yes,' she said quietly, 'I am very happy.'

Tim doodled thoughtfully with a pencil. And then, almost shyly, he put the back of his hand lightly against Vita's cheek. He held her eyes. 'I'm so sorry,' he whispered. 'For the misery I caused you.' He didn't want her to look away. 'For doing what I did – and not doing what I should have done. I'm a cunt.' A tear started and stopped in the corner of his eye.

356

Vita gently took his hand away from her face. 'That's a bit harsh,' she said. 'Let's settle for a tosser and a twat.'

He laughed a little. 'I hope he treats you well, Vita.'

'He does.'

'Good.' He paused. 'That really is good.' Then he put his head down. 'I'm insanely jealous!' His voice cracked. 'I regret so much.' He shook his head at himself. 'I'm beyond jealous.'

'You're not,' said Vita, 'you're just nostalgic, perhaps.'

He shrugged, nodded. 'I *am* happy for you.' He was trying to smile warmly but his eyes betrayed him. They were hollow with sadness. 'I wish it was me. But I know it's not about me. I know that. It's you. And I hope you have the chance to be truly happy – to be loved and cherished and respected. I hope he'll keep you safe. I'll kill him if he doesn't.'

Vita laid her head lightly on Tim's shoulder and he slipped his arm around her and gave her a squeeze.

'You look after Suzie,' she said and she marvelled at the genuine emotion she was putting behind words she'd so long assumed she'd be incapable of saying.

'I'm not making a very good job of it,' he mumbled.

'So – try harder,' Vita said. 'This is your chance to take what happened between us – and put it to good use.'

They sat in a silence that was as steady as it was awkward. Then Tim tapped the table. 'Right!' he said. 'I'd better be off!' He kissed her clumsily on the forehead but he kept his lips there. 'I love you,' he whispered. 'Always have. Always will.'

And then Tim left.

It no longer crossed Vita's mind to even wonder where he'd be going, let alone fret about it. All she wanted to do was to lock up and go home. She was doing chops and chips for supper, for Jonty and Oliver. And they were bringing the dessert.

Parenting

'What's up?' Oliver had been watching Vita for a few minutes, lying next to him in bed, her eyes busy tracing imaginary patterns on the ceiling. It was mid-November. Fireworks and pumpkins were gone, many of the trees were bare but it seemed the world was in good spirits and just starting to gear up for Christmas.

'Nothing's up.'

'Fibber. I know you, Vita.'

'Nothing's up. Actually, I was just thinking we ought to get up and start thinking about lunch because Mum is usually early.'

'Fibber. It's nine o'clock on a Sunday morning. I might be cack-handed in the kitchen but not even I can take three whole hours to prepare a roast.'

'Actually, I was just wondering if we ought to ring Jonty, you know, to see if he wants a lift back. I should hate for him to be late.'

'Fibber. He won't be late – he likes her. Remember how well they rubbed together at his school fireworks? Anyway, my son's abnormally prompt for a teenager – and you know that too.'

358

Oliver propped himself up, placing his arms either side of her, dipping his face to kiss one nipple and then the other.

'What's up, missy?'

'I don't want to tell you.' She turned her face.

Oliver used his nose, his lips, to nudge it back to him. 'You can tell me anything.' He could see how hard she was trying to fathom out if she really could. He returned to his side of the bed, lay on his side and stroked her hair. He liked her new cut, it really suited her. It had been Michelle's idea. She'd pampered Vita with all sorts of treatments on her birthday last week. Oliver had bought her a watch and Jonty had given her a T-shirt emblazoned with the PainMeister album cover on it, because Vita was always saying she thought they were cool.

She turned to Oliver. 'I'm very nervous about saying this.'

He nodded.

They nestled down into their pillows.

'What's up?' he asked again. She looked into his face and knew she could tell him.

'I have come into a family where there is one child – by choice.'

'You don't like my boy?' Oliver smiled gently and managed to coax one out of Vita.

'I love your boy, silly,' she said. She put out her hand and touched his face, ran her fingers along his arm and found his hand under the pillow. 'I mean – you wanted one child, didn't you? You and DeeDee chose to have Jonty as your only child.' She could see that Oliver was concentrating hard on what she was saying. 'It's just – it's just. I have – Oh God – if I say this it's going to change everything.' She took a deep breath. 'Oliver – I would like to have a baby. That's the problem. That's what's up.'

'You're now thirty-four,' he said.

She nodded.

'Seems perfectly natural to me.'

'But – you? Jonty?'

'What about us?'

She paused. 'It's not what you want.'

Oliver found his eyes wandering to the invisible maze on the ceiling that Vita had been scouring earlier on.

'How do you know what I don't want?'

'Because you said – you told me. About being Bourne Three – you and DeeDee only wanted one child. The problem is, I want one too. Perhaps more than one.'

'Are you saying you'd like to have a baby with me?'

She nodded. 'I would really love to have a baby with you.'

'Wow,' he said, staring fixedly at the ceiling.

'That's the problem,' Vita whispered. 'I know it's not what you want. I know your life plan with DeeDee was for just the one. And Jonty is so perfect. Plus, you've done the nappy thing and the sleepless nights and the potty training and teething – all of it. I'm frightened, Oliver. We want very different things.'

Oliver spoke quietly. 'You are quite right – fifteen, well, I guess almost sixteen years ago – DeeDee and I, together, decided on one child. But that was with DeeDee. Vita – you and I, together, can plan another. And another – if we so decide.' He turned to Vita. 'It doesn't have to follow that what was right for DeeDee and me, need be right for you and me.'

'Really?'

'Truly,' said Oliver.

'But Jonty?'

'Free babysitting?'

'Seriously!'

360

'He's a beautiful boy – and if it wasn't for him, I'd still have your cagoule in the back of my car.'

'But the disruption, Oliver?'

Oliver shrugged. 'It's part and parcel, Vita,' he said.

'I'm nervous,' she said.

'I am too.'

'How do we do it?'

Oliver smiled. He kissed her nose, found her mouth. 'Well, we have a kiss and a cuddle, then I put my manhood in your lady bits and we jiggle about for a while and then—'

'Stop it, you daft bugger!'

He was kissing her neck. 'We just practise – practise until we make something perfect.'

'Are you *sure*?'

'I make great babies – you can trust me.'

'I mean, are you *sure* sure?'

'Vita – I am positive. In every sense of the word.'

And she was kissing him back. The winter light which silvered its way into the room spoke of thick frost outside, giving them all the more reason to hunker down under the duvet. The condoms remained in the bedside drawer. The sex was intense and silent, illuminated by the grins they gave each other which turned lovemaking into baby making. As Oliver came, both he and Vita marvelled at the closeness two human beings could attain.

* * *

Ruth Whitbury brought dessert. She made trifle because Jonty had requested it, having tasted her speciality when first meeting her at lunch at Vita's some weeks ago. She'd also come, with Oliver and Vita, to his school fireworks display a couple of weekends ago. That time, she'd brought with her hot baked potatoes wrapped in cloth napkins just to hold, to keep their hands warm, and Jonty had decided that she'd make an excellent surrogate granny.

'Do you think they'll mind – Gran and Grandad?' he'd asked Oliver a little while ago. 'Do you think they'll mind that I like Ruth so much?'

'You know, Jonty, I didn't know what they'd think – how they'd feel – when I told them about Vita,' Oliver confided back. 'But they're brilliant people – and they seemed genuinely happy for us.'

'So they won't feel left out if I have Ruth too?'

'I think they'll be very pleased for you. After all, you never knew my folks. Anyway, I think they'd all get on famously, don't you? Grandad especially – Gran can chinwag to her heart's content and he'll be able to doze off in front of the telly without being poked the whole time.'

'True.'

'Shall we invite them all for Christmas?'

'Shall we?'

'I don't know – that's why I'm asking you.'

'How the heck are you and I going to do a whole Christmas lunch – for *guests*? It was all right, last year – we ate what we wanted.'

Oliver remembered the mountain of Marks & Spencer ready-meal trays by the close of Boxing Day. 'The beauty of extending our family is that we'll end up doing less. Ruth will say, What can I bring? Gran and Grandad will come laden anyway. And Vita will do that bossy thing of hers and shoo us from the kitchen. You and I can kick back and watch *Harry Potter* because we've been all but told to.'

'Genius!'

'Is that the plan, then, Jont?'

'Cool.'

'Done a list for Santa yet?'

'It's only just been Guy Fawkes, Dad – you're as bad as Tesco. Anyway, Santa doesn't exist.'

'Oh, don't say that!'

'Dad – you're so lame.'

'Is *lame* a good thing or a bad thing?'

'Dad!'

And Oliver thought, How much more blessed can a man be than to have the love of close family all around him?

He left Vita preparing lunch while he collected Ruth en route to picking up Jonty. Ruth didn't know where Jonty's friend Mark lived and so was unaware of the detour Oliver took.

'I love your daughter very much,' he said. They were listening to *The Archers* omnibus so his statement appeared to come out of the blue. To Ruth, at least. Oliver had been on the verge of saying it many times during the course of the journey. 'And at some point soon I'd like to ask her to make an honest man of me.' He kept driving, sensing Ruth's eyes on him, quietly assessing his words.

'Thank you,' she said at length, and she tapped his leg. He tapped hers back. 'You're just what she needs,' said Vita's mum.

Jonty gave Ruth a guided tour while Oliver got under Vita's feet in the kitchen, picking at things and asking her to make plenty of gravy. He was summarily banished to the sitting room. He could hear footfalls creaking around upstairs and he wondered what Ruth would make of Jonty's room. Would she in any way judge his parenting skills by his condoning black and red paint

363

and posters with skulls and daggers and band names like Rodekill and HellWhole. DeeDee would have laughed and called him silly. Which is pretty much what Vita did. How was he so lucky that the love he'd found in his life had been with two such different and yet similar women?

It won't ever be Oliver's style to consider how luck has played only a part; to credit himself for inspiring the love that's come his way.

'Ruth saw the Rolling Stones in Hyde Park!' Jonty blustered into the room.

'Did you?'

'I did. July fifth, 1969.'

'And the Beatles,' Jonty exclaimed.

'Hammersmith, tenth December 1965,' said Ruth. 'Couldn't hear a thing though – all that ridiculous wailing and screaming. Myself included, I hasten to add.'

'Have you heard of PainMeister?' Jonty asked her. 'They're awesome, Ruth. I bought Vita the T-shirt for her birthday. I'll play you some, if you like. I'll make you a CD.'

'I have cassettes and vinyl.'

'What's that?' Jonty asked. He shrugged. 'I'll lend you my iPod.'

'What's that?' Ruth asked.

'Your ears will bleed,' Oliver warned her.

Ruth winked at Jonty who grinned back.

She looked out of the window to the garden. It was as dull and dank outside as it was warm and colourful inside. She turned her attention into the room and politely complimented Oliver on the comfort of the armchair, the pleasantness of the colour schemes, the impressive quantity of books.

'What a monstrous television set,' she said.

'Thanks!' said Jonty and Ruth laughed.

Then the photos caught her eye. 'Come and tell me who's who,' she said and Jonty went over to the shelves with her.

Oliver thought, Clever lady – you want to hear him annotate them, for you to deduce whether I'm rushing the child into accepting another woman in his life. He wasn't offended. He knew Ruth was acting both as a mother to a child who had been hurt, as well as a parent who'd lost a partner when her own child had been a similar age to Jonty.

'Wasn't your mum pretty as a picture,' she said.

'I have her eyes,' Jonty said.

'I'll bet you have so much more than just her eyes,' said Ruth. She was touched that Oliver and Jonty had a photo of Vita framed and placed next to one of DeeDee. She wanted to tell DeeDee, You can trust Vita, dear – she'll look after your boys. She wanted to tell her late husband, you'd be so proud of your daughter, she's done very well for herself. And she wanted to tell Jonty something too.

'You know, Jonty, despite everything, you are lucky,' she said to him. 'You've had a lot of love in your life.'

Jonty nodded. Then he looked gently confused. 'Bit mental, then, isn't it – that I like bands called Deathdrive and Rodekill and Slicer.'

Ruth shook her head. 'I'll bet you, under those angry shouty voices, if you analyse their lyrics, they mostly sing about love.'

'Grub's up,' Vita called.

'Would you like some help?' Oliver asked.

'Please,' said Vita. 'Everyone can take a dish in – that should do it.'

'Ruth,' said Oliver, 'please, take a seat.'

365

'Nonsense,' said Ruth, bustling off into the kitchen ahead of him and Jonty.

Father and son looked at each other. Christmas had the potential to be very good indeed.

Elsie Mackenzie

'He's a very funny guy, your Oliver,' Michelle was saying as she piled items on the counter in Vita's shop. 'That was a top night, on Saturday. Chris really likes him. I *love* him. Oh – and Jake wants to be Jonty when he grows up. God – these are gorgeous! Are they porcelain? Have you any more stars? They'll look stunning on the tree.'

Vita went to the shop's Christmas tree and unhooked two more porcelain stars. 'Will two do?'

'I'll take more – if you can spare them.'

Vita took down another two. 'I'd better leave some.'

'You mean for the general public who don't get a discount?'

Vita laughed. 'Something like that.' She started running the items through the till.

'So – Boxing Day will be fun,' said Michelle. 'Candy's lot are coming after lunch – but you come whenever you're ready.'

'And it's OK for Mum to come?'

'Of course! DeeDee's parents can come too.'

'Oh, they're coming at New Year now. Are you sure

you want twelve of these?' Vita held up a small wooden angel made from an old-fashioned clothes peg.

'Quite sure,' said Michelle.

'That'll be – oh God – I can't charge you that!'

'Now look, I can spend my money here – or I can go to John Lewis. And by the way, that's too much discount. Ten per cent is more than adequate.'

Vita acquiesced, reluctantly took Michelle's credit card and popped it into the reader. 'Would you like anything gift-wrapped?'

'Great idea – can you wrap the scented hangers and the wall sconce?'

Vita opened the drawer where the paper, scissors, sticky tape and ribbons were kept. And she stopped.

'You OK?'

'Yes,' she said slowly. She brought something out onto the table. It was wrapped in Christmas paper. 'I did this ages ago – and she hasn't been in.'

'Who hasn't?'

'My mad old lady.'

'The kleptomaniac?'

'Yes.'

'Take it round to her.'

'I don't know where she lives. I don't even know her name. She hasn't been in for over a month. That's not like her.'

'Maybe she's gone to family, for the festive season?'

'I hope so,' said Vita. 'I hope she's OK. I told you about the Trysting Tree?'

'You did, my dear.' Michelle laughed.

'Many times?' Vita cringed.

'Many times, V.'

'It's been a long year,' Vita said. 'And I'm tired.'

'Tired?' Michelle gave her a knowing look. 'What kind of tired? Sore-boobs-and-morning-sickness tired?'

368

'Not yet,' said Vita, 'but not for want of trying.'

'That's my girl,' said Michelle.

*   *   *

No sooner had Christmas been and gone and the New Year welcomed in and helped on its way with sales, discounts and slashed prices, than Vita found herself in a sea of love. She was surrounded by hearts and cherubs and turtle doves and many other items variously in pinks and reds when a gentleman came into That Shop carrying a box. She assumed it was a delivery – Valentine's Day was big business and the merchandise tended to be small and pricey, invariably wrapped and packed to the nines.

'Love is a licence to print money,' she'd told Oliver and Jonty.

'Dad doesn't do flowers,' Jonty warned. 'He'll probably buy you a sapling or something.'

'That'll do,' Vita laughed.

Oliver had pretended not to be listening. Damn, and the sapling was already hidden behind the shed at work.

Now, sitting in the shop in a tangle of pink ribbon and lovey-dovey froth, Vita wondered what else she could possibly have ordered that hadn't yet been delivered.

'Are you Vita? The owner of this shop That Shop?'

The man was like a Dickens character. His voice, extravagantly deep and quite pompous, complemented a bulbous nose and a three-piece suit, the waistcoat stretched tight over his corpulent stomach.

'Yes – that's me.'

'Mr Reddington-Foulkes,' he said, looking round for somewhere to put the box so he could shake her hand. He had to make do with waggling the ends of his fingers at her.

'Am I expecting you?'

'No one ever expects me,' he said. 'May I put this down somewhere?'

Vita motioned to the side of the table where the till was. 'I'm here on behalf of Elsie Mackenzie.'

And Vita was just about to say, But I don't know an Elsie Mackenzie, when he spoke again.

'The *late* Elsie Mackenzie.'

Vita still didn't know an Elsie Mackenzie; early, late, living or dead.

'Are you sure you have the right person?'

'Oh yes,' he said. 'She left you some items. In her will.' He motioned to the box. 'These are for you. I have another box in the car, which I shall now go and collect.'

Vita thought of phoning her mother, to ask her if Elsie Mackenzie rang a bell. But curiosity saw her head directly to the box.

There was a label on it.

Messrs Reddington-Foulkes & Smythe
Estate of E. Mackenzie

She took one of the mother-of-pearl-handled letter knives and sliced through the tape over the flaps. Inside, wodges of shredded paper. And beneath those, items of varying sizes wrapped in plain newsprint paper. She took one, peeled back layer after layer and when a wooden duck appeared Vita thought, How funny! I used to stock these right here in the shop! It was only when she unwrapped the next and found an unopened tube of Gardener's Handcream, that she sat down heavily and stared at the box in stunned silence. Mr Reddington-Foulkes had come in again, with another box, only slightly smaller.

'Are you all right, my dear?'

'Is it?' said Vita. 'Was she? Has she *died*?'

'Yes, my dear.'

'But when?'

'December the twelfth. Peacefully, I am pleased to report. At the St John Hospice.'

'I didn't know her name. I thought of her as my Mad Old Lady.'

The solicitor tipped his head. He'd heard it all, over the years. Heard a hell of a lot worse than Mad Old Lady.

'All this stuff,' Vita said, 'why is it for me?'

'Because it was hers,' the man said. 'She'd organized everything. She had it all packed with notes dotted here and there. Very clear, she was, very clear indeed – about who should have what. Not that there were many beneficiaries.'

Vita wasn't going to tell him what these items were.

'Sign, please.'

She signed.

'Good day.'

'Goodbye,' she said. And when he reached the door she cried, 'Wait!' He turned. 'Do you know, please, where she's buried?'

'At the Wynford North cemetery.'

'Thank you,' said Vita, 'thank you very much.'

It surprised Vita just how sad she felt. She'd phoned Oliver, asking him to collect her at closing time on account of the boxes to take home and she sobbed all the way back. Jonty made scrambled eggs for everyone. After they ate, they listened to Vita reminisce about Elsie. After that, while Oliver loaded the dishwasher and made tea, Jonty helped Vita with the unwrapping. Many of the items she'd forgotten about, others she was quite stunned to see again.

'How on earth did she fit *that* into a pocket?' Jonty asked, marvelling at a barley-twist candlestick.

'Look!' said Vita unwrapping another. 'She swiped the

pair of them!' She paused as she looked around her, it was like sitting amidst a history of That Shop. 'She said to me once that she just liked *pretty things*.'

Oliver came in with tea. Jonty passed Vita the tissues.

'That's the lot, I think,' said Vita as the three of them wondered whether they'd have to pack it all away now.

'Mrs Blackthorne is coming tomorrow,' Oliver said. 'I'm sure she won't mind.'

Vita looked at him aghast – just the way DeeDee used to when he'd say, Oh, leave it for Mrs Blackthorne.

'But what am I to do with all of these?' Vita said. 'They've already been written off in various stocktakes over the years and anyway, it seems inappropriate to sell them – they're *possessions*.'

'Why not donate them?' Oliver suggested. 'Why not contact the hospice who looked after her? They'll have fund-raising events, I'm sure.'

'Hang on – there's one more thing left,' said Jonty, 'right at the bottom.'

It was flat, too flat to be a book and too smooth to be a photo frame. Vita unwrapped it. It was a piece of wood, a slither an inch thick, about the size of a shoebox lid.

'Gorgeous grain,' said Oliver. '*Sorbus* – whitebeam at a guess. What did you sell it as?'

'I didn't,' said Vita. 'This isn't one of mine.'

'Odd.'

'Yes.'

'A plain piece of wood,' Vita said. 'I love how the ends are unpolished and rough.'

Then she turned it over to find it wasn't plain at all. It was inscribed, beautifully.

> *I nor wealth nor titles bring,*
> *But I love, and love I sing.*

'I know those lines,' Vita murmured, wracking her brains for how.

'I know where they are,' said Oliver, tracing his fingers over the engraved lettering. 'They're on the Trysting Tree.' He took the plaque over to the bookcase, moved a photo of DeeDee and Jonty along a little and positioned it carefully on the shelf.

*   *   *

There was one gift Vita wouldn't be donating to the hospice, one gift she wanted Elsie to have. And so, when the craziness of Valentine's Day was over and That Shop paused for breath before gearing itself up for Easter, Vita went to Wynford North cemetery, taking the unopened Christmas gift with her. Elsie wasn't easy to find but when Vita finally located her she broke into a broad, teary smile. Vita had always thought of Elsie as slightly batty – but also as a loner; a mad old spinster, perhaps, who probably lived in a flat with piles of newspapers and all the ill-gotten gains.

Not so.

The headstone told a very different story. Robert Mackenzie had died twenty-seven years ago. Beloved husband of Elsie. And under his dates were Elsie's. Elizabeth Mackenzie. She'd been seventy-eight when she died. Vita stooped and placed the gift, unopened, on the grave.

'There you go,' she said. 'From me to you. Sorry you didn't have it for Christmas.' She paused. 'I shall miss you.' She paused again. 'But I'll think of you often. And especially next time I go to the Tristan.'

Epilogue

Alice Johnson had moved into Pear Tree Cottage after Easter. The letting agent had warned Vita against her, saying that this potential tenant could not afford the top whack they'd placed on the house. However, as Vita had thought all along that kind of money had been unrealistic, she didn't mind. And, when she met Alice for her second viewing, she knew the house would be right for her.

She'd come down from the North, she told Vita. She needed a fresh start – she'd found herself a new job and just wanted somewhere homely. Somewhere, Alice said, where she could find her wings again. Vita recognized in Alice a weariness, a vulnerability, but also the seeds of determination to take chances and start anew. Vita felt confident Pear Tree Cottage would be perfect for her.

'This place was very good to me,' Vita said, laughing to herself that if the letting agent had been here today, he would have steered her away from such musings to focus on the stripped floorboards and original features.

'I'd had a very challenging time,' Vita told Alice. 'I left my ex – but I finally found my feet here, at Pear Tree Cottage.' Alice, suddenly wide-eyed, appeared to be on the verge of tears so Vita steered the conversation away and on to the mystery of the floral wallpaper in the little room upstairs. They went on into the main bedroom.

'That tree is *amazing*!' Alice said and certainly, bedecked with blossom the pear tree was a stunning sight against the vivid spring sunshine.

'Let me tell you about that tree,' said Vita and the two of them sat on the bed and Vita told Alice everything she knew.

*   *   *

That was last year. It's Alice's second summer now and she is very happy at Pear Tree Cottage. Her job is going really well and, just recently, she started seeing someone lovely. Her landlords are great, Vita especially – and Alice has become a regular at That Shop. Nothing is too much trouble for the Bournes and Alice is grateful they took a chance on her. She was even invited to Oliver and Vita's wedding when they finally married in the spring.

School's out. Jonty sailed through umpteen GSCEs last summer and has just completed his first year at sixth form college. Once again, he's working for his dad over the holidays, on the days of the week which don't start with a T or an S. Oliver is thankful that he is; with so many changes at work and home, the extra pair of capable hands is more than welcome. Tinker went back to Canada in the spring, just before Oliver and Vita's wedding, but his cousin's buddy Red recently came over. He's a rookie when it comes to trees, but he's strong and hard-working and Boz and Spike like him.

There's a busy day ahead. An old oak needs to come down – it's not dead, but it's not safe. It will pain Oliver to fell it – but he will do it with all the expertise and sensitivity of a vet putting to sleep some aged old shire horse. Though the tree will be felled, it will continue to be a tree of life – its wood providing plenty of fuel next winter, its stump somewhere for children to clamber for generations to come.

'Jonty, I put a couple of bottles of water in the fridge – can you take them out? I'm just going to take a cuppa up to Vita.'

'Have you got the list, for Spike and I?'

'Pardon?'

'*Do you have* the list for Spike and *me*?'

Oliver smiles and Jonty play-boxes him as he passes.

The kettle has boiled; Oliver brews tea in a pot and takes it upstairs on a tray.

'God, I'm a lazy mare,' Vita says sleepily.

'Nonsense,' says Oliver, 'it's little past the crack of dawn. Relax.'

'Tea,' she says. 'You are lovely.'

'I'll call in at Pear Tree Cottage on the way home – it's time to put the wasp traps up.'

'There's beer and jam downstairs,' says Vita.

'I thought I'd try marmalade this year.'

'Alice says she's counted six parakeets,' Vita says. 'Her second summer – and yet she's welcoming the blighters back as if they're as delightful a symbol of the season as the swallow!'

'She's mad.'

'She's great and we're lucky to have her.'

'Will you phone her and let her know I'll call by with the wasp traps after work?'

'Sure.'

'It's going to be a beautiful day.' Oliver walks over and peers through the drawn curtains.

'You can open them,' says Vita.

Oliver opens the curtains. The light streams in. He looks over to the bed and his heart surges. Over he goes to settle himself by Vita, dishing out kisses as though they're on special offer this morning. She'll take all he has to give. But there'll always be more.

From the chest of drawers opposite, DeeDee looks out from the photograph. She doesn't appear to be looking over Oliver's shoulder this morning, but straight at him. He's between two women again. He's snuggled there, with Vita on one side and his month-old daughter, Georgia Danielle Bourne, on the other. And all the while DeeDee has continued to smile. She'll always be smiling. Outside, the breeze works its way through the leaves of the copper beech. It sounds as though a million pairs of hands are applauding the day.

Acknowledgements

Writing *Chances* coincided with an absolute pig of a year for me personally. This book would never have been written were it not for the unwavering and extraordinary support extended to me by some very special people. Sarah Henderson, Jo Smith, Kirsty Johnson and Jessica Adams – thank you, from my heart. Profound gratitude too, to Alan and Leslie Dunn, Jane Sutcliffe, Emma O'Reilly, Kate Holmes, Tamsin Pearce, Lucy Smouha and Clare Griffin. I would like to thank Ron and Ruth for putting their heart into my home; also the Cucumber girls, especially Souki; the St Jo's ladies (if you can call them that), Lisa W., Mel B. and the Real Michelle Sherlock, also Emily H., Toria C., Hilary and Nick. My family – thank you, Mum, Dad, Dan, Osi. My children – Felix and Georgia – thank you for being the best cubs this lioness could hope for.

This book is a co-production . . . I simply wrote it. That it has made it to you is due to the sterling efforts of unsung heroes behind the scenes. To Jonathan Lloyd at Curtis Brown, aka JLlo, aka Mr Big – it's been quite a ride and all these years later it's still a thrill. At HarperCollins – thank you Ben, Lee, Damon, Ollie, Roger, Penelope, Kate,

Belinda, Victoria, Hana and of course my editor Lynne Drew (eleven down, quite a few more to go . . .). With thanks and respect to Sophie Ransom at Midas PR who puts up with my flapping, and to Mary Chamberlain who ensures I never split an infinitive.

My sincerest thanks to Martin Hugi at Eco Tree Care and Kate Hugi, not just for assisting me in my research for this book, but also for my beautiful orchard and hedge.

Finally, deepest gratitude to Professor Woodhouse and everyone at the Royal Marsden who looked after my mum and helped her beat that sodding disease.

In memory of Liz Berney 1968–2005

www.ancient-tree-hunt.org.uk
www.ecotreecare.co.uk

Inside:

- Up close and personal with Freya
- Don't miss Freya's other bestsellers
- www.freyanorth.com

Up close and personal with Freya

Freya invited fans on her official facebook page to submit questions. Here are her answers.
www.facebook.com/freya.north

Q. *Do you think you can 'learn' to write a book, or is a talent that people have?*
(Rachel Howard Hornbuckle)

I'm often asked if I took any writing classes – the answer is no. However, that's not to say that there aren't many wonderful courses out there and some fantastic, bestselling authors who attended. Personally, I believe there's no right or wrong way to write – you find the method that works for you. I hope unpublished writers out there are encouraged by this concept. I don't plan my stories – but I know other authors who meticulously plot each and every chapter. I write sequentially, from Chapter 1 to The End – but some writers I know might start with the middle section first, then the ending, then the opening. Some writers can only write under pressure and cram it all in to the last few weeks leading up to a deadline. Others want their editors or friends to read the work in progress (not me – no one is allowed even a peek until it's complete!). Some authors write only at night. Or only in the day. Or only after a yoga class, or a bottle of gin...

What unites all 'true' writers is the desire to write, rather than the notion of 'being a writer'.

Q. *Where do you get your inspiration from?* (Katie Macleod)

Ideas can come from the most unlikely sources. *Pillow Talk* was inspired by a tiny news article I read about a 15 year old girl waking up in her nightie along the arm of a crane... thus began my fascination with sleepwalking. The idea for *Secrets* came when I was on Saltburn Pier licking an ice-cream – why not have a runaway Londoner coming up here to hide but discovering the delights of the seaside town for herself. Sometimes, it's a case of rather cheekily indulging my own passion for a subject – and being given carte blanche to research it and then witter on for 130,000 words about it. Hence bridges (*Secrets*), trees (*Chances*), the Tour de France (*Cat*), sculpture (*Fen*). Massage was a good one – I simply HAD to have a lot of massages, all in the name of research, for *Love Rules*!

Q. *If you could write a novel with another person, who would it be?* (Alison Jones)

Charles Dickens because my characters would then have the most fantastic names. Or Lynette, from *Desperate Housewives* – all those genius quips and put-downs. Actually, I don't think anyone would want to write with me because I'm extremely secretive, proprietary and somewhat moody whilst writing.

Q. *What is your favourite tree?* (Colette Shaw)

Hornbeam – some writers blow their advance on diamonds or a snazzy car or a luxury holiday. I bought a hornbeam wood. It's an old, old coppice and very beautiful. As firewood, it's the best as it burns very slowly and very hot. Traditionally, it was used for charcoal for this reason – to fire the malting kilns in Hertfordshire, Bedfordshire and Essex.

Q. *Are your characters in Chances based on real people and, if so, would they recognize themselves?* (Justine Quinn)

My great friend Paul Broucek sent me a gift from the USA. It's a hand painted plaque which is now in my study: "*Careful... or you'll end up in my novel*"! I don't tend to base characters on people I know, but I firmly believe one writes from experience – even if subconsciously. The pen is mightier than the sword, and all that... It's a writer's prerogative to have the last laugh – if anyone double-crosses me or my loved ones, they'll find themselves as an odious character, though I may distort a surname or hair colour to keep the libel lawyers at bay! In *Chances*, Vita's pal Michelle Sherlock is based on a lovely lady called... Michelle Sherlock – a birthday present from her husband which raised a lot of money for our school! Generally, I find it more rewarding to make up characters – especially the hero...

Q. *Would you like any of your books to be made into a film or TV-serialized?* (Susan Hetherington)

The film rights to *Polly*, my third novel, were optioned for a while. Yes, I'd be really tickled if any of my novels made it to the screen – be it the silver or smaller version. I wouldn't want any part in the adaptation though – I'm a novelist and scriptwriting is a whole separate skill and discipline. I would, of course, insist on my red-carpet moment – not to mention a walk-on cameo appearance! I think *Pillow Talk*, *Chances* and *Secrets* would work well – because they are very visual (though it would take a brave film crew to keep the cameras rolling on top of the Transporter Bridge). My stories, though, are conceived as books – I love the look of words on a page. But that's not to say I don't watch a movie and find myself thinking ooh! You'd make an excellent Joe (Rufus Sewell) or a wonderful Vita (Andrea Riseborough). But I don't think I could trust anyone to truly capture Uncle Django from my earlier novels *Cat*, *Fen*, *Pip* and *Home Truths*...

Q. *Do you always have a set 'path' for your characters? Or do you allow yourself to be led by them and their own actions? Has a book ever ended differently to how you intended?* (Jennie Atkinson)

I always think I have a path for my characters to follow – but by about chapter three, they don't take a blind bit of notice of my opinion and ultimately, I'm little more than their secretary, typing out their story for them. In fact, when I switch on my laptop each morning, I'm always surprised to find the characters exactly where I left them the night before – I'm sure they'll have gone off gallivanting behind my back. That's why I enjoy writing without a plan – I love the rings my characters run around me. In my mind's eye, there's a queue of them, waiting to sit with me and tell me their tales – I guess I still haven't moved on from the Imaginary Friends of my childhood. I was quite frustrated with Vita at a couple of points during *Chances* – so I was pleased that the supporting cast gave her a ticking off. The ending of *Love Rules* was contentious amongst my readers – but I had to respect my characters' personalities and thus could not have changed it. Halfway through *Secrets*, I had a good shout at Tess. In my fifth novel (*Fen*) the eponymous heroine has to choose between two lovers: one young, one older, one rich, the other poor, one from the city, the other from the country. I was slightly disappointed with her ultimate choice. Though I appreciated that Fen ended up with the right chap for her, I would've had the other one, myself...

Q. *What's your fitness mantra?* (Emma O'Reilly)
Walk the dog. Ride the horse. Chase the kids. Spinning classes three or four times a week. And then eat chips.

Q. *What song always gets you on the dance floor?* (Leslie Dunn)
Beyonce's *Crazy in Love*, Nickleback's *How You Remind Me* and Fat Boy Slim's, *Praise You* – a fantastically bizarre combo, really. Anything by The Rolling Stones and anything by Primal Scream. The children and I go crazy to *Jolie Dragon* by Le Tone – a weird but addictive tune.

Q. *What's next?* (Emma Anderson)
My 12th novel will be entitled *Rumours*. It's the first time I've had the title before I've written the book. I'm researching it at the moment – I'm hoping it'll be something of a 21st century Downton Abbey... but there again, who knows what my characters have in store for me this time!

Q. *OK...In your honest opinion, does true love exist?* (Susie Purser)
I bloody well hope so. Excuse my French.

secrets

Freya North

They drive each other crazy.
And they both have something to hide.
But we all have our secrets.
It's just some are bigger than others...

Joe has a beautiful house, a great job, no commitments –
and he likes it like that. All he needs is a quiet house-sitter
for his rambling old place by the sea.

When Tess turns up on his doorstep, he's not sure she's right
for the job. Where has she come from in such a hurry?
Her past is a blank and she's something of an enigma.

But there's something about her –
even though sparks fly every time
they meet. And it looks as though
she's here to stay...

pillow talk
Freya North

The sleepwalker.
By day, Petra Flint is a talented jeweller working in a lively
London studio. By night, she sleepwalks. She has 40 carats
of the world's rarest gemstone under her mattress
but it's the skeletons in her closet that make
it difficult for her to rest.

The insomniac.
Forsaking a rock-and-roll lifestyle for the moors
of North Yorkshire, Arlo Savidge teaches music at
a remote boys' boarding school. But, like Petra,
ghosts from his past disturb his sleep.

Putting the past to bed.
Petra and Arlo were teenage
sweethearts. Now, years later, in a
tiny sweet shop one rainy day, they
stand before each other once
more. Could this be their
second chance?

Winner of the
Romantic Novel of the Year 2008

home truths
Freya North

*Our mother ran off with a cowboy from Denver
when we were small.*

Raised by their loving and eccentric uncle Django,
the McCabe sisters assume their early thirties will
be a time of happiness and stability.

However, Cat, the youngest, is home from abroad to begin a
new phase of her life – but it's proving more
difficult than she thought. Fen is determined to be
a better mother to her baby than her own was to her –
though her love life is suffering as a result.

Pip, the eldest, loves looking
after her stepson, her husband,
her uncle and her sisters – even if
her own needs are sidelined.

At Django's 75th birthday party,
secrets are revealed that throw
the family into chaos. Can heart
and home ever be reconciled for
the McCabes? After all, what
does it mean if suddenly your
sisters aren't quite your sisters?

love rules
Freya North

Love or lust, passion or promise?

Thea Luckmore loves romance and lives for the magic
of true love. She's determined only ever to fall head over heels,
or rather, heart over head.

Alice Heggarty, her best friend, has always loved lust – but she's
fed up with dashing rogues. Now she's set her sights on good,
sensible husband material. And she's found him.

For Thea, a chance encounter on Primrose Hill ignites that
elusive spark. Saul Mundy appears to be the perfect fit and
Thea's heart is snapped up fast.

However newly-wed Alice finds
that she's not as keen as she
thought on playing by the rules and
she starts to break them left, right
and centre. At the same time, a
shocking discovery shatters Thea's
belief in everlasting love.

When it comes to love, should you
listen to your head, your heart, or
your best friend?

Keep up to date with Freya

Log onto **www.freyanorth.com**

for the latest news, reviews and photographs

You'll also find details on all Freya's books – including sample
chapters and what happened next to your favourite characters
– plus Freya's journal, an advice page, videos, the chance
to win signed copies of her books, and much more.